Where's the Ivy?

A Novel
by
Marc Cullison

NEW
FORUMS
Stillwater, Oklahoma
U.S.A.

This book may be ordered in bulk quantities at discount from New Forums Press, Inc., P.O. Box 876, Stillwater, OK 74076 [Federal I.D. No. 73 1123239]. Printed in the United States of America.

Edited and designed by Katherine Dollar

Library of Congress Cataloging-in-Publication Data Pending

International Standard Book Number 10: 1-58107-221-X
International Standard Book Number 10: 978-1-581072-11-21-1

For my wife, Janet, who does so much for me, enduring the silence while I read and write. It is her unique outlook on life that inspires me to write about it.
And a special thanks to the members of the Just Write writers' group. Their piquant critiques tamed my writing into something readable.

About the Author

Marc Cullison is a baby-boomer who grew up in an era when education was everything. After serving time as helicopter pilot with the U. S. Army Reserve, including time in Vietnam, and earning a masters degree in architectural engineering, he honed his technical skills as a professional engineer. Then into quality control at a manufacturing plant which led him into computer programming. He is currently a math and science instructor at Connors State College in Warner, Oklahoma. He lives with his wife in a self-built log house near Sallisaw.

The day you stop learning is the day you start dying.
- Marc Cullison

Chapter 1

The first time I saw the girl was in the Wal-Mart parking lot of Elkridge, Oklahoma. Of course, at that time I had no idea who she was. I had just left the store having passed by the greeter, a smallish old man with a grave disposition who had given me no greeting on the way in and scowled at me on the way out.

She was in the outer region of the lot, no vehicles within a hundred feet, sitting on an upturned tub of something between two laundry baskets full of something else and staring into space. Even the long, print dress, a well-worn cotton thing, unusual for the sweltering heat, did not conceal her stooped frame, elbows on knees, unmoving. I thought she might be ill, but wondered what she was doing alone in the middle of an empty parking lot. I slowed my car and stopped in front of her.

"Miss," I said. "Are you okay?"

She didn't move. I repeated my query and her eyes slowly looked up at me like she was descending from some plateau of ecstasy.

"Are you ill? Do you need a lift somewhere?"

She slowly shook her head back and forth. Then the thought occurred to me that she might be disoriented from heat exhaustion, but there were no tell-tale signs of excessive perspiration.

"Is there some reason you're sitting in the hot sun in the middle of a parking lot? Are you waiting for someone?"

Again, she shook her head and returned her gaze to whatever she was staring at before. By this time I was confused. I drove my car back to the store and approached the cheery greeter whose suspicious look indicated that he remembered me.

"Excuse me," I said as pleasantly as possible. "Where would I find the manager?"

I thought I saw a glimmer of fear streak through his eyes as he hesitantly turned and pointed toward a short, rotund woman talking with an employee near the beauty shop. The greeter's body fell into relief as I offered my thanks and turned away.

"Excuse me, ma'am. Are you the manager?"

The woman turned suddenly, and if eyes could impose impending doom on a person, then hers were fatal.

"I'm sorry to interrupt, but there is a young lady in the outer region of your parking lot sitting alone in a rather precarious situation. She seems to be ill with no one around to assist her and she's not exactly lucid. You might want to send someone to check her out in case something happens to her while on your property."

The manager's eyes narrowed and her mouth slowly opened to speak.

"Well, if she's way out there, she's not going to be our concern. A lot of folks loiter in our parking lot. That's why we have signs posted saying they can't do that."

After the shock of her response wore off I tried again.

"I just figured you might want to avoid any liability in case of injury."

After a brief stare-down I figured a response would not be forthcoming, so I turned to leave. That's when I saw the reflection of a middle finger in the glass in front of me. Now I began to wonder if everyone in Elkridge was this unhappy. If so, I had just made a huge mistake. I kept walking out the door and made a mental note to avoid returning to Wal-Mart. I concentrated on the meeting at the college in an hour.

*****

I saw them sitting there, through the small window in the door, an institutional kind with blonde finished wood, thick, stark, and surrounded by a metal frame. The kind that offers little suggestion of comfort, but rather arduous trials of obligatory social interaction. Since much of my life had been spent within this dour state of existence, it seemed no contest to me to whisk myself into the center of it all and take my rightful place as a subject of scrutiny

The door was stiff, giving reluctantly to my shove. Then it hammered my head when it stopped abruptly and I didn't. Fortunately, the blow wasn't hard enough for a concussion. I could see everyone in the classroom staring at me as if I had just intruded upon some intimate confidence. I tried to ignore them as I squeezed in through the still unyielding barrier and launched my body toward one of the desks. I sat rigidly, contemplating the inauguration into my new career. I had never thought seriously about what teaching would be like. Or, not to the extent that I would actually be doing it. It scared the hell out of me.

I was meeting the other faculty members of the Math Science Department of Hartmann College who were, as of yet unknown to them, my esteemed colleagues. I had looked forward to many happy hours of intellectual discussions and personal enlightenment. Although I had envisioned the grandeur of Ivy League magnificence, I was also aware that such grandeur would not exactly be one of the strengths of a college like Hartmann. However, as an unrenowned entity in the collegial world, I could expect to entertain a host of camaraderie that would feed my spirit, open the eccentric doors of academia, and part the ivy on the walls. But then I'm often given to folly. And as I sat there, a mere bump on the façade of higher education, like a wart on the Pope's nose, my reverie quickly mutated into delusion.

I studied the faces in the room wondering why they didn't seem like the faces of prominent scholars I had envisioned. The inquisitive eyes behind the benign countenance; a slight cock of the head as if infusing one's mind with knowledge and wisdom. No, none of that. Only the stale, unremarkable faces like those I had seen at sales counters, insurance offices, and audiences. It appeared as though I had wasted a good deal of anticipation. At the same time, though, in spite of anticipation and excitement, I was dreading my impending failure as an instructor. That was something to which I was not accustomed: failure. Not that I had been a raging success in any of my careers. I had made my share of blunders, but I had managed to learn whatever I had to know to do the job. I've never given serious thought to why I have done many things. Perhaps they seemed appropriate at the time, or were reactions to something, mostly the latter. And that is what gave me cause to worry about the future. I had known such anticipation on only two previous occasions: my wedding and the exam for registration as a professional engineer.

A fifty-seven year old man, I suspected, would always have trouble fitting in to a new environment and this one, could be tough. The remote affability forced me into the isolated company of my own thoughts. I wondered how these favored individuals, as unlikely as they appeared to be able to inspire the intellect of anyone, much less the fickle minds of undergraduate novices, could sit there so unconcerned with the regal stations they held as college professors. How could they ignore the importance of what they were doing and face each other with expressions of primal ignorance? I couldn't help notice that none of them **was** facing me. Except for my maladroit entry, I'm not sure they were even aware of my presence. I stared at them, and worried.

I had expected to see Stanley Kutch there. I met him during my interview. He showed promise as a mentor and his presence would have calmed my anxiety about the meeting. Since I had no idea what was expected of me, I sat still with my mouth shut and listened.

Claudia Cooper, the department head, tramped into the room with her butt in the air as though it were held aloft by a string. She stopped at the lecture desk and stood there, busy with her briefcase, obviously a souvenir from a past conference, with only her arms in motion as if the string that held up her butt also supported the rest of her and allowed movement only from her shoulders forward. Her dress, resembling a nondescript sack bound with a cord around her mid-section, revealed little of what lay beneath except for a noticeable abdominal bulge. Her austere appearance was unchecked by makeup and, as much as I prefer natural beauty to colored faces, her stark presence was intimidating. Her hair fell in long, graying strands; lifeless, like a pelt casually thrown over her shoulder. As I would discover later, a perfect complement to her character. Her gray-green eyes, as dull as ash, flitted over the room with unexpected quickness. And, in keeping with her lack of elegance, her wire-frame glasses, held in place by the hooked tip of her nose, did not impose on her otherwise Spartan fashion. I had not placed much credibility in the notion of witches, but I began to wonder if there might be something to it.

She ruffled through a fistful of papers, looking at one and muttering some sort of confirmation to one of the instructors, then another.

"Now, August, I only have you down for sixteen hours." I was not even to get an introduction. She didn't even look at me. "We had a conflict with Mr. Smithers," she continued. "He can't teach the one-ten class, intermediate algebra, and you have that time free, but that would give you nineteen hours."

Then she looked at me. Or rather, stared. No, glared. Glared at me with those lifeless eyes that could reach through my body and yank my soul straight into Hell. Like most other folks, not actually having been in Hell, I was only surmising the authenticity of my vision.

"I really have no idea what to expect, here," I said, "since I haven't done this before." And I wondered if I had humbled myself sufficiently to avoid any displeasure that might have been at the root of her dispassion.

"I mean, nineteen hours is a lot," she explained. "But most of us here do this sort of thing every semester."

The glimmer of evil peeked from her mythical eyes. And that led to other apprehensive stares, as if waiting for me to either protest in fury or rally to Claudia's cause and accept whatever arrangement she thought best.

"All I can say is I'll try it and see how it goes." I scanned the room for some sign validating my response, but the uninspiring faces yielded nothing. "All I need is time to prep for the calculus class before it meets."

The mood in the room suddenly fell into calm, satisfied that I had surrendered my virtue.

"Oh! You know," she said. "I forgot to tell you. I need you to teach general physics. We lost the instructor who did that last year and according to your college transcript you've had quite a few physics and science courses."

The turmoil of my wrestling brain seemed to lock my mouth shut, allowing a good deal of time to pass within the solitude of my now vacant mind. Enough time for everyone to perfect the mental image they would form of me and size up my gumption. Without even looking at them, I knew they were all staring at me again, an evil spirit hovering over my life waiting for me to reveal my weakness, then striking with a decisive blow to crush my resolve. I had been there many times. "General physics?" I asked.

"Yes. General physics. Mr. Aydelott decided at the last minute he wanted to work on his doctorate, so he left to go back to school. That means we don't have anyone to teach it and we have…" she rifled through some other papers on the desk, "sixteen enrolled in it this semester."

I'm normally not given to panic, but I had only signed on to teach math and general physical science. Physics was not even a consideration, nor had I had much to do with it for several years. However, my background as a structural engineer gave me a good head for physics and, hell, I had read the old calculus book I had resurrected from my stash of college memorabilia and felt confident that I could deliver effective instruction on the subject. What would be so difficult about physics? All I needed was a book.

"Do you already have that in my schedule?"

She went back to the first stack of papers.

"No. General physics is scheduled for the one-ten slot. I guess that means I'll have to find someone else to take the intermediate algebra."

She apparently was determined that I was going to have a general physics class regardless of what I said. I figured it would be best not to fight it and jeopardize any possibility of forming even a marginal alliance with the division chair.

"Okay, general physics it is," I said. "Is there a lab?"

"Lecture is one-ten, Monday, Wednesday, and Friday. The lab is at one-ten on Thursday." She rifled the papers again. "You don't have anything then, so I guess this will fit."

I had already left the meeting, at least mentally, and didn't hear the next bomb she dropped.

"August? August, did you get that?"

"I'm sorry, no. I was thinking."

"Well, I forgot to tell you that I have you down for intermediate algebra at Boyd Atkins on Monday night from five till seven-thirty."

I was right in the middle of digesting the wad of crap about physics and this new chunk of news stuck in my gullet like a plug of tobacco that had inadvertently slipped down the wrong way. I was beginning to understand how Hercules must have felt when he faced his twelve labors. I had not been an avid student of mythology, but I knew enough to recognize that the ancient personification of conflict was not in itself, entirely mythological. It still stalked the courage of modern man.

"Exactly what is Boyd Atkins?"

"Oh, it's a prison just outside of Springer. We teach several classes out there. All of the teachers say the students are very nice to work with."

The word "prison" startled me and I had to think for just a moment about what she said. And she said it without any change in her expression. Prison? Classes? Students who undoubtedly are prisoners? Nice to work with? I would be teaching prisoners? What if they took me as a hostage? Did Hartmann's benefits include additional life insurance? And what about riots? Prisoners? Claudia had tossed out this information so casually, as if it were something I might encounter every day.

"Prison?"

"Oh, it's minimum security. They don't have any hardened criminals or anything like that there. It's completely safe and all of the instructors who have been out there have really enjoyed the experience."

I couldn't get my mind off the word "prison." And I was alarmed not so much at the idea of a prison, but rather the prospect that I might actually be in one. Somehow I just couldn't accept the use of both "prison" and "enjoyed the experience" in the same context. Claudia acted as if she was really serious, but I wasn't quite able to accept that, either. I was familiar with education programs in prisons but I had never made the connection that regular, everyday, ordinary teachers did that. And I wasn't even a bona fide teacher, yet. I figured that anyone who had the strength of character to teach in a prison must have undergone training in such things as how to quell riots and insurrections and been given some sort of assurance that his personal effects would be taken care of should anything happen to him. While I sat there blowing all of this through my mind, Claudia rallied to my confusion.

"You seem like you don't really want to do this."

She stared at me with eyebrows raised above her glasses, much like my third grade teacher who used that technique to threaten her students into submission. I had the feeling that if I didn't accept the class there would undoubtedly be some sort of retribution. I didn't want to be the subject of retaliation the first day on the job.

"Oh, I don't think I'll have a problem with it, I've just never done that sort of thing before." I lied about the problem thing.

"Well, if you're uncomfortable with it, I can probably find some-one else to take it. It's just that I would have to juggle the schedule a lot and rearrange several of the other instructors' classes…"

They were all staring at me again. I knew it. It was like cosmic rays streaming through a haze of censure and slowly transforming my body into a horrid, insubordinate creature. Who was I, but a mere novice instructor, to question the solidarity of their purgatory? The longer I hesitated to accept the assignment, the more severe my denunciation of their ideals.

"No, it's okay." I lied again. "I'll give it a try this semester and see how it goes."

"Okay, but I don't want to push you into anything you don't feel comfortable with."

I think she lied, that time.

"By the way," I asked. "Where is this Boyd Atkins?"

"It's just outside of Hathaway."

"Where is Hathaway?"

"Okay. If you go to Springer, then take Sixty-two west, you'll run right into Hathaway. Boyd Atkins is just on the other side of town."

She seemed pleased with her explanation. I wasn't.

"If you have any questions, you can talk to Ricky Smithers. He's taught out there for several years."

"Okay, who is Ricky Smithers?"

"One of our instructors. He teaches intermediate algebra, too. You can catch him this afternoon in class."

"Where is his office?"

"Oh, it's in the Math Science Building, but he's never there. He just kind of hangs out."

So, she told me where he wasn't. She was really going out of her way to be helpful. Claudia had moved on to the next item on the agenda and everyone else seemed to have affirmed their faith in my resolve to be one of them. After such intense anticipation I wondered just what event actually marked the point at which I became one of them. Was it when I sold out my resolve to the tyranny of unconditional submission to academia, or could it have been when I merely entered the door?

The meeting ended soon after and I was left to grapple with uncertainties on my own behalf. No one offered any assistance, knowledge, or kind words. Somewhere during the meeting I had missed the intellectual discussion and personal enlightenment. And the host of camaraderie I had anticipated had not given me a kind welcome. The intellectual discourse seemed to have been drowned out by the chorus of indifference. And any personal enlightenment I might have found did nothing for my current state of wisdom, which was faltering gravely toward wanting to be somewhere else. If the folks there were really the faculty I would be working with, any expectations I might have had about success had just been abruptly pruned from the fragile limbs of my ego. I wondered if this is the way the girl in the Wal-Mart parking lot might have felt?

Chapter 2

F resh air replaced the unanticipated discouragement from the meeting, and the sudden burst of chimes that overtook the campus fell into steady, rhythmic beats, long and bold, reverberating across the grounds. The peals, one by one, powerful and majestic, died slowly to near quiet just before the next plunged into the air to replace it. I could almost feel the vibrations. There I was, belched from the jaws of mortality and into the great ivy-covered walls of academia and the pomp and circumstance that bespoke its sanctity, humbling me with prominence.

I wandered through the small campus and found myself in front of an abandoned foundation. I stared at the bolts protruding from the top of the stone. Rusted stubs of metal, cocked at an angle and reaching upward as if toward some divine salvation from their destiny that held them fast in solid pools of mortar. The statue that had graced the campus there on that foundation portrayed the founder of the college, the late Dr. Johannes Avery Hartmann, and that was some time ago. According to the book about Hartmann College I purchased a couple of weeks earlier in the campus bookstore, no one seemed to know what happened to it.

The two bolts at the apex had moored the good doctor to his station overseeing the daily and nightly affairs of the college campus. It was said that the nightly affairs could be quite lively at times, causing serious concern among the local citizens of Elkridge. Of course, the good doctor would not have been aware of much of it since he was destined to look in only one direction: north. It made sense, then, that the legendary uprisings took place predominately on the south campus.

From my position squarely in front of the brick structure, I could picture the old boy standing there, his feet bolted fast to the base, long coattails blowing in a breeze as rigid as his likeness, and his hat shadowing the hard and distinguished face. The moustache overhung delicate lips, almost touching a stately beard that, according to numerous photographs, was surely better kept on the statue than on the old man himself. Each hand tenaciously grasped a lapel and the figure was focused on what was purported to be, by the inscription that remained on the base, the future of Hartmann College. Why it would have lain to the north I have no idea, but that's where the good doctor looked for it. Hartmann College had had its future; it just never happened into really good fortune, as Dr. Hartmann always believed it would. I, like the good doctor, was looking for a future, too.

So I stared at the statue that wasn't actually there. Like my life. I remember a lot of it. I just knew that it wasn't normal, or what I envisioned normal to be. Of course, my limited exposure to the many facets of society undoubtedly gave my perspective of normalcy short-shrift. My wife, Alexis, and I had had a home and jobs. She had seemed content until about three years ago. That's when I also stopped being content. And I have no idea why. And that is when I began to forget all that I had been. It overtook me slowly, like a disease that creeps through the body, manifesting itself in the organs and ultimately, the body's behavior. At first, I wasn't aware of it. Then Alexis began making observations that seemed odd to me. As it turned out, they weren't so odd. After my wife left, I finally realized that I had this… affliction, whatever it was, like something drove me to commit random stupid acts. I had to get rid of it. I was determined to expunge it from my life and mind.

I had given up a good position at a growing company. I had forgone seniority, friendships, and a promising financial future. I had assumed a significantly smaller salary, no acquaintances, and no financial prospect. All of this in order to teach at Hartmann College. I didn't exactly understand, at that moment, why I had done that.

But, there I stood, in the campus square, the object of odd looks, and I was staring at an image of something that wasn't even there. And I wondered if what I saw in Hartmann College, whatever that might have been, wasn't really there, either. And if whatever was choking the life out of me would respond to the change and give me back my life.

I figured I was better off than Hercules, having been burdened with only two labors instead of twelve. Then I thought of the lesson plans I had not yet completed. And I wondered how the hell I was going to teach physics. And what had happened to the girl in the parking lot?

Chapter 3

I didn't quite see how I was going to get fifty-five calculus lectures into only forty-four class periods. And for each of the forty-four lectures, figuring out how to abbreviate the material into a fifty-minute class with something of substance pretty well finished off my enthusiasm. I sat at my desk, scarred from years of abuse from college, thinking of my old professors, who surely had been as frustrated then as I was, and contemplated the trauma I would experience after severing what was necessary from my lectures to fit them to the short term. I was just finishing the plan for Calculus and was on my way to the restroom when I met Horace Klieburn.

One might believe that such a small woman had her growth stunted from an addiction to coffee and smoking at an early age. Large glasses rested on an almost indiscernible nose leading me to wonder what was preventing them from falling off her face. A plump midsection gave definition to her small frame. Her voice, a rendition of acute laryngitis, was remotely similar to a bullfrog. Instead of the calm, genteel eloquence of a petite lady, one was greeted with a deep patois having the sharpness of barbed hooks. A volley of sentences, heavy with spurious grammar, accompanied the croaking.

Stanley had mentioned that she was the second oldest professor at Hartmann College; one of those professors who never faced a challenge that required ambition. She was perfectly content to reign over her ignorant wards, imparting the virtues of American government and history to what she considered the sordid lives of today's generation. She was neither creative nor effective in her methodology, but for some reason most of her students managed to skim through her classes with some knowledge of the content, or at least, that's what the annual faculty recognition awards indicated.

"You must be the new professor, ah… ah… now someone just told me your name…"

Horace was unlocking her door, studying me while her mouth

spewed words like gravel through the air. I had just left my office and could almost feel the chat hitting me in the face.

"August," I said. "August Lane."

"Ye-es," she said, beginning the word in an upper octave and letting it slide to a bass pitch. "August. I'm terrible with names."

She labored with three books that would have been little more than an inconvenience to the larger stature of most people. She had been working at her door just long enough for her perfume to bite my nose with an acute sweetness, almost as severely as her rough voice sanded my ears.

"I've seen you on campus but I didn't know who you were. I asked Francis who that handsome man was and he didn't know, either. I'm glad you're going to be one of us."

Any comfort I might have gained from the promise of my new career was distressed by her innuendo of the battlefront: the "us" and the unmentioned "them."

"Well, I hope that will be a good thing." I smiled. "I would hate to think that I brought unrest to the honorable world of academia."

"Well, you know," she started her sentence again with an upper octave bleat, "unrest is not always undesirable. There seems to be a lot of it in my classes."

She let loose a hideous laugh that bore an impact like someone had slapped their hands over my ears. The concussion left me dazed as she continued laughing to herself and disappeared into her office.

I turned to continue my journey to the restroom trying to dissipate the ringing in my head when the elevator door at the end of the hall opened and a silhouette of a curious figure waddled toward me. It was a short and squatty man with what appeared to be an extremely large head. Each step was a deliberate attempt to balance the disproportionate weight above each stubby leg by swaying its mass from side to side, much like a toy robot.

"Good morning, good morning," he wheezed, spending the words as if each was worth a month's salary. "Are you one of us?"

I could almost feel the sluggish words hover in the air like he was trying to reign them back in. And, there was the "us" thing again. I wondered if there was really concern for confrontation.

"Good morning. Yes, I'm August Lane."

"August who?" Heavy glasses framed squinting eyes, his entire bulbous face taxed by the question of my identity. He did not stop waddling, since the momentum of such a large mass would continue to carry him forward in spite of any attempt to halt it.

"Lane."

I paused so it would have time to find its way through the tangle of hair sprouting from his ears.

"August Lane."

"Oh, yes," he wheezed. "Yes. You're the ah … ah … math guy, aren't you?"

"Yes," I said. Perhaps my prominence was more than just apparent. "Yes, I am. And you are…?"

"Frank."

I waited for the rest of it but by the time he had waddled another ten feet, I was certain that there would be no more information offered.

"Is that your first name, or last name?"

"Oh, you're one of those people who are inclined to find need for a given name." He waddled three more steps while his words drifted toward me. "Able. Frank Able. In fact, just to put things accurately, so you don't become confused, my name is actually Francis Able. But, after hearing that, I'm sure you'll understand why I go by the name of Frank."

While my bladder wore at my discomfort, his oration wore at the time. He managed to finish the sentence just as he reached the end of the hall and tottered into his office.

The name was familiar to me because I had heard it mentioned often, and I had come across it in a book written about the college. He must have been the Francis who Horace mentioned. No one I talked to could remember his not being there. I had seen him at least once, not knowing he was one of the more colorful legends of Hartmann College.

The men's restroom was one flight down on the second floor. I stood at the urinal in welcome relief reading the various passages of wisdom left on the wall by previous patrons. I was puzzled by some of them because of the fresh appearance of the ink, although the quips dated back to my own college days. Contemporary youth still recognized the value of generational graffiti. They had not been able to better it.

The glass in the windows, cracked from old age, I suppose, began vibrating in a subtle hum with the chimes that rang outside. It was time to start the games.

*****

Chapter 4

I have since learned that the first day of class in any semester is a wash for the students and hell for me, especially if I am unprepared for it. I wish I had known this then. Having four different classes on that very first Monday in August would have been difficult for a seasoned instructor. In spite of burying myself in my office two hours before my first class, I could not grasp the magnitude of the day's labors.

I was charged for calculus, but astuteness eluded the students at eight-ten in the morning. Bombarding them with high-level mathematics only compounded their plights. I had survived the same tribulations at their age, and it had not been easy for me then, either. I had always been in awe of the professors' seemingly endless well of knowledge. No matter how much I had managed to extract from that well, there always seemed to be more to fill the bucket. I wondered if my students, fraught with the business of learning, felt the same way about me. Or did they tolerate me as just another obstacle to their collective happiness?

The calculus students were almost eager to learn. I say almost, because the average student displays a slight hesitation toward fully committing himself to the task of learning. And, the environment of a college like Hartmann stifled any inclination a student might have to open a book and study. But these students, who politely listened to my opening remarks and actually opened their books to follow my lecture, appeared to be a better lot than I expected, in spite of their sluggish motivation. The anxiety that rested like a sphincter around my gut relaxed a bit and I thought for a moment that this teaching thing might not be so bad.

Then came general physical science, or GPS, as it is referred to in collegiate parlance. It is one of those colorless courses, devoid of any perceived value to the student, but considered necessary for general education requirements mandated by the powers of higher education. The students who enrolled in it generally considered it an unnecessary invasion of the pursuit of pleasure. They are the students who avoided science in high school and saw no reason to learn that friction was what prevented their one-hundred-fifty dollar sneakers from slipping out from under them and causing bruises on their butts.

My entrance into the classroom had little effect on the chatter. Only a few students actually turned to the front and looked at me. I was invisible to the rest of them.

"Good morning," I said, cutting through the profuse babble on my way to the lecture table at the front of the room. "This is general physical science. If that's not what you expected, you should probably find where your class is being held."

Finally, the din receded.

"What was that?" a girl from the rear of the room asked while pulling on a strand of bright, green gum that was anchored by her teeth. She had been engaged in a lively interchange with her neighbor.

I trained my eyes on her and the green strand of gum wrapped around her finger. "If you want to know what I'm saying up here, you'll need to pay attention." That should set them right, I thought.

"I said this is general physical science. If that's not what you're here for, you're in the wrong room."

Poking the wad of gum back into her mouth, she and her neighbor promptly got up and left, leaving snickers in their wake.

I would have a hard time getting used to the somber faces and indifference to the cosmos. That was certainly not the way I had envisioned my foray into teaching. Where were the boisterous, excitable electrons of youth that zoomed about the ideology of the classroom in undying curiosity? Where was the multitude of questions about the meaning of life and the wisdom of mathematics and science? Maybe I was in the wrong place.

Once I had established rule over my kingdom, I took roll and passed out the syllabi. I immediately followed with a one-time lecture about classroom protocol, emphasizing that they would be expected to learn something.

I'm pretty sure it was shock that held them there with faces drawn and nettled for that few moments before the mumbling spread through the room. I could see that I would not be popular. I would learn later that I had just destroyed one of the legacies of Hartmann College: GPS as a "pud" course, or one of those that requires only the presence of a warm body in a chair. That sort of thing is long remembered by a student body. The typical student relies on a core of non-challenging courses that he can breeze through without the unrealistic expectation that he actually learn something. And since he really wasn't expected to learn anything, his grade reflected only the fact that the professor recognized his name enough to honor it with a grade. A more familiar name might warrant an A. A less familiar one, a lowly B.

My lecture to an unreceptive and rude audience was interrupted when a young lady walked into the classroom and placed a paper on the table in front of me. She stood there like a predator watching her prey. And I stopped to watch her. I really couldn't help it. She would have been an attractive girl had a mass of colorful makeup not obscured her face, the long blondish hair that caressed her shoulders, almost teasing them. The short, tight-fitting skirt barely covered her essentials, and her blouse, appearing a size too small, could not have been donned without considerable effort. The fabric was cut unmercifully low to reveal two enormous breasts that looked like they would become dislodged if she were to so much as pull back her shoulders.

"This is general physical science," I said to her. "Is this where you need to be?"

"Yes. I have a form from Dr. Tipton," she said, almost cooing

I read the form she had deposited on the table. Apparently, she had registered a learning disability with the Dean of Student Affairs and the letter specified certain requirements the faculty must meet on her behalf.

"You are Melanie Parker?" I read the name from the form.

"Yeah?" She shook her head.

"Okay, Miss Parker, suppose you take a seat and I'll discuss this with you after class."

She nodded again and sashayed to a desk while her skirt revealed a perfect outline of her derrière. It took just a moment for me to re-cover.

The remaining thirty-five minutes, which seemed like thirty-five hours to both myself and, I'm sure, the students, brought little more than scowls and apathy. They might as well have been foreign students that spoke no English at all. The chimes delivered salvation to my waning valor.

I don't like to admit that I'm easily intimidated, but by the end of the class I felt like I had surfaced from the depths of a lake with lungs on the verge of collapse from the lack of air. I think I was almost gasping as I reached my office. I'm not prone to hyperventilation, but I've no other explanation for it. Those young, smart-assed bastards were going to be tough. But, I could be tougher. After all, I was the instructor. I made the rules. Of course, that didn't guarantee they would follow them. And I never stopped to think what would happen if they chose not to. I had burst the idea of GPS as a course that students used to grease their transcripts. I was going to be that "son-of-a-bitch professor" who screwed them out of a grade.

Miss Parker followed my heavy, erratic breathing to my office after class as I was weighing heavily the impact of her presence in my classroom in her absurd outfit, considering all of the stories I had heard concerning faculty-student relationships. A feeling of insecurity surrounded me and clutched my lungs and I suddenly found myself straining for air.

I sat in my chair, a creaky, threadbare relic, and she sat in the guest chair facing me, her book on her lap, fortunately concealing what her short skirt didn't. I scanned the dour beige walls, scabbed with blotches of white where paint used to be. The suspended ceiling tiles festooned between the metal tracks as if the dirt embedded in the worn carpet had some collective gravitational attraction pulling them toward it. It was unbelievable when I first laid eyes on it, and I kept hoping that maybe it was just the shock that made it look so depressing. It wasn't.

I read the letter, again. It spelled out requirements for supplementary auditory materials and visual aids.

"Miss Parker, I understand what the letter is saying. But I have to be honest with you. Other than a few demonstrations, we don't have any of these materials available to us here for physical science." I looked at her hoping for empathy. "In fact," I continued. "I'm not aware of materials like this for any science course we offer."

"Oh, that's okay?" She said, waving me off. "If you could just like speak plain and not go too fast, I should be okay?" She smiled wickedly, not in an evil way, but deliciously, like eyeing forbidden fruit hanging from a tree, and then she spoke very slowly. "Oh, and sometimes I'm a little slow?" She leaned forward. "I may need some extra time on the tests and things like that?"

I was still trying to recover from her smile and overcome my sudden surge of testosterone, at the same time wondering why she ended her sentences in questions.

"I don't see a problem with that. You can take extra time after class to complete your exams. If I go too fast with my lectures and demonstrations, just let me know."

"And," she added, "I might need some extra help, like tutoring or something like that?"

"My office hours are posted on the door. I'll be happy to help you if I'm available."

It seemed like it took her an unusually long time to agree to the terms. I can't remember a thing she said after that, but I certainly remember what she did. After conveniently dropping her books on the floor, and being from a conservative generation to which chivalry still has some significance, I began retrieving them and she knelt down beside me there in the middle of my office. And she bumped into me, I'm pretty sure intentionally. Several times.

"Uh-oh," Stanley said as he swept into the office. In spite of the weak enrollment, office space was short at Hartmann so most of the faculty shared offices. Stanley shared his office with me.

I clumsily placed the books into Miss Parker's arms and we both rose.

"I'll see you in class on Wednesday," I said. "If you have any questions, let me know."

"Thank you, Professor Lane," she cooed, just before she turned and strutted out. I didn't think there had been quite that much swish in her hips before. I wished I had said something to her about her choice of clothing.

Stanley Kutch was a tall, lanky sort with graying hair advanced beyond my own. His long, affable face gushed with paternal wisdom and anyone meeting him for the first time would quickly draw him into his confidence. The tall chin, pulled by years of its own weight, balanced the high forehead and long bridge of a nose that was not even slightly askew as one would find on most faces. The lips, thin and appearing even thinner between the tall nose and large chin, neither smiled nor frowned, but held a firm line noncommittal to both common and uncommon attitudes that he might encounter. Without his glasses, I imagine Stanley would have seen little of the world. Behind the heavy lenses danced eyes that seemed to be unscathed by what lifetimes usually bestow upon their owners. Together with the graying hair the overall effect was a portrayal of wisdom and serenity. I needed both.

He sat at his desk, bent over course plans and, and in spite of his experience, was resisting any inclination to start on them. His legs were too long for his chair and only one would fit beneath the desk. I stood there awash in a conundrum waiting for Stanley to say something.

Finally, he spoke. "She looks like she might be a problem."

"You really have no idea how much of a problem," I said. "She has a learning disability. Her official requirements are visual and audio supplements to the lessons." I sat down. "For science."

The haughty smile radiating from his face annoyed me. Not because of him. But, because of myself. I had just allowed a little vixen do a number on me. I looked at Stanley's smug face.

"You think this is funny, don't you?"

"Let's just say that I have a fondness for watching someone come of age."

I leaned back in my chair trying to be nonchalant. I knew that he knew I was upset. "You like to watch people struggle?"

"I do."

I was wrong to think that his smile could not get larger.

"Especially new college professors." He dropped part of the smile and looked at me sincerely. "It's a different world in here. It's like a void in the universe that God forgot about. The rules you live by in the real world don't apply so much here. College has its own rules."

I pondered the weight of his words. At the time they certainly made sense. I just didn't understand why. Stan's advice hung in my mind, taunting me with some hidden meaning that would serve as extra baggage I would have to lug around while I gained maturity as a professor.

"So, other than the typical student come-on, how are you doing?" He said.

"I'll be better around four-o'clock."

"Oh, they're getting to you already, are they?"

"Hell, the day started that way."

I moved my GPS books to the top of whatever was laying on the table behind my desk. Alexis keenly observed that I did not necessarily subscribe to the notion that everything had a place. At least, not the place she would have selected. I did try to keep some order about my affairs, but not in the neatest fashion. One day into the semester and the table already overflowed.

"You know," I said. "I really thought teaching would be a grand experience. One of those revelations in life that recharges your confidence in humanity and leaves you with some satisfaction that our future leaders will be competent enough to know the difference between responsibility and excuses."

Stanley gently laid down his pencil and slowly turned his chair toward me. He leaned back as much as he could, since his chair didn't do that, and he smiled.

"I sense that you are not completely in tune with modern education," he said.

"The only thing I'm in tune with right now is my own foolishness."

"Oh, come on, now. You're not going to let these simple-minded adolescents predominate, are you?"

"Easier said than done." Vulnerability sucked my body into the chair. I could feel it pulsing, eager to latch its claws into my integrity. "I'm definitely not prepared."

"No, that's something that's going to take a lifetime," he said, waiving his finger. "You can't get prepared for something you've never experienced."

Stanley was right. Due to all of the unpredictable circumstances of the job, there's no way I could have prepared for it. I had envisioned myself as the Don Quixote of education. I was ready to charge ahead with my lance of knowledge and topple the flailing arms of ignorance. I would set right the mistaken notion that learning was trite and unnecessary. But, I found myself charging in the wrong direction with a broken lance. And Stanley was having a good time with it.

"Well, I don't really have time to mope about it now," I said. "I've got to find out how to get to Boyd Atkins. Then I have to find out what the hell I'm supposed to do if I actually get there."

"Boyd Atkins?" Stanley said. "That's the prison, isn't it?"

"So I'm told. I think I'm teaching intermediate algebra."

"Gee, I've never taught there."

I emptied my cup into the trashcan and filled it with fresh coffee. Well, it wasn't exactly fresh, but it was better than the dregs that had been spawning new life forms in the bottom of my cup.

I found my way to the Dean of Academic Services. I had interviewed for the teaching position in his office. Administration Building, first floor at the end of the hall. Mary Einhorn, his secretary, was sitting prim and proper at her desk guarding the door to Dr. Gaines' office. During my interview, she had advised me on key matters of protocol.

"Ms. Einhorn?" I said striding up to her desk. "Good morning."

"Professor Lane," she said as if talking to a child. Her eyes looked like large green marbles inside the white, retro glasses that had somehow escaped from the sixties. "It's good to see you again. How do you like Hartmann College so far?"

"It's a very … quaint college, isn't it? I've settled in but I'm not sure I'm quite up to a full day of the rigors of teaching."

Tightly gathered auburn hair rested in a bun on her head giving her the appearance of a holy roller. I used to call them "bun ladies" when I was a kid. The style was typical of the non-denominational church down the street from us that would flood the neighborhood with screams of absolution and song every Sunday evening. Her hair was not unattractive, but unsettling. I wondered what it looked like when unleashed from its holy bindings. Her sweet face showed much more promise.

"Oh, come on now," she said. "The first day is not that bad is it?"

"No, I guess not. It could be a lot worse."

"I suppose you would like to see Dr. Gaines?"

"No. I actually came to see you."

Mary raised her eyebrows, put down the catalog she was reviewing and tapped a pencil on her hand. "What can I do for you?" she asked through a coy smile.

I caught a whiff of the most delightful scent. Not strong. Just a hint of something bold, tempered with sweetness, but not too sweet. And spicy. Almost masculine. It spoke kindly of her.

"What can you tell me about Boyd Atkins?"

"What do you want to know?"

"For starters, how do I get there? Who do I see? What do I do? What do I take with me? And anything else you think I should know. Oh, and can you tell me where Ricky Smithers hangs out or where his classes are?"

She opened a drawer and took out a map. "First of all, you are here," she said, opening it flat on her desk. "You take this highway to Springer," she said, tracing her finger along the route, "then turn west toward Price. The prison is on the far side."

"I think I have a map in my car," I said.

"I don't know the administrator's name, but just ask at the guard's window."

"Do I need to take anything with me?"

"Just your driver's license," she said, raising an eyebrow and smiling, "but I'm sure you always carry that."

I ferociously jotted notes in the notebook I cleverly thought to take with me. Between notes, I took in her mysterious attractiveness. She was not the cover-girl type, nor would I expect to see her strutting down a runway in a fashion show. But there was something striking about her appearance that held my attention. Like how a missed phone call taunts you to wonder who it was that called. And what it was they wanted.

While she explained the workings of Boyd Atkins and distance learning, in spite of her charm, my mind intermittently rambled into other areas of interest. Like Alexis. And why she left. And what I could have done to prevent it. Questions kept popping into my mind. Things that continually nibbled at my confidence.

Alexis and I had practically no social life. Very few friends. And very little in common. And I couldn't really remember what had drawn me to her in the first place. Each year of our marriage it seemed she found more shortcomings in my demeanor, and she made certain that I was aware of them. Perhaps that was why I was unworthy of friends. Or, at least, her friends. Even when she asked for a divorce, she wanted nothing else. No alimony, nothing except the house and car. Of course, she made more money than I did anyway, so I was not entirely surprised. I let her keep the house. I didn't need it. I wanted to get far away.

Then I thought about what possibilities might lay at Hartmann. Like, how I would go about establishing a network of friends. And, if luck was to play any part of my new life, maybe even a close acquaintance. A pretty one. A smart one. Someone with whom I could communicate. I looked at Mary more closely.

As I left her office, an elderly man, heavy-set and slump shouldered, brushed past me. The aroma of well-worn tweed followed him and his sidekick, a younger man in black, all black, sporting a pony-tail. They conducted a lively interchange with flaring voices and occasional glances around them as if they expected someone to be eavesdropping. I thought I recognized the larger man as Dr. Damascus, a cornerstone of the college. He certainly looked impressive. Perhaps academia would manifest itself in my own appearance one day soon. As I stood there staring at him, he glanced back at me, stopped and stared briefly. I can only say that I have never seen that look on any benevolent face. A chill flashed over me just before he turned and continued down the hall. I had no idea what had just happened, but I knew I didn't feel any better for it.

I had acquired from Mary a wealth of knowledge that I should have been able to find in simple documentation. A user's guide. A policy and procedures manual. Or something in print. But I wouldn't have found it. Not at Hartmann. I always thought of an institution of higher learning as a place where knowledge was sacrosanct and freely shared by all who sought it. But like most other conceptions I had formed during my fifty-seven years, this was entirely wrong. The sharing of knowledge went only so far as the student, and that was marginal. The faculty was left to struggle with the unknown. It was much like a scavenger hunt. If you knew where to look, you might find what you were looking for.

*****

I found Ricky Smithers in the Math Science Building between classes.

"Boyd Atkins, huh?" His playful eyes looked at me with a smirk that echoed the ruffled hair. The tousled look seemed to conceal the gray that was slowly overtaking his head, as well as much of his ears.

"You say that like it's something I shouldn't be doing."

"Oh, no, it's not that," he chuckled, the small dimples just visible. "I just wonder why they stuck you with something like that?"

"What do you mean?"

"Well, hell, Boyd Atkins is a good forty minute drive from here. From the look on your face I'd say nobody bothered to fill you in on the details."

"So, maybe you can?"

Since Ricky was of my own height, I didn't have to strain my neck up or down to watch his articulated explanation of the prison. His lips, which any woman might have found irresistible, seemed to form each word perfectly so as to reduce the strain on my defective hearing to understand him. He also warned me about potential situations that could throw my classes awry. I also asked him about the general demeanor of the typical algebra student I would find there. I would not normally be concerned about this detail except that the students I asked about happened to be in prison. And they were sent there for some reason. I just hoped it wasn't for assaulting a teacher.

Suddenly without banter he said, "You know, these guys have never been around math much. Most of them are fairly young. Most never completed high school. They're trying to make up for lost time."

He paused to make a deposit of tobacco juice in a Pepsi can, which obviously no longer contained Pepsi. A few more chews and he continued.

"Those guys are in that class because they want to be. I mean just getting into that class is a privilege. Not just anybody can do it. They have to be on their best behavior. You just have to take it easy with them and start with the basics. I mean," and here he started drawing out his words, "the – real – basics. I usually can't get everything in I want to in the semester. I have to leave something out or I'd be going so fast I'd leave them all in my dust and they wouldn't know which way I went."

While I listened to Ricky orate on intermediate algebra, my elation with being a college professor suddenly turned from its soaring circles of adulation and started a nosedive toward fear. I went back to the office to eat lunch and prepare for my trip to the prison that evening. The chimes rang out against the peculiar silence of the campus. Each peal exuded the essence of academia and soothed my apprehension with hope. There, within the walls of an institution of higher learning, was sufficient justification for me to grasp at the slightest chance of instilling in even one fledgling the spirit of learning. Of course, I always had been naive and somewhat gullible about such matters, and being the sort that is inspired by the underdog's triumph, I usually find myself in wait for that very thing to happen. I am usually left to wait a very long time.

The chimes. I loved the chimes. I loved the way they reverberated across the campus. I loved the domination of those few seconds of each hour. The forceful resonance that drove all within hearing distance to take note of their ethereal aura. Even when the sound stopped, it didn't. Not for me. I still heard it, echoing in my head as if it had never ceased. It drove me onward into the afternoon.

I joined Stanley, who was already halfway through his two packages of cheese and crackers, apple, and snack bar. I warmed my frozen entree in the microwave and tore into the meager helping of vegetables and two small pieces of chicken that might have been put in the plastic tray by mistake. And I thought about my next general physics class.

Chapter 5

I always liked to rummage around old houses and building, especially hardware stores, the kind that has the creaky, unfinished wood floor that might have been built during the Renaissance, and merchandise hidden beneath layers of dust and stacked so that you have to dig through several tiers to see what's there. The storage room behind the physics lab was very much like one of those hardware stores. I had looked through the room several times and had not even come close to exhausting its store of goodies. I remembered seeing an optics demonstration kit buried beneath one of the many stacks of boxes. It had light sources, mirrors, and lenses and a zillion accessories that handily stuck to a magnetic board. All it required was a power supply, two of which stared at me through the glass in one of the cabinets in the lab. A demonstration of the power of light, mirrors and lenses would have the students bowing to me in awe and begging for more.

I attempted to test the apparatus before class, having carefully arranged the equipment on the whiteboard and set the power supply for twelve volts according to the instructions taped to the inside of the box. I flipped the switch to preview the dazzling display and nothing happened. The power supply did not work, so I exchanged it for the other one after adjusting the controls. The chimes alerted me to the start of class in ten minutes and I did not have time to test the equipment. Hopefully, I would have only to flip the power switch to put the show in motion.

Of the sixteen students, nine girls and seven boys, only one of them possessed any propensity at all toward being there. I can't say that I blamed the rest of them for their lack of enthusiasm. I was not exactly taken with the coldness of physics lectures when I took the course. I had, however, captured their interest with the maze of equipment that was stuck to the large whiteboard at the front of the room.

"Physics is one of those things we often take for granted," I lectured. "You experience physical phenomena every day of your lives without ever realizing that these things are happening and affecting you. You get up in the morning and your body kicks into action. Well, that might be the case for some of you, anyway. Even your body relies on the laws of physics to make it work for you. Everything you do, see, hear, smell, and feel is controlled to some extent by the laws of physics."

I unloaded my introductory monologue giving them time to adapt to my style, if I even had one, and get comfortable with the idea that they were there to learn, even though I knew well enough that most of them weren't. The anticipation grew in open and curious eyes that locked onto me without even blinking.

"Now, we're going to see how one of these phenomena actually works."

With the students eagerly anticipating the forthcoming scientific production, I turned off the overhead lights and flipped the switch on the power supply. In the split second that followed I had no time what-soever to react to the brilliant flashes of light and sudden explosions that occurred in the light canisters attached to the whiteboard. I barely had time to dodge the spray of glass fragments that flew by my head and sprinkled the floor.

I turned toward the class and saw nothing but eyeballs. Even in semi-darkness, eyeballs larger than any eyeballs I had ever seen, except in science fiction movies. Eyeballs that glared in the likenesses of hu-man anatomy, frozen from total astonishment at the spectacle that had just occurred before them.

"Is anyone hurt?" I blurted.

At first there was no response. The eyeballs remained fixed on the curls of smoke that were barely visible in the dim light coming in from the covered windows and that fell on the spoils of the physical "phenomenon." The acrid smell of the electrical burn wafted across the room and one by one the strained faces relaxed and mumbling started. Then giggling. Then all out laughter erupted.

I turned on the lights, which fortunately still worked, and took stock of the damage. Smudges above the smoking light canisters painted an abstract landscape on the whiteboard, and glass shards that had peppered the front of the room gave the carpet a shimmer. The power supply had thrown its breaker and sat quietly on its cart as if nothing had happened. The damage was confined to the light canisters and the whiteboard.

Upon examination of the power supply, I immediately noticed my error. I had forgotten to adjust the voltage multiplier when I exchanged the units. The unit was set to provide twelve-hundred volts.

In the midst of the laughing, still in a state of euphoric ferocity, I couldn't see my face, but I felt quite sure that by that time it would be red. A couple of deep breaths stalled my embarrassment enough to regain control of the class.

"I had every intention of demonstrating to you how light rays are refracted and reflected as they encounter various media. But, I think it might be more prudent to discuss the hazards of electricity."

Stillness overtook the room as the drone of my voice lulled them into cocoons of disinterest. My shoes crunched their way to the whiteboard. "We're not due to study electricity until the second semester, but this might be a good time to mention some of the dangers involved."

Even in the light of the amusing mishap, they remained largely an unmotivated assemblage of uncaring and misdirected souls. Even the mention of the effects of various levels of electric current on the human body, as unpleasant as they may be, were met with only moderate enthusiasm.

When I had finished, a gradual silence settled over the class as they apparently were just beginning to ponder what had happened during the errant demonstration.

"Professor Lane?"

Ah, a question. At last, some sign of intelligence.

"Yes?" I had no idea who the young man was who spoke. I hadn't yet any notion of what their names might be.

"How would that make the bulbs explode like that?"

"As you will learn when we study electricity, the function of a light bulb comes from putting a resistance in the path of electric current so that electrical energy is transformed into light and heat energy, mostly heat. In fact, a typical incandescent light bulb is only about ten percent efficient at producing light. The rest is expended in heat. In this case, the sudden surge of electrical energy was too high for the materials to withstand and something had to give. Rapidly."

I didn't want to waste the moment, so I continued with the first lecture about the scientific method and measurements. That soon took the edge off of the excitement and put them back into their trances.

"For Wednesday, read through chapter one and begin working on the questions at the end of the chapter."

The mention of the assignment set off the alarm for them to begin stuffing their equipment into backpacks and notebooks in preparation for speedy exits.

"And when I say read, I mean study. When you come back

Wednesday I will expect you to have some idea of what I'm going to be talking about."

I could just as well have yelled out the window at the students passing by. They were already making their way for the door mashing bits of glass deeper into the carpet. My career was not getting off to a good start with the janitorial staff.

As I collected my notes I noticed a young lady sitting near the center of the room. She looked up at me with sad eyes that projected skepticism, curiosity, and perhaps, even anger. The dress looked familiar, and so did the girl. Wal-Mart. The girl in the parking lot. Without a doubt, it was her. She looked almost as forlorn in the classroom as she did in the parking lot, although more lucid. The oversized dress hung from her shoulders in folds beneath long, dark hair that cascaded around a very white, simple face.

"Can I help you?" I asked.

"Allison." It came from the doorway. I caught a glimpse of a girl's face peeking around the jamb. "Allison, come on."

Without changing the emotionless expression on her face, she immediately snatched her books, then quickly left. A strange one, she was. I looked at my class roll and found the name Boyer. Allison Boyer. The only Allison in the class. The girl from the parking lot.

College algebra was a change of pace from the complexity of science, but it, too, was a dismal failure. I could tell by the time I reached the second section in the review chapter that they had chosen to pursue other interests, such as daydreaming. They sat listlessly, like worn-out robots, staring blankly at random parts of the room with glazed eyes. Perhaps the day had been too much for them. It had certainly overwhelmed me. When the hour approached I was certain they would be incapable of enduring anymore math. I dismissed class a few minutes early to save them any further anguish. I saved myself a lot of it.

The chimes fell on the hour and whatever was in my head, confusion, uncertainty, wisps of regret, dissolved into the rhythm of Westminster's melody. The collegiate anthem was hypnotizing. My mind flushed itself of the day's trials as I walked down the hall to my office.

I caught the phone just before it quit ringing. That would have happened after the third ring. It was supposed to go to voice mail, but I didn't know how to set that up. So, if voice mail caught the call it would have disappeared into some unknown far corner of the universe. I made a point to call the operator later and ask about it.

"Hello," I was still transfixed by the chimes but I'm pretty sure my voice sounded cordial and not too nerd-like.

"Hi, August. This is Claudia. I just wanted to see how your first day was going."

Claudia. She actually called me to inquire about my first day at Hartmann. I have to admit that I was surprised at her consideration. Maybe she was actually going to be of some help to me.

"From what I have learned," I said, "I would surmise that it has been a typical day, so far."

"Well, I'm glad you haven't had any catastrophes."

I decided not to bring up the incident in general physics. No need to rock the boat. It already had a hole in it.

"By the way," I said. "What do we do about learning disabilities? I got hit with one today."

"Learning disabilities?" The inflection of her voice was enough to tell me that she had no idea. "I guess you would have to talk to the Dean of Student Affairs. I think she is the one in charge of that."

"That's Dr. Tipton, isn't it?" I asked. I didn't wait for an answer. "Well, I have this letter here that requests audio and visual supplements to the lessons for GPS. Hell, I thought we were doing good just to have a textbook for the class."

"Well, talk to Dr. Tipton. She will know about it. Oh, and by the way, don't forget about Boyd Atkins. Do you know how to get there?"

"Yes. Ricky Smithers was kind enough to explain that to me."

"Good. Do you think you'll have any problem with it?"

"Only the fact that you failed to mention the forty-mile trip to get there."

"Oh, that." She paused. "I didn't mention that?"

"If you had, I wouldn't be mentioning it now."

"Okay, sorry. But, good going. I've got to run to class. I'll probably see you tomorrow."

I held the phone to my ear wondering if she really did hang up. The dial tone hummed while I considered her motive for not telling me about Boyd Atkins.

I found a map in my car, the origin of which I have no recollection, and I planned my journey for the evening. The intermediate algebra class at the prison started at five-thirty and I had one more class that afternoon. Many decisions lay ahead: the route, supper plans, what to take with me, what would I do when I arrived, and not the least of my worries, how do you teach prisoners?

I wandered out onto the campus thinking I might find some bit of inspiration that would stall my sudden charge toward despair. The demonstration in general physics had completely undone my ego. I had made a total ass of myself and, barring any further embarrassment, I had probably squashed any possibility of developing a meaningful relationship with my students. I would have to be more careful, although I had no idea how I would do that. I walked absentmindedly with my head lowered as an appropriate manifestation of my state of mind, kicking rocks from the sidewalk. It's a good thing there were no stray dogs in my way.

My mood had sunk through excitement and eagerness to feed on the underbelly of humility. I tried to find something to lighten my self-pity enough to see the rest of the day through while the chimes softened my apprehension. I returned to my office to find the history book and read more about the college.

I found the book under several layers of magazines and papers on my desk, so it had been at least a day since I had looked at it. "The Unofficial History of Hartmann College," it was called. The cover said that it was "unofficially written by Francis H. Able." Thinking about how other folks had described him, I realized that the author of the book fit those descriptions perfectly. Stolid and sarcastic with an abundance of dry humor. I'm sure the book only heightened the animosity between him and the administration. Considerable mention was also made of Dr. Damascus. The prose seemed to conflict with his general reputation as a hallowed professor, instead describing him as a philandering hypocrite. Well, there certainly must be a story there, I thought.

I found my previous stopping place and continued to read while unconsciously worrying about an evening at Boyd Atkins.

Chapter 6

Highway 62 ran west through Springer and past the turnoff that would take me to Boyd Atkins. Mary and Ricky told me it was just on the other side of the town. What they didn't tell me was that the road had very little pavement, most of it having succumbed to an expanse of potholes, each overlapping the ones next to it. Six miles of skipping along the roadway brought me to the edge of what I assumed was Price. The pock-marked road brought out a symphony of sounds from my car that I had never before heard.

Just as I was about to cross into Price, a car tore past me in the opposite direction dancing spiritedly from hole to hole. I thought I recognized the driver as Mr. Hillford from the history department. I had met him during my interview. Even the dirty windshield did not hide the scowl hanging on his face.

Price was one of those places one might consider a non-town. I had seen better habitats among the tar-paper shacks of Mississippi and Alabama. But in Price, the feebleness of humanity lay open like a gaping wound, festering with trash, broken toys, un-drivable vehicles, and black children, mostly toddlers, running wildly among the ruins of fences and yards that were either buried knee deep in weeds or totally devoid of vegetation. The road wound through the small town like a sewer might twist underground through the bowels of a city, carrying waste from one point to another leaving accumulations of debris along the sides.

On the other side of Price, just as Ricky said, a large sign pointed toward Boyd Atkins Correctional Center. Other signs clearly marked the route for visitors and I carefully followed the instructions. As I pulled into the parking lot a white prison van packed with, what appeared to be prisoners, pulled by me and disappeared into the yard behind a huge chain link gate that slid closed behind it. Although not exactly cheery, the faces behind the windows were not necessarily the grim, sinful icons of crime I had expected. They were the faces like those of students in my classroom, people I had worked with, and casual acquaintances.

Why would decent people like that be in a prison van? I parked my car and lugged my briefcase to the visitor's station and stood directly in front of the hole in the glass.

"I'm here to see Dr. Eigenhurtz." I almost yelled since the guard inside had not removed the barrier from the hole and I wasn't entirely certain he was going to. But, after making a multitude of notes in his binder, he finally came toward me and removed the wooden board.

"You here to see somebody?"

"Yes," I said. "Dr. Eigenhurtz."

"Here," he said, stuffing a logbook through a small door at the bottom of the window. "Fill this out and I'll call her. I'll need your driver's license."

I wrote in my name, college, appointment and time in the book and placed it on the shelf with my driver's license. The guard yanked them in through the door.

"She'll be right here."

I said, "Thank you," even though he wouldn't have heard it since he had already slammed the board back in front of the hole.

I was commending myself for my early arrival and at the same time becoming agitated at what seemed like a long wait. Then I finally saw a woman, heavy, and short, moving sluggishly along the sidewalk toward the gate, each step a deliberate and ungraceful effort to move forward. I could only assume that it was Dr. Eigenhurtz. The white hair suggested an elderly lady, not as agile as she should be to traverse the grounds of a prison, unguarded and seemingly unconcerned for her personal safety. I waited patiently while she inched toward me.

"Professor Lane?" Her words crept as slowly as she did to meet me. I moved forward so her extended arm wouldn't tire before she got close enough to shake hands.

"Yes, I am. And you must be Dr. Eigenhurtz."

She gently bobbed her head once. The gesture reminded me of a sloth.

"I really wasn't expecting you," she drawled with excruciating annoyance. "That's why I wasn't here to greet you."

"What do you mean?" I asked.

"Why, a history professor just left. He said he was supposed to teach American history tonight but I explained that our schedule plainly was for algebra."

"That must have been Mr. Hillford I passed on the way in. So, when is history class?"

"History is scheduled for Tuesday nights."

She turned slowly and sidled toward the gate.

"Okay. So, where is the classroom and what do I need to do?"

She stopped her retreat about as fast as a fully loaded train would stop on ice-laden tracks and turned toward me.

"Oh dear, you can't teach tonight," she explained oscillating her head side to side like an old fan. "Since they sent a history teacher, I thought you weren't coming and I've already sent the students back to their dormitories."

I tried to think of something to say with a diplomatic tone, and not accusative or rude. My mind kept stumbling over insulting innuendoes, so I said nothing.

"I'm sorry you had to drive all this way," she muttered, resuming her crawl back to whatever had given her up to greet me.

I signed out at the window and retrieved my driver's license. The guard was just as pleasant as he was when I signed in. I got in my car, and charged out of the parking lot, much, I suppose, as Mr. Hillford had done.

I wasn't aware that I had even driven home. My mind was concocting a strategy to deal with the communication that dried up like a drought-ridden river bed before it ever reached me. I had been mortified by an aging monolith of arrogance and inconvenienced with over two hours of wasted time. And since each two and a half hours of class at the prison was equivalent to one week of regular classes on campus, I was already a week behind in the class and I hadn't even met the students.

My consternation boiled. The conversations I had planned for Claudia were distorted by visions of hands around her neck choking the life out of her. I didn't know her that well, but the short exposures to her character should have been adequate warning. I had been taken in and, as I saw it, screwed. Some measure of vengeance was in order. But how does a college professor extract vengeance upon a colleague without divesting himself of honor? I had much to learn.

Chapter 7

The Math Science Building was strategically located in the geographical center of the campus, presenting to those who worked there a formidable cross-country hike from the parking lots that were located nearer the buildings around the perimeter of the campus. But, I enjoyed walking. In fact, I enjoyed exercise. I don't even know what the insides of most elevators look like because I rarely use them. I habitually take the stairs. Both directions. But that didn't excuse the notion that the folks who worked in the Math Science Building were denied convenient parking. Another thorn beneath the saddle of academia.

My early arrival at my office was planned in hopes of avoiding any quick-tempered reaction that might lead me to jump up and down on Claudia's desk. An e-mail would have been easier, but the cloud of mystique that hung over Hartmann College pervaded the policies with sordid and bizarre conditions, especially those regarding information technology. The computer on my desk was left from the previous occupant. However, I had no access to the campus network. In fact, I couldn't even log onto the computer to use it without the network. The odd thing was that I wouldn't be able to do that until I received my first paycheck from the college. And that would be in another two weeks. It was policy.

I made my way to the Life Science Building and left a note on Claudia's office door. It would be eleven before I would be free to talk to her. That would give me most of the morning to stew about the Boyd Atkins incident.

My office was of little value to me except for a battered desk, two unstable chairs, ancient bookshelves cluttered with obsolete textbooks, and a computer I couldn't use. Of course, there was Stanley. I brought my own laptop to use until the IT gods determined that I was fit to use one of theirs. So, I had two computers on my desk and room for little else.

Eleven o'clock came sooner than I wanted.

"August." My name sounded almost plastic when Claudia spoke it over the phone. "I found your note on my door this morning."

She paused as if waiting for me to acknowledge her. I didn't.

"From the tone of your note I sense that you're upset about something."

I didn't think she could have read my indignation from a simple note. This woman was good.

"Yes, Claudia," I said in my best patronizing tone. "I am rather upset about something."

"Well, are you free now? Why don't you come on over and let's talk?"

It sounded more like a command than a suggestion, which was all right with me. My note probably seemed more like a command than a suggestion to her, as well.

During the course of fabricating scenarios in my head, I must have taken larger steps than usual because I arrived at the Life Science Building before I realized I was there. That threw my logic awry, because I hadn't time to actually decide upon an argument. In a sudden flash of enlightenment I figured I should just be honest about the matter and not offend her. I took the stairs two steps at a time and reached the second floor, hardly breaking stride, in hopes of not changing my mind before I arrived at her office door.

"August, come on in."

Her chipper mood heightened my anxiety. "I went to Boyd Atkins yesterday evening."

"Oh, good." She was suddenly excited. "How did it go?"

"It didn't."

The surprise on her face gave me an edge.

"Just before I got there, I passed Mr. Hillford as he was leaving."

"What was Mr. Hillford doing there?"

"In spite of history being scheduled for Tuesday, our schedule with Boyd Atkins showed him teaching history on Monday evening. When he showed up to teach history, Dr. Eigenhurtz dismissed the class because they were the algebra students. I never got a chance to teach class."

"Why would he be scheduled to teach history on Monday?"

"Well, there I'm stumped, Claudia. I mean I realize that by the end of my first day I'm expected to know everything around here that everyone else has had several years to find out about. But I have to admit that the teaching schedule for Boyd Atkins has completely eluded me."

I knew before I had finished speaking that my remark would draw fire. Her eyes seemed to narrow a bit and muscles tightened the already rigid face, making her glare more alarming.

"August, I'm sorry." Her tone became authoritative. "Why don't you check with Dr. Purdy. He's the director of distance learning."

So much for my good intentions. At the moment I didn't care if I offended her or not.

"Claudia, I have been given a job to do with absolutely no resources to do it. The instructor that had my classes left nothing. Not even a current textbook or any kind of notes. No classroom materials, nothing. I can't even use the campus network. I have to use my own computer. I've had to find everything I need on my own. I have had practically no help from anyone in this place to do anything. And I sort of figured that your job as a department head would be to facilitate my job as an instructor. And now, you're telling me I have to do that for myself as well?"

The rigidity of her face nearly solidified into stone. I had done it again. I hated myself for doing it. She didn't deserve that. I could have relayed my concerns without personal accusations.

"Look," I took a deep breath, "I'm sorry, but you've got to admit the situation I'm in is just a little bit overwhelming. I need some help, here. But, yes, I will contact Dr. Purdy and resolve the issue at Boyd Atkins."

I left immediately before she could respond. I was completely unaware of the loose sense of responsibility within the world of academia that left duty flapping in the breeze of consequence. Contrary to best business practices, those who should have had responsibility seemed only too anxious to dispose of it by means of delegation, or in Claudia's case, neglect. This meeting was probably going to loom over my teaching career as a sort of specter of ineptitude. A constant reminder of my fragile confidence.

The skirmish soured my mood and I made it back to my office in less time than it took to get to Claudia's. I threw myself into my chair and sulked. Self-pity came easily. It waited just beneath the surface of integrity, beckoning me to lift it from its shroud of pride and wrap my injured ego in it. It felt good, but it stung. Much like a foot going to sleep and feeling the relief of being able to move it again while also feeling the needling nerves that enable it.

The chimes rang out the noon hour. The longest chimes of the day.

Note by note, the pity I was culturing withered, and I regained some of my composure. Each peal of the hour added another asset to my store of self-worth. I was a professor. Or, at least, an associate professor. I was teaching in a college. An institution of higher learning. A place of knowledge, sacrosanct ideals, and integrity. And I was a part of it. In spite of its demons and illusory promises, I was a part of it.

I would take care of the Boyd Atkins incident. A college was a business. It could be run like one. And I knew how to solve that kind of problem.

I called Dr. Purdy.

Chapter 8

Humility is a great teacher. She watches you; she assesses you; and with ever sharp justice, she strikes when you least expect it, toppling your towers of pride and integrity. Contrary to my presumption, the first day of classes had not been the worst. In fact, each day seemed to be more treacherous. I soon realized that whatever hole I was digging for myself was getting deeper and my shovel larger. But I couldn't stop digging.

"Professor Lane?"

I think it was the second one that got my attention. That and the soft knock. Melanie Parker posed in the doorway, one hand raised to the doorjamb and the other spread out over her breasts, either pointing at them or holding them in. I wasn't sure.

"Yes, Miss Parker?" I didn't exactly stop working, but I did pause and turn toward her as she advanced into the office and sat in the guest chair which had been divested of its previous glory as a prominent furnishing in some dean's lavish office at some time rather long ago. She leaned over toward me and almost spilled the contents of her very low-cut top into my lap.

"Professor Lane, I missed the last class?"

I have encountered many situations that offered temptations of lustful satisfaction, even without possibility of consummation. Fortunately, my ability to avoid relationships with teenagers has prevented a serious mistake on my part. And, besides, I didn't particularly care for large breasts, regardless of their degree of perfection. I've always fancied legs. And butts.

"I recall noticing that your seat was vacant on Wednesday," I told her. "You're not exactly getting the semester off to a good start."

Her eyes opened into the purest blue, played up with mascara, eye shadow, and liner expertly applied, no doubt, in preparation for this very occasion. If one dared look below, her cleavage screamed "SEX" in a silent burst of maddening exposé. Her arms rested on her thighs and pushed the two delightful breasts together so that they bulged with allure that even appealed to a leg-man such as myself.

There was the question thing, again. "Well, I'm sorry?" She relaxed a bit and extruded her lips into what I think was supposed to be a pucker. "You know, science is just not my thing?" She said, almost apologizing. "And, with my learning disability and all, I don't think I am going to have enough time to study and do my homework?"

I raised my eyebrows in preparation to counter with sage advice. I reached to pick up my cup of lukewarm coffee and missed the handle sending the contents over the lecture notes I was preparing. I mopped up what I could of it and turned toward her hoping that she didn't notice what she couldn't help but have noticed. She showed no reaction to my clumsiness and continued her plea for mercy.

"I have to work late in the evenings and I just don't have time to study?"

"And exactly where do you work?"

"I have this real neat job at a store and it pays real good? If I didn't have this job I just don't know how I would ever be able to go to college?"

I think she was intentionally vague about the job she probably didn't have.

"I'm well aware of your plight, Miss Parker. Many students have to work to get through school. But, you're going to have to make a choice, here. Either you want an education, or you want to work in a menial job for the rest of your life, or you don't want to work at all."
As difficult as it was to avoid the breasts that were projecting dangerously from their confinement, I searched her face for a sign of comprehension. Surely she had some ethical attributes bound up somewhere in her tight garb.

"I'm giving you the benefit of the doubt that you actually have a job that requires a great deal of your time."

It became more difficult to resist glancing over the top of her blouse. During our conversation she had managed to scrunch her shoulders closer together allowing the blouse to drop even lower. I could tell without even looking that her breasts were in a state of suspension, free from any restrictions other than the flimsy material of the blouse.

"But, Professor Lane, I just don't have time. And if I don't pass this course, I won't get to graduate next semester?"

She turned to look toward the door and swung back around, launched herself from the chair and knelt in front of me. No matter how I looked at her, my eyes could not escape the spectacle of her open blouse.

"I… I really can't afford to fail this class."

A statement, this time, instead of a question.

Her pouty lips and sad eyes would have tested the reckoning of any compassionate soul. And the view down her blouse would have tested even an uncompassionate soul. Since my own compassion lent itself more to the fortune of animals lower in the food chain, I did not see the tears that she undoubtedly believed to be there.

"And…"

At this point she rested her hands just above my knees and moved back and forth as if shuffling for position. In addition to providing a gentle stimulation of my sensory awareness to her femininity, the movement caused her robust breasts to sway inside her blouse in a provocative manner. I did not dare let on that at least part of me was responding. She was good at this.

"… I… I will do anything to pass this course, Professor."

She squeezed my legs.

"Anything…"

I kept waiting to hear the climax of her oratory but she stopped before she had really finished speaking and she never got to exactly what anything was, although I knew what it meant.

We had nearly entered no-man's land when I realized that she was serious. I had heard many tales, or more appropriately, jokes about the innocent professor and the hot student who takes him for a ride. I wasn't about to get on that horse.

"I think we need to speak to your advisor," I said, picking up the phone. "I'll give her a call and let her know we're on the way over." Just as my finger pressed the first number she was on her feet, arms straight at her sides, hand clenched. Her pouty mouth and sad eyes had instantly become flashes of anger.

"You – you're mean," she said. In curt staccato words. "You – are – so – very – mean."

I stopped dialing since I really didn't know who her advisor was, anyway.

"You have no right to keep me from passing this course," she almost screamed.

Her clenched fists tightened. I wondered if she thought they were around my neck.

"You professors … you just try to make our lives hell, don't you?"

I still held the receiver in my hand while she ranted on.

"Obviously, I'm not good enough for you."

Her lips took on a peculiar curl, evil-like, and I could see the white of her teeth, like an angry pit-bull. Then her eyes widened and her mouth fell open.

"You're hitting on Allison, aren't you?" she said.

I had no idea who Allison was, but I assumed she would be another sexually-charged vixen, possibly an acquaintance of hers.

"That bitch! I knew that little whore was up to something." She jammed her hands into her hips and looked at me wide-eyed and aghast.

"You mean you like that skinny bag of bones more than me? You couldn't put a prick in her without splitting her in two."
Just before hysteria overcame her, I flashed the phone and dialed security.

"You uppity bastards are all alike," she ranted. She leaned forward and started to launch another volley.

"Security," finally came from the other end of the line.

"This is Professor Lane. Math Science Building, office 302. I need you. Now!"

The person on the phone probably would not have taken me seriously had it not been for Miss Parker's screaming. Then, she moved one jump ahead of me.

"Stop it!" she screamed. "Stop it, Professor. Get your filthy hands off of me!"

"Hurry, NOW!" I yelled into the phone.

I hung up the phone just in time to receive a slap across my face. I had never been slapped before so I wasn't sure of the proper response. In the few seconds I needed to collect myself, Miss Parker had turned and run from the office, pulling her blouse down off of her shoulder on the way out of the door.

The little bitch was good. Almost too good. I sat in my chair, stunned by what had just happened. A few minutes later I heard heavy footsteps and creaking in the hallway.

"I got here quick as I could."

A short, plump, black woman in a uniform hung from the doorjamb, gasping.

"You missed her," I said.

"What the hell happened in here?" she said between wheezes.

"I'm August Lane, by the way. I'm glad you came quickly."

"I'm Wanda," she said. "Glad to meet you Professor. So, what's the ruckus?"

"Miss Melanie Parker. You know Miss Parker?"

"Oh, yeah," wheeze, wheeze. "Me and that girl," wheeze, "go back a long ways."

"Well, Miss Parker is upset because she thinks she will probably receive a failing grade in my class. She's probably right. She tried to come onto me. I supposed you heard her rendition of a damsel in distress over the phone?"

"Professor L," she always called professors by the initials of their last names, "I'm not exactly sure what it was I heard." The wheezing slowed a bit. "What was that girl screaming about? Take your hands off me, and such?"

I looked at Wanda with a less than concerned expression on my face and cocked my eyebrow. "That young woman is dangerous. She doesn't belong in college. And she certainly doesn't belong here."

"Professor, what went on in here?"

I could see that Wanda might have doubts about what I said. Maybe someone else had heard the commotion, but there were no signs of life in the hall. No squeaks of the floor, no talking, no nothing. No one had been near that I knew of.

"Wanda, the girl made a play for me in hopes of getting a passing grade. The door was open and the lights on. Of course, that doesn't mean much when no one else is around. And I assume no one else was, or there would be a convention in the hall by now."

"Do you want to take disciplinary action against her?"

"No. Let's just wait and see what develops."

"All right, Professor L." She turned to go. "But, you remember," she said. "Melanie's smart. I don't mean book smart. I mean street smart. She can do a job on you."

With that, squeaking floorboards followed her like a shadow down the hall toward the elevator. I was sure she would not be taking the stairs down.

I had not been too concerned about Miss Parker until Wanda's warning echoed in my mind. The office suddenly seemed cooler, like an evil spirit hovering over me. What possible inclination would anyone have to believe a cock-and-bull story conceived by a less than aspiring student of marginal success? Who in their right mind would believe such accusations against a college professor, a reputable member of the educational community dedicated to schooling those young individuals? How could I be accused of betraying them? For a moment, any such notion was unthinkable. But, then the pedestal teetered a bit and I realized that some of the staff and faculty who occupied the hallowed halls of Hartmann College were not necessarily IN their right minds.

That thought gave me cause for worry.

I immediately documented everything I could remember about my encounter with Miss Parker. I carefully reconstructed every detail of our meeting, even my conversation with Wanda. I didn't think she would mind. In fact, I figured she would be impressed by my diligence to detail. I had not been at Hartmann long enough to learn all of the intricate twists and turns of its political system, but, I knew that there, within the hallowed halls of ivy, dark corners would be waiting for me.

"Hey, man." Stanley glided in the door. "You look pretty serious."

I shook my head in agreement. "I think I'm about to be initiated into the depths of disharmony. My song of jubilation here at Hartmann, even with minor discord, is about to become a score of sour notes."

"Why, whatever do you mean, dear colleague?"

"I just had an encounter with Miss Melanie Parker."

"Ah, the sex-pot you frolicked with on the floor the other day."

"Well, she was certainly in good form today."

I relayed my account of the event while he sat calmly at his desk trying to stifle laughter. I might have embellished a few minor details, but it was in good faith that I conveyed Miss Parker's exact intentions. I hadn't yet succumbed to emotional repression and was actually enjoying my performance when Stanley broke in.

"Before you get too comfortable with your unfounded security as an irreproachable pillar of academia, I would like to give you some unsolicited advice."

I was grateful for anything a veteran of scholastic combat had to offer on the subject.

"I had a similar experience with a female who would stop at nothing less than getting what she wanted. She was one those gorgeous types that made you wonder, if you know what I mean."

He stretched his long legs out in front of him and reared back with his hands behind his head.

"She was failing the course, didn't come to class very often, flunked all of the exams, and generally didn't do any work at all."

"Yes," I said, "that sounds just like Miss Parker."

"Well, about two weeks before finals, she came to my office. I had noticed her lurking in the hallway but she didn't come in for a long time. And it wasn't until everyone else had gone that she finally came in the door. Then the waterworks started and the sob story followed. She was really very good at it. And I did feel a pang of sympathy for her."

"You know," I interrupted. "I wonder where these kids learn that? If dear old mom is coaching her, there's a real problem in our society." I waved off my observation. "I'm sorry, please continue."

"Well, after so many attempts to sway my judgment, she finally got desperate and said, 'Mr, Kutch, I'll do anything. Just anything,' with particular emphasis on the 'anything'. That was when I said, 'I think we need to go see Dr. Morril,' who was the dean of academic affairs at the time. Well, that pretty much did it for her."

Our laughter brought Horace out of her office.

"What on earth is going on in here?" she rasped, while staring at me through her oversized glasses.

"Stanley was just replaying one of his almost misadventures with a student."

Horace pulled in her chin and gave Stanley an accusative look. I'm sure she would have raised her nose at him were she not so short, but her straight-on eye-shot was meaningful enough.

"Oh, yes, I suppose you GUYS have some very sordid tales."

"Now, now, Horace," I said, "it's all in good fun."

She snapped her head toward me and glared.

"We are not the kind of crass, Hunnish vermin who prey on innocent students," I explained. "We were merely discussing the various tools some students use to achieve what they consider acceptable grades."

"Well, there's only one grade that's acceptable to me, and that's the one they earn." Her head never wavered and she stood erect and proud, as serious as a judge on her bench.

"Yes, Horace," Stanley drawled, "I agree. If a student earns a grade, it doesn't matter so much what it is. That's the measure of his accomplishment." Then he added, "or hers."

"Well, for your information, I happen to know Miss Parker. She is in my American government class. She's not exactly a bright student, but she's doing all right. I just wish I could get her to wear a different style of clothing."

Stanley and I looked at each other and burst out laughing. Horace stiffened from the affront and lifted her nose at us in spite of her short stature. Then Stanley began an oration about the true meaning of learn-ing.

Ah, the sweet, sweet babble of academia. Chimes rang in the background. Just listening to a fellow professor rattle on about the idealistic world of education sent me into euphoria. I soon forgot about Miss Parker, although, the promise of her offering would haunt me many times. I would always wonder what it would have been like.

Chapter 9

Distress over Miss Parker's lechery consumed most of my week-end. It wasn't so much the enticement, because any old fart like me, beyond the foible of youth, enjoys being the subject of flattery now and then. No, it was the fact that it was deceptively delivered. That I could resist it fortified my integrity, otherwise, I would have been as big a fool as a weaker soul who would have succumbed to the ruse. Aside from her obvious ploy to railroad me into giving her a free grade, I couldn't escape the thought that I had been tempted to take advantage of the young vamp. I could only wonder what new tricks she could show an old dog like me. However, as a slave to common sense and reality, notwithstanding Alexis' assessment of my virtues, and having successfully deflected Miss Parker's advances, I relinquished my dreams to prudence.

But, the fact that I was drawn to her troubled me. I didn't re-member ever feeling that sort of attraction for Alexis. Although not as well endowed as Miss Parker, her body was attractive enough, but it certainly did not warrant salivating lust, or at least mine. But then I can't remember any advanced state of lust in my life. Maybe I just hadn't encountered the right woman. So, what was it about Miss Parker? Had I been too remote in my marriage? Did Alexis actually have some alluring qualities that I never noticed? Was I too busy with my work to be a real husband? Or a real man?

I never had time to realize what my wife needed. But, then she never seemed to need anything. At least, not from me. Even during our honeymoon she was completely independent and left me with menial responsibilities that I suppose most brides are left to deal with. And so went our marriage. See seemed to handle everything, including bringing home a larger salary than I did. I never saw any competition between us, but maybe I just wasn't looking.

A gentle rain scuttled Monday morning's briskness, leaving it in a nasty state, stifling, sultry, and murky. I could almost swim through the mugginess that stretched door to door between buildings. By afternoon, additional heat made the disagreeable day even more so. And due to the lack of proper ventilation in the men's restroom on the second floor of the Math Science Building, odors there hung in the ruthless air like fog over a noxious swamp, foiling any attempt to pass more than a few minutes in leisure and relief.

That's where I happened to be when Francis Able entered and waddled to the urinal next to me. Since there were only two, it was necessary to break restroom protocol that dictates leaving one urinal free between patrons.

"Good afternoon, Frank," I stole the first greeting so as not to appear intimidated. Of the men at a stand of urinals, the one who speaks first assumes the position of alpha male. It is seldom disputed by the others.

Being a male, the mechanics of emptying a bladder into a urinal came naturally to me. However, it occurred to me while watching Frank standing there with his huge belly stuffed between the walls of porcelain, how on earth did he know exactly what he was doing under there? Of course I suppose he could get adequate aim by feel. And then there was the sound. If you aimed just right there is this kind of gurgle from the drain that tells you you're on the mark. Otherwise, you might be subject to naughty spatters that leave telltale spots on your trousers.

I made a point to try it without looking the next time I was alone at a urinal.

"What was your name again?" He wheezed.

"August. August, the math guy."

"Oh, yes." Wheeze. Wheeze. "I suppose you're finding things all right?" Wheeze, hiss, wheeze.

"Well, I must admit that teaching is a little different than I thought it might be."

"Different from what?" Wheeze.

"I suppose I had envisioned teaching to be a sort of passive, perfunctory exercise with a rewarding satisfaction of sharing one's knowledge. What I'm finding is that most students neither want me to share it nor want me to be satisfied doing it."

"Ah, you have already reached the pinnacle of self-doubt that every good professor must pass." Wheeze. "Some pass it more than once," wheeze, "but once was enough for me," wheeze. "I'm a quick learner and I figured out," wheeze, "that it wasn't worth trying to perform miracles," wheeze, "on this mass of ignoramuses, har, har, har." Wheeze.

"I think I see your point. But, you'll forgive me if I try to at least impart some wisdom to a select few."

"Oh, the few I grant you." Wheeze. "Just be sure you have the right few." Wheeze.

I had just tucked myself in when Frank appeared to start leaning backward and kept moving. I lunged over behind him to arrest his fall. Fortunately, he had nearly finished his business so he was able to get his bearings quickly.

"Thanks, ah… math guy." Wheeze. "I guess I wore myself out just thinking about those miracles, har, har, har."

"No problem. Do you fall often?"

His arms were stretched downward as far as they would go and he was slumped forward in order to find the zipper on his trousers and close it. He accentuated the act with a slight hop at the end of it.

"Once in a while I'll topple over, but it doesn't happen very much," wheeze. "High blood pressure. I forgot to take my pill this morning." Wheeze.

"Be careful."

It was nearly time for college algebra. I scuffled through the throng of students in the hall and upstairs toward my office. In place of the usual scowls on the students' faces, there were hints of smiles and I could swear I heard a giggle or two. I hoped they were smiling at me, but I'm sure it was just that I was consumed with vanity. I rushed past Stanley uttering a hasty greeting, grabbed my algebra book and rushed out of the office before he could say anything.

I slowed to a controlled march just before I reached the classroom door and entered with the dignity of a king. My subjects were all watching the minute hand on the clock creep toward the four, which would be three-twenty. Had the hand ever made it to the four, the unofficial ten-minute rule would have been evoked and they would leave class without being counted absent. The hand had only one minute to go. My sudden appearance drew sighs of disappointment from the girls and the scowls from other students bathed the rear of the room in gloom. They had already collected what meager books and supplies they had brought to class to make ready their escape at twenty after. They dropped them to the floor in disgust.

"I'm sorry I'm late, but some of you are usually late and I don't complain about that, do I?"

I marched directly to my desk and opened the textbook to the section on polynomials.

"Are there any questions about what we covered in the last class?"

I knew there wouldn't be, but I always gave them an opportunity to clear up any misunderstandings, should any of them wish to break tradition and actually ask a question. "Well, then, let's talk some more about polynomials. If you look on page seventy-five of your textbooks you will see some examples of polynomials. I'm asking you to follow along in your books because I know very well that this will be the first time many of you have seen this information, in spite of the fact that you were supposed to read it before coming to class."

I wrote examples on the whiteboard, explaining them as the marker flew across the field of white. The rustling of paper and groans of discontent filtered through the wisdom that emanated through the room. I moved in front of the desk. Then the giggling started. I remember thinking that with this jovial mood, it might turn out to be a halfway decent class.

I hurried my lecture a bit, since I had only about thirty-five minutes left in which to work my magic. I did not take much time to solicit responses from the students, and I doubt that I would have received any, what with all of the giggling. Then long before I expected it, the chimes rang just after most of the students had collected all of their belongings to rush for the door.

"Do your homework. Exam on Friday," I shouted as the throng forced its way through the portal to freedom, still giggling with some outright laughter.

I erased the board, grabbed my book and started back to my office.

"Hey, Math Man," wheezed Frank. He was waddling toward me from the elevator. "Say, ah…" he stopped, "are you trolling for something?"

I noticed his left hand pointing discreetly at my fly. I looked down to find it open.

"Oh, I see." I yanked up the zipper while, I'm sure, turning red, and thanked him.

"No problem. I just don't want you to get into any trouble for illegal hunting, har, har, har."

I fled for my office and fell into my chair and sat there helplessly while the fulfillment I had briefly enjoyed disappeared behind a vision of my head trapped between the teeth of a giant zipper while it closed slowly toward me. Then Stanley arrived.

"What's the matter with you?" He asked, pausing at the door.

"Did everyone pass one of your tests?" He laughed as his own joke.

"No. Had that actually happened, I'd be breaking out the keg in the classroom and celebrating with the students."

He folded his long frame into his chair and looked at me, apparently waiting for an explanation for my despondency.

"Well, I approached my algebra class, the one with all of Satan's disciples in it, with a fair attitude and the determination to teach them something about math. And when the giggling started I thought I had finally broken through that shell of resistance that held me at bay."

I relaxed a bit and turned toward him. "You know, I really felt like I had established some sort credibility with them. I thought this was going to be a good class, after all."

Stanley said, "and then ..."

"After class I met Frank in the hallway and he shattered all of my euphoria by simply pointing out that my fly was open."

Stanley's laughing and bouncing in his chair set up a sort of resonance with its support springs which soon led to a fit of coughing accompanied by a horrid, almost inhuman, croaking sound. My embarrassment completely overtook me and I sat fuming at my desk waiting for calm to be restored at Stanley's end of the office.

"You know," I said, "I don't know which is worse. Having an open fly, or being told that your fly is open. If someone points it out to you, then you endure immediate embarrassment and find some way to control your emotions and behavior within an acceptable frame of reference to your company. At least this afternoon I was spared the public embarrassment, but I wonder what all of them must think of me, now?"

*****

I had not given much more thought to the class at Boyd Atkins until I approached the guard at the entrance. A different one, this time.

Before I even spoke he snatched the board from the hole in the window and bellowed, "You need somethin'?"

"Yes," I said. "I need to sign in to teach class at the Program Building."

He tossed the log book through the door at the bottom and waited. I filled out the information as quickly as I could and passed it back to him along with my driver's license. He said nothing and turned around to talk to someone behind him. I turned and headed for the gate. I figured I was on my own.

I pressed the button on the post, the gate clicked open and I entered the yard carefully closing the gate behind me. I walked in the direction I remembered Dr. Eigenhurtz following. I kept my eyes moving from side to side. There were inmates everywhere and guards nowhere. The dreary institutional red brick buildings sat like dreadful fortresses of doom that stole away any pleasure that might have been extracted from such a dismal environment. The inmates clad in disturbing gray garb looked like large drugged laboratory rats crawling about, in and out of the various openings, searching for some morsel of food left there for them to find.

My short paces were unsteady and, at times, misdirected. It was like wandering through a spook house waiting for something to pounce. A group of them approached me. I kept walking with one eye on them and the other on my path straight ahead and away from them.

"Good evening sir," one of them said in a mellow voice.

Sir? Did a prisoner just call me sir? I looked at him and forced a nervous smile, the kind I wield to anyone I don't wish to offend. They walked on past with expressions that seemed happy. I walked on, insensibility taking over my mind. Another inmate passed by with a happy greeting and almost a salute. The smile on his face seemed genuine. Was this really a prison? The folks there were actually human.

Once I found the Program Building, Dr. Eigenhurtz explained, in very basic terms, the drill. I surveyed the classroom and prepared for my lecture. The students still had no textbooks, as I figured, so I had brought along photocopies of the first chapter. If I had to, I could always procure books from the bookstore and charge them to the Math Science Department. Claudia might get pissed, but hell, the students had to have books.

They wandered in, one by one, and took a seat. Their discerning eyes studied me as I studied them. Except for being a few years older, they appeared no different than my other students. I introduced myself and class began.

The two and a half hours passed quickly and I was almost euphoric by the end of it. The students actually listened and followed along in their handouts. They asked questions. Intelligent questions. These were real, honest-to-God, students. I had completely put out of my mind the fact that I was in a prison. By the time I left, I had made up my mind that the inmates were really human after all. In fact, I would go so far as to say that they were better humans than most humans I knew. How ironic that they should be incarcerated there while the real assholes of the world were left unattended.

The drive home passed quickly. It always did when I worried about something. Especially what a fool I had made of myself in front of the algebra class earlier that day. What did they think of a professor, a man of learning, one of society's prime examples of success, a man who left his fly open? It would be two days before I saw them again. Maybe they would forget and the incident would pass without mention. All I wanted was to share my knowledge with those students and prepare them for success. I caught myself. The thought of sharing knowledge seemed so corny. Share my knowledge? Prepare them for success? It was obvious that most of them didn't want the knowledge. And they certainly had no notion of what success even was. And most of them probably didn't care.

*****

The books pulled at my arm, the weight as immense as the one on my heart. The void where Dr. Hartmann's statue used to be gave me a chill, or it could have just been the cool morning air. I wondered what he would have thought about my situation. It would have been comforting to have a confidant, an associate, or hell, even an enemy, give me some advice on my future. I had entered this job with all of the determination and ambition of a man set to remove the debilitating ignorance from the world's population and to cure the lack of motivation and confidence that had befallen our struggling youth. I had found only the means to become a humiliated muddle of uncertainty.

My innocence in the world of academia was my biggest liability. I needed to know what went on at Hartmann. I had to become familiar with the policies and procedures. I had to understand the political forces that ruled the campus and learn to play the game. I had to get into the mindset of the students. Who were they? What did they expect? What was important to them besides a liter bottle of Mountain Dew and the incoming call on their cell phone? How could I reach into their minds to squeeze out the consummate selfishness and unbridled fantasies of adolescence and leave them with a passion for learning? What had become of the values of my own generation? I had no answers as I reached my office.

I barely heard the soft knocking at the door.

"Professor Lane?"

Andy Dixon stood in the doorway, hand raised, head down, and his backpack slung over his left shoulder like he had just been furloughed from a long and arduous war. His uniform, long, tattered shorts, held a number of pockets, each unzipped and apparently, like most others, holding nothing.

"Come in, Mr. Dixon."

I motioned for him to enter and he sneaked toward me, stopping in front of the guest chair. I made a quick check of my crotch for any telltale signs of activity.

"What can I do for you?"

The poor boy, confused and intimidated by my presence, expounded on a lengthy explanation of his visit. It wasn't until the mention of algebra that I caught on to what he was trying to tell me.

"I didn't have good enough grades to get into college algebra," he said, "but the advisor let me in, anyway."

"You seem to be doing okay with it."

"Oh, well … that's what I wanted to tell you."

He finally raised his head, almost proudly.

"I never got this stuff in high school. But in your class I'm starting to understand it."

The shock lasted only a moment. I always wondered what it was like for a teacher to experience some instance of ardent gratification. Would it be an epiphany of the soul? A rising of the inner spirit to some new lofty pinnacle of success? What would one feel like after such an extraordinary event? But there it was, laid right in my lap. It was mine. Given to me freely. I was stunned. And it was all of the things I had imagined. Even more.

"Professor Lane?"

I snapped out of my trance and smiled at him.

"Andy, I'm glad this is working out for you. Once you get this first bit of mathematical jargon under your belt, I think you'll find the rest of it gets much easier."

"I hope so," he said through an enormous smile.

I had not seen such an enthusiastic expression on a young man's face. At least, not at Hartmann College. I decided that if he was going to be enthusiastic about learning, then so would I.

"I'll tell you what," I said leaning forward, "if you need any help come see me. My hours are posted on the door and my phone number is on the syllabus. I'll be glad to work with you anytime that I have free."

"Gee, thanks, Professor."

He shot up out of the chair yanking the backpack after him and he stood there smiling like an idiot.

"Thanks," I said. "For the compliment."

His smile dropped to perplexity.

"What compliment?"

"Where you said you're getting it. You have no idea what that simple statement means to a teacher. After all, that is our job, isn't it?"

"Oh, yeah," he shook his head and smiled again. "Well, thanks, Professor."

He turned and strutted out of the room of much different spirit than when he entered. And I had a much different attitude than when he entered. I had wasted much of the morning concerned about my effectiveness as a teacher. What I didn't realize is that there might only be a few real success stories in any class. Andy would be one of them. Melanie would not. As for the others, time would be the only thing that would reveal the outcome.

I still had to prepare for the physics lab the next day. There was no sink or running water in the lab. No gas supply for burners. No air supply. Only a rickety table that served inadequately for demonstrations and student tables with four legs and nothing else. I had mentioned it earlier to Claudia in hopes that she would see fit to correct the shortcomings. Since nothing had happened, I decided to pursue the cause again. That, and the textbooks for Boyd Atkins.

I caught Claudia shortly after my last class. She was getting ready to leave.

"If you can spare a few minutes I have some things I'd like to talk about," I said.

A briefcase dangled from her hand, the one with "OCAA" on it. She put it back on the floor and sat down behind her desk. I sat opposite her.

"I was just leaving," she said. "But I'm not in a hurry. What's on your mind?"

"You know, I realize that our budget is somewhere between pennies and pure vapor, but I really need to get the physics lab upgraded. Like running water and a sink, and gas, air, tables. I know that's not possible this year, but when *would* that be possible?"

"Yes, I'm aware of lab. In fact all of our labs need upgrading. It hasn't really come up yet, but I can talk to Dr. Gaines about it and see what he has in store."

"I would appreciate that. If there's something I can do to help things along, I'd be glad to do it."

"Well, I'll let you know what happens."

She picked up her bag and started to stand.

"Oh, and there's one more thing. It's the second week of classes and the students at Boyd Atkins still don't have textbooks. Do you have any idea what is going on?"

"Oh, dear, no. I can't imagine them not having books by now. The prison staff is supposed to provide the books. Maybe you need to talk to Dr. Purdy. All of those things go through him."

I hadn't really expected to get anything resolved. But I did expect her to pass the buck to Dr. Purdy.

"Well, I knew you were going to tell me that. I just thought you might have some interest in improving the effectiveness of the department. But, I'll talk to him about it."

Her meager intellect failed to pick up on the barb I threw at her since she showed no signs of being offended. I would talk to Dr. Purdy in the morning and perhaps have books by Monday. Even if I had to buy them myself and take them with me.

The five-o'clock chimes rang sweetly through the air as I wandered back to my office. A renewed sense of purpose tamed my apprehensions about teaching, but doubts about the profession nipped at my confidence. I figured it would be a good night to layout plans for the new physics lab.

Chapter 10

Thursday's physics lab polished off my energy, confidence, and patience. No matter how well I explained a concept during lecture, I could just as well have been talking about three little pigs. When they reached the lab they were supposed to have some idea of what would be going on. The young minds needed to see it; experience it; touch it. Lack of equipment crippled my effectiveness and it was time to do something about the shameful facilities that held back the advent of a brilliant physics program. So that Friday morning, after calculus, I marched over to Claudia's office with all of the determination of a charging rhino.

She greeted me with a hearty smile which must have been a terrible strain on her dreary face. I sat in the chair opposite her desk and we looked at each other for a moment. I sized up her plastic façade.

"Well, August, how's it going today?"

Her manufactured zest scraped at my disposition like a coarse grater into an orange peel.

"For the most part, I'm still getting my feet wet."

"I'll bet you have your hands full right now," she droned, sitting upright with her hands on her desk like a tarot card reader.

"Well, it's not that I have so much to do, which I do. It's the juggling that makes it so difficult."

Her eyebrows bent into sharper arches over her witless eyes and her inelastic mouth formed an oval.

"What do you mean?"

"As I mentioned on Wednesday, physics and GPS are my main problems. These courses are based upon the fundamental idea that the students should be able to experience some of the concepts they are expected to learn. That means I have to be able to actually demonstrate them and the students must be able to experiment with them."

"Okay," she said, her eyebrows forming an almost acute angle.

"In order to do these demonstrations and experiments, it is customary to have access to a variety of equipment, not to mention sinks with running water, gas lines for burners, and compressed air. None of those facilities are available in the physics lab or classrooms. I mean, I do try to use common materials, but some utilities are still necessary."

"Yes, August. I'm aware of that. And I told you I would talk with Dr. Gaines, but I haven't had the opportunity yet. None of the instructors before you have ever had a problem with that."

"Do you mean to tell me that no one has ever asked for water, gas, and air in the lab before?"

"Well, no."

"Then they have asked?"

"Yes, but I told them the same thing I just told you."

"And why did these instructors leave?"

"For better opportunities, I suppose. I mean, Hartmann is a good school, but there are more expensive ones that might offer better opportunities."

"And how would you rate our physical science program?"

"Well, it's certainly not the best, either, but it getting the job done."

She sat there, immobile, her stare becoming more focused beneath the angled eyebrows, obviously annoyed. I continued.

"I can't very well speak for the instructors before me, but I can tell you that in order to effectively teach this kind of class, I need those facilities." I felt bristles stirring on my neck as her stubbornness set itself into an unyielding stance. "You admitted yourself that the program is second rate."

"That's not exactly what I said," she bit back. "It is mostly offered because some of the engineering and science students needed it."

"Would you consider it a top notch program?"

"No, I wouldn't go so far as to say that."

"A mediocre program?"

"Since you are rebuilding it, I guess you could consider it mediocre for now. That is, until you bring it up to snuff."

"So, it isn't very good."

"I didn't say that it wasn't good."

"If it's not capable of teaching students what they need to know, it's not very good."

"Well, I think our instructors haven't quite given it a lot of priority."

"Not to mention the administration."

"August, that's not fair."

"Why not? Do you have water, gas, and electricity in your chemistry labs?"

"Why, yes."

"Then why don't I have it in my lab?"

"The chemistry labs are newer. Those things were put in when they were built."

"Did you have them before that?"

"Of course not."

"Well, if you got along without them for so long, why didn't you leave them out to save money?"

"Because we needed them. That should be obvious."

"Well, there's the rub, Claudia. You just admitted that water, gas, and electricity are needed. If you need them, so do I. Obviously, by your own implication, the program is not as good without them."

A pencil from her desk became prey for her menacing hands as she snatched it up like an exposed rodent in the claws of a hawk. She worked it furiously.

"And, I can tell you why other physics instructors left," I said, leaning forward and resting my arms on her desk. "You see, if one doesn't have the necessary equipment, it is really futile to try to accomplish much. So naturally, one's priorities are going to be directed to whatever he can do most effectively. And apparently, in the case of prior instructors, that wasn't physics. Not at Hartmann at any rate."

"August, the college can't afford to completely renovate the physics lab. The building is old and it would cost a small fortune. The biology lab is in worse condition than your physics lab and we can't even afford to refurbish it until next year."

"At least the biology labs have running water, gas, and air."

Her face pulled itself into a frightening witchy look. I had gone too far.

"Okay," I said, "I understand the money thing." I sat back in my chair. "But, if I'm going to build a physics program at Hartmann, I've got to have some support and the facilities are going to have to be upgraded. If we had a decent program with state of the art facilities, we could draw more science and engineering students here. That would help the college, would it not?"

"Yes, I suppose it would."

"No one is going to want to come to a rundown college with obsolete facilities. Our reputation as an educational facility is at stake here."

"So, you think we could increase our enrollment in science if we upgraded the physics lab?"

"Look, right now there is a transition taking place in physics education. Physics is a tough cookie for most students to chew and the current tide in physics education is problem-based learning. This is where the students sort of teach themselves and the instructor provides guidance and facilitates the class with minimal lecture. A discovery type of learning. For the kind of students we get here, this approach is ideal. Most of these poor kids don't know how to learn because they've never been taught that. This would give them the opportunity to discover that they really can learn."

"August, you're talking about the students as if they are stupid. I sense resentment in your tone."

"I don't resent anything except the rotten deal they get when they come here and have to endure the crummy facilities. And, no, they're not stupid. Just deprived."

"But, you don't talk like that. What I'm getting from you is all negative."

"I'm only negative about the college. And let's face it. When something sucks, it's negative. I am positive about its future. The one it doesn't have right now. But, the students are my main concern. We are here to help them learn. In order to do that in science, they need more than just a book. They need to actually see some of these things and experience them so they can relate them to their lives. It's all about problem solving and that's hard to do from just a textbook. Why do you think biology students dissect these poor animals? Could they learn as much from a book?"

"Okay, I see what you mean."

The wheels were starting to turn. She leaned forward and her empty eyes had an unusual luster to them. The plastic façade transformed into curiosity.

"Let's try this," she said. "I neglected to tell you, but this spring all of the faculty presents a project plan for the next three years. It's an outline of our problems, strengths, weaknesses, and how we are going to solve the problems. What you need to do is write this up on your project plan and that way we might get funding allocated for it. Now the funding probably won't come for a couple of years, but that gives us a chance to plan for it. What do you think?"

I felt fortunate that I had taken the time to talk with Claudia before instigating a mutiny. At least she presented a viable option for getting what I needed for the physics program. It would take time, but so would the design of a viable program. I was curious, though, as to why she had not mentioned it earlier.

"If that's what I have to do, then I really don't have much choice, do I?"

"Good. Now that that's settled, what else is new?"

"Well, it's not quite settled, yet. What is the project plan, where can I get a copy of the last one, and when is it due?"

"Oh, yeah, that might help. Let me find last year's copy and I'll either send it to you or e-mail it."

"Well, e-mail won't do me much good because I still don't have a computer that I can use."

"Oh, that's right. I'll just get a copy to you."

"That's probably enough for one day. I'll look forward to seeing the project plan."

I got up to leave and she rose with me.

"I'm going to mention this to Dr. Gaines. I think he will be excited that we have someone on our faculty who actually wants to get involved in the future of the college." The plastic smile was on her face, again.

"I think we will need all the support we can get. Thanks."

I left feeling better and worse. She agreed with me in principle. But no concrete commitment was forthcoming. Whatever doubts I didn't have before, I certainly had now.

The following confrontation with Dr. Purdy left me with a casual implication that he would get an authorization for the textbooks for the prison to the bookstore. They would be charged to Boyd Atkins and would be available after the authorization had been approved by the bookstore manager. He assured me I would have the books by Monday.

*****

Stanley and I sat alone in the cafeteria at a table adjacent to a window, a rare occasion for either of us. I kept watch on the natural beauty outside expecting that at any instant it would succumb to the vile atmosphere of Hartmann College and turn to a landscape of desolation. I also kept watch on the growing line of patrons eagerly waiting to be deceived by what was supposed to be nourishment.

"I see Mary Einhorn in the line," I said. "She seems to be staring at our table for some reason."

Stanley looked toward her, then at me. He smiled and shoved a large bite of tasteless beef tips into his mouth.

His smile baffled me since I failed to see any humor. Mary joined us at our table.

"Do you boys mind if I join you?"

I jumped up and pulled out a chair for her. "Please do," I said, taking in the sweet aroma of whatever she was wearing. It masked the reek of ill-prepared food.

She sat gracefully and arranged the plates on her tray. She had selected the chicken Ceasar salad, as had I, with a wheat roll, as had I, a bowl of fruit, as had I, and cookies, also as had I. I felt a little odd at the coincidence, but flattered that we had the same culinary tendencies.

I looked at her, more carefully. The brown hair, done up tightly in the customary bun, rested on her head like a crown, tipped back slightly. It gave her an air of dignity, but robbed her of the subtle beauty that would have complimented her engaging face. Actually, it was the glasses that engaged me. A more classic pair of wire frames would be more appropriate for her face, not that it needed enhancement. On the contrary, it had an ordinary beauty. Not the kind that knocks you off your feet at first sight, but the kind that subtly gets your attention, teases you, then beckons you to learn more about the person behind it. It was meant for a more amorous purpose than her hair or glasses afforded it. In fact, I found her more attractive than Alexis.

"Dr. Gaines told me Claudia called him," she said just before placing a piece of chicken between her unadorned lips, which needed no adornment.

"I just talked to Claudia this morning. She said she was going to call him. I'm surprised that it would be so soon."

"It appears that you might have a nice feather to put in your bonnet."

"I really didn't' think she would actually do it." I stuffed a wad of suspicious looking lettuce into my mouth and gnawed on it before swallowing. "What do you mean by a feather in my bonnet?"

"Oh, you're being touted as the salvation to Hartmann's science program."

The sudden surge of ego was smacked smartly with the realization of expectations I would be forced to achieve. If that's the idea she left with Dr. Gaines, I would most certainly wind up a failure. I was staring out the window as if it offered a vision of my shattered future when I saw the fellow with the ponytail, the one in all black, talking with a student. Because of the violent gestures from the "ponytail guy" I surmised the meeting might be more of an admonishment. The poor student, awash in fear and confusion, mouth open and frozen in place, watched wide-eyed as thrashing arms pantomimed his transgressions, whatever they might have been. I couldn't help but wonder what would justify such abuse of a student.

"…August?" I heard my name and turned toward Mary.

"Exactly what was it you promised Claudia?" She repeated.

I explained my conversation with Claudia, and I discovered from what little Stanley did say during my many pauses, he was more versed in corporate politics than I, and he understood that to get something you wanted you had to work around the system, above it, or below it. Working within it seldom resulted in any degree of satisfaction except to impart credit for your own hard work to someone else. I think he was actually laughing at me while I rattled on about my plans.

So, his eyes tittered at me behind his thick glasses as I expounded on grandiose plans to resurrect the physics program. Mary made frequent glances toward me in approval. I think that during my oratory I actually began to dream. I don't even know if Stanley listened to the whole presentation, but I remember seeing the hands on the clock approach the hour and I halted my bombast in anticipation of the chimes.

My eyes followed each jump of the second hand as if my watching it would enable it to speed to the top of its path and release the carillon from its bindings of time. I had carefully synchronized my watch with sounding of the chimes so that the minute and second hands both reaching the twelve simultaneously would mark the beginning of the melodious song. The hand crept around the dial and it seemed to slow near the top just as my anticipation grew. Then it passed the twelve. There was no fanfare. No chimes. Nothing. The hand kept moving, sweeping out its arc in uneasy silence.

"Something wrong?" asked Stanley.

"Yes," I said, still staring at my watch. "My watch shows noon. What time do you have?"

He looked at his watch.

"Twelve." He sat forward and stretched to read the time from my watch. "It looks like you're right on the button."

"Yes, I have twelve, too," said Mary.

"I know. That's what's wrong."

"What do you mean?" she asked.

"Do you notice anything about the passing of the hour?"

They sat frozen for a moment then looked at me.

"You know," said Stanley, "the chimes didn't ring."

"Exactly." I shook my head in agreement. "I wonder what happened?"

Chapter 11

My lunch settled to the bottom of my stomach like a torpedoed battleship. The ruminations ceased leaving the lump of partially digested cafeteria waste there to loiter in its depths. My short residence at Hartmann had addicted me to the hourly fanfare of regalia, but now there would be no peal of the Westminster tune to calm the churning sea of digestion. I had begun to rely upon the chimes as reassurance of my haughty distinction as an elite member of academia. The chimes affirmed my worth as a part of Hartmann College. It would have been easier to have lost a principle body part.

After several phone calls, I learned that the Information Technology group maintained the chimes. The notion that these folks, trained in electronic wizardry, were charged with the menial chore of maintaining something as conventional as simple chimes, challenged my sense of logic.

However odd it seemed, the chimes had to be fixed. I called Ed Fulkrod, the IT guy.

"Ed, this is August Lane. Math Science."

"August?" he said. "I think I remember hearing your name somewhere around campus."

"Well, I hope you heard it in a good light."

"I never have good light. And it is preferred that you go through the help desk."

Help desk? I thought for a moment and it dawned on me that even amid the archaic rudiments of information technology that had found the way to Hartmann College, they just might have a user support group. "Ed, I never thought about there being a help desk because as of yet I don't even have a computer I can use. And since there is not phone directory listed for the college, and since, I'm sure you know by now, that I am relatively new here, I had no earthly idea that a help desk existed, much less, how to contact it. And my question does not concern a computer. Can you help me?"

"So, what's the problem?"

"I understand that your group is responsible for maintaining the chimes here at the college."

I waited for him to say something. "Ed?"

"Yeah?"

"You do take care of the chimes, don't you?"

'Yeah."

"Well, it appears that they have quit working."

"That's probably because we shut them off?"

"Uh, is there a problem with them?"

"I thought you said this wasn't about a computer."

"It isn't."

Over the munching in the background, I heard, "Well, it is."

I passed off his remark because it did not make sense. "So can you tell me why they're down?"

"Yeah. We had a complaint about them."

"A complaint? What kind of complaint could there be against chimes?"

More munching. "She didn't like them."

"Excuse me?"

"She didn't like them. Said they were annoying and they interrupted her classes."

"Exactly who is 'she'?"

"Oh, that's ah…" The rustling of paper overtook the munching for a moment. "That's Dr. O'Mally."

"Dr. O'Mally? I guess I don't know her."

"You probably don't want to."

"Oh? Why is that?"

"Let's just say you don't want to get on the wrong side of her," *munch, munch, belch.* "I mean this gal could chew you up and spit you out without even moving her mouth."

"I'm getting the picture. So, what about the chimes?"

"Look pal, all I can say is that Dr. Gaines told me to shut them down."

The mention of Dr. Gaines removed any inclination I had to pursue the matter with Ed. "Well, thanks for the information. I should get over to meet you."

"Yeah, well, suit yourself."

It was almost like the handset was slammed down on the cradle. Like one of those things you can't hear but you instinctively know is happening. I was not exactly happy that I had called Ed, but at least I knew what had happened. Kind of.

I called Dr. Gaines' office. Mary answered.

"This is August Lane."

"Yes, August, I know who you are." Her voice was soft, sweet, and melodious, but it also had a subtle warning against saying anything improper.

"Oh, hi. Is Dr. Gaines in this afternoon?"

"Yes, he's in. Do you want me to transfer you to him?"

"Thanks, but no. I would prefer to speak to him personally. If he's in, I could come over now."

"Just a minute and I'll see."

A click and then the white noise of nothing. I thought of just how I would approach Dr. Gaines without appearing to be complaining or whining.

Click. "August?"

"Yes," I said jumping out of my trance.

"Dr. Gaines will see you."

*****

Mary Einhorn sat at her desk like a hinged board. Her back, straight and vertical, didn't even touch the backrest. Her arms moved as she shuffled papers on the desk, but her head and torso remained motionless. The bun on her head almost glistened, a radiant auburn. Her face, attractive and almost childlike, was a very pleasant welcome to the office.

"Mary?" I said.

"August?" she said.

I had not previously noticed the small frames that displayed photographs of some attractive children, who I supposed were hers, probably taken some time ago. She didn't have to look up to see me. All that was necessary was for her eyes to rise slightly over the tops of her glasses. Then perfectly white teeth glared at me from between two very plain lips that stretched into an easy smile. And the aroma of her sweet cologne caught me.

"He didn't run away, did he?"

"Just go on in. He's expecting you."

Her eyes stayed on me as I moved toward the door, kind of like one of those painting of Jesus where the eyes appear to follow you around the room. Not judgmental eyes, but curious ones.

"Come in, Professor Lane."

I heard the timid voice before I actually saw Dr. Gaines. Although he was not a small man, the vast expanse of desktop dwarfed him. The chair, in grand proportion to the monster desk, towered over his large, balding head. I couldn't help but notice the loose threads around the ends of his jacket cuffs.

"Dr. Gaines," I said reaching over the desk to shake hands. I had to reach much farther than usual.

"Ms. Einhorn tells me you wanted to see me."

"Yes, I do."

"Please sit down and tell me what's on your mind."

He motioned toward one of the two guest chairs facing the desk. I sat, leaned back, placed my hands on the arms, and began.

"If you have noticed, this afternoon has been rather quiet."

He looked at me, obviously puzzled with my visit.

"Yes," he said, "it has been a very quiet afternoon."

"That's due in part to the fact the chimes are no longer sounding."

"Oh, that. Yes, I had them shut down."

I knew as much, and he probably knew that I knew.

"Now, I don't mean to be disrespectful." I paused and looked at him like a humble beggar. "But, I have enjoyed listening to those chimes. They break up the day and offer a small opportunity for reflection each hour."

I tried to keep my voice as soft and modest as possible.

"The chimes are sort of a symbol of academia. They lend an air of authenticity to the environment. They make the campus complete. Sort of like a finial on a lamp. Or the period at the end of a sentence. Folks enjoy hearing that familiar melody every hour. It kind of breaks up the day for them."

I could see his eyes sort of melting in sympathy for me. His face lengthened and he fell back in his chair. I went on.

"They remind me of my own college days and give me inspiration. I mean, we all need a kind of pick-me-up throughout the day, sometimes. Well, the sound of the chimes is what keeps me going."

"You know," he said, shaking his head. "I experienced the same thing. When I hear them I always stop what I'm doing and just listen to them. It's really quite delightful."

"Well, it's not happening anymore."

"Yes, I'm afraid I took care of that, didn't I?"

"Look, I know Dr. O'Mally has some sort of issue with the chimes. You see, I called Mr. Fulkrod. He informed me that due a complaint from Dr. O'Malley, he had been told to stop the chimes."

"Yes. Dr. O'Malley said they interrupted her class."

"Exactly which class is that?"

I shifted in my chair to lean toward him.

"It was primarily the noon class."

"The one that doesn't start until twelve-ten?"

"Yes, that's the one."

"But if the class doesn't start until ten minutes after the chimes play, how can they be disrupting the class?"

I could see him thinking deeply about that question. He obviously had not interrogated Dr. O'Malley about it.

"I see what you mean. There really shouldn't be a problem with the class because it starts at ten after the hour."

"Now, I don't want to stir up a hornet's nest, but there are other people on this campus who enjoy the chimes."

"Well, I have to agree with what you're saying, Professor Lane. But, I need to gather some information about the situation before I can say with any certainty what I think is right."

"Dr. Gaines, I trust your judgment."

I hoped it wasn't too obvious that I was kissing his ass. I could have played him much stronger but it would have been unfair to take advantage of such an easy mark.

"Let me see what I can find out and I'll let you know."

"Thank you," I said. I got up to leave.

"By the way, I've heard a lot about you. You seem to have great plans for the science program."

"I'm working on it," I said modestly. "Hopefully we can get our science enrollment up."

"That would be a welcome change. I hope you succeed."

It wasn't so much what he said that bothered me as much as what he didn't say. There was a conspicuous absence of any offer of support for my effort to improve the science program.

I felt it was time to leave before I made a fool of myself. I left a compliment with Mary as I passed by her desk and departed swiftly into the hallway still savoring the delightful aroma of her fragrance. In my hurry to escape, I collided with a woman who had just come out of a doorway I was passing. I might have been a little close to one side of the hall.

After the surprised "Oh" from the woman, I said, "Excuse me. I'm sorry."

I was ready to grab her if she showed any signs of falling, but it wasn't necessary.

"Are you all right?" I asked.

The slim woman, festooned with several necklaces of beads, bones, and other curious objects from what could have been burial grounds, gathered herself and straightened her clothes and without looking at me said, "You should really look where you're going."

Not having considered myself to be the transgressor, I was shocked by her arrogance. Just as I opened my mouth to speak, she said, "You men run down these hallways like you're driving a hot rod."

The blaze from her angry, beaded eyes blinded me to the harsh features of her face, which I remembered after the course of dubious guilt passed. Coarse, dark hair; long nose; drawn eyes; time-pressed wrinkles; and lips as thin as wire bent into an eternal frown. A crab if I ever saw one. I wondered if each of the female faculty was as homely as the ones I had encountered.

"I'm sorry," I repeated. "By the way, who are you?"

She snapped her eyes toward me. "I'm Doctor O'Mally," she said, with emphasis on the "Doctor."

So she was the infamous chime slayer. I had a fleeting impulse to confront her about that very subject, but due to the conflict at hand, reason overcame my emerging crusade and I quelled the urge. "I'm Professor Lane. And, by the way, it is customary for one to assess existing traffic in a hallway before entering it. Perhaps you should try it sometime. Good day, madam."

I left her in front of the door from which she had bounded, glaring at my exit.

*****

In spite of Dr. Gaines's intentions, the bookstore had not received his authorization for the algebra textbooks I needed for Boyd Atkins. The manager agreed to let me sign for the books myself. They would be charged to the Math Science Department, which would get credit for them when they were turned in at the end of the semester. I lugged the books to my car and dumped them in the rear seat. Claudia could worry about what to do with the account deficit until the end of the semester.

Through my dingy office window, I watched what appeared to be the flag blowing in the wind. Even that did not inspire me. I worried about Hartmann. Instead of the bright, feisty youths who should have been eager to learn, the campus crawled with costumed shells of students who had no earthly notion of the meaning of education.

Little more than shadows against the window's veneer of grime, the students moved slowly across campus, on their way back to their dorms, I supposed, to plan a heady evening of partying and boozing. It seemed like a fitting end to the day, but I had to leave for Boyd Atkins.

*****

The prison guard closely inspected the box of textbooks I brought. He finally satisfied himself that I was not going to instigate a mass escape and waved me through the gate. I almost collapsed from the weight by the time I reached the classroom. The students were waiting for me.

"Hey Perfessor," one of them said, "is dem our books?"

"As a matter of fact, they are. I had to practically steal them, but I got them, nonetheless."

A round of cheers hailed from the room and they rushed up to grab a book. Each of them sat down at his desk and devoured the text in front of him. I had never seen such enthusiasm over a simple textbook. They gestured to each other as they soaked up their newfound knowledge. These fellows were indeed eager to learn. I figured they would be my best students, just as Ricky had said. Their prison uniforms, though the same as before, now made them look like scholars.

I wish I could say the same for Hartmann students.

Chapter 12

By mid week, I would have expected fate to ease its stabbing humiliation of my ego, having had its fill of fun with me on Monday. However, Wednesday was particularly arousing to my vexation, especially when I found Miss Parker on the front row of the classroom in all the glory of her youthful exuberance. It was her first appearance in my class since the incident in my office. I was surprised to see her there, to say the least. The moment I looked at her she crossed her legs.

I was not surprised at her attire. She was half dressed, with the other half practically hanging out. That was her top. As for the bottom of her wardrobe, the skirt was minimally functional. Her ensemble was even more provocative than the last time I saw her. I took roll before I addressed her appearance, trying to keep my attention on the grade book instead of on her breasts.

"Miss Parker, may I speak to you in the hall, please?"

I didn't even look at her. I just closed the grade book and proceeded to the door. She followed me out of the classroom and stood before me with her arms behind her back and her chest thrust toward me as if trying to launch one of her breasts from its flimsy support.

"Miss Parker, if you read the student handbook, you will find a section about student dress. Read it. On Friday I will expect to see you in more appropriate attire. Now, gather your things and leave. I cannot allow you to sit in my classroom in that condition."

I looked in her eyes the entire time I spoke and during those few seconds I saw the song of seduction turn to the winds of indignation and then to the fire of silent rage. Angry lances danced in her eyes ready to hurl themselves toward me.

"I'll see you on Friday," I said as I returned to the classroom.

The moment I entered the room, the din ceased immediately as if someone had turned off a switch. Forty-six eyes were trained on me trying to discover some clues as to what had just transpired in the hall. They were spared a lengthy wait when Miss Parker dramatically reappeared with both hands clasping the tissue that was daubing at her weeping eyes and concealing the sniffling nose that worked adeptly at audibly signaling her imaginary distress. In all honesty, I couldn't imagine where she had room in her scanty attire to keep a tissue. The young men in the class were snickering, and the young ladies seemed to take Miss Parker's performance in an entirely different context. I could see a river of pity exude in demonstrations of sympathy and bolster Miss Parker's rendition of the innocent victim to a crescendo of wails and sobs as she hastily snatched up her books and fled from the room.

I immediately addressed the class. "Any questions about what we discussed on Monday?"

I tried to recapture the proper tone of the class as quickly as possible, but all eyes were drawn toward the door in the melodramatic wake of Miss Parker's hasty exit as if expecting an encore. Even though an agnostic, I found myself praying for no such event to occur.

Finally, pair by pair, eyes reluctantly turned from the door and rested either on me or on the desks in front of them. The following forty minutes could have been one of the longest classes of the semester. It was, however, one of the shortest.

My oration of educational wisdom withered rapidly into drivel and I thought it best to forgo the last fifteen minutes of class. It seemed more appropriate to spare the students the misery of listening to non-sense. I wouldn't have stayed to listen to it myself. I was back in the office well before Stanley arrived.

The hall was quiet enough for me to hear the floor creak beneath Stanley's long strides making their way toward the door. From there, it took him only one step to arrive at his desk. I looked at him, probably with a forlorn face, and nodded. His smile, an unusually wide one, did nothing to dislodge my despair and was almost annoying.

"Well, you're back early," he said, smiling. "Bad day at Black-rock?"

"You remember that movie, too, huh?"

"Hey, Ernest Borgnine was one of my favorites."

"Well, I can't say that I had an affinity for him, but he was a good actor. Of course, back then I hardly knew the difference between good acting and crap."

"Gosh," he said, "you're right. That was a heck of a long time ago. What would it have been ... fifties?"

"That sounds about right. Black and white, short, corny dia-logue."

"You know, I don't know what made me think about that." He oozed himself into his chair, kind of like sitting in a hole, his long arms and legs resembling a spider that had fallen into a tiny bucket.

"I don't think it would have been as good in color." He looked at me and I looked at my desk.

"Yeah," I said. "Bad day at Blackrock."

"So, what on earth happened with what's her name… Parker?" he asked.

"Yup, that's the one."

"The scuttlebutt is that you made an advance on her in the hall during class."

"What?" My chest felt like a vacuum cleaner was sucking the air from it.

I didn't think his smile could get any wider, but again I was wrong. I was also shocked. I wondered how the hell he could have known about something that happened not more than thirty minutes earlier.

"Some of the girls are saying that you made a pass at Miss Parker and she left the class in hysterics."

"Oh, she is good. That little bitch showed up for class today wearing practically nothing. I asked to speak to her in the hall and told her she wasn't going to stay in class in that outfit. I told her to take her things and leave."

"Oh, I figured that when I saw her outside the front door in the tramp costume. She was talking to some of the girls."

He tried to sit forward in his chair but it wouldn't lean with him.

"Apparently," he grunted as he reached for a bottle of water, "they were the last ones to know. As quickly as she works, I imagine the entire campus knows about it by now."

Before Stanley arrived I was depressed. After hearing his report, I was frightened and depressed.

"You know, you might want to call Dr. Tipton and sort of update her on what's coming her way."

"Good idea."

Her performance as a slut didn't bother me as much as her trying to suck me into it and make me the buffoon. I had successfully contained the temptation, and of course, her not being my type helped immensely. But I would have to watch myself very carefully. She would be using this escapade to her advantage. I just didn't know what advantage that might be. A passing grade for the course was my first thought.

But, what if the real motivation was not necessarily self-serving, at least for the sake of ambition? What if she had personal issues that drove her to that peculiar behavior? What if I were merely a target of her vengeance? A grade would be of no concern to her. Only my ass being burned, my ego trampled, and my credibility refuted. There was real motivation. And that's when I began to worry.

Chapter 13

In spite of all the things wrong with Hartmann College, one of the few things right was Ricky Smithers. His long tenure mellowed him into an easy-going type. I was never able to comprehend how one can just simply ignore transgressions against his person, his ambitions, and his duties and continue to serve in the capacity of dedicated instructor. Such behavior is foreign to my notion of propriety, and I admire anyone who can do it. Not that I would choose to do so myself. My capacity for benevolence ends when my ego is threatened. The mere act of allowing someone to trample on my good name without reprisal would enlist more strength of character than I could find within my pathetic self-righteous soul. I had heard more than once about Ricky's mettle and considered him a reasonable role model for my own success. So, it was the least I could do for Ricky when he asked me to cover his intermediate algebra class for him while he attended a funeral.

I reported to the classroom at 9:10. Instead of the usual instructor's desk standing in front of a whiteboard or chalkboard, I encountered a console affair that contained a plethora of electronic equipment. Several large display monitors populated the walls and any other available floor space. I figured the room was a high-tech classroom for some kind of science course. I only wish I had such luxuries with which to spread the wisdom of science. I opened my textbook on the console in front of me, being careful not to touch any of the electrical equipment, and prepared to begin the class.

"Excuse me, sir." A young man in the second row had raised his hand. "Aren't you going to include the other class?"

It is not often that a student can ask something that confounds me, but due to my new station as an instructor, this question had me stumped.

"What do you mean?"

The young man looked as confounded as I was. "The other class, sir."

Seeing no other classroom adjoined to the one I was in, I gave no response to his answer.

"The class in Binkerton," He said. "This is an ITV class."

Shit. I could have had no other reaction. Just shit. That pretty much said it all. I had not taught an interactive television course. I didn't want to teach one, and I saw little point in teaching one. And now I would have to. The young man probably thought I was a dolt. Ordinarily, this would be a fairly straight-forward task, since I teach college algebra and the intermediate class is only a dumbed-down version of it. But the fact that it was an ITV class compounded the issue, and its significance bore heavily on my confidence. I think the students sensed my profound ignorance of the situation. Fortunately, I had not told them my name. I was not inclined to volunteer that information just yet.

I surveyed the desk and its myriad electronic boxes, monitor, and no fewer than four remote control units that I could see. Heaven only knows what was beneath the desk in the concealed compartments to either side.

"Sir, would you like me to connect the session for you?"

This young man was a gem. I looked at him in amazement while trying not to appear as foolish as I felt.

"I would appreciate that. I have not had much experience with ITV classes."

He quickly walked to the front desk, picked up one of the remote controls, pressed several buttons and the monitor flashed twice then displayed a message that the session was connecting. Then, all of a sudden an image of another classroom appeared on the monitor.

"Thank you," I said to the youth as he slithered back to his seat.

Okay, I had the other class on the monitor. So, now what?

"Good morning," I said to the monitor.

I expected at least an acknowledgement of my greeting but I saw no movement whatsoever among the images.

"Good morning," I repeated.

Nothing.

"Ah, sir, your microphone might be muted," said the same young man. "You'll have to turn it on."

That made sense. Surely there was a button labeled "MUTE" somewhere. I picked up the control the young man had used and there it was: "MUTE." I pressed it.

"Good morning," I said once more.

I heard varied responses from the remote site and all seemed well. I turned to the chapter on adding polynomials.

"Now that we seem to be in order, I'm Mr. Lane. I'll be filling in for Mr. Smithers, today. He is attending a funeral."

The faces in the room gave no indication that anyone really wanted to be there or that they would be interested in anything I had to say. In many ways, it was just like one of the college math classes I had endured as a student long ago. Had their faces been hidden, I wouldn't have known the difference. They seemed to dismiss my presence as they would a tiny gnat flitting about the air. I wondered how Ricky handled such rejection.

"Can anyone tell me where you left off during the last class?"

Nothing. Not even from the monitor. Most of them looked like they were ready to drop into a bed or had just crawled out of one.

"Well, that's okay," I said. "I think I know where we need to begin."

I turned around to the whiteboard with the intent of writing an expression. I saw that drawing anything on the whiteboard would not be possible since there were no markers in the tray. My building frustration had just escalated to the threshold of anger.

"Well, this is going to be one fun class," I said as I faced the audience. "It appears that no markers are available for the whiteboard."

The helpful young man thrust his hand into the air.

"Yes?" I looked at him.

"Sir, Mr. Smithers uses the document camera to draw."

I saw the thing on the desk that looked like a hungry praying mantis. A document camera. Yes, it all made sense. I pressed the "ON" button. Nothing happened and I was about to press other buttons when the contraption flickered and came to life with a brilliant show of light on its surface. Now, I had to figure out how to get it to the monitor so the students could see it.

"Button number two on the remote switches it to the document cam," said the young man, who I would have adopted if given the chance.

I picked up the remote again and pressed button number two. The screen immediately went black. The wretched episode was not going to end. I had changed something. I just didn't know what.

"The lens cap might be on the camera," said the young man.
My God, to have a son as intelligent as that! I couldn't tell if he was

toying with my ignorance or was annoyed by it. Sure enough, when I removed the plastic cover from the bottom of the camera the screen displayed a brilliant white image of the empty platform beneath it. I have to admit that I was intimidated not only by the technology, but also my own inability to manipulate it. I brought nothing in preparation for this class except my textbook and the pen in my pocket.

I'm sure I didn't cover as much material as Ricky could have, since only about thirty minutes remained. And much of that was consumed with switching the monitor back and forth from the instructor camera to the document camera. The chimes, had they not been disabled, would have signaled the end of my adventure. So, in addition to the complicated manipulation of electronic controls, I had to remember to check my watch occasionally. I still don't know how they did it, but by the time the hour arrived, most of the students had packed their gear and were jumping out of their seats like they were hooked to a static line waiting to bail out of the cargo door of an airplane. With all of my knowledge of physics, I am still at a loss to explain this phenomenon.

I pondered the possibility of some internal function of their bodies like electro-location or bio-magnetism that enables some animals to navigate.

The young man who helped me through the period was not of the lackluster quality that graced the rest of the class and he took his time collecting his things.

"I want to thank you for your assistance, today," I told him.

"Oh," he grinned, "I was glad to help."

"I'm sorry today's class was probably less than exciting and probably deficient in content. I'm sure Mr. Smithers would have done much better. I'm just not used to the ITV thing."

"Oh, that's okay."

While slipping the textbook into his bag, he looked up at me briefly with coy eyes. I could see a smile behind the course, black hair and figured he got some measure of entertainment from my bungling skills at ITV. He was not exactly the nerdy type, but I could picture him hovering over a textbook, devouring every morsel of knowledge from the cryptic figures on the page. He slung his backpack over one shoulder and kept smiling.

"What's your name?"

"Jacob Zamudio," he said.

Then he was gone.

According to my watch, my GPS class should start in one minute.

It wouldn't. Not knowing what to do with all of the technology that had screwed my day around, I left it as it was. If it was so damned smart, it could figure out what to do with itself. I hurried to my office to change books and arrest the flow of students from the classroom who would have seen fit to leave if I failed to arrive by twenty after.

Chapter 14

I rushed into the classroom with the GPS exams in hand and quickly passed them out. Stillness settled in as I took my seat at the front of the room. I should have brought something to read but I didn't dare leave this bunch of heathens unattended. So, I entertained myself by studying them. One by one, I looked at each student. Some were busily reading, marking, erasing, remarking, erasing, then pausing since they had no clue as to the correct answer. Though most of the questions were structured so that even an educated guess would render a correct answer, such a feat was beyond their mental capabilities. Even simple calculations that required only the move of a decimal point escaped their mathematical prowess. The sad scene repeated itself as my eyes roved over the rows of students.

There were, however, a few of them who could actually interpret physical science and understand the meaning of it. They were the ones who confidently checked off each answer without much study and finished the exam in good time.

Those who finished earliest in the period were the ones who had no intention of learning physical science as they probably considered it to be an unnecessary infraction of their freedom. So, they merely checked whichever answer looked appealing.

Then there was the back row of the classroom. The athletes. Due to previous encounters with athletes, I would make a note to compare their exams, since I suspected they would all be identical.

While I endured the silence, I considered the intricate jumble of electronic devices in Ricky's ITV classroom as nearly as I could remember. I also wondered how it was possible for any instructor to effectively deliver a lecture with such a diverse collection of devices, each of them requiring a different mode of operation. Even though the monitor displayed a good view of the remote classroom, the poor resolution made it impossible to recognize the face of any one student. The image appeared more like a blob than an actual face. And the sound was very much like what I experienced as a child while talking into a whirling fan. And the use of a whiteboard or chalkboard was definitely out of the question since the students at the remote site couldn't see it. The document camera had a small drawing area and required a bold pen to draw anything that would be visible on the monitor. Drawing small figures with a fat pen made the images impossible to decipher.

I figured the presence of a videocassette recorder and a computer meant that multimedia could be presented as well, but I dared not think of what would be required to do that. I made a note to talk with Ricky about ITV and see what it was all about. If I was ever going to be required to do this, and even as badly as I hated the thought of doing it, I damn sure wanted to know how.

After class, I contacted Ricky, which was not easy. Since he didn't stay in an office, I left word with Mary that I wanted to talk with him, and she spread the word around campus. Eventually, he called me in my office. We were to meet at four-thirty at Jim Bob's. I had no idea who Jim Bob was or what his place looked like. I got directions from Ricky and jotted down some notes.

Since the science exams were multiple-choice with three essay questions, it didn't take long to grade them. There were only six from the athletes. I could have sworn there were seven of them in class, but I hadn't paid that much attention to who was there.

As I suspected, the athletes' papers were identical. And so were their scores. All Bs. I was troubled that they didn't try for As. If they were going to be cunning, they could have made it worth their while. If their motive was to avoid invoking suspicion, I underestimated their abilities at that game. But, the mere similarity of six exams would put even a novice teacher into alarm. And the fact that the students sat adjacent to one another would leave no doubt.

I started preparing the next exam for GPS. My experience as a student in college revealed the cunning nature of some athletes and I suspected that disposition had not changed significantly in one generation. I had to find some way to outsmart them. But how to do it? It was almost time to meet Ricky.

*****

The main road through the campus passed beneath a gate that at one time had been a grandiose affair. An intricate iron scrollwork arched overhead between stone columns at either side that bore elaborate carvings of ancient scenes in totem-pole fashion. The gate had been a remarkable hallmark of an institution of higher learning. But after decades of neglect, the columns had blackened from grime and soot, and from a distance appeared to be little more than mundane obelisks holding up a dilapidated mass of twisted and rusted iron. I began to see more and more of the true character of Hartmann College in its environment.

When I drove through the gate a shiny sign caught my eye. The speed limit sign, reflecting the sun, glared at me and I could just make out the "25" on it as I passed by. I could have sworn its mate across the road was "35" when I had come to campus that morning. Then I saw the flashing lights of the city police car ahead. The speed limit had been lowered and no notice had been offered to the college community. A typical move, I later learned, for Elkridge which already had wide notoriety for its speed traps along the highway that bisected it. Strangely enough, the practice was condoned by both the east side with its lavish green areas with large gaudy houses, and the west side, devoid of greenery, with smaller houses, more like shacks, huddled in groups resembling villages.

As a result of many maneuvers by Elkridge to unjustly extract revenue from the local students, Dr. Dennison, the president of the college, had reportedly met with the city council many times to plead for consideration since the college was responsible for the majority of the jobs in the community. But, the city council figured it unlikely that the college would pack up and move overnight. There was nowhere for it to go. There was little the college could do in retaliation, so the faculty and student body largely boycotted the local businesses.

The poor sucker who had unwittingly failed to observe the new speed limit, most likely because of the reflection of the sun, was slowing down and pulling to the shoulder just ahead of the flashing red and blue lights. Since luck usually eludes me, it bolstered my ego to think that I had the good fortune to escape a traffic ticket.

Near one end of town, a gaudy neon sign perched on a bent steel pole near the shoulder of the highway read, "Jim Bob's." Its tacky theme was echoed by a similar sign that dangled from the front of a pre-fabricated metal building clad in vertical stripes of white and faded red and blue. From a distance, no other hint was given as to the nature of the establishment. I considered the possibility of a private club. I never liked that sort of thing. It made me feel guilty at having to segregate myself from decent people to cavort with arrogant and pompous assholes that hung from the bar, thinking they were worth more as human beings than those who actually were.

The only two windows that graced the barren facade appeared to be darkened and held lighted signs advertising Budweiser and Keystone. Advertising labels plastered the metal door, advertising various brands of alcoholic beverages and tobacco products. I pulled on the well-worn doorknob and, even though I thought it might have separated from the door, it held fast and the dented, metal slab opened.

Soured yeast. That's what it smelled like. Enhanced with a bouquet of malodorous grease that must have been used to fry vile delicacies. The air, dank and heavy, seemed to hold me back while my eyes searched through the dim lighting for some glimmer of amenity amid the bare concrete floor, tin walls, and ceiling. A jar of pickled-eggs on the counter did it for me. I was almost nauseous.

Ricky was leaning over the bar opposite an older woman with a shock of disheveled hair. They both turned to watch my entrance and the parched face of the woman smiled at me. I wondered how it kept from cracking.

"Is that 'im?" bellowed the dry face beneath the strange hair.

"Come on in, August."

Ricky motioned me to the bar stool next to him. I couldn't help but stare at the woman and wonder what history had formed the ancient face. She was certainly not attractive, and probably never had been, but she wasn't unpleasant to look at. It was more like anthropology. I tried to imagine what kind of hell she had been through.

"You must be August," the old dame shouted with a British brogue. "'ave a seat. They call me Cindy. That's sho' for Cinderella."

Now, there was a mystery. The smile never left her face. It was comforting. Not that the smile was anything special. It was just that I didn't like waiting for her face to break if it were to change expressions.

"What's y'pleasure?" the voice hacked out.

Before I answered her question, I surveyed the lineup of bottles behind her. I was surprised to see an impressive display of scotch, vodka, gin, and several liqueurs. I took a chance.

"I don't suppose you would have Glenlivet?"

"Now, there's a man's drink," she said to Ricky. "Why didn' you tell me you knew a bo'y who 'ad real class?"

She reached under the bar and a bottle of Glenlivet slowly surfaced. She held it aloft for just a moment, staring at it like she had just killed it, then lowered it over a glass with her creviced hand, carefully pouring a shot. Then she made it a double and gently pushed it in front of me.

"I don't sell a lo' of this stuff. No' many ask for it. Hell, I don't think anyone around 'ere even knows wha' it is."

She smiled at me again and I smiled back with a curt thank you.

"Well, Gov, Ricky, 'ere, tells me you're one 'ot shot professor."

Her British dialect was completely out of character for the bar and seemed foreign to the mouth that spoke the words.

"Well, I don't know about being such a hot shot. But, the professor part, well I guess you could call me that, in spite of what the students say."

Her laughter roared through the room, since the corrugated metal panels on the walls did little to abate the sound, especially when she started coughing.

"Sense of 'umor, too." More laughter. "Ricky, by God, y'r coming up in the world."

I looked at Ricky who seemed unaffected by her innuendos. He calmly sipped the beer in front of him and showed no expression of concern one way or the other. I was curious about her name.

"So what's the Cinderella story?"

She laughed again. "Well, let' just say 'at I earned it after I stumbled into some good luck."

"Fair enough. Where did you find it, if I may go there?"

She roared again. "Damn, Ricky, this'un's precious."

She har-har-harred to the end of the bar where she bent over in another fit of coughing.

"Let's grab a booth," Ricky said, slipping off his stool.

I put a twenty on the counter. Ricky grabbed it and shoved it back into my hand.

"Put this on my tab," he yelled to Cindy.

I followed him to the side of the room and sat opposite him. The seat sort of grabbed onto my clothes and held on, twisting my trousers around me. I rested my arms on the table, also sticky. I wondered how I would clean the leather patches on the elbows of my jacket. The pants, I wasn't worried about. I needed a new pair, anyway.

"Nice place, Ricky."

"Cindy was right. You have a sense of humor."

"I'm glad you took it that way. What's the story with Cindy?"

"Oh, well years ago she married a GI who was stationed in England. A pilot. It was one of those one-night love affairs that somehow ends in marriage. The next day they discovered they really didn't really like each other. But before they could do anything about it, he was killed in a plane crash. As it turns out, his family was loaded. Shortly after that, his parents died in a fire. Some attorney finally found out about their son's marriage and went looking for his wife. Cindy inherited everything. So she pulled up roots, moved to the U. S., and settled down here in Elkridge. No one knows exactly why, but that's the story."

"You know, this town is just plain weird." I took another sip and contemplated Cindy's history. "Is this place the best Elkridge has to offer?"

He took a swallow of beer. His long, tranquil face smiled at me. "It's the best for me."

"Why is that?" I said, grimacing from a sip of whisky. It had been awhile.

"It's sort of a woman thing."

I was not prepared for a new acquaintance to open up his personal life to me. But, as long as he dangled the carrot, I would follow it.

"Bad experience, or bad luck?" I asked.

"Both. Due to bad luck, I had a bad experience once and I haven't had the nerve to get involved with another woman since."
"I'd think a bar would be the last place to avoid women."

"It's highly unlikely that a woman will make a pass at me, here."

Being tall and fit with a manly face, Ricky was attractive enough and successful, if you consider a lifetime of teaching successful. And he could hold decent discourse with just about anyone. I figured he was good bait for some women.

"Why not?

"Notice anything peculiar about this place?"

I looked around, this time in earnest. It looked like a bar. Any bar.

"Nope."

"What kind of people do you see?"

It was then that I noticed the two men kissing in a back booth. I had nothing against gays. In fact, I had a couple of very good friends who were gay. But, the thought of what they actually did to each other was a source of considerable discomfort. Not that it was distasteful. Just uncomfortable.

"Oh. So what is a gay bar doing in a town like Elkridge?"

"Elkridge is a curious place." He took a drink of his beer. "Well, of course it has its token rich, poor, and everything in between, including war mongers, pacifists, and followers of about any cause you can think of." He took another drink. I did too. "But, you see, the crowning glory of Elkridge is its distinction as a refuge for the undesirables. The cast-offs from neighboring communities. They finally formed an alliance and persuaded one of their well-to-do patrons to invest in this land and build a bar."

"That must have been some time ago, from the looks of this place."

"Many years. The city has tried to get rid of it, but it lays just outside the city limits. They can't touch it."

"Why don't they just annex it?"

"Oh, they tried. But the owner brought suit and the state said the city would have to provide utilities and city services if they did. Well, that stopped it because Elkridge didn't have the money. Over the years they just gave up."

I wasn't sure just how comfortable I would be in a gay bar. But, I hadn't even noticed it when I first came in. With that observation out of the way, I focused on my objective.

"So how the hell do you make this ITV thing work?"

I sipped the whisky and held the welcome relief in my mouth just long enough to cleanse the day's harshness from it, like fire sterilizing a cauldron. The sweet burn did its job and I sank back into the stickiness as much as the adhesion would allow.

"ITV," he echoed. "Well, partner, it's like this."

He took a drink, another long one, and leaned forward over the table. His smile would have been comforting had it not been for the mischievous eyes.

"You know, our administration is not exactly an award-winning team." Another drink. "And, I'm sure by now you have come to accept even a small bit of mediocrity as a mainstay of your objectives." Another drink. "And, in all fairness, I have to wonder why a man of your integrity and competence would even have considered such a place as Hartmann College."

This time I took a drink. A long one.

"But to answer your question, you don't. You don't make it work. You let it. It will work when it wants to."

I had set myself up for a complex answer rife with technical jargon and complicated words. I had even read what I could about it in several trade publications. But, Ricky's answer was beyond complex. It was bananas.

"What the hell are you talking about? Let it?"

Ricky took a huge gulp of his beer and leaned back. The smile had not changed.

"You have to, old chum. That's all you can do."

Then he started laughing. It began with a chuckle and gradually increased by gasps and chortles into cackles and finally into howls. A series of roars echoed from the end of the bar as Cindy joined in his exuberance.

He finally calmed himself enough to take another drink. The smile returned.

"I'm sorry, August."

He almost began laughing again but squelched it with another drink that emptied the mug. He raised it above his head.

"Cindy," he yelled. "We're dry, here."

I self-consciously sipped my whisky hoping I would understand what was going on before my pride started looking for a hole to climb into.

"Look." He sat forward and leaned toward me as far as the table would allow. "I don't mean to be patronizing, but I don't often get the chance to release a lot of rapture about much of anything around here. Like you, I have to endure the awkwardness of ignorance and incompetence every day. And then there's the students on top of that." He laughed again.

I hadn't heard Cindy approach with the drinks but she gracefully set them in front of us and turned to leave. Then she started laughing. The cackle followed her all the way back to the bar.

"Thanks, Hon," yelled Ricky. "Now, about ITV. You see, every room in that blasted place that's wired for ITV is different. There are different boxes, different controls, different cameras, different monitors, different computers. Hell, everything is different."

"I wouldn't know. I've only seen one of the rooms. And I wasn't too impressed with that."

"Well, buddy, just wait. You don't know how unimpressed you can be."

He started in on the second mug. I finished my first glass.

"So, how do you know how to run all of this equipment?" I asked while his nose was buried in his mug.

"That's the beauty of this system, August. You don't do that, either."

"But aren't there some kind of instructions or training?"

"Wait a minute." He set his mug down and sat upright. He looked at me straight on. "Instructions? Training? What do think this place is? An institution of higher learning?"

Then he laughed again. Harder, this time, almost choking.

"I'm sorry August. But this is just too much. Boy, you're really green."

He took a drink and stifled his coughing.

"No. There's no training. And no instructions. Oh, there are a dozen manuals scattered around somewhere that explain the operation of the equipment, but who the hell has time to read them? Much less, understand them."

We passed the late afternoon by approaching a hearty inebriation and expounding the tribulations of Hartmann College. I frequently thought about Dr. Hartmann and how he might have reacted to such apathy. How did the college get this far? How could it function as an institution of higher learning? Unless, of course, it wasn't really functioning that way and I was too stupid to realize it. Perhaps it was just being allowed to happen that way. Like ITV.

I was wishing I could hear the chimes. That would at least have signaled the passing of another day of enlightenment. Somehow, I couldn't let go of the thought that what I was doing had some justification and purpose. Even in the depths of such confusion and languor, was there no hope for education? The chimes. I needed to hear the chimes. I needed their magic to keep my faith alive. Faith in education. And faith in my worth as a teacher.

Chapter 15

M r. Armany," I said to the young man with the sly grin. "Suppose you assist me with this projectile launcher."

The entire class watched as he jumped up from his seat in the rear of the physics class and strutted toward the demonstration desk in the front of the room. His medium height and attractive features of his hard, chiseled face gave him a distinguished look for a young man, but in an evil sort of way. It was mostly the eyes, dark and deep as if hiding something. I wouldn't have been concerned about him except that he was one of the more troublesome students in the class. Not that he was disruptive, but he continually made comments to his neighbors about, I suppose, the dorky professor. I figured he might learn something by participating in the experiment.

"The apparatus you see here is a projectile launcher. Mr. Armany is going to elevate the launcher to an angle of forty-five degrees from the horizontal. A spring firing mechanism will launch a steel ball from the tube and we will observe the path of the projectile, noting where it lands. Then he will change the angle and repeat the experiment."

I turned toward Mr. Armany.

"Now, I want you to fix the angle of the tube at forty-five degrees. Be careful because it's heavy. You can see the scale on the side of the support stand. Then you insert a steel ball into the tube, pull back the lever, and secure it by pushing the lever into the notch below it. Then when I say 'ready' you can release the lever."

He nodded and the smile on his face was not unlike that of a criminal who was planning a lucrative heist. His eyes sparkled with keenness.

While I prepared a bucket to catch the projectile on an adjacent desk, I heard him adjust and load the launcher and I turned around to inspect it. I heard the clank just before I felt the impact against my forehead, a dull, hollow thud that echoed through my skull. Oddly enough the force from the small steel projectile hurled my head backward in approximately the same trajectory, I suppose, as the ball would have taken, and I fell into the other desk that held the bucket intended to receive the ball. The back of my head struck the edge of the table, and I'm not entirely sure what happened after that, but I seem to remember a sudden universal gasp that filled the classroom.

When I opened my eyes, Mr. Armany was hovering above me, a fiendish curl to his mouth. His eyes, trained on mine, looked as if he had just witnessed some thrilling, macabre event. Then I saw two other faces leaning over me.

"Professor Lane?"

I was conscious. At least, I thought I was. The emerging pain in my head told me that much, even though I was lying on the floor.

"Okay," I said. "Help me up from here."

I struggled to my feet with the assistance of the students. Once upright, my knees immediately buckled, but their firm grasps on my arms prevented me from falling again. I stumbled to my stool and plopped down on it.

"Professor, you're bleeding," said a blonde-haired girl. I had no idea who she was, even though she must have been one of my students. At that point in time I wouldn't have recognized any of them. Except Mr. Armany.

They all leaned in toward me, I suppose, to view the bloody wound.

"The back of your head. It's bleeding."

I took a handkerchief from my back pocket and pressed it against my head. I looked at the blood-soaked cloth and pressed it harder against the wound.

"I guess I should cancel the rest of the class and get this looked at."

"Ah... Professor," said the blonde-haired girl, "everyone has already gone."

I looked at the empty classroom and thought how nice that they were concerned for my well-being. Only the strange girl, Allison Boyer, sat alone in the middle watching me. Not a top-notch student, but at least she seemed to be attentive to my lectures. And accidents. Her mesmerizing eyes, black and severe, seemed to prod me as if analyzing me, as one would poke a carcass to see if it were alive. Very different than her state in the parking lot. Her long face, stern and sallow, seemed to scoff at me. All in all, I changed my assessment of her. She was not a pleasant girl. In fact, I had just realized that she was the girl I saw in the Wal-Mart parking lot.

The name Allison also struck something familiar deep in my

mind, that part that usually sees little daylight. The blow to my head must have jarred it loose. Then it hit me. Melanie Parker. Was this the Allison she referred to? I couldn't believe there was a connection with this shy, strange girl.

I remembered that I was injured.

"Thanks, guys. I'll just walk over to the nurse's station."

I managed to stand on my own. A little fuzzy, but competent.

"I'm sorry, Professor Lane," Mr. Armany suddenly yelped. "I … I… I don't know what happened. I… I… I guess the lever slipped."

I looked at his frightened face. Or it could have been a sneer instead of fright. Sometimes they look the same.

"It's all right. I'm sure you didn't do this dastardly thing on purpose."

He recoiled as if I had accused him of shooting me. I gave him the benefit of the doubt in lieu of any evidence to the contrary.

"I'm kidding," I said. "Everything is fine. Things like this happen and I certainly won't hold it against you. Relax."

I picked up my books and I think I said, "I'll see you on Wednesday," as I stumbled out.

Slowly, I made my way out of the classroom to my office, then toward Caftan Hall.

*****

I was fortunate that Caftan Hall was in an adjacent building because no one else was available to help when I exited into the cool air and bright sun. At least I didn't have far to stagger. My tipsy state challenged me to stay on the sidewalk. Using one hand to press a handkerchief behind my head interrupted my already flawed sense of balance.

Caftan Hall was a dilapidated structure, aged by decades of neglect and several piecemeal renovations that served only to conceal more of the rotting material that magically supported the building. The main door seemed to be jammed, testing my weakened dexterity to force it open, but I managed to pass through it. The building directory listed a number of offices, most of which were stepchildren of the college, like campus security and the training office, which no one claimed or wanted near them in other, more prominent buildings. The nurse's office had been relocated from the administration building to this huddle of misfits, I was told, because Dr. O'Mally was offended by the smell of antiseptics. And she thought sick people should be isolated in case one of them happened to carry a deadly disease that would suddenly eradicate Hartmann's population. I wondered what other pleasures and human frailties besides chimes and illnesses annoyed her.

The office was just past the directory on my right. The handkerchief did not seem to be abating the bleeding from my head, so I hurriedly grabbed the doorknob and turned it while starting forward with good momentum to enter the office. Due to my debilitated state and bad luck with doors, the doorknob did not turn and the momentum of my body was stopped abruptly. The collision smacked my nose and bloodied it. Then blood was pouring from the back of my head as well as the front, and there I was with only one handkerchief. I saw a restroom next door to the office and barged inside for paper towels. I removed most of the visible blood from my face and grabbed some towels for my nose. Then I thought of finding a phone to call for assistance.

I pushed on the door but it didn't give. Then it dawned on me that it opened inward and both of my hands were occupied. I stood facing the door for an instant pondering whether I should use my left hand to open the door and let blood trickle down the back of my neck, or the right hand and let blood flow down my face. Just as I assembled enough nerve to use my nose hand to reach for the door handle, the door was thrust open and I was knocked to the floor in one clean blow. While I wallowed about among bloody towels I heard a scream and managed to direct my vision toward the door. There stood a girl, obviously a student, with both hands in front of her mouth as if stifling another scream. Her eyes, distended well beyond their limits and very familiar, glared at me in a state of fear.

"What you do in here?" She almost screamed.

"That's alright," I said. "You don't have to be sorry." I tried to sit upright. "I could ask you the same question."

The poor girl dropped her hands and looked at me like I was a buffoon.

"I want to use restroom," she squeaked.

While puzzled by her broken English, I quickly looked around the room and even in my impaired condition I was able to discern the lack of urinals hanging from any of the walls. I looked up at the girl. I finally recognized her as Allison Boyer, the shy girl from my physics class, and the Wal-Mart parking lot. This being the second time I heard her speak, I surmised that she was a foreign student, but from where I had no idea.

"Young lady, I am truly sorry. I had no idea I had wandered into your restroom. As you can see, I have an urgent situation here."

"Oh," she gasped. "I sorry. You okay?"

"Well, actually, I don't think I am."

With a series of complex and, I'm sure, ungraceful moves, I managed to stand somewhat erect by pulling myself up on a sink.

"Would you mind showing me to the nearest phone?"

She watched suspiciously as I stumbled past her into the hall. I stood there waiting for her to regain her composure. I had stopped worrying about my own.

"Phone down here," she said as she led the way.

She turned halfway around, the black eyes watching me. I wasn't sure if she didn't trust me or if she was wondering what she could do to help. I followed her as best I could. She disappeared into an office somewhere ahead and I kept plodding forward. Then I saw her head peek from inside the doorway, I suppose to ensure that I was still interested in finding a phone. When I made it as far as the door, she pointed to a desk.

"There," she said.

I sat on the desk and dropped my nose towel to dial the phone while blood dripped onto my trousers. I called Claudia. The phone rang the token three times before the voice mail broke in with her coarse message. She was probably in class. I hung up and dialed Dr. Tipton. Voice mail. I hung up and dialed Dr. Gaines.

"It appears that you and I might be the only two people left on campus, today," I said to Allison who, by this time, had lost some of her apprehension about my presence.

She seemed to wince when I said that. I suppose that if I were a girl and someone who looked like he had been in a skirmish trespassed on the sanctity of my restroom and tried to convince me that I was going to be alone with him, I too would be a bit concerned with my safety.

"I'm sorry, Miss Boyer," I said. "I didn't mean to upset you."

Then Mary Einhorn answered.

"Mary, this is August. I'm trying to find the nurse. The door to the office is locked and I have no idea where she might be. Can you give me a hint as to where I might look?"

"Oh, my, August, is a student ill?" she said with some concern.

"No, it's not that."

"Is someone hurt?" Her voice had a hint of urgency. I paused, not wanting to admit that I was the victim.

"Well, yes, as a matter of fact, I have fallen and hit my head. And my nose. I think that's all. I need someone to assess the damage."

"Where are you?"

"I'm in a …" I looked at Allison. "Exactly where are we?"

"One-fifteen," she said.

"I'm in office one-fifteen in Caftan Hall."

"I'll be right over. You stay there."

She hung up. Allison had sat down by then, I don't know if she was afraid to leave or just wanted to see the outcome of my situation.

"How did you know this office was here?" I asked the girl.

"I work here part-time."

"I'm really sorry. I didn't mean to frighten you. I think I'll be fine until Ms. Einhorn arrives. If you need to go to the restroom…" I nodded in that direction and left the question open hoping not to have to finish it. She got up and darted from the office.

It seemed like only a few seconds since I had hung up the phone when Mary barged into the office, her body straight as a board, the bun hair resting on top of her head like a beehive, her eyeglasses screaming to be returned to the sixties, and a first-aid kit tucked neatly under her arm like a courier with a dispatch. The striking maroon dress, with its distinctive epaulets, gave the impression of a uniform. She couldn't have been more beautiful.

She rushed toward me as I sat there with one hand holding the handkerchief behind my head and the other holding towels to my nose.

"What in the world happened?"

"It's a long story. I just need to know if I'm going to live."

"August, you shouldn't joke about such things."

She pulled my hand from my nose and blood began dripping again.

She went about her business cleaning the blood from my face and inserting a gauze plug.

"Is the back of your head injured?"

I pulled my other hand free and held out the blood-soaked handkerchief.

"Oh, dear. Why don't you sit in the chair over there so I can get a look at it?"

I slid off the desk and plopped into the chair. She scurried around behind me and I felt her probing fingers, gentle, but very effective.

"We need to get you to a doctor. I think you'll need stitches."

With that said, she placed gauze on my head wound and instructed me to hold it there. She helped me to her car and off we went to the hospital.

"Sorry to be such a bother," I said, staring at her alluring profile. She looked good driving that car. A Mazda. Larger than mine, but sensible. "Thanks for rescuing me. I'm not sure anyone else on campus would consider me worth the trouble. Least of all, my students."

"August Lane, why do you say that? Anyone here would be willing to help in this sort of situation."

She said it with a slow, deliberate enunciation. My name seemed to roll out of her lips like a cloud over a mountain. I had never heard it pronounced that way.

"You say that so nicely."

She looked at me and smiled. A genuine smile. Sincere. I began to feel uneasy. And very foolish.

*****

The first task on my mind when I returned to campus was to corral Claudia in her office. When I relayed my experience with the nurse, or at least her absence, she immediately launched her defensive shields.

"But, Claudia, the nurse is supposed to be on duty just like everyone else on this frigging campus. If she's being paid to do a job she should do it."

The anesthetic was beginning to wear off and the back of my head stung from the three stitches that held my scalp together.

"Hell, you expect me to do my job, don't you? I mean it's not like I'm being paid this huge salary for nothing, right? What would you think if I just decided not to show up some day?"

"All right, August, I get your point. For your information, I saw the nurse in the coffee shop by the Student Union earlier. But I don't have anything to do with the nurse. I certainly can't give her an order to report to her office, if that's what you expect."

"Fine." I wondered if my boiling blood was spurting from the stitches. "So who does our virtual nurse report to?"

"I don't know. You might try Dr. Tipton. Student affairs probably takes care of that job."

"Then that's where I'll start." I got up to leave.

"You're not going to sue the college, are you?"

"The thought never occurred to me, but thanks for mentioning it. And, by the way, thanks for taking care of this for me."

I left her alone with her scowl.

*****

The secretary answered my call to Dr. Tipton. She informed me that Dr. Tipton was not in. After pressing for her whereabouts, I was directed to Dr. Gaines' office.

I proceeded to the Administration Building. I had never met Dr. Tipton, only talked with her on the phone. But her reputation for goldbricking was universally known.

Mary greeted me as I entered the office.

"August, how are you feeling?"

"At least I'm walking. Thanks again for rescuing me."

"I was glad to do it. Are you here to see Dr. Gaines?"

She began looking at the appointment calendar in front of her with a puzzled look on her face.

"No," I said. "No appointment."

I studied her serous eyes as they scanned the calendar. It might have been the pain medication I had running through my body, but she seemed more attractive. Just something about her graceful movements. And the maroon dress. I was always partial to darker reds. I suppose it might have had something to do the fact that I tended to bleed a lot from the frequent self-inflicted injuries.

"Actually, I'm here to speak to Dr. Tipton. That is, when she finishes with Dr. Gaines."

She gave me an odd look.

"Okay, let me buzz him and he'll let her know you're waiting."

I selected a chair in front of Mary's desk while she made the call. It was not long until Dr. Tipton came marching out of Dr. Gaines' office like a British general after a de facto victory. Her short, stocky body seemed to bob up and down like a giant ball of Jell-o bouncing on the floor. The ball stopped in front of me. I remained seated so I didn't create a spectacle by passing out when I stood up.

"Yes, Professor Lane?" she said looking down at me, though slightly, due to her very short stature, with huge white eyes that seemed to be illuminated from inside the black face; sort of like one of those Halloween lanterns. Her pug nose was turned up. The sharp, raspy voice was as unpleasant as her demeanor.

"Dr. Tipton, thank you for seeing me on short notice."

"What can I do for you?"

The words were rapid, staccato bursts, much like an automatic rifle fire into a rusty barrel.

"I was very surprised to find that the nurse was not on duty during her office hours earlier today. Was there some sort of emergency that came up that required her presence?"

"The nurse, you say?"

"Yes, the nurse. The one who has an office in Caftan Hall and who is supposed to be on duty from eight in the morning until four in the afternoon."

"I'm not aware of any emergencies, no."

"Then is there some explanation of why she was not there?"

"Why do you want to know?"

I did not foresee the deployment of such rapid defense. "What difference does it make why I would want to know?"

I tried to be as reserved and polite as I could. Of course, the best behavior I was capable of at that time was tainted with animosity. Mary was making gestures behind Dr. Tipton, I suppose in an effort to get me to remain calm.

"Professor Lane, I am not obligated to justify the behavior of any employee in my charge to you or anyone else at the institution without a need to know."

"Excuse me?"

"What did you not understand about what I just said?"

Any restraint I might have been able to exercise was quickly eroding.

"What I don't understand is how the nurse is being paid for not doing what she is supposed to be doing."

She drew back from me, looking more like a fat midget with enormous nostrils.

"Professor Lane, I am not responsible to you for the hours my employees keep."

That was it, game time was over. Now it was war. I jumped out of my chair and stood in front of her. I fought to regain control of my wavering.

"You damned sure are responsible to me when that sorry-assed lazy nurse over there is not available during her working hours to treat a wound in the back of my head that required three stitches to close."

I turned my head to show her the bandage, then I glared at her while she tightened up even more. Behind her, Mary had her hand over her mouth, shaking her head in abandon.

"And, since she was not there, I bloodied my nose trying to open her office door, which was locked. And if that isn't enough, I incurred further injury in a restroom from another door that was opened in my face. Hell, I could have gone into shock, or suffered a severe infection.

Or I could even have bled to death. Then who the hell do you think you would be responsible to?"

I stood there waiting for her to regain her composure. She didn't, and said nothing, merely grinding her teeth, obviously searching for a comeback that would justify her position.

"Dr. Tipton, one of your employees charged with ensuring the safety and well-being of the students and staff at this college neglected her duties. Unless you can provide some justification in her defense, and I strongly doubt that you can justify her sitting on her ass in the coffee shop at the time I went to see her, I intend to carry this matter as far up the ladder as I can get it."

I watched the anger slowly turn to concern in her face. Her hands had compressed the notebook she held in her arms into a wad of paper and cardboard.

I continued my attack. "There was no note on the door and no indication of when she might return. There was no phone number posted for emergencies. That nurse should be available to everyone here during her office hours. Now, if you persist in this game of self-righteousness, I will have no alternative but to take this to Dr. Gaines or the President. And I think you must surely realize that would mean an all out investigation of this incident. And I really don't think you're prepared to give up your cushy little job here reigning over your empire."

She stood motionless, glaring back at me like a cornered snake waiting for a chance to strike.

"So, let's make a deal," I suggested.

She cleared her throat with a short burst of obnoxious sounds.

"What do you have in mind?"

"You call that worthless nurse on the carpet. You tell her to get her lazy ass in gear and the next time I go over there for any reason during her hours, I'd damned well better be able to find her there."

She looked down in defeat, but still clinging to a bit of pride.

"And," I continued, "the next time I see you, I expect to be treated with respect. I'm an employee of this college just like you are. We're working for the same team, Dr. Tipton. It's not them and us. It's just us. You're no better than I am, lady. And if you think I'm going to treat you like royalty, you're out of your mind."

I relaxed my stance and fought the urge to collapse. "Fortunately, no serious damage was done, here. But I think you have to agree that it could have been disastrous had a student been seriously injured and no help was available. Can this college afford that kind of a lawsuit and notoriety?"

She still stood there, almost in shock from having her world turned upside down.

As I was leaving, I offered one last word, "Oh, by the way, you're just damned lucky I don't sue the shit out of this college. And you."

I drove home a bit slower than usual, much to the dismay of the local constable I saw hiding behind a row of trash cans. I tried to piece together how I could repair my reputation in the physics class. I had not exactly presented a professional image. And I certainly didn't expect them to believe anything I might say after that embarrassing incident. It would have been difficult for me, as a student, to have any faith in a fool for a professor.

Then I thought about the long night ahead at Boyd Atkins. In my condition, it would be very long.

Chapter 16

As I turned to write an equation on the whiteboard, the whispering and giggling started. I had expected better of my calculus class. After all, they were sophomores with at least one year of college under their belts. After I explained the equation and its application, one young lady raised her hand.

"Professor Lane, what happened to the back of your head?"

I had not paid much attention to the bruise on my forehead. However, the gash in the back of my scalp felt like someone was still sewing stitches. I was aware that the wound, emblazoned with a shining ring of shaved scalp and a glaring bandage, would be a beacon to my chagrin. A curse to be borne by my self-esteem, which was already dwindling beneath the stares of my students.

"I had an accident yesterday. Nothing major. Just a few stitches."

"Is that what happened in your physics class?" a young man asked.

"Yeah," from another, "everybody heard about it."

"As a matter of fact, it is," I said, keeping my disturbed ego intact. "It's nothing to be concerned about."

I continued lecturing and each minute seemed to loiter before passing. I had already toyed with the thought of canceling afternoon classes. Since the pills the doctor prescribed for pain had done little more than deflate my checkbook, I wouldn't have lasted through another class, much less a lab. The previous night's class at the prison had completely sapped my endurance. The prescription was for only a few pills to be used "sparingly," the doctor said, "as needed." I don't think he had any concept of the meaning of the word "needed." Or, "sparingly," for that matter.

I checked my watch often hoping the chimes might surface and blast through my sordid misery, but I knew I would not be hearing them. Even if the chimes were operable, they probably would not have restored my spirit to its keen state. On the way out the door I uttered a few words about the assignment for the next class and fought my way down the hall to my office.

"Hey, August." Stan was in too good of a mood for me to want to respond. "I heard you had an accident yesterday."

"Yup." I made no effort to clarify my reticence as I passed by him on the way to my desk.

"Ooh, that looks like a dandy there on your head. Well, since you're walking, I guess that means you'll still be around."

"Yup." I yanked the bottle of pills from my attaché case and struggled to open the childproof lid. My frustration led me from innocent attempts at twisting the lid to vigorous pulling, and finally to the use of a small screwdriver to force the lid off. I extracted a pill from the scarred remains of the bottle and gulped it down with a swig of cold coffee.

"You know, I could have done that for you a lot easier," he said.

Stanley was enjoying my performance. He relished my fits of frustration. He would sit calmly, leaning back in his chair that didn't lean, while I went through various maneuvers evolving from annoyance, to confusion, anger, frustration, and as an encore, stupidity. He would never say a word, just watch like an anonymous member of the audience who expected to be entertained. It pissed me off.

"Yes, I'm sure you could. And, I could have kicked your ass, too, but as you can see, your not getting involved with the pill bottle spared you that embarrassment. It all would have been for naught, anyway. These pills are worthless."

"Oh, aren't we in a feisty mood?"

"If that's what you'd call it," I said plopping into my chair and leaning back into it and mashing the wound on my head.

"Of course you realize that you're the talk of the campus, right now." He got up to pour a cup of coffee. His lanky frame towered above me. I looked up at him looking down at me. "But then, you seem to be making that a habit."

He took a drink of coffee, still holding the carafe in his other hand. "Are you feeling all right?" His eyes oscillated between his cup and me. "Can I freshen you up?"

"No, but thanks for offering. What I really need is a belt of whisky."

"Why don't you go home?" He sat back down. "You look like hell."

"Professor Lane?"

The darling voice came from Melanie Parker who was standing in the doorway with an armful of books. The picture did not seem right. The straight skirt, a decent looking one, at that, certainly couldn't have been her idea. But the blouse? Yes, the blouse was hers. The trademark blouse, opened wide, mind you, in a naughty way to reveal more than a hint of her intriguing breasts.

"Miss Parker," I said. "Come in, come in. Mr. Kutch, you remember Miss Parker?"

"Yes," he said, trying not to look too keenly toward her open blouse. "How are you, today?"

"Oh, I'm fine, Professor Kutch?"

She flashed her eyes and a devilish grin spread across her face. When her first performance ended, she came toward me and sat prim and proper in the guest chair in front of me.

"Professor Lane," she began with an alluring voice, "I heard about your accident yesterday?"

Here, I could swear that her face actually showed some hint of sincerity.

"Are you all right? I mean this isn't going to keep you out of class or anything, is it?"

Oh, she was good. She was probably wondering if she should bother coming to class the next day.

"No, Miss Parker. I'll be fine, but thank you for your concern."

I winked at Stanley who had sat down and seemed to be thoroughly enjoying our interaction.

"I want to apologize for the way I behaved the other day?"

She was careful not to lean forward since, I suppose, Stan would be able to bear witness to such a provocative move. In fact she was careful to be very proper and endearing. It was most aggravating to sit there expecting to revel in the pleasures of enticement and receive only teasing.

"Thank you, Miss Parker," I said casually. "At least you have improved your attire if only marginally."

"Oh, that. Well, I'm trying to find some other clothes? I just don't have a lot to pick from?"

She flashed her eyes again and lowered them to my crotch, apparently for a status check.

"You see, I don't have a lot of money to spend on clothes since most of it goes for tuition and books and things like that? It's just hard to find good clothes that I can afford?" She looked me in the eyes. "And, besides, I only want to learn all I can from you?"

Having her back toward Stanley, she licked her lips, slowly, her moist tongue gliding around the opening like she was savoring the trace of chocolate that might have been left there. Or something else. I got the message.

"Well, since that's the case, you should do well in class Wednesday."

It was obvious from her face that this wasn't what she wanted to hear. But, she was a real trooper and kept her composure. She got up to leave and stood for an instant looking at us both.

"Well, thank you professor, for seeing me?"

Then she turned to Stan.

"And it was very pleasant to see you again, Professor Kutch?"

Her politeness was sickening but commendable, although I thought I noticed Stan lusting for a moment. Her performance was well planned and flawlessly executed. We both watched as she swished out of the room leaving behind the barest hint of perfume. We still watched even after she had gone. Then we looked at each other and blasted our laughter throughout the third floor until my head was hurting so badly I had to stop. Professor Able popped his head in the door.

"What have you guys been doing to that poor little wretch?" He crept, one waddle at a time, into the office. "She looked like she was ready to jump on anything that moved." He laughed between fits of coughing and wheezing.

"She's just playing her little game," I said. "You missed one of the finest performances I have ever seen."

"That's right, Frank," said Stan. "You would not believe the theatrical endowments of that young lady." He leaned back in his chair.

"And her other endowments aren't exactly second rate."

"Why, do I detect indecent contempt in you mean old men?"

"No," I said, "that's certainly not what you detect, here."

He cut loose with a barrage of hooting that followed him out the door and down the hall. The levity ebbed and Stan leaned forward in his chair.

"What are you going to do about Miss Parker?" He leveled his eyes at me and they stayed there, suspended in his worried face, probing me for an answer.

"I really don't know."

I think we both knew what was coming. We just didn't know how it would be orchestrated or when it would begin.

"I guess," I said without any insight into the severity of the situation, "I'll just keep my nose clean and not give her an opportunity to make anything happen."

"That could be hard to do, you know."

"It hasn't exactly been easy, so far."

"Yeah, but you're going to have to watch that little vixen. She's out to do you harm, my boy."

"You just had to say that, didn't you?"

"You're such a nice guy. I hate to make you grovel for my opinion."

"Thanks," I said, turning back to my desk. "Not that I appreciate it or anything like that, you see. It's just that some folks can be too thoughtful."

"I try. I try."

When some dreadful event like that hangs over me I tend to focus on everything but what I should. But the problem with Melanie Parker just couldn't find its way into my sphere of priorities, especially with a head that felt like it was going to blast off of my neck.

"August, you know you might want to check with Dr. Tipton to get an update."

"Yeah, I called her earlier but I haven't heard anything further."

"As long as you stay on top of it, you won't be surprised."

"You might have a good point, there."

I dialed the Dean of Student Affairs. I figured the sooner I did that the better it would be for my potential situation with Miss Parker. But, I wasn't sure how receptive Dr. Tipton would be in light of our recent confrontation.

"Dr. Tipton," I said when she answered. "This is Professor Lane."

"August. How nice to hear from you."

Sarcasm screamed from the phone. She apparently took our last meeting seriously.

"You can probably expect another visit from Melanie Parker."

"Funny you should say that, August. She's here now."

"Well, she certainly didn't waste any time. Have you talked to her yet?"

"No, she's waiting outside my office."

"Well, don't keep her waiting too long. It will just give her more time to think up a better plot."

"Do I sense more trouble between you two?"

"I think it's going to amount to a bit more than just trouble."

"All right, suppose you tell me what happened?"

"She's doing poorly in general physical science. She needs the course to graduate. She probably won't. She made a play for me to get a grade. I didn't bite. And she's been doing everything in her power to antagonize me into a situation. Mostly, seduction."

"So, you think Miss Parker is going to file a sexual harassment complaint?"

"You got it."

"You might want to come in so we can talk later. If that's what she does, I'll need to report it to the administration."

"I know the drill. Not that I've been in this position, before. But I read the few pages of the faculty handbook. I was a good boy."

"Let me talk to her first. Of course, you realize, that after I talk to Melanie and if she does file a complaint, any conversations we have will have to be witnessed."

"Do whatever you need to do. I'm just letting you know what to expect so you're not stunned when she drops the bomb."

"Thank you, Professor Lane. I'll let you know if anything happens."

I wondered how equitable she would be about my circumstances. Considering our volatile meeting at Dr. Gaines' office and her probable contempt for me, I wouldn't be surprised if she should lean toward Miss Parker's favor. The fact that I had no idea what to expect kept me on edge. But, I figured I knew what would ultimately happen. I just had to come to terms with it and prepare for the worst.

I wished the chimes were ringing instead of my ears. Their melodic ringing was like the Siren of Greek Mythology that lured sailors to their deaths. Not that I would be in danger of expiring, but I would be calmed and set back on the path of good character. I seemed to be having difficulty staying on that path lately.

I eventually put Miss Parker to rest and concentrated on the ITV class I had unwittingly agreed to take for Ricky again that afternoon. It would be a bit of a rush, but nothing I couldn't handle. Besides, I had grown fond of Ricky. I'm not sure of the reason for this anomaly in my behavior, since I rarely have a fondness for anyone. But, there was something genuine about his character. He lacked the pretense that I found so often in people, myself included, and he was able to live with the knowledge of what was going on around him without being consumed by the urge to correct it. This, to me, was a remarkable trait in any human being. I envied Ricky.

The first ITV experience, as unpleasant as it was, did provide an excellent educational opportunity. Since I could reasonably expect to become more proficient at this thing if I did more of it, I reluctantly agreed to take his class. However, this time I would be prepared. My equipment included a notebook for recording each difficultly I encountered, especially the various parts of the system that did not work as expected. I would be spending a great deal of class time documenting the failures of the ITV infrastructure.

I picked up my books and was on the way out the door when the phone rang. Unfortunately, I went back to answer it. Whenever I do something like that I always wish I hadn't. There is something about a ringing phone that penetrates the core of human curiosity, leaving an insatiable compulsion to know who is calling. And why. And being human, I usually succumb to it.

Claudia summoned me. I agreed to stop by before the ITV class, since it was in the same building as her office. Her assent indicated that it would be a short meeting and, therefore, of little consequence. As it turned out, it was, in fact, a short meeting. I was wrong about the consequence.

Claudia was determined to schedule an ITV class in GPS for the next semester. I was determined not to let it happen. I fought my best battle, but superior rank usually wins. In this case, it did. But I was not finished fighting.

Ricky's ITV class presented the opportunity for gathering feedback from the students about the technology that was robbing them of an education. From all of the comments and complaints, I learned that the sound was so horrible that students in the remote classroom barely understood what was said. The video resolution was so poor I couldn't even recognize who the students were in the remote classroom, and they had a great deal of following what was drawn on the document camera. The image froze frequently and by the time it resumed, I had already written an entire equation with no hint of what happened in between. I was convinced that I was onto something big. If I could expose the failure of ITV to deliver quality education, I could improve the state of affairs for the students.

So here the students and I had the opportunity to grasp the reigns of higher education and guide it onto the path of reason. A collective desire to achieve some good in its own behalf. A noble task for ones so young and untried. We all would be heroes.

But, not until I took Horace and her history club on their road trip to Norman on Saturday.

Chapter 17

I walked through the brisk morning air that bathed the campus in serenity, contemplating the complicated sequence of events that had thrust me into the guise of Good Samaritan. I had volunteered to drive Horace Klieburn and her history club to the Sam Noble Museum of Natural History in Norman. Well, I hadn't exactly volunteered. I have always made a point not to overextend my capacity for good deeds. It was more like boasting that resulted from Horace's initial inquiry about my driving ability.

I had, on occasion, passed along to her my critiques of other drivers, but rarely did I brag about my own refined driving techniques. Notwithstanding this obvious omission, she must have been led to believe that I was an excellent driver, which I believed myself to be. On the other hand, Horace, believing herself to be a very poor driver, was apprehensive about the upcoming field trip with her history club. Of course, the manner in which she presented her case intrigued me and I made the mistake of asking her to explain.

She said, "I just know I'm going to do something bad, especially around the road construction just outside of Norman. Do you have trouble there?"

Like any self-righteous macho male, I had to respond with, "No. Why?" It wasn't until the words were leaving my mouth that I realized my error. Somewhere in that fraction of a second between, "No" and "Why" I had conjured visions of her erratic control of a vehicle and compared it to my own expert command of mechanical devices and, wanting to flaunt my superiority, I succumbed to the bait. She had me.

She countered with, "Well, perhaps you should drive us."

It was done. I was the designated driver. Since that innocent exchange, I had a week to consider some way of retracting my claim, but to no avail.

So, there I was, just outside the motor pool, which was little more than a garage and small parking area bordered by a chain link fence, parts of which were still erect. The gate, secured with a chain and padlock, appeared to have been in that state for at least a decade, since the lock was only a mass of corroded metal. To one side of the gate, where the fence folded over itself to the ground and disappeared beneath a stand of weeds, a well-worn path provided access to the lot.

I found the van, number one-two-zero, that matched the number on the key tag and trip log. The key was a tight fit in the door lock but it eventually did go all the way in. But as hard as I tried, it didn't turn. I forcibly retracted it and tried again with the same result. So, a flash of logic told me to try the other door. Same result. I walked around the van to find another lock and examined the key. That's when I noticed the Chrysler logo on the key that was not compatible with the blue oval with the letters F-O-R-D on the van's grille.

The motor pool office was closed. So, I fired up my cell phone and called the motor pool supervisor. I got voice mail. I searched the directory on my phone and there were no other numbers for anyone on campus who could be of help. I trampled back over the folded fence and walked to my office.

I called Claudia. Voice mail. Then the motor pool supervisor, again. Voice mail. Then, thinking that maintenance was located next to the motor pool, I called them.

"Maintenance," said the surly voice.

I wasn't expecting an answer, so, my mind was already working on the next number I would call.

"Hello. Maintenance."

This time it sounded annoyed.

"Hello, this is August Lane. Math Science. I was supposed to take the History Club on a field trip today but I was given the wrong key to the van. I can't seem to get hold of anyone at the motor pool. Do you think you could notify them for me?"

"Yup," the voice said. "I can call Marney. He's the super over there. I got his number right here. Where you going to be?"

"I'll be at the motor pool."

I gave him my cell phone number, thanked him, and hung up. So, Marney supervised maintenance as well as the motor pool. He might have been busier than I gave him credit for.

I heard a click instead of a good-bye. I copied down some phone numbers from the directory on my desk and returned to the motor pool.

I looked at my watch several times each minute while my anger accelerated to a near relativistic state. For fifteen minutes it gouged my ego and poked at my stomach leaving what remained of my breakfast in a suspended state of digestion. Then a maintenance truck raced up the path across the weeds.

"Understand you got a problem," the driver yelled from outside the fence.

I walked to his truck and handed him the key to the van.

"This is a Chrysler key. I've got a Ford van. Number one-two-zero."

He looked at the key.

"This is a Chrysler key," he said. "You won't be able to start the Ford with a Chrysler key. I'll see if I can find the right one."

I don't think he heard my thanks since he was already backing away to leave by the time I said it. During the next fifteen minutes students began arriving. I broke the news to each of the girls upon her arrival and assured her that I would have a key shortly. Oddly enough, the situation seemed to have little effect on their attitudes. They sat on what pieces of curbing remained around the lot and began their undecipherable chatter that is so characteristic of the modern college student. Due to my slight hearing impediment, I had no clue as to what they were saying. They could have been talking about me for all I knew. That perturbed me even more.

Then a motor pool truck arrived and stopped in the same place the maintenance truck had stopped. I wondered if that's what that worn spot was really for since it seemed to have been devoid of grass and weeds. I walked to the truck.

The driver looked at a clipboard. "You... a... Avgurt?"

"August," I said.

"Oh, yeah. Well, we can't find the key. I called Marney. He'll be here in a little while to straighten out this here thing."

Then with a shake of his head, he too was gone. I walked back to the huddle of students.

"Okay, so I lied," I said, standing over them with my hands in my pockets, a dejected soul. "I don't have a key and it will be a little longer than shortly."

With that, I sat down beside them. It was then that I heard Horace's screech as she hurried toward us waving like a lunatic.

"Good morning," she burst out, "why aren't y'all in the van?"

"We can't get in," I said as calmly as I could.

"Well, why not?"

"The key I was given didn't fit."

"Is somebody getting us a key?"

I looked up at her. "I think so." I motioned for her to sit. "At least someone is supposed to be looking for it. Have a seat."

"Oh, that's all right," she said. "I'll just stand. I'm going to be sitting for a spell anyway."

I listened to idle chatter for at least ten minutes before another motor pool van arrived, this time driving over the collapsed fence and into the lot. It stopped in front of our assigned van. I refused to let myself get excited and slowly walked toward it. A large, rotund man stepped out and walked toward one-two-zero.

"Did you have any luck?" I asked Big Boy who was poking a key into the door with hands that looked like inflated gloves. He didn't respond right away, but examined the key with a puzzled look on his face.

"Hell, this here key ain't going to work." He held it out to me. "This here is a Chrysler key. You got a Ford van."

I had to give the motor pool gang credit for at least being able to recognize a problem. And the amazing thing is that they were all able to zero in on the same conclusion. That small bit of mastery on their part seemed remarkable to me, but it did nothing to put us on the road toward Norman. I kept my thoughts to myself and looked at him with disinterest.

While I was marveling at his adroit troubleshooting skills, the other two bozos returned, each in his own vehicle, flying across the folded fence and coming to a halt behind the first van. Each got out of his truck and stood behind Big Boy.

He turned around to them and smiled, shaking the key up and down as if he had just discovered that the Earth was round. "The secretary must have given him the wrong key," he said to them.

The bozos shook their heads in agreement.

"Actually," I said, "if you look on the tag attached to the key, you'll find that the number is one two zero. The same as the van."

He looked. He laughed. I scowled.

"Well, I'll see if I can find another key. Back in a minute."

The bozos watched him mount his truck and start to back up, then stop abruptly.

"Y'all going to have to move so I can get out," he yelled out the window.

"Oh, yeah," the bozos said, and they scurried to their trucks and backed out of Big Boy's path.

He left behind a cloud of exhaust fumes that drifted over the students through the heavy, stale air. Horace slapped at the fog in an attempt to dissipate it, but only succeeded in swirling it into a small vortex around her and the students. The bozos got back out of their trucks and stood beside one-two-zero, hands in pockets, watching it as if expecting a grand revelation to occur. Neither spoke.

I rejoined Horace and the students. We chatted. I found that the museum tour was not scheduled to begin until after lunch, so the impact of our delay would be minimal. However, they were planning on shopping at one of the malls before the museum tour, and our delay was definitely having an impact on that.

Almost an hour after I first arrived at the motor pool, Big Boy flew back across the fence, skidded to a halt behind one-two-zero, jumped out and rushed for the door. He inserted a key in the lock and the door opened. Naturally my anxiety recoiled, stifled by the existence of a key.

"Okay, guys," I said, standing up," let's go."

Big Boy handed me the key.

"I'm sure sorry about the mix up. We'll find out what happened and get this here straightened out".

I thanked him and unlocked the passenger's door and then tried the sliding door on the side. It wouldn't budge. I tried the key. It wouldn't turn in the lock. Just before Big Boy actually made it back to the fence in his truck, I was able to flag him down. The truck raced back toward me, again skidding to a halt. I approached his door.

"I can't get the side door open."

He killed his truck and we walked to one-two-zero. He tried the handle. It wouldn't open for him, either. He tried the key in the lock. It wouldn't turn for him, either. He reached around from the passenger's door and slammed the lock plunger up and down until something clicked inside the door. Then it opened.

"Okay, there you are. I'm sorry about that. Jake just worked on the latch and I guess it's a little tight."

"Will we be able to open it again?" I asked.

"Oh, sure," he said. "It'll be fine, now."

By that time everyone was loaded and waiting for me to assume my position behind the wheel. I gave Big Boy a nod of thanks and climbed in the driver's seat. One-two-zero started and I filled out the pre-trip paper work. Then we were off.

Being one of the oldest vans in the fleet, if you could actually call an assembly of scrap vehicles a fleet, the rattles made it all but impossible to have a normal conversation. The students seemed to adapt well by using some sort of sign language. And Horace, having a rather robust voice, had little difficulty making herself heard. But my voice, no matter how loudly I yelled, did not seem to carry past the edge of my seat. Horace would respond to each of my comments with a "Huh?" and I would lean toward her to shorten the distance my voice would have to travel. The second or third iteration usually met with success.

A new road construction zone had been installed at our entry point to the interstate so we drifted along at an idle pace. My fears had been abated by then and I felt some degree of comfort with one-two-zero. At the end of the zone I increase the speed to cruise mode, around seventy, and all hell broke loose.

The front of one-two-zero suddenly went into convulsions, bouncing up and down violently, and it was all I could do to restrain the vicious oscillations of the steering wheel. Of course, all manner of discourse had stopped, since everyone's eyes had opened to capacity and their hands were clenching the nearest piece of metal that was attached to something reasonably solid. What rattles had annoyed us before had now become dreadful clangs and clatters. Poor Horace was holding on to the grab bars, her slight frame bouncing uncontrollably in the seat like she was sitting on a trampoline. My head began to ache. I thought for a moment the extreme impulses delivered by one-two-zero might cause my concussion to recur. I checked the back of my head for blood. My hand came back dry.

I slowed gradually until the undulations of the van were endurable.

"Okay," I said, "it looks like we're not going to make very good time on this trip. If the ride gets too bad, let me know."

I kept the speed around sixty and one-two-zero shimmied along the road like a giant vibrating Barca-lounger. The grimy windshield had become annoying and my natural inclination was to turn the button below the icon of a windshield washer. I did. The fluid sprayed generously against the windshield and the wipers began to sweep across the glass with the effect of distributing the grime in a less uniform fashion. In fact, the moisture seemed to have made it into a more workable paste that easily coated the entire surface of the windshield with concentric arcs of filth. More fluid, more filth. By the time I thought I had exhausted the fluid reservoir, some clearing had taken place and I was able to see the pavement again. It was a long time until Norman.

*****

"Okay, guys," I said getting out of one-two-zero. "Everybody out."

I had just locked the driver's door and Horace was still teetering in her seat trying to make the plunge to the ground. Then I heard banging on the side door glass.

"We can't get out," the voices said in unison. "We can't get the door open."

I pulled on the latch. It wouldn't give. I helped Horace down from her perch and tried jiggling the lock like Big Boy did, but it wouldn't jiggle.

"Well, you guys are going to have to climb through the front seats and come out the passenger door."

Amid the whining and grumbling, one by one they passed through the seats and climbed out the door. Once assembled we headed for the restaurant. After lunch we would hit the museum.

"One benefit of having a defective vehicle like this," I said to Horace, "is that there is one less door to have to lock."

Her eyes narrowed at me but not a word escaped her mouth.

*****

The journey back to Hartmann was quiet except for the metallic symphony of the one-two-zero's parts banging, rubbing, and squeaking against one another. At first I hoped some of them might fall off and relieve the clangor, but I quickly realized that one of those parts might be the one that actually enabled one-two-zero to run. We shuddered our way back to the college, the students clawing the handles in order to stay in the seats. Even Horace seemed preoccupied with disgust. I was thinking about all of the entries I would be making in the trip log about the vehicle.

By the time we reached Hartmann, my temperament had settled to a simmer. I plowed across the folded fence into the motor pool and parked one-two-zero in its original spot. Everyone slowly disembarked through Horace's door while I completed the log. I had to attach an extra sheet of paper to make sure all of my concerns were duly noted. I folded them with the key and placed them into the envelope for delivery to the motor pool secretary on Monday.

Before heading home, I hit Jim Bob's. Ricky was there, sitting at the bar.

"Hey, Perfessor!" Cindy yelled. "Come on over here and I'll fix you up."

Everyone in the room looked in my direction. Even the fellow exiting the restroom zipping his trousers stopped and zeroed in on my presence. I'm sure at least a few seconds passed before I thought to move. So I went to the bar and took an unoccupied stool next to Ricky.

"I'm glad you come back," she barked. "What with more the likes of you around here, my clientele might improve."

With that she cut loose in a roar of laughter followed by a coughing fit. Then more laughter. Then more coughing.

"August," he said, "I'm surprised."

"Why?"

"You came back even though you know that this is a gay bar?"

"Oh, yeah. I don't have anything against that. The dweebs in here can think what they want. That's the least of my worries. Apparently, it's also among yours."

Cindy slid a shot of Glenlivet in front of me. I took a sip and laid a ten on the bar.

"You're all right, Perfessor."

Ricky downed the last of his beer and signaled Cindy for another. She slammed a fresh mug down in front of him and turned toward me.

"Ready for another, Gov?"

I shook my head and held up the glass hoping she would see that it had almost as much in it as when she brought it. She nodded back and lumbered to the end of the bar.

"I just needed someplace to crash and drink out my frustration."

"Oh yeah," he said. "You drove Horace to Norman today."

"If that's what you want to call it. How did you know?"

"Horace and me, we talk some. That means you met the motor pool crew."

"How would you know that?"

"Hell, no one ever takes a campus vehicle without some major catastrophe."

"I wish you had alerted me to that fact before I went on this mission."

"Nonsense," he said tipping his mug for a longer than usual time. "Just consider it valuable combat experience."

"It was certainly that." I took a longer than usual sip of whisky. "Now I have to debrief the commander about how bad his troops are."

"August, I'm going to give you some advice." Another drink. "Now, mind you, I don't normally make it a habit to dispense unsolicited advice. But, I've grown fond of you and I'm only thinking in your best interests."

I said nothing because the suspense precluded me from thinking of anything to say.

"Don't make waves." He leaned over the bar and shielded his mug between his arms as if protecting it from attack.

"What do you mean?"

He turned toward me.

"Look, this is a small time college. Our funding is barely enough to keep the place from closing its doors. The people they've got working for them aren't exactly Rhoades Scholars. And, frankly, I think we're lucky to have even the decrepit pieces of shit that sit in that motor pool. Otherwise, we'd all be walking or taking a bus. Or, Heaven forbid, driving our own vehicles and not getting reimbursed for it."

I got his meaning. I didn't like it, but I got it.

"So, you're saying don't blame the help for being the ignorant creatures that they are?"

"Damn, you're fast." He held his mug up. "Hey, Cindy!"

She barked from somewhere in the back of the room.

"And the point of your advice is that no matter what I say or do, nothing will change?"

"By God, did you used to be a rocket scientist?"

We both laughed. He quelled my anger and I could go home with a decent attitude, at least toward my misfortune. I would talk with Marney on Monday morning. And behave myself.

Chapter 18

I stole some time after calculus class on Monday to walk to the motor pool. Before I got within a hundred feet of the building, Marney came scurrying out of the door toward me.

"Professor Lane!" He ran a few more steps. "Professor Lane, I'm sorry about Saturday."

We met just outside the folded fence and he erupted in a profuse apology. I opened my mouth to respond, but I never had an opportunity. He stood there like a beaten dog, head down, looking at me from the tops of his eyes. If he'd had a tail, it would have been between his legs.

"We found the key. There was a problem with some of the keys last week and the secretary put new tags on most of them. As best we can figure, she just put the wrong one on the key to that van."

He gasped a couple of times trying to catch his breath.

"Anyway, I think we've got it straightened out, now."

He looked me in the eye with a pleading expression.

"Oh, hell, I understand." I lied. "Things happen. We got there and back."

"Well, okay. Thanks for filling out the trip report. We'll get right on those problems." He nodded. "Usually, when folks bring back these things they don't put anything down and we never know anything is wrong."

I wanted to believe him, but I couldn't imagine how anyone couldn't know something was wrong with that van.

We chatted about maintenance, which consisted mainly of Marney expounding on what he considered to be the excellent condition and reliability of the motor pool vehicles. I had reason to argue the point, since I'd suffered mechanically-induced trauma with the "excellent condition" of one of the vehicles. But, I behaved myself, heeding Ricky's warning. For some reason, Marney took this as an excuse to open the door on a shower of delusory self-compliments.

We exchanged salutations and I returned to my office satisfied with the outcome of the encounter, but not comfortable with it. It might seem illogical that the results would be satisfactory, but by not making a major deal out of the motor pool's deficiencies, I had recruited an ally for future need. Something told me that would be more important than my being right.

I had just enough time to grab my notes and textbook and head for general physical science. Only half of the students bothered to attend class that day. Those present consisted mainly of the successful ones with a few determined souls who, for some undetermined reason, just couldn't get it. Those that didn't want to get it rarely showed up. I could read the eagerness in some faces and the despair in others. I felt confident that some of them had at least read the material about the pendulum, but I knew that most of them hadn't.

The apparatus for the demonstration was already in place in the classroom. The week before, after much pleading, I had the maintenance crew install a large hook in the ceiling near the center of the lecture area, from which desks were moved to the front or back of the room. From the hook I hung a 300-pound-test rope. The other end of the rope supported a bowling ball, which had been drilled to accept another hook. When released, this simple pendulum would carry its oscillation from side to side of the room through the majority of the fifty-minute class. I had moored the ball to the wall at one side of the room.

In the middle of my preliminary lecture, "The Matador" erupted from a cell phone. It was quickly answered by Cleetah Shoaven under my scowl. I pointed toward the door but the obstinate girl did not take my hint. When not in class or a boy's dorm room, Miss Shoaven was always seen in the presence of Melanie Parker, who sat in front of her.

"Miss Shoaven, hang up the phone and turn it off," I commanded.

She looked at me like I had just asked her to disrobe in front of the class. After a curt good-bye, she put the phone down.

"Turn it off, period," I said.

I continued my lecture amid frightened stares from the timid, inquisitive gazes from the enlightened, and glares from the scorned. I had become adept at ignoring visual cues from students that were disruptive to the class. Not that the cause of those cues didn't bother me. They did. I just forced myself to maintain my decorum so as not to let them know that they bothered me.

Then "The Matador" cut loose again.

I rushed to the young lady's seat and ripped the phone from her hand just as she was saying her hello.

"Hey," she yelled. "What are you doing?"

I turned the phone off and put it on my desk.

"One of the rules of this class is no cell phones. They are to be turned off when you enter this room. This information is in your syllabus and I went over this at the beginning of the semester. I asked you before to turn off your phone and you didn't. You may retrieve your phone when you leave class. It this happens again I will confiscate your phone and leave it with the Dean of Student Affairs.

The stares, the same as before, intensified, except for a storm boiling within Miss Shoaven, who seemed like she could launch small lightning bolts toward me.

I had carefully measured and tested the pendulum beforehand with the assistance of one of the students. I led him to the wall where the bowling ball was secured.

"Your job," I explained to the fellow, as well as the rest of the class, "is to stand here perfectly still. You must not move."

I loosened the bowling ball from its mooring near the student.

"This bowling ball, as you can see, is attached to the rope suspended from the ceiling. If any of you bowl, you know that this ball is quite heavy."

My assistant positioned the ball in front of his face.

"My assistant will release the pendulum and will be keeping an eye on the ball, but will not move from his position."

With that, I released the ball and it swung gracefully to the other side of the room in a great swooping arc, leaving a black smudge of its presence in the vision of each student and stopping just short of the wall as intended. After it paused, as if taking a deep breath for the return flight, it swung back toward my assistant. Logic told me that he would not be harmed. But, just in case, I stood close by to yank him out of the way should something not go according to plan. It never occurred to me that I wouldn't be able to rescue the poor boy. But, the ball glided swiftly toward his head. Just after gasps of alarm erupted from the class, it stopped in mid air an inch from the tip of his nose and very large eyes while his fingers clawed at the bare wall. The ball seemed to hang in front of his face for a bit while all of the gulps in the classroom were exhausted, then slowly started its return trip.

I thanked him for his participation and sent him back to his seat with a broad smile on his face. I had acquired the attention of the class. The ball completed two more trips across the room.

"As you witnessed, the law of conservation of energy is still with us today. It explains why the pendulum rose no higher at the far end of

its arc than it did at the near end, and stopped short of my assistant."
I moved toward the rear of the class to reinforce the lesson, delivering an oratory that exceeded even my own standard of excellence. I'm sure the pendulum swooping back and forth behind me only enhanced the awe and mystery of my academic prowess. But there were equations. I had to show them the equations. I turned to go to the whiteboard behind the lecture desk, pausing briefly to go around a pair of feet in my way.

I tuned again to the side and heard another rush of gasps just before the bowling ball struck me squarely in the back and slammed me against the wall. That, in turn, slammed my face against the wall. And that, in turn, produced a torrent of blood rushing from my nose, much as it had done the week before.

The gasping had been replaced with screams and utterances of various pitches alarming Horace, who was in the classroom just down the hall. I don't remember exactly when she appeared, but I do remember her trying to pick me up from the floor. Two of the students assisted her and I was plopped into a seat at the nearest desk. I yanked a handkerchief from my rear pocket and crammed it against my nose. I made a mental note to buy more handkerchiefs.

Stunned by the blow, I looked up at the wall from which I had just ricocheted. As hard as it had seemed at the time, I had only managed to hit the bulletin board, sparing my forehead any serious injury, but not sparing the board. The prominent depression there would surely fit my nose and forehead.

"… August?"

I heard someone calling my name.

"August, are you all right?"

I looked up at Horace who was leaning over me like a buzzard waiting to see if its meal was still alive.

I think I disappointed her when I said, "Yes, I'm fine."

I tried to get up, faltered, and fell back into the seat.

"Okay, guys," I said to the class. "Let's pick it up here on Wednesday."

"Do you need to see the nurse?" Horace asked.

"Sorry, Professor Lane," I heard one of the students say on the way out. Other condolences were offered by passing students.

"No, Horace. I think I'm all right," I said trying to stand again. "Besides, the nurse is probably not in her office, anyway. I just need to get my nose to stop bleeding."

In the silence that followed I watched the bowling ball still tracing its lazy arc in the air, although shorter than before, transfixed by the permanence of inertia and gravity that held it to its path. I could have used some of that.

The doorway was suddenly jammed with students, and other instructors were forcing their way through. In all of my humility, I had not wanted to be the center of attention. I did not need the embarrassment. I'd had enough of that already. I just wanted to be left alone.

"August? August, are you all right?"

I recognized Claudia's voice. I didn't look up.

"What happened?" she asked.

I still didn't look up. "Just a slight mishap."

"What on earth is that bowling ball doing swinging in the classroom?"

"Well, you pretty much guessed it," I said. "It's swinging."

"Is this another one of your experiments?" She said, with this peculiar tone she used when annoyed.

I did look up just long enough to catch a glimpse of her incensed eyes.

"You remember the last time when you got hit in the head with some kind of marble or something."

"Yes." I groaned. "I remember quite well. It was my own fault. A person doesn't easily forget stupid things like that. And I doubt seriously that I will forget this one. At least not until the wound to my ego heals."

After a short pause, during which loud murmurs filled the room, I managed to stand up.

"And, yes, this was another of my experiments. A damned fine one, too."

We all looked at the ball still swaying to and fro, oblivious to anyone or anything around it. Finally, Stanley stepped forward to stop it and it hung there, motionless, suspended in the air by the rope. I sensed its restlessness.

The sound of the chimes would have been nice, about then. I could have savored their sweet melody and distracted myself from the embarrassment. Of course, they might also have been celebrating my clumsiness. But, in spite of my misfortune, I was still convinced that I was a good teacher. If the students hadn't learned something from that day's class, then they had no business being in college. I just wondered exactly what it was they might have learned.

*****

"August, I just don't like the way you're conducting your classes," Claudia insisted. "It's just dangerous."

She got up from behind her desk and, unlike her traditional vagarious march, the sack dress glided calmly back and forth across the floor. However, she worked her hands in front of her like she needed a chicken's neck to wring. Her eyes remained focused on the floor in front of her path. I wasn't sure if she intentionally avoided looking at me, or if her words were that difficult to find. Her monologue was dry, drawn out, and for my worth, pointless.

"This college has a responsibility for the safety of its students," she said, turning to me with a scowl. "And, for the safety of its employees."

"Tell that to the nurse," I said, squirming in the hard chair.

Her eyes snapped toward me like a hawk honing in on its prey. She kept pacing and talking. And wringing the poor chicken's neck.

"I can pretty much control any serious behavior issues with the students. We have policies in place to deal with most things."

I listened patiently, wishing for a quick end to the reprimand. In view of the stupidity that gave rise to this meeting, I figured a lot of patience would buy some relief from censure. It didn't. And the reprimand wasn't quick.

"But, I don't seem to be able to control your behavior," she continued.

With that, she stopped just to the side of me. I looked up at her. It seemed like I was looking up at people a lot, lately. Then a pause in the verbal flagellation gave me an opportunity to offer a small gesture of penitence.

"Yes, I'll admit that the bowling ball thing might have been a bit... unorthodox. I should have thought it out more thoroughly."

She did not move or offer any sign of accepting my explanation. Perhaps if I were to humble myself further.

"Okay, so I'm accident prone. Things happen. And I know you think I'm a bungling idiot. Well, I probably am. But, that's just the way it is."

She turned up her head and glided back behind her desk. She still said nothing. Seeing that she was not going to be receptive to any capitulation of pride, I took a bolder approach by appealing to her sense of achievement, if she had any.

"Look," I said leaning forward over her desk, "I'm still trying to put this program together. I had nothing to start with and I've had to do a lot of trial and error things to find something that works. These students aren't an easy audience."

I offered a pause in hopes that she would provide some feedback. I hadn't a clue as to what she was really thinking. Or wanting. I tried humility, again.

"All right, so the bowling ball thing was a little dangerous. Next time I attempt that, I'll take the class outside. I can have maintenance rig up a hook under the fire escape behind the building."

The ridges in her forehead finally smoothed a bit. She directed her seething eyes at me and sat behind her desk, resting her arms on it.

"All right, August," she said in a less stern voice. "That sounds like a reasonable compromise. I don't want you to have to give up your demonstrations. But I do expect you to exercise some caution."

So, she had some sense of reason, after all. Another modest offer of compromise might be in order to cement the accord.

"Thank you," I said. "I'll look over my other demonstrations and modify them, if necessary. I'll even run them by some other folks in case they have notions of something that can go awry."

"I think that is an excellent idea," she offered with hesitation. She picked up a folder, beaming with satisfaction. "Now, there's one more thing I want to discuss with you."

A switch somewhere deep inside of her psyche had been thrown and the stormy, displeasure suddenly metamorphosed into affability. She opened the folder and handed me a copy of my schedule for the spring semester.

"I've have been thinking about the fact that you are attempting to rebuild the science program. In view of that, I think it's only fair to allow you time to develop your curriculum. So, I'm keeping you at fifteen hours next semester."

The submission on her part stunned me. I wasn't going to gloat. At least not in front of her.

"I very much appreciate that." What could I say? I was flabbergasted. And gracious. "Perhaps next year I will be more adept at this and I can take on an additional class."

I was about to let my weaknesses overrun my ego. I forced myself not to make any further concessions.

"I'm hoping you will, too," she said.

The momentum had turned to my favor and I wanted to ride it as far as it would take me. It was an appropriate time for risk and I mentioned one of my ideas.

"And, I had an idea about recruiting. I'm going to see Jerrod Baines this afternoon and get his take on it."

This was not exactly a concession. It was for my own benefit, as well as Hartmann's. I stood in preparation to go. But first, I dropped the hook.

"If it pans out, I think we can increase our enrollment."

She seemed pleasantly surprised by my offer. Our meeting ended with mutual pleasantries, including an inquiry about my nose, and I left.

Despite Hartmann's size of over eight thousand students, there was only one recruiter. Jerrod Baines was it. And even if they did have only one, there could be none better than Jerrod. I had only seen him a couple of times, but everyone knew of his skills. How he would have wound up at Hartmann falls beyond the realm of comprehension. His tall, virile frame lent an air of authority and dignity to his presence, and a distinguished face that would be considered handsome by most standards gave him mass appeal. If not slightly intimidated, most students were at least aroused by his commanding performance at the Hartmann College display. No question went unanswered and the logic imbedded in his arguments left little room for the student to decide on another college. He was like a gravitational magnet attracting all of the loose debris in the universe to the doorstep of Hartmann. Had there been more of him, Hartmann's enrollment would surely have been vastly more than eight thousand. The only thing that prevented a higher enrollment was Hartmann College itself.

Chapter 19

When I parked my Mazda the next morning, Mary was in the parking lot. She locked her car and walked to the Administration Building, her brown, pleated skirt swishing in rhythm with her graceful, short-paced gait. She could have been a dancer. I caught up with her.

"You sure are an early bird." Her sweet, alluring voice drifted toward me on the vapors of her perfume.

"I'm a morning person," I said. "How about yourself?"

"Well, I usually get an early start, but not this early."

"Is there a big project in the works for Hartmann?"

"No, I just felt like coming in early. You put on quite the show the other day with Dr. Tipton."

"Oh, I'm sorry about that. I forgot you were sitting there. Please accept my apology."

"Oh, an apology isn't necessary," She smiled. "That's the most entertainment I've had in ages. I'm just amazed you got away with it."

"What do you mean?"

"Why, Dr. Tipton is one of the most domineering figures we have on this campus. No one talks to her like that."

"Yeah, well, I did. She had it coming."

"You have a great deal of fortitude." She lifted her head and carried it aloft as if gloating. "I like a man with fortitude."

With that she stopped at the door to the Administration Building and turned toward me and smiled. Even her eyes smiled. I smiled back. Then she disappeared through the door I was holding open for her.

*****

I was never sure of Jerrod's stature in the Hartmann community. Few people ever spoke of him and he was rarely visible because of his travels to surrounding schools. But his effect on the students was unquestionable. All but math and science students, that is. No one seemed to be able to explain the drop in enrollment in the Math Science Department over the last two years. I was hoping Jerrod could.

I had arranged the meeting a week earlier. It would be one of the few times he was on campus. I had met him once and seen photographs of him in action in the college brochures and publicity material.

"Professor Lane?" He said, towering over his desk as I walked into his office.

"Mr. Baines," I said. "It's a pleasure to see you again."

"And I, you," he said graciously, in a smooth, deep voice. "Please, sit down. Call me Jerrod."

"August," I said.

He had all of the charm of a recruiter and a persona that would make even a scoundrel feel welcome. But his gestures had a peculiar bearing.

"You said on the phone you were concerned about math and science recruiting?"

"That's right," I said. "We don't seem to have much."

His expression never strayed from its personal level. His eyes, trained on me, drew me in as though I were the only important thing in his life.

"Yes." He narrowed his eyebrows. "I've seen the numbers drop."

"I was hoping you might be able to offer some insight as to why? I mean, you're out there in front and see what's happening in the public schools. I just thought you might know something we don't."

He chuckled behind his charming smile. It was one of those that I suppose would drive any young girl into frenzy.

"No, I'm afraid I don't believe I would know anything proprietary about enrollment trends. Hartmann is not the only college facing a decline in math and science enrollment."

He leaned forward in his chair, apparently more comfortable with the flow of our conversation than I. He rested his elbows on the desk and put his hands in a double fist beneath his chin leaving some fingers exposed to flap in the air. His right hand flashed a large silver ring with a blue stone of some sort that matched his eyes. There was no ring on the other hand. The tips of the flapping fingers sported highly polished nails, not colored, mind you, just polished. And as I looked more closely, the cuticles were neatly pushed back. I'd never tried that, thinking only women, eccentric millionaires, and gay men solicited manicures. The thought suddenly occurred to me that Jerrod was gay. That would explain his scarcity in the social circles.

"In fact," he continued, "it's pretty much statewide. It appears that there is a lack of interest in science and math in the schools. Most of the high school counselors I've talked to make little effort to encourage math and science courses."

I kept pumping him for information and he continued to deliver plausible explanations. I couldn't help but notice his precisely aligned teeth that almost glared from their perfect whiteness, and his hair was held in place by some invisible constraint that allowed not one strand to escape. And his eyebrows. They were too perfect. His face looked more like a retouched photograph than a real person. And his mannerisms struck me as odd. Fluid, deliberate, and exact. They bordered on effeminacy. He was definitely gay.

"I've seen you recently," he said, turning up his nose a bit as if knowing he was right.

Uneasiness crept over me and I felt the need to retreat into a shell, like a crab threatened by the incoming tide.

"Well, I don't believe I remember seeing you recently, but that certainly doesn't mean you couldn't have noticed me. I do get around campus quite a bit."

I explained the plight of the Math Science Department and suggested some corrective actions. Jerrod continued to stare at me with a dreamy gaze. Had he been a woman I would have expected him to ask me out on a date. Of course, he wasn't a woman and I feared he might ask me out, anyway.

"Jim Bob's!" He burst out. "Jim Bob's. I knew it. That's where I've seen you."

My body just seemed to lock up and my brain could not deliver one word of sensible discourse. The son-of-a-bitch was gay. Jesus!

"Yeah," he said, "about a week ago. You were talking with Ricky Smithers. I was going to come over and introduce myself, but you both seemed so involved I thought it best not to intrude."

"Oh, that," I said, wondering how red my complexion had become. "Well, we were just discussing the ITV thing. I'm having trouble accepting that as a viable teaching method."

"That's all right, August. I understand."

His smile grew larger and my embarrassment grew heavier. Did he mean, "I understand that you're gay and don't want me to acknowledge it?" Or did he mean, "I understand you're not gay, that you were just meeting with Ricky since he frequents Jim Bob's?" I had to get out of there.

"Look," I said, "how about if you forward the names of prospective math and science students to me, or anyone even remotely interested, and I will follow up with personal letter inviting them to the campus."

We agreed on the plan of action and I hastily removed myself from his office.

*****

I could hear Stan's typing from well outside the office door. He was pounding at his keyboard with unusual fervor.

"Are you trying to beat it to death, or what?" I asked.

"August," he said. "How are ya?"

"Ever met Jerrod Baines?"

"The recruiter?"

"That's the one."

"Oh," he said, still pounding. "No, can't say as I have." More pounding. "Should I?"

"You might not want to. I think he's gay."

"And how do we know this?"

"I just met with him. He sat across from me with stars in his eyes the entire time. It reminded me of the old black and whites where the girl is hopelessly in love with this handsome hunk of guy she just met."

He stopped banging on the keyboard and turned to face me, grinning that evil grin of his.

"Why August, I didn't know, you handsome hunk, you."

"Oh, cut it out."

"So, the guy has the hots for you?"

"God, I hope not."

"Well, do me a favor and don't bring him around. I mean I don't consider myself an Adonis, but I wouldn't want to take the chance of mistaken identity." He laughed. Then again, louder.

"Okay, have your fun. Sorry I mentioned it."

"By the way," he stopped laughing long enough to ask a question. "Why is he coming on to you?"

"It appears that he saw me talking to Ricky Smithers in Jim Bob's last week."

Stan kept looking at me as if waiting for something.

"Jim Bob's," I repeated.

"That's the gay bar down the main road? Near the end of town?"

"Yup."

He smiled, again. "You know I've always wondered why there's a gay bar in Elkridge, Oklahoma, the center of universal conservatism. Are you implying that Ricky is gay?"

"No, no, no," I blurted. "Ricky just goes there to unwind and not be picked up."

Stan looked at me, perplexed.

"By women. Look, it's a long story." I turned around toward my desk while Stan laughed. "Just let it suffice to say that neither Ricky nor I are gay. I'm pretty sure Jerrod is."

I pulled up a file of lecture notes on the computer but my mind was hovering over Jerrod. Had he come on to me? Had he actually been a woman, I think I would have recognized it. But not being familiar with the protocol of the gay community, I had no idea how to interpret his behavior. He was very cordial, so I assumed that he found me somewhat pleasant. But how pleasant?

I have to admit that he was quite attractive himself, but I couldn't picture myself in bed with the fellow. I looked out the window at the blurred image of Dr. Hartmann's vacant berth. The poor fellow had no idea what his good intentions had wrought. I listened for the chimes to play through Stan's laughter and give me strength to ignore it. I wasn't going to hear them. And I couldn't ignore Stan. I wondered if the good doctor was laughing at me.

I went to see the old boy and I stood in front of the statue's base pleading with the spectral image for a favorable assessment of my value as a teacher. I thought I had made a good impression on him and I also wondered if it was good enough to ask Mary out. I skirted that issue with the good doctor thinking he was not the proper source for such counsel. On the way back to my office I was overcome with the problem of the athletes' cheating on an exam.

*****

I arrived in the office early the next morning. Stan was already there.

"Stan, I need some advice."

He pointed to the coffee pot and leaned back in his chair that didn't lean back.

"Now, I know you're not adverse to parting with your valuable wisdom you have amassed over the years when asked to do so."

He pointed to the coffee pot again and I filled my cup.

"So, I'm going to beg for your indulgence."

"Well, if you put it like that, I suppose I have no choice but to consider your request."

I sat in the guest chair facing him.

"I need to foil the athletes in my GPS class. I know they're cheating; I just have no way of proving it. They're good."

"What have you tried, so far?"

"Nothing. I thought it would not be prudent to waste a lot of time reinventing the wheel, so that's why I'm humbling myself in front of you."

He elevated his nose and cast his eyes down on my presence like a king passing judgment on a servant pleading for mercy.

"Well, there was this one time I had an algebra class," he began.

When he started his oratory in this fashion, the rest of the story usually took a while, so I made myself comfortable. It was a half hour until calculus. Surely he could wrap it up by then.

"They were on the baseball team. Two in the first class, the rest in the second. Both morning classes two hours apart. The first class usually did pretty well. The second class stunk. Until the third exam. Then their collective knowledge of algebra seemed to blossom overnight with scores as high as the first class."

He had me hooked. I had to know the details.

"And being the skeptical sort," he continued, "I looked at the exams. The answers from the athletes in the second class were all identical to the exams from the first class. Every problem they answered was given in exactly the same way. I figured they had to have had a copy of the exam."

"Well, hell," I said, "that should have been an easy fix. Just rearrange the exam each year."

"That was the problem," he said, leaning toward me. "I did."

I sat slumped in my chair, puzzled and disappointed that a veteran such as Stanley could be duped so easily.

"And?" I prompted.

"And, on the next exam, I watched them all like a hawk. I mean, I did not take my eyes off them for a second."

We both took a slug of coffee and leaned back into our chairs.

"I didn't see a thing," he said with confidence. "Nothing."

"What do you mean?"

"I mean, I saw nothing. No evidence of any talking, signaling, or communication of any sort."

"But if they had copies of the exam, couldn't you have seen them looking at them?"

"Well, if they had copies, I certainly couldn't tell it."

"So, is this going to be a dead end story?"

Stan leaned back and laughed.

"Oh, no. I tried one more exam to discover their secret, but no dice."

"Okay, you are going somewhere with this, aren't you?"

"Well, for the next time, I made special exams for the athletes. I rearranged the questions and put a key on each one so I could identify it."

He got up and filled his coffee cup and stood there at the pot while he finished his story.

"When I graded the tests, all of the answers were right. But, they were given to the wrong problems. They all seemed to correspond to one of the exams from the first class. And that exam was never turned in to grade."

"So, how did they do it?"

"I didn't have an exam for one of the athletes. Although I thought I remembered seeing him in class for the exam, I never got one from him, so I counted him absent. I mean, why take roll on an exam day. If they don't turn in an exam, I just figured they weren't there."

He walked back to this chair, or rather, took one step, and sat.

"When the missing student came in to ask about the makeup exam, I asked him where the other exam was."

Here, Stan smiled and raised his cup as if offering a toast.

"I had him. After several unsuccessful attempts to evade the question, he admitted that he had taken the uncompleted test with him, sacrificing his grade until the makeup exam. He copied the test and gave it to the second class."

I was astonished at the ingenuity and complexity of their plan. It must have taken considerable coordination on their part to pull it off. My complacent regard for their craftiness seemed to have left me vulnerable. But Stan's solution of making each exam unique had merit. For the few athletes I had in the class, it could easily be done.

"Stan, you have restored my faith in the virtue of the teacher. The real teacher."

"I'm glad I could be of service. That was one of my better battles. Oh, I've won most of them. But this one in particular I hold dear. It took me nearly an entire semester to better them, but I consider the experience a valuable lesson. An investment in my career, if you will."

"Yes," I said. "It's symbolic. The victory of knowledge over ignorance. The veteran over the novice. The old farts over the punks."

It would have been fitting to hear the chimes ring out through the brisk morning outside the murky window. Each peal would have renewed my spirit and bolstered my resolve. But, the air was silent and it was time for calculus. I marched to the classroom with vigor only slightly less than what the chimes would have imparted.

Following a robust calculus class, I spent the next hour preparing the GPS exams, making certain that the seven different versions for the first class had the keys to the exams cleverly embedded in the first question. That way they would not be able to tell the exams were different. I was ready for them.

Being a Friday, class attendance would be sparse. Skipping class on Friday has become a tradition in some schools, being carried over from generation to generation. Some things are just like that. They have withstood the test of time and new generations try it and like it. So it perseveres. Like the beer parties that took place behind the baseball stadium out of the watchful eye of the late Dr. Hartmann. And the weekend binges that left the students debilitated on Monday, unable to fathom any words uttered by an instructor.

So, on that Friday, about half of the first GPS class showed up in spite of the exam that was scheduled. It wasn't until twenty after that the seven athletes strutted in the door. As they passed by my desk, I handed each of them one of the keyed exams. I thought I saw them smile all the way to their seats.

The exam was a simple presentation of multiple-choice questions that a moron could have answered had he read the text. But still, some resisted that basic task in favor of expending more time trying to find a way not to have to even open the book. And then there are those who just didn't want anything to do with it at all. Like Cleetah Shoaven. The Matador, again.

I didn't even speak to her. I just went directly to her desk, plucked the phone out of her hand, and turned it off.

"You can pick this up in the office of the Dean of Student Affairs."

The slight look of surprise quickly gave way to the glare of annihilation. She must have been practicing. And, I suspect daring me to actually take her phone from her. In only a few minutes order returned to the classroom and everyone was occupied with the exam.

At the end of the class I briefly looked through the exams. There were only six from the athletes. I was sure that seven had entered the room. So, Stan knew his stuff.

The second GPS class showed as much initiative as the first with about half in attendance. The seven athletes in this class were there on time. I gave each a keyed exam and the games began. I watched them carefully as each focused on the exam and expertly selected answers. There was little hesitation and they completed the exams well before the other students. I looked through them quickly to verify that all of the answers were identical, probable with one of those from the first class.

Anticipation is one of life's sweetest rewards. It rarely disappoints, offering at least some serendipity. The initial vision of grandeur brings one to a euphoric state just before the thrill recedes to joy, and then to contentment, and finally, pleasant wonder. My reward was too grand to play itself out as a typical emotional high. This would mean victory. It would manifest an elemental superiority of wisdom over impetuousness. Another benchmark for my distressed career.

I almost thought I heard the chimes on the hour, even though they didn't ring. The victory peals would have been a sweet kiss of favor from the gods of education, if there were such a thing. And the confidence one often takes for granted, and loses among the trivial quests for purpose, is fortified by the validation of the business of education.

I charged into my algebra class with unheralded fervor. Although the students had no clue as to the reason for such demonstrative lecturing, they sat through the class, attentive and engaged, probably more as a result of confusion than intent.

A fine note on which to end the week. A teacher lives for such affirmation of his powers of education, and the faith that manifests itself in his dedication to expanding the horizons of knowledge, even if it merely results in only one student learning how to think. I could face the weekend with a clear conscience and the satisfaction that I was doing the right thing. This newfound fortitude was just what I needed to tackle the ITV thing. I grabbed all of the material I had collected and headed for home. Next week would be different.

Chapter 20

Isaw the large man approach the Student Union. Tall, heavy, bald, round face. Ed Fulkrod, the Information Technology Supervisor. I caught up to him about thirty feet from the door.

"Ed, you got a minute?"

He stopped and turned toward me, squinting through the thick glasses that echoed his round face and made his eyes look like billiard balls.

"I need to talk to you about the chimes."

"Humph," he said and started walking toward the door with a lumbering gait that looked like it was painful.

"Hey, I just want to know if you've heard anything else from Dr. Gaines?"

"Nope."

He picked up his pace, as awkward as that must have been for such a large man.

"I talked with him about the chimes," I said. "He said he would look into the matter a little further. I haven't heard back from him."

"Good for you."

"You seem to be pleased that they're not working."

"I am."

"Why is that?"

He stopped just in front of a flock of students coming toward us. We staged ourselves in the center of the sidewalk making them go around us.

"Look." He directed his thick glasses downward toward me. "I got enough problems what with the fanatical idiots around here that don't have sense enough to turn on a computer, much less use one. And the printers that jam. And idiots that don't bother to back up their data."

His arm suddenly became animated.

"And the crappy network system we have here doesn't work worth a shit, and who do think has to keep screwing with it to keep it alive?"

Then both arms began flailing.

"And then there's all these damned students that pull every trick they can think of just to download porn off the Internet and clog the system with stupid emails and disgusting videos. I spend most of my time telling people how to do what they should know how to do and fixing problems that aren't really problems. I don't have time for no goddamn bells. I got enough of them in my head as it is!"

He stood there in front of me, his torso as rigid as a statue and his arms whipping the air like a distressed hummingbird. His magnified eyes wanted for something to bore holes through. For a tall nerdy type he was almost intimidating. But in a funny way.

"Okay, look. What if I were to assume responsibility for the chimes?"

"What!" He screamed. "Are you nuts?"

I put my hands up to reassure him I meant no harm.

"Wait," I said. "What if I were to take over the chimes? That would leave you completely out of the picture."

"What the hell do you know about that sort of thing?"

"What's there to know?"

"Why the hell are you wanting to do this?"

I took a deep breath and smiled at him. "I like the chimes. Believe it or not, they actually give me strength to get through the day."

He squinted his eyes again and looked at me as if puzzled. "Boy, are you ate up with it."

"Yeah, I know. Many people have told me that."

We walked on in silence for a moment.

"You know," he said. "I got to tell you, I sort of liked them, too." Ah, a soft spot in the heart of the ogre. "Yeah, I like them," he grunted. "Just don't tell anybody I told you that."

"Ed, I wouldn't breathe it to a soul."

He turned and continued his clumsy gait toward the door to the union.

"So, you really want to do this, huh?"

"Yes, I do."

"Fine by me. I'll tell Dr. Gaines."

He disappeared inside the door leaving me standing alone outside wondering what I had just done. It was settled, then. I would have to talk with Dr. Gaines. Maybe I could do that in the afternoon after I talked with Claudia about the ITV thing.

Between classes I managed to assemble the documentation from my ITV research. Claudia's faith in ITV as the savior of education would not be easily shaken. As repulsive as ITV was to me, I vowed to keep an open mind about its usefulness in the classroom. I had to admit that some courses thrived beneath the technological union of two geographical locations by invisible waves screaming through the air. The classes suited to the distance-learning thing were more aligned with business, math, and biology, which all lent themselves to easy adaptation toward ITV. But, science was another story.

From my office I retrieved the notebook of documentation and the bag that held the overflow of miscellaneous material. The hazardous trip to the Life Science Building did not distract my thoughts about the impending meeting with Claudia. I was careful to hang on to my book and bag during the numerous encounters with blind or thoughtless students who seemed to be continuously thrown off course by waves emanating from the cell phones plastered to their ears. Since they had no predetermined paths, I couldn't very well have one, either.

One young lady, in particular, was determined to derail me from the sidewalk in spite of the fact that I had the right of way. Of course, I really wasn't looking where I was going, either. The collision left our books scattered across the walk. She apologized and, for some odd reason, so did I.

"You must be Professor Lane," she said, as she bent down to pick up her books with one eye looking up at me.

I was still reeling from the impact and I had to wonder how she knew me. "As a matter of fact, I am. Have we met?"

"No. I mean with our bumping into each other and all, I just figured…you know…"

She never finished her statement, assuming, I suppose, that I should know. Then it hit me. Had I suddenly gained a reputation as the campus buffoon? I hadn't thought much about the implications of the circumstances. But my pride sprang a leak and oozed from my ego, spilling over my shadow on the concrete among the books.

Since the collision had already distracted me from my mission, I figured I could at least help her gather her belongings and get her the hell out of my way. The incident on the sidewalk not only delayed me several minutes, but dashed my confidence, as well. Those few minutes must have given Claudia just enough time to fire up her tainted logic.

"August, I don't understand your attitude toward ITV."

"It's not really an attitude. It's more of a conviction of faith in the appropriate use of resources."

"What did you just say?"

My mouth was working faster than my brain. And for Claudia, that would never produce anything meaningful. I sat in the guest chair across from her desk.

"ITV is well suited to some courses. For example, you seem to be very successful with it in chemistry. Others have used it well for English lit and math."

I had no idea if she was successful or not. But, I certainly didn't want to shed poor light on her own ego, so I made the concession of giving her the benefit of the doubt. I went on with my case and presented the other evidence of equipment malfunction I had collected with the assistance of the students in Ricky's ITV class. I must say I was persuasive. I finally achieved a breakthrough when she agreed to get with Dr. Gaines and discuss possible alternatives to the ITV system. And I promised to gather more information about ITV classes and study possible improvements.

The walk back to my office was more of a march. A victory march. Like a general heralding a defeat over the archenemy. As I passed Dr. Hartmann's post I smiled up at where the old fellow would have been. I could swear I saw his image smiling back at me, although it was hard to tell because of all the facial hair and shadows that would have been beneath the hat.

When I reached the office I looked out the window toward the statue's base. Through the grime I could just make out its dark ruddy outline against the grass that still bore part of its summer green.

"Well, Stan, I have triumphed over ignorance."

Stan looked at me, his head low, eyes peering over his glasses.

"What's the matter with you," I asked.

He shifted his eyes toward the door and back to me.

"I heard that you might be the subject of a rather nasty charge."

The exhilaration that had supported my ego disappeared and I plummeted into the depths of anxiety.

"Miss Parker, I presume?"

"That's what I gather, my boy."

"And where did you hear this tasty bit of information, if you don't mind my asking?"

"I ran into your buddy, Ricky. He asked me to warn you. He said if you needed anything to give him a call."

"So, Ricky has a pulse on the grapevine." I fell into my chair and let myself spill over it. "You know, Ricky seems to know just about everything and everybody here. How he does it?"

"I don't know, but you should think seriously about garnering some support for your cause. You haven't exactly been a stellar example of academia, what with all of the accidents."

"You may have a good point, there. A student bumped into me today and seemed to intuitively know who I was."

"My, you have acquired a reputation, haven't you?"

"Well, it's something I can't very well help. Hell, I know I'm arrogant, impatient, and clumsy. But those sorts of things require traumatic ordeals to change. I don't plan on having any of those. Of course, they'll probably happen anyway."

"Okay, buddy boy, I'm not one to say I told you so, but just remember you heard it here first."

"Thanks. I'm sure you'll remind me."

Beneath all of my troubles and expositions, I still wondered when I would hear about the chimes.

Chapter 21

W hen I arrived at my office the next day, just after tripping over my feet in the hall, a lady of about my age was waiting by the door. Average height, chunky, graying hair, and a nondescript beige dress. She wasn't pacing or moving any part of her body, but just standing there, staring at my approach with hungry eyes. As I got closer and noticed her face, a basset hound came to mind.

"Hello," I said. "Are you waiting for me?"

"Yes, Professor Lane." she said. "Yes, I am."

"Have we met?"

"Why, no. I don't believe we have. I'm sure I would remember it. I'm very good with faces. They're sort of like words and sentences to me. And I'm very good with words and sentences. That's because I teach English, you know." She stood motionless while talking, moving only her mouth. "I can look at a face and it instantly conjures an image of some word or phrase. Sometimes I can construct a face into an entire sentence. Of course, that doesn't mean that I will remember them any better than the others for whom I don't have complete sentences, but I can remember them just the same. I'm very good at that, too."

During a very short lapse in her chatter, I broke in.

"If I may ask, how did you know who I was?"

"Oh, that."

I unlocked the door and motioned her inside.

"Well, you see everyone knows who you are. I mean you have become very notorious for your…let's say, your adventures in the classroom."

I felt my self-esteem slip. It was bad enough that she knew me and I didn't know her. It was also disconcerting because of how she knew me.

"Please have a seat." I grumbled.

She bent herself into the guest chair. Somehow, it just didn't seem right without Miss Parker there. I plopped into my desk chair.

"My adventures?"

"Oh, yes. That has become… ah, let's say, ah… your trademark here on campus."

"My trademark?"

"Yes. You see, everyone here at Hartmann has some distinguishing characteristic that sets him, or her, apart from everyone else. Some… trademark that belongs to no one else. Yours is your…awkwardness, if you'll forgive me for being candid. You're really quite fortunate that we found something so quickly. Most folks require some time before we can find anything special about them. But, you just sort of popped right out all at once."

"Excuse me, but I'm at a disadvantage, here. You know who I am but I have no earthly idea who you are."

"Oh, silly me," she said with a hand on her chest. "I've been running on like this and you don't even know who I am. I'm Samantha Crumb. I teach English literature and freshman composition. Actually, I'm the English department chairperson."

She paused, I suppose, so I could form an impression of her credentials.

"As you have probably figured out, I like to talk. So, if I get to rambling too much, just stop me."

"Okay," I said. "Exactly what can I do for you, Ms. Crumb?"

"Sam, please. And I wanted to ask you how you would feel about writing a science column for our campus newspaper. Well, I said science column, but it could be anything you thought that might be appropriate. Now, by appropriate, I mean anything that relates to the students here at Hartmann. And, come to think of it, that could be just about anything now, couldn't it?"

I broke into her drivel. "I didn't even know there was a campus newspaper."

"Well, you're right, August. You don't mind if I call you August, do you? I always like to call people by their first names. Last names seem are so impersonal, don't you think? But no, we don't actually have a campus newspaper. At least, not any more. We used to have one years ago, but it sort of died when nobody read it. You see, that's why I'm here. I want to start a new one."

I could see where this was leading. I was about to be duped into providing free labor for the benefit of Hartmann College. I had nothing against campus newspapers. In fact, I enjoyed reading them when I was in college. But I was not prepared to offer my scant time for such an endeavor.

"August, in order for us to have a newspaper, we need something to put in it. There are a few events here at Hartmann, but most of them seem so trite for a college newspaper. And other events aren't suitable. At least, not the paper I want to publish. So, you see, I'm looking for something of substance. Something that would be meaningful to the students. Something that might help them get through their four years they spend with us, or at least most of them. Some of the poor darlings stay on another year or two to finish up. And, of course, something entertaining for them."

She seemed to be dragging it out before she got to the part where I was supposed to help type it and distribute it. I figured students would be doing that and I had already resigned myself to not giving in. I had too many other things to do.

"Now, what I propose is to ask someone from each department to submit an article for each issue of the newspaper. The article should have something to do with that person's area of expertise, obviously, and informative to the student. Well, I guess it would have to be informative to the staff and faculty, too, since I intend for them to read it as well." She leaned toward me and held out her hand, palm up, as if calling a dog.

"So, August, I would like to ask you to make a contribution in the physical science area."

Having thus been invaded, I met it head-on with cold-blooded relegation. It took only a few seconds, however, for the horizon to clear and I could actually see myself gaining celebrity status as a writer. An article might be a way of neutralizing my disconcerting clumsiness. My clever and exacting article would astound the campus and bring awareness to just what a gem Hartmann had in its midst. But, then reality shook my thoughts and I had to wonder who would want to read about physical science? The students hated it enough as it was. They damned sure wouldn't want to read about it in the news.

"Ms. Crumb… ah… Sam, I'm flattered that you would consider my professional talents worthy of publication."

I leaned forward toward her, mirroring her posture. I rested my arms on my knees, clasped my hands in front of me, and tried to prevent a chuckle from escaping.

"But, I have to tell you, the students who take physical science classes don't necessarily do so of their own volition. You see, it's a general education requirement. They have to take some kind of science to graduate. And to some, physical science is less repulsive than other science classes. For others, it's the only option they have."

"Yes, August, I realize that physical science is not popular. Land sakes, I hear enough whining about it in my own classes. Oh, dear, I'm sorry. I didn't mean to say that your classes are bad, or anything like that. In fact, the students talk about the…clever demonstrations you do and all. And, in view of that, I was hoping you would be able to contribute something out of the ordinary to the paper."

She sat straight up in the chair and pulled her hands into her lap, apparently pleased with what she considered a compliment. Then she went on.

"Something that would shake up the campus and get folks talking. Something wild and unexpected. I didn't mean to imply that I was after the mundane list of scientific facts that bore them to death in the classroom. Oh, I'm sorry, I didn't intend to imply that your classes are boring, again. I mean, I've never sat through one of your classes, so I would have no way of knowing if you're boring or not."

She jerked her hand to cover her mouth. I jerked my hand to my head in order to scratch it, wondering about the enigma before me. A scatterbrained woman, who looked like a basset hound, given to English literature, and who wanted something bold and daring from a science instructor. The bizarre situation gave me reason to be concerned about anything I might unintentionally surrender.

"Oh, my," she said. "I've done it again. You're going to have to say something, August, before I let something out that I shouldn't have said. I'm really –"

"Sam, it's okay. I'm a bit confused, though. Exactly what do you mean by something wild and unexpected? Hell, science is not exactly unexpected. We confront it and live with it every day."

"Oh, yes. I think I see what you mean. But from what little I know about science, I do know that there are many mysterious things we take for granted that have simple explanations."

While she rattled on, I leaned back and thought about how to interpret what she had said. Something wild? Unexpected? I would have to give that some more thought. The idea was intriguing.

"Okay, Sam, let me think about what I might be able to do. I can't promise anything, but out of the wealth of scientific phenomena, there is surely something that someone would find to be wild and unexpected."

She offered profuse thanks. So profuse, it was another fifteen minutes before she left. Then I sat at my desk pondering the acclaim that would soon be mine. The anticipation was a pleasant diversion from the rigors of lecture notes. I just had to figure out how to realize that acclaim. The phone killed my fantasy just before I had formulated a plan. I answered it immediately to stop the obnoxious ringing.

"This is Ed," the voice said even before the receiver was against my ear.

"Mr. Ed," I laughed. "What can I do for you?"

"Very funny. I'd better not hear you call me that in public. Especially not after the huge favor I just did for you."

"And to what bit of serendipity do I owe gratitude?"

"The chimes are all yours. When do you want the crash course in pulling the rope?"

My euphoria escalated to unknown heights. I was in the arms of Lady Luck relishing a warm embrace against her bosom. Ah, those sweet mounds of delight. I could feel myself falling into them, wallowing in ecstasy.

The chimes were mine. I would be the one to ring them. I could almost feel the vibrations and hear the crash of the clapper against the bell. I would be master of the sacred chimes of Hartmann, as well as, an author of renown. I had just begun my journey toward immortality.

"Anytime you're ready," I told him. "The sooner, the better."

"I've got a few minutes before I go home. How about now?"

"When and where?"

"Do you know the door on the third floor in your building that is at the top of a short run of stairs?"

I had to think. The only door I could remember at a stairway was the one with the words "Cop Room" left on the glass with a space that a "y" had once occupied. It sat at the top of six steps that led up from the third and uppermost floor of the building. There was no fourth floor. I often wondered what was behind that door since I was told there was no copy machine in there.

"Yeah," I said. "The one that says 'Copy Room'?"

"That's the one. I'll meet you there in twenty minutes."

"Why there, if I may ask?"

"Because that's where the computer is that controls the chimes. The speakers are on the roof."

"Speakers?"

"Yeah, speakers."

"You mean, there're no…bells?"

"What do you think this is? Westminster Abby?"

"Okay, twenty minutes."

I started to hang up, then, "Oh, Ed."

"Yeah."

"Thanks."

The click started the twenty-minute countdown. My hands shook as I packed up my attaché case to leave. I would take it with me on the way out. The restricted door was down the hall from my office just off the main stairway. At least it would be convenient to maintain. I locked the office door and strutted to the "Cop Room".

Exactly twenty minutes elapsed and I heard the elevator. Ed emerged and lumbered toward me carrying a computer. He unlocked the "Cop Room" door and led me inside over crackling bits of plaster and glass.

"Just ignore the trash. It won't hurt a thing."

The room appeared to have been an office at one time. Bookcases along the walls held rows of books in a protective cloak of dust from years past. A large Palladian window opposite the door looked over the portico of the front door to the building. So that's what the window was. It was a prominent feature on the building's facade, but I never saw the window from any of the rooms inside.

"This is the old computer that broke. I brought a surplus one I had laying around. I'll load the software on it and you should be in business."

"You know, Ed, I really appreciate you doing this."

"Yeah, well don't thank me yet. Wait until you get the call from Dr. O'Mally, because you'll get one."

"I'll bet I can handle Dr. O'Mally. Just show me what I need to do."

It took only a few minutes for Ed to load the software and demonstrate the operation of the chimes. It was coming up on the hour and we gave them a test run. The computer started making the funny clicking noises it makes when it does something and the air was filled with music. Everything worked perfectly. I stood at the window and absorbed the vibrations that stole through it. My soul was restored. My passion rekindled. I wanted to hear them again, but I had an appointment in town. There would be time enough the next day. I took the key to the door from Ed and went home.

Chapter 22

After an unpleasant encounter with Claudia, as if an encounter with her would actually be pleasant, I trudged through the doors of the Education Building into the overcast autumn, the brisk wind lobbing the smell of damp leaves into my face. She had confronted me about the sexual harassment charge. There wasn't much I could tell her except to deny it, but that didn't seem to appease her suspicions.

Then, as if the gods had heard my plea for delivery from the grasp of certain collapse, the chimes blasted forth their fanfare of rectitude, bathing the campus in a flood of academe. I stopped, as did some others, and looked toward the speakers on top of the Math Science Building as they filled the chilled air with a call to observe the sanctity of our institution.

"They really sound nice."

I had not heard the young lady who had stopped nearby, and spoke to me.

"I'm sorry," I said. "I was listening to the chimes."

"Oh, I know," she squealed. "Aren't they great?"

"Yes. Yes, they are. Great."

"Say, aren't you Professor Lane?"

"I'm afraid I am."

"Oh, then you're the one who got them fixed."

"Yes, that would be me," I said, basking in the gratitude that flowed from that dear angel's lips.

"I think it's just wonderful to hear them again. They just sort of, like, you know, make this place seems so, like college?"

"I'm glad you think so. And thank you for your praise."

I rendered a small salute and began strutting toward my office wondering how a student unknown to me would know about my business with Ed. I passed by Dr. Hartmann's station and looked up at where he should have been. I saw his smile materialize in the brisk air. He was listening to the chimes, too.

Once in the office, I suggested lunch in the cafeteria and Stanley agreed. Off we went to join the other victims that foolishly followed their primal need for nourishment into a pretentious repast. I suppose one would be hard pressed to find a decent meal for four dollars elsewhere in Elkridge. And, impossible to find a good meal in the cafeteria, but we ate there in spite of its deficiencies. It was easier than fighting our way into a crowded restaurant, and there weren't many of those in Elkridge. That's why they were always crowded. Obviously, the general population of Elkridge had unrefined palates.

More empty tables than usual filled the stained floor. I imagined the carpet had not been replaced since old Dr. Hartmann himself had eaten there, if he ever had. We thrust ourselves forward to the line at the first station. The poor girl there was trying to explain to a suspicious student the origin of the blistered mass of brown matter suspended in her tongs. Although the sign above the pan read "Chicken Fried Steak," I don't think anyone believed it. The student reluctantly allowed her to drop it onto his plate, and then foolishly asked for mashed potatoes and gravy. Then green beans. I had the same. So did Stanley.

We stopped at the salad bar to harvest our ration of wilted greens and assorted vegetable-like items. Then to the drink station for some water tainted by an atrocious blend of minerals and unknown chemicals unique to Hartmann's water plant.

The disappointing meal was complemented well enough by stories from the crypt as told by Francis Able, who joined us shortly after we arrived. Frank seldom missed lunch in the cafeteria, since he lived alone and did not cook and was too cheap to pay for better quality food.

"You know," he said. "I've had better food out of a trash can."

"When did you eat out of a dumpster?" I asked.

"I was in the army, once," he began. "Oh, I know I don't look like it now, but I cut quite a dashing figure back then."

He paused for a drink of the mineral water. Oddly enough, the foul liquid didn't seem to faze him.

"When we were in Vietnam, our unit never had much fresh food. One day Charlie took out our mess hall and all of the food stores in our storage trailer. That's when we all changed our religion and were introduced to fasting, har-har-har-har-har."

He looked around the table to make sure everyone was still paying attention to him. He even smiled when Mary asked if she could join us. I invited her to sit next to me.

"A pleasant surprise," I told her in a low voice. "You might not want to stay here, though."

"Oh, Frank?" She whispered. "Hey, I'm used to it. He doesn't bother me."

Frank recovered his dominance of the conversation and continued.

"Well, since we didn't have any food, we had to find something that we could eat without puking until battalion could send us rations. So, we took to searching all of the trashcans around the post. We were actually quite amazed at what some of the guys threw away. Did you know that our CO used hair coloring? Even in a war zone? Har-har-har."

During his coarse belly laugh, he leaned back so far in his chair it almost tipped over.

"I guess he had to look younger than he was so the hooch-maids would come near him, har-har-har."

It was obvious to me that the others at the table were trying to tune him out. It was not obvious to Frank. Food roiled in my stomach from his continual barrage of crass jokes and anecdotes. I was fascinated how he was able to consume his food while spouting forth such crusty tales.

I caught a whiff of Mary's perfume over the ghastly smell of the food. Or, it could have been cologne. It could have been anything. I was not well schooled in the devices of women's toiletries. Even Alexis hadn't bothered with much of the stuff.

Her hair, still in a bun, was immaculate, glowing beneath the harsh light. Her delicate nose was perfectly proportioned to her crisp profile, slightly pink at the tip, and cute. Sexy. Her face was an alluring beacon. She was inviting. And I was timid.

Frank raised his moustache toward me.

"Hey, ah… what's your name?" He said.

"August. August Lane."

"Well, August Lane, I've got to confess that I am confounded by your dedication."

"What do you mean?"

"I mean the chimes. Hell, I liked the things and then one day they didn't work…eh?"

"Oh, that. Well, yes. I agreed to take on this project. We acquired a new computer from Ed and now it's in business."

"A computer?"

"Yes, a computer. You see, it's all electronic. A computer controls the timing and the melody."

"A computer?" He repeated.

Frank's reaction was entertaining to Mary. She kept a coy grin on her face while watching him. I wondered if that's the way she watched me. Then I wondered if she ever watched me at all. Somehow, I felt a pang of guilt at staring at her, my eyes soaking up the beauty that exuded from every bit of her body, not knowing if she felt the same way about me. Then I wondered, what if she didn't? I felt stupid. Then Frank's voice broke my trance.

"What's a computer got to do with anything?"

"I see you're having difficulty with this." I said. "Where did you think the music came from?"

"Why... ah... the bell tower. I don't get around campus much."

"No." I said, "No bell tower. Just the speakers on top of the Math Science Building."

"Speakers, huh?"

"Yup. Speakers."

"There's probably a bell tower around here, somewhere." He grumbled.

Stanley and I collected our plates to leave. The chimes rang out one solitary peal. Francis looked up in suspicion.

"They probably hid it someplace," he grumbled after us.

*****

"August, are you busy?"

Samantha Crumb invited herself into my office. I had not expected to see her again, since few people ventured to the third floor of my building. And being the middle of the week, I wasn't in the mood for her visit, anyway. It would be difficult enough to conduct classes while my focus was on what Miss Parker was concocting. The morning had been a bust and I had no hope that the remaining classes would fare any better.

"You don't mind if I call you August, do you, I mean Professor Lane is quite a mouthful and seems a bit distant. I always prefer to maintain a sense of closeness to those with whom I talk."

"Not at all... Sam," I said. "I believe we covered that avenue during our last meeting. Come in."

She sat in the guest chair at perfect attention, legs together like a proper lady, and hands on her lap. Her basset hound face looked lonely.

"August, I just dropped by to tell you...well, to ask you, really, if you were still willing to contribute an article to our college newspaper? I had asked you earlier, I'm not sure you would have remembered, so I wanted to remind you that I am still excited about your writing for us."

"Yes, I remember."

"Oh, good." She dragged out that word as if extending its meaning and relaxed her composure a bit. "I was so afraid you had forgotten. I mean, what with the difficult courses you teach, that must place a formidable demand on you. I mean, English is not that –"

"Yes, it does somewhat. Tell me, Sam, tell me again what kind of article it was you were expecting?"

"As a newcomer to Hartmann I thought you might like to share your impressions of the college and some of your first year experiences you've had here. It needs to be something out of the ordinary. Something daring. Different. Sometimes the introduction to something new presents the ideal foundation for stories and humor. That reminds me of –"

"I would be most happy to contribute an article," I interjected. "When do you need it?"

"Oh, August, I can't tell you how thrilled I am. You have no idea how many folks here have turned me down. I mean it's not as if I asked them to write a book, or something. I figured they could at least write a short article."

That is where her composure failed and her arms began echoing her words in almost obscene gestures.

"You see, the others in the English Department told me they didn't think you would write an article for us. Oh, just wait until I relay the good news. They will all be so surprised."

"Ah… when did you say you needed the article?"

"Oh, silly me," she said hiding her mouth. "How thoughtless. I just get on a tangent and just sort of ride away with it."

I was hoping she would find another tangent and ride it out of my office.

"The article?" I asked again.

"Oh, yes. The paper will be printed in about two weeks, so I need to have the draft next week. Will that give you enough time to write it?"

"Yes, I think I can manage that. Next week."

I turned around and made a note in my planner.

"August, I'm just so happy to have you here. You know, most folks we ask to do articles turn us down. And I don't understand why."

She seemed genuinely clueless, as if she had expected them to react like they had been asked to contribute an article to the New York Times. My pity for her basset hound face justified my agreement for an article. It would temporarily satisfy her delusion until I could think of some excuse to use for any future requests.

"By the way," I said as she rose to leave. "Are you familiar with a Miss Parker?"

"Why, yes." She gleamed. "She is in one of my classes." Then the smile melted into a frown. "She's not a very motivated student, but I do see some promise in her. I just wish she would do something about those clothes she wears."

"Are you aware of any relationships she has with other students? Like Allison Boyer?"

"No, she keeps pretty much to herself. Except that there is one young lady…a Cleetah Shoaven that she is with much of the time. Is there a problem with Miss Parker?"

"No, no. I just have her in one of my classes and, as you mentioned, I am also alarmed at her choice of wardrobe."

"Well, you never can tell about the young folks today. They come to class wearing their pajamas."

Samantha did eventually leave after I learned about her daughter's progress in college and her late husband's business, the control of which she had relinquished to a management firm because she did not have adequate business training. Oh, and the annual booklet of poetry the English Department published, featuring works by students and faculty. It was mostly for the benefit of the faculty, who could not manage to get published anywhere else, but some students also found enjoyment in sharing their visions with others.

*****

The evening had turned warmer than usual and I sat naked on the sofa in my apartment with a broken air conditioner watching a program about World War II airplanes, nursing a glass of Glenlivet, and waiting for the ceiling fan to dry the sweat that continued to run down my chest. Even my fascination with the aircraft on television could not compete with my musing about Miss Parker. Why would she be pursuing a formal complaint? What good would it do her?

It was then that I considered the possibility that someone was out to tarnish my good name and destroy what I had done to build the science and physics program at Hartmann. I had forgotten for a moment to consider if I actually had a good name at Hartmann. I had barged my way through opposition to realign the physical science program with a more contemporary flair. I had taken over the calculus class from a complacent instructor whose only ambition was to hand out worksheets and give exams. I had riled several members of the administration by bypassing their intricate web of processes and resolved issues by taking them directly to whoever was ultimately responsible for them or who-ever could authorize it, whether or not it was his actual responsibility. My good name might not be held in very high esteem. Miss Parker's affair loomed over me like a plague. It couldn't be just her.

The longer I sat there in a hypnotic state, more possibilities occurred to me. An instructor takes issue with another who steals a cherished class from him. And few of them appreciated my determined efforts at reviving the physics program for fear it would awaken the administration to their own stagnant curriculum. Even those people with whom I had developed a measure of trust became suspect. Had it not been for the previous two single-malts that kept my mind hovering over the sofa, the list would not have been as long.

Who would be the sneaky sort? Who would stand by while an innocent victim was tortured for some fabricated act? This is where it got complicated. A host of names filled my mind. The power of my own imagination frightened me. Here I was, near the heart of academia and all I could visualize was a throng of contemptuous, backstabbing hypocrites, who, by day, appeared to be normal visions of intellect. Of all the names that occurred to me, none seemed likely. The whisky was doing a fine job.

Chapter 23

The atom is a wonderful mystery. As the foundation of the universe, atoms in combination with other atoms determine the nature of a substance: its color; its state; its identity. And yet we can't even see them. We aren't even aware that they are there. That's what makes it so difficult to explain to the typical science student who lives in a cosmic world of visualization and self-gratification.

Tangible evidence can be manipulated with curious hands, or even hands that aren't curious, and viewed with discerning eyes, or sleepy ones. Hollows of a student's mind don't easily digest abstract notions, so I used demonstrations to assist in visualizing what happens. Actually seeing an event frequently removes part of its shroud of mystery, and sometimes drives the mystery deeper into the cosmos.

Although they had just arrived, the GPS students waited listlessly for the end of the fifty-minute period. Miss Parker was dressed in her trademark regalia, unconcerned with any of her surroundings. Except for me. Her sultry eyes, hungry for gratification, clutched at every movement I made. I tried to ignore her.

The chapter about the atom caught most of them by surprise. They were familiar with the term but, like most mediocre students that endured a mediocre education, they blew it off in high school, if they were ever exposed to the subject at all. Just like most other subjects they were encouraged to learn. So, I reduced my lecture to an elementary form.

"You all know, then, what we think the model of an atom might look like," I explained in front of the whiteboard. "The nucleus containing the neutrons and protons are surrounded by clouds of negatively charged electrons that balance the positive electrical charges of the protons."

This was where I animated the illustration of the atom by drawing swirling lines around the nucleus to simulate the paths of the electrons in their virtual orbits. I followed the articulated lecture with a demonstration of an electron gas tube. I had the power supply connected to the apparatus and ready to turn on. I asked one of the students to turn out the lights and I flipped the switch on the lamp. The show began.

The sudden darkness woke those who were asleep and captivated those who weren't. They all watched quietly as the tiny electrons streaked through the tube in tiny trails of light. The "oohs" and "aahs" started and the din of excitement filled the classroom. Oh, that blessed sound of discovery. Music to a dispirited professor. I revered in my performance and the rapport that developed during that short time. I wanted them to leave feeling satisfied with their time spent in the classroom. Not that it happened often, but fulfillment gives way occasionally to statistics and even the most oppressed of us find some relief in the laws of probability.

The chimes reverberated through the silence signaling the end of class. I asked for the lights to be turned on and reached for the power supply to turn it off. In the darkness, I missed the switch and my hand fell on one of the cables connected to the unit. Had it not been for the fact that I was leaning on the metal frame of the whiteboard, and the fact the cable's insulating cover was split leaving a wire exposed, I would not have heard the loud crack that accompanied the ten-thousand volt charge that briefly surged through my body and left me standing in a state of total bewilderment. The circuit breaker in the power supply disconnected as did the circuit breakers for the third floor of the Math Science Building, casting us into complete silence and near total darkness. The only sounds were exclamations of surprise from other classrooms. Then, to my astonishment, the emergency lights threw their glare into the hallway.

I'm sure the students were puzzled about what had just occurred. Although I was beyond being puzzled and was in a state of shock, I was able to steady myself enough to remain erect.

"Professor Lane?" One of the students asked. "Are you all right?"

I believe it was me who said, "Yeah."

"Should someone go for help?" One of them said.

"No," I was able to say as I felt the blood still draining from my head. "That's all for today," I dragged out.

Someone said, "Look, his hair is standing straight up!"

I managed to hold on to the edge of the desk until everyone left. Then Horace rushed through the door into the dim room.

"August?" She squawked. "August, I just lost my video. Do you have electricity?"

Just then, I lost my hold and collapsed to the floor. I propped myself against the wall with my butt planted firmly on the carpet while I tried to think.

"Oh, my God!" She said as she rushed over to me and tried to kneel down.

"August, what happened? Are you all right?"

On her way down she lost her balance and tumbled into a heap beside me. While she lay there wallowing with me on the floor, Frank happened by and stopped to view the performance.

"Har-har-har," he pointed at us. After wheezing several lungs' full of air, he was able to speak. "Are you two frolicking about in the darkness or do you need help?"

"Francis, for God's sake, help us up." Yelled Horace. "I think August has hurt himself."

Frank waddled over to us and offered Horace a hand. Before he was ready to execute the maneuver, she yanked on his extended arm and he, too, fell into a heap at my feet covering Horace's legs.

"Goddamn it, Horace, wait until I'm ready," he growled.

"I thought you WERE ready."

The impact must have dislodged something in Frank's chest because he had succumbed to a fit of coughing and hacking while Horace tried to crawl out from beneath him and at the same time keep her dress in a decorous position.

I sat there dazed and, except for the presence of Horace and Frank, unconnected with my surroundings. It was like watching Laurel and Hardy. I wanted to laugh but I wasn't sure how to start doing that. No part of my body seemed to do what I wanted it to do. So I continued to sit and watch Horace and Frank wrestle on the floor like two turtles trying to mate while belly up on the beach.

The day had started with anticipation of worldly deeds and feats of grandeur. But, I was outflanked by fate and obliged to retreat to a sultry attitude. The defeat left me with little confidence to face the rest of the day. I had been put down. My revelry quelled, and my outlook soured.

I staggered my way through the rest of the day leaving the students pretty much at their own discretions. I was unable to regain complete control of my disheveled hair, tame the sting of my hands, and some of my students might have thought I had become mad. There were no questions, quizzes, exams, or homework. And I can't help but wonder if I ever did lecture in those classes at all. The only thing I do remember is the sweet melody of the chimes every hour. It was almost as if something, or someone, were calling, beckoning me toward some alter-existence in another world.

Eventually, the last class dispersed and I was left to reflect on the day. Even after several replays, I was unable to make sense of it. And my hands hurt. I needed help. Not anything to do with analysis. Just a little boost to pick up my awareness. I headed for Jim Bob's.

*****

"Hey, Perfessor," Cindy called as I teetered in the door. "Boy, y' loo' like something bagged ya."

I found a stool and stood in front of it looking at her, hoping she might tell me what to do with it. I couldn't recall how I had gotten there.

"Hey, August."

I heard my name but I had no idea where it came from.

"August," again.

I stood there holding onto the stool not knowing what to do. A hand on my shoulder drew my attention toward Ricky's face. It had popped up out of nowhere and I thought how nice of him to greet me.

"Are you all right?" His lips seemed to ask.

"I don't know," I said. "I honestly don't know."

"God, what happened to your hair?"

"My hair? What's wrong with it?"

"Come sit down," he said pulling me along with him toward a booth. "Cindy!"

"I got 'im, hon," she yelled.

In what seemed like a very short while, but then of course I had no sense of time, a glass appeared in front of me. The vapors reached up to my nose and performed their magic. Glenlivet. The elixir for all ills. The cure-all that can almost resurrect the dead, and maybe it could even do that. I hoped I didn't have to die first for it to do its work. With a shaky hand, I managed to capture a sip of it. It burned so sweetly, scorching my mouth and scalding my mind out of its disordered state. Another sip and I knew where I was.

I melted into the booth's stickiness and Ricky looked me over shaking his head.

"What the hell happened to you?"

"That reminds me. I need to get the power supply in the physics room repaired."

"Power supply? What power supply?"

"Oh. The ten-thousand-volt power supply I use for experiments."

"So, what's wrong with it?"

"It leaks." I took another sip.

"What do you mean, it leaks?"

I looked at him without saying a word. And I took a sip of the whisky. Then another. And another. Then it was gone. And so was I.

"Now, what's up with you?" I asked just before I broke down laughing and wailing while convulsing like a madman. I had just enough sense to motion to Cindy for a refill.

"August, can you handle that?"

"Ricky," I said almost lying over on the table in front of him. "I need all the help I can goddamn get."

Cindy hacked her way to the booth and set the drink in front of me. She brought Ricky a fresh beer, as well. Then she pulled up a chair and sat at the end of the booth. She hacked so violently I thought something might launch itself across the table. Ricky focused a serious look at her.

"Cindy, you got a bad one, there."

"Hack-hack-hack. I know, hon. It's those damned cigars. Hack-hack. Got to quit."

"Cigars?" I asked.

"August," Ricky broke in, "what about the power supply? How does a power supply leak?"

"Oh," I leaned back in my seat. "Well, you see, one of the wires is cracked and wouldn't you know that's the one I grabbed."

"You mean it shocked you?"

"Yeah, man. Just like a bolt of lightning came out of the box and zapped me. It was awesome."

"Let me see your hands."

I turned loosed of my glass and held my hands out for inspection.

"Hell, you're burned. You need to get something on that."

I looked down at my hands. Sure enough, the fingers on my left hand had been seared by the wire leaving a crisp black line across them, just like a fresh fillet off the grill. That explained why my hand hurt. My right hand had a shadow on it where the frame of the whiteboard pressed against it.

"I think I've go' some stuff in the back," Cindy said. "I'll go fetch it."

Cindy hobbled off hacking her way to the back of the bar.

"Buddy, you need to get home and get some rest."

"Yup," I shook my head. "You're absolutely right."

I heard Cindy hacking her way back to the booth. I held up my glass.

"You sure you want another one of those, Gov?"

"Hell," I said. "I can't walk worth a damn anyway. Who'll know the difference?"

She dropped the first-aid kit on the table and went to refill my drink. Ricky administered an antiseptic and placed a bandage around my left hand. He had done that before many times, I would guess.

"'Ere you go, Gov."

Cindy plopped the whisky in front of me and sat down.

"Are you going to be okay for classes tomorrow?" Ricky looked at me like a doctor examining his patient.

"I think so. Nothing a little sleep won't cure."

"Well, I was going to ask you to cover my algebra class, but that's out of the question."

That reminded me that I needed to find out more about the ITV thing. "Say, as long as you brought up the subject, what do you know about the rest of the faculty's problems with ITV?"

"There are plenty of them. They all curse it in one breath then turn around and praise it whenever anyone even remotely responsible for their paychecks is around."

Ricky was more than willing to talk about the rotten situation surrounding ITV classes. His indifference was beginning to wear down. He revealed the suspicious meetings that Professor Bartholomew had with students in his ITV classes in social science, many of whom boasted about the "A" they received instead of the "C" they actually earned, more or less. He had a trail of athletes behind him who always seemed to make excellent grades in spite of their poor overall performance, even if they had, in fact, attended class. And Ricky hinted about some dark mystery surrounding Professor Bartholomew, although I wasn't quite alert enough to comprehend its significance at the time. And, of course, there were numerous accounts of canceled classes because the equipment didn't work or the line dropped, or a dozen other reasons.

I should have taken notes, but I didn't have a pencil or paper. And, besides, I wasn't sure I could even write at that point. The clandestine information was compelling enough to become a permanent memory. I had already forgotten about the incident in GPS class and my mental acuity had been partially restored. Of course, the Glenlivet might have had something to do with my sudden change of behavior. Tomorrow I would start prying into the ITV thing. There had to be more.

Chapter 24

I sacrificed a few minutes at the beginning of each class to survey those students who were enrolled in an ITV class. Except for a few praises, the majority of the comments were indifferent or critical, most of them critical. Other students wrote barbs about the time wasted in ITV classes and the poor instruction. The actual phrasing varied, but for the most part certain expletives were commonly used to express their displeasures.

That afternoon, after my last class, one of my college algebra students stopped by my office. The short bundle of energy shot into my office and nearly jumped into the chair.

"What can I do for you, Miss Workman?"

She looked at me with luscious brown eyes that were filled with concern. "Well, you said if we have anything to say about the ITV thing, you know, to come see you."

"Well, I'm glad you decided to drop by. What is it you would like to tell me?"

"It's about my class with Professor Cooper."

"What class is that?" I asked.

"Chemistry."

"Is there a problem with it?"

Her eyes narrowed and the concern turned to anger. "Her class is a joke."

"In what way?"

"It is just so much crap. I can't see what she's doing with the sketches and I can't hear what she's saying about them. None of other kids can either. I asked her about it, you know, but she just said to pay better attention."

I made sure to get that comment down accurately for my next meeting with Claudia.

"Miss Workman, I appreciate your sharing this with me. I wish I had something to offer you in return, but I'm afraid I have nothing."

"Oh, that's okay, Professor Lane. It just feels good to be able to gripe about it to someone. I know nobody's going to do anything."

"Ah, but that's why I'm conducting this survey. If I can get enough information together, I'm hoping I can change the ITV classes into something useful, or get rid of them altogether."

"Yeah, well good luck," she said as she slowly got up and walked out.

A young man had been waiting in the hall when Miss Workman left. He marched in and abruptly sat in the chair in front of me, placed his books in his lap, and looked me square in the eye with a slightly upturned nose.

"Professor Lane, I'm Shawn Crandall. I'm in your GPS class." He spoke with authority. I recognized him as one of my better students.

"You said if any of us had any comments to make about ITV classes to come see you."

"Yes, Mr. Crandall. Several students have expressed concern over the quality of the ITV classes. I take it you have some issues you would like to bring to my attention?"

"Yes."

He shifted in the chair slightly, but did not relinquish his authoritative posture.

"You see, I take social science from Professor Bartholomew. It's okay, I guess. But I don't like him."

"I see."

I searched the gray, almost black, inert eyes for a clue as to where he was going with this. There was nothing. It was like looking into a bottomless well. A poker face.

"Is this a personal dislike or is there some professional issue we need to discuss?"

"Both."

I felt the sharp edge of fear flash in my mind and my mouth turned sour. I wasn't sure I wanted to hear what the young man was going to tell me, but I had to know. It was like folding a decent poker hand without knowing what the winner's hand held. You always wonder if you could have won.

"Professor Bartholomew is a crook." He stated it bluntly and without emotion. I don't think his eyes even blinked.

"Would you like to explain what you just said?"

His face broke with just a twitch of an eye and a tear formed at the corner. "Professor Bartholomew is…"

Then the boy froze. I had no idea what he wanted to say. He opened his mouth as if to speak again but nothing came out, teasing my patience.

"Not knowing exactly what it is you want to say, I understand how difficult it might be. Whatever it is, if there is any way at all, I will try my best to help you."

He jerked his lips in a slight grin, perhaps, then sniffed once.

"I…"

Then he lowered his head, concealing his face. I saw a tear fall on the book in his lap.

"…I know it's wrong," he muttered.

I listened carefully. I was ready to lunge after the bastard at the mere mention of any injustice done to the boy.

"It's wrong." He paused and sniffed. "What he does."

More tears fell. His hands were busy arranging the books in his lap, his confidence drained.

"What do you mean?"

"I don't do too good in his class. Social science. I don't make good grades in that kind of stuff. But I got to have good grades to keep my scholarship. He said he'd give me a good grade if I… I… it's just wrong."

I began to realize what was going on. I had rarely experienced the effect of fear, pity, anger, and anxiety at the same time. But I will remember that day forever. My body seemed to compress itself into a knot so tight my lungs clenched, starving me of air, and I felt like a board that had been broken and dropped into my chair. I wanted to help this young man but I had to find out the nature of what was confronting me.

"Is he making unrealistic demands of you? Is he making you do something you are uncomfortable with?"

The head slowly nodded up and down as well as it could from its restrained position against his chest. I waited until he spoke again.

"He wants money. I have to…pay him to get an A in the class." Of all the things I had expected to hear, that wasn't one of them. Did he say what I thought he said? This boy was paying Bartholomew? The bastard was extorting money from his students? I got up and closed the door.

"Do you mean to say that Professor Bartholomew is extorting money from you in order to earn a grade in his class?"

"Y…y…yes."

Then he looked at me, head up, eyes focused, with the same proud look he had when he first sat in the chair, like he had conquered the great heights of a mountain. I sat there still unsure if I should believe this young man. Why would he admit such a thing to me instead of the authorities?

"Shawn, why are you telling me this?"

"You said you wanted to know if any of us were having problems with ITV classes."

"Well, this isn't exactly what I meant."

His bearing broke. His eyes almost melted as they watered around the edges.

"No, no," I said. "What I mean is that I was really after information about the quality of the classes." I leaned forward and looked straight in his eyes. "But, I think we have a bigger problem here that needs some attention."

He swallowed hard and kept staring at me.

"Let me ask you something, Shawn." He blinked his worried eyes. "Why are you in Professor Bartholomew's class?"

"That's the one Dr. O'Mally put me in. She's my advisor. She said I could probably get a decent grade in his class."

Ah, there it was, an advisor making overt implications about a student's success. How did she know he would get a decent grade? Now another hole opened in the floor beneath my already unstable feet.

"You did the right thing. Talking to me about it, I mean. Have you told anyone else about this?"

"Just a couple of my friends."

"Have they discussed the situation with anyone?"

"No. We just kind of keep it a secret. We're afraid to let anyone else find out. He said he would have us expelled if we told anybody."

"Are your friends in the same situation?"

"Yes."

"Same teacher?"

"No."

Oh shit. There was more than one of the bastards. Was Hartmann a breeding ground for criminals?

"Do I need to know who the other instructors are?"

"There's only one." Shawn looked away from me and raised his head back to its prominent position. His courage had obviously found its way to the surface. "It's Dr. Damascus."

If my chair hadn't been under me I surely would have fallen completely through to Hell. I felt the blood fall from my head. Visions danced through my head of the stately old professor with a pitchfork and horns. It was a moment before I could say anything. Dr. Damascus was a cornerstone of the college. His reputation was almost... well, it almost WAS the college.

"What do you want me to do, Shawn?"

He turned toward me and tears fell from the corners of his eyes.

"I want it to stop," he squeaked. "I want to be left alone. I don't care about the scholarship anymore. I just want to be left alone."

I had to help this boy. I wasn't sure how the system worked, but I knew I would have to have evidence of this atrocity. The administration would think it was one word against the other.

"Okay, here's what we're going to do. You're going to have to help me. First, don't give in to any more demands by Professor Bartholomew. I know that's going to put you on the spot. Do you have any of your exams or any material with a grade on it from his class?"

"No. He keeps everything."

Smart man. At least he can doctor the papers if anything happens to implicate him in the affairs.

"Okay, then, do you work the exams in pencil?"

"Yes. That's what he requires us to do."

"Why is that?"

"I don't know. That's just what he wants."

"Then, do your next one in ink."

"But, he'll fail me."

"Look, as long as you answer the questions correctly, he can't fail you for using ink instead of pencil."

His eyes screamed anxiety, but his face begged for help. This was going to be difficult. I hoped that he would be stable enough to handle this.

"I know this is not going to be easy for you. But, I will try my best to get you through this. You're going to have to trust me. I know that's asking a lot, seeing as another instructor has already betrayed your trust. I'm not sure I know exactly what I'm going to do, but I can figure something out."

He shook his head and his face relaxed a bit.

"Just keep your nose clean and do what you're told. Except for giving money to anyone."

Stanley came in shortly after Shawn left. His chipper attitude made me feel better about what I was going to ask him.

"Stan, I'm glad you're here."

"You look like hell. How's your hands?"

"Right now I feel like I've been dragged through Hell. And my hands are still attached."

"Rough day?"

"You want to close the door?"

After a funny look, he pulled the door shut and sat down.

"I just had a frightening talk with one of my students. He claims Bartholomew is extorting money from him for grades."
I wondered if my face looked as shocked as Stanley's when Shawn told me his story.

"What? Bartholomew? The guy with the pony-tail?"

"Yup. That's the one."

"You mean he's forcing the students to buy grades?"

"It appears so."

He said nothing for a moment, but just stared at the ceiling.

"You mean this kid comes in here and accuses an instructor of extortion?"

"Well, actually, I was soliciting comments about ITV classes and this student starts unloading about this."

"What are you going to do?"

"I told him to follow orders but not to turn loose of any money. I'm going to talk to Dr. Damascus, first, and see what I can find out."

"What has Dr. Damascus got to do with this?"

"Oh, he's the other culprit that's preying on some friends of this kid. I think Bartholomew works for him."

Stanley slumped back in his chair and his mouth fell open.

"So far, he and Bartholomew are the only ones I know about. But, you know, they do tend to be together a lot."

"I'll be damned," he said. "We have a little Peyton Place right here at Hartmann. I wonder what the hell else is going on."

"I'm sure the good doctor is rolling in his grave."

Meeting with Dr. Damascus meant confrontation and that is something I have always tried to avoid. I hate it. It is stressful and generally disagreeable. And it usually leaves both parties less happy than it did before. Just like Alexis and me.

Each of our confrontations usually began with what I perceived as an innocent inquiry from her. Of course, I naively answered with no intent of wrongdoing or offense. And as many times as I had been victimized by my own ignorance, I never looked beyond the first question. But behind it all, lurking like a demon, was some ulterior motive born of some greater significance to the situation than I afforded it. And I always bore the only wound of battle. Her intent was entirely different than what I had assumed. I had little problem with other people. They are willing to explain if they perceive that my response is not in character with their request. But Alexis, being possessed by some malignant form of absurdity, never presented a question that any reasonable person could respond to correctly.

The chimes worked their magic, driving Alexis back into the past. My ego found new mettle and I felt confident that I could handle confrontation without making a total fool of myself. I would make a point to visit Dr. Damascus in the morning.

In the meantime, midterm exams were scheduled for the next week and I had done nothing to prepare for them. I sequestered myself in my office and put together test questions and surveys.

I had collected a healthy number of surveys and spent the entire evening at home tallying the responses. Two instructors seemed to pop up frequently. One of them, Dr. Damascus, was unexpected. He didn't seem like the type of professor that would take to ITV classes. I was surprised that he was teaching two of them.

And Zanzio Bartholomew, the social studies professor. I had seen him swishing around the campus in a gray tweed jacket, black turtleneck sweater and a pony-tail that just screamed "unconventional." Each comment about Bartholomew had a bizarre quality that begged closer scrutiny. I couldn't nail what it was, but something just wasn't right. I had seen him socializing with Dr. Damascus and that made it stranger. Perhaps Shawn was on to something.

Chapter 25

If Shawn Crandall was telling me the truth, it was a very well kept secret. But how could it be such a secret with so many people involved? I wanted to talk to Shawn's two friends. There had to be more than what Shawn was willing to divulge.

On my way to Damascus' office, I thought about how I would bring up Shawn's allegations. That sort of thing isn't something that one just blurts out without provocation. I didn't know how easily he could be provoked. Perhaps if I just mentioned Bartholomew.

The old boy was sitting behind his desk grumbling to himself. His thinning gray hair left a shiny spot of scalp on top to reflect the dim light in the room. The quick jerks of his hand indicated he was grading papers. I wondered why the teaching assistants had not been given that laborious task. I knocked on the door, having no idea what I was going to say.

"Yes, yes," he snorted from behind the desk. "What do you want?"

"Dr. Damascus," I said moving toward the desk. "I wonder if I might have a few minutes of your time?"

The old codger looked up at me through bushy eyebrows and scowled.

"Well, what is it you want? I haven't all day."

"I understand Professor Bartholomew works in your department."

"Yes, of course he does." He returned to grading papers. "What of it?"

"I believe he teaches an ITV class in social science."

"If you say so."

"I do. One of his students came to see me." The old fart gave no sign that he even heard me. I continued. "He wasn't very happy. In fact, he made some disturbing allegations concerning Professor Bartholomew."

He raised his head just enough to peer at me through his eyebrows, but said nothing.

"How well do you know him?"

"Who?" He barked. "Bartholomew? Or your student?"

"Since I didn't give you the student's name, that leaves Professor Bartholomew."

He shook his head and one corner of his mouth smiled. "I know him well enough, I suppose."

"From what this student tells me, the professor may well be leaving himself open for criminal charges."

The old man's eyes widened and the scowl returned. He dropped the paper he had been grading and clenched his fists. "What in the world are you talking about? And, by the way, who the hell are you?"

"I'm sorry. I failed to introduce myself." I bowed slightly. "I am August Lane. Math Science."

"Now, Professor Lane, what the hell is it you're talking about? Student? Bartholomew? Criminal charges?"

"Precisely."

"And why would you be speaking to me about it?"

"Professor Bartholomew does work in your department, doesn't he?"

"Yes. I've already said that he does."

"Then that pretty much makes this your problem, does it not?"

"I still haven't any idea what you're talking about."

My dislike for Dr. Damascus was growing, notwithstanding his prominence within the college hierarchy. He was trying my patience, but I kept a lid on my composure. "Look, here it is in a nutshell. A student in Professor Bartholomew's ITV social science class claims that he is extorting money from the student for a passing grade in the class."

He jumped up and pounded his fist on his desk. "Just who the hell do you think you are to barge in here and accuse one of my professors of that sort of conduct?"

"It's not me who is accusing Professor Bartholomew. It is his student. And I didn't barge in here. I knocked and asked permission, which you gave me."

"Why you smart-assed son-of-a-bitch. I ought to teach you a lesson about respect."

His left eye twitched. That worried me. Whenever someone's eye starts twitching, it has been my experience that they are unpredictable. I backed off and let him cool down.

"I'm sorry if this conversation is not to your liking. But, the fact of the matter is, a student has made a serious allegation against Professor Bartholomew. I'm just relaying to you what I know."

He marched around his desk and stood in front of me. His chest swelled with a deep breath almost as large as his belly and strained the already taut buttons on his shirt. His tie, much of its length consumed by the girth of his neck, stopped a good four inches above his belt. His scowl waxed into a hostile grimace while his jowls inflated. I could see something happening soon.

"And," I went on, "as you know, as a member of the faculty I am obligated to forward this allegation to the Dean of Student Affairs."

I didn't know if that was actually true, but it brought a blaze to his eyes. His body stiffened and if his mouth had bound itself any tighter, it would have altogether disappeared from his face.

"You have no idea what you are getting into," he almost whispered through his teeth.

I had struck a deep nerve beneath the old boy's tough skin. I figured it was time to drop the last bomb and depart.

"Oh, and by the way, this student also mentioned something about some of his friends being in a similar predicament with you."

I was so pleased with my success that I left myself completely unguarded. That's when the blow knocked me backward into the chair that was behind me. At the time I didn't know what had happened, except that I was suddenly sitting down.

"Get out of my office, you despicable imbecile. You don't know who you're dealing with. You're out of your league. Go back to your haven of cretins and dole out your pity on the unfortunate souls."

I was able to see that he was pointing toward the door with his left hand. His right one seemed preoccupied with pain from the jab it had landed on my face. I slowly got up and left, keeping myself as erect as possible so as not to show him any signs of defeat. Even the toll of the chimes did nothing to bolster my confidence. I treaded from his office with as much dignity as I could muster. I had lost all the feeling around my left eye.

I got back to my office just before the morning GPS class was to start. I grabbed my books from the table and turned toward the door. That's when Stanley noticed my eye.

"What happened to you, now?"

"Later," I said rushing past him. "I've got class." I would have to endure his interrogation sometime before the end of the day. My main concern was getting through GPS.

"Today, we talk about magnetism," I lectured. "Not the animal kind, mind you. The force kind."

I hoped they would take to the lecture and ignore whatever blemish might be growing around my eye. I knew better, but I was always a sucker for hope. Even as a kid I always hoped I would turn out to be Superman, or some other super hero, much like every other boy did. It never happened, of course, but that did not deter me from hoping my life away on frivolous fantasies. The one about being a teacher came closest to reality. I have no idea whatever possessed me to dream about that unless it was my tenth grade English teacher. Every boy in her class who was anywhere near sexually maturity had erections for the entire fifty minutes. I think she knew because she always seemed to recognize us by looking down at our crotches instead of at our faces. Since heralding the grade book as an instructor, I didn't know what else the attraction could have been at that stage in my life.

The students weren't all listening. I saw them staring at me. I knew they were wondering why I had a swollen eye, which would surely have been turning black by then, and my field of vision was narrowing. Even Miss Parker seemed intrigued by my appearance. She was probably conjuring another of her fantasies where I ravish her.

The giggling started. Then my anxiety started. Then laughter broke out. Then my anger broke out. Then Cleetah Shoaven's cell phone started its serenade of the Matador.

I immediately stopped talking and marched to her desk. Just as she flipped open the phone and poised her mouth to speak, I ripped the offending device from her hand, marched to the window, opened it, and promptly threw the phone out of it. She snatched up her belongings and headed for the door. It appeared as though she was going to try to beat the phone to the ground.

The entire class seemed dumbfounded as they stared at me. Their eyes followed my every step like thirty scared animals cornered by a vicious predator. I picked up my lecture where I had stopped and continued until the end of class. There were no further interruptions or interactions with the students except the bombardment of my dry lecture on their shocked minds.

Stanley was waiting for me in the office.

"Okay, it's later," he said. "What's up?"

I fell into my chair and laid my head back against it.

"I had a chat with Dr. Damascus."

"It appears that it might have been more than just a chat."

"As it turned out, much more."

"I take it he wasn't too pleased to see you."

"I don't think the man could be pleased about much of anything."

"Certainly not you."

"No. I mentioned Bartholomew to him."

"And?"

"Well, that wasn't too bad. Not until I brought up the extortion thing."

"I'll bet that did it."

"That it did. While I was on a roll, I also mentioned the student's friends and his allegation about the doctor."

"Boy, you are one gutsy fellow."

"Yeah, too gutsy. That's when he gave me his right jab."

"You mean he actually hit you?"

"He's got a mean punch for an old fart. I must have struck a nerve."

"So did he? Do you really think there's something going on?" Stanley's face fell long over his chest and worry enveloped his eyes. I hadn't given much thought to it up till then. I had been caught up in the excitement and challenge, having no consideration for the students involved and what other consequences might follow.

"Yes. There's something going on. I'm just not sure what. And the strange thing is that he was actually grading papers when I walked in. Wouldn't you suppose a professor, a doctor of his status, would avoid such menial tasks? I mean, that's what teaching assistants are for."

I closed my eyes and inhaled. The stirring air of dread settled heavily in my lungs. I had jumped into the middle of the fire and would, I was certain, be badly singed.

"But I'm afraid Shawn Crandall is telling the truth. I just wonder how many other students are involved."

"Oh, Geez!" Stan said. "You know, this thing could really be one big can of worms."

"Why couldn't I have just let it go?" I said. "But you know, something else bothers me about Damascus."

"And what would that be?"

"I heard that he's pretty well fixed. That's because of his wife. She was the one with the money. I couldn't imagine what sort of battle-axe would choose to live with someone like him. Because of his volatile nature and all. I mean he's divorced, but still, there's just something not right about all of this."

"Is that his Mercedes parked in the lot at the Admin Building?"

"Yeah. That's it. His finances must have been pretty darned good if he can still afford one of those things, especially after a divorce."

The phone rang. It was Mary.

"August, are you alone?"

"No, not exactly."

"I have to tell you something very important."

"Oh, it's just Stan here with me. What is it?"

"Dr. Damascus was just here. Dr. Gaines asked me to schedule a meeting day after tomorrow at ten-thirty. It is something about sexual harassment."

"Why would they be doing that? The hearing hasn't even been scheduled as far as I know. And what does Dr. Damascus have to do with that?"

"I don't know. That's why I wanted to let you know."

"Mary, you shouldn't have put yourself in jeopardy like this."

"But I'm worried that they are going to pull something funny. Oh, August, I'm getting worried."

Neither of us spoke for a moment.

"August, I have to ask you something."

"Sure. What?"

Here was another of those moments. The kind where I keep hearing things I expect to be said but aren't. In fact, I heard absolutely nothing. Not even the crackle of the phone line. Dead time and dead silence. Then for an instant I begin to think of what she could possibly have to ask me that might be so profound to warrant such hesitation.

"Are you involved with one of your students?"

There it was. The slam. Probably the only thing I had not expected to hear. She could have asked if I was gay. Or asked about my divorce. Or maybe if I drank. And how much. Or even how many times I went to the restroom during the day. But messing with a student?

I realized that my credibility had fallen from its precarious perch of fine repute, if it had ever been there. But the thought that Mary might believe something so terrible about me was like a hundred-thousand volt shock to my ego. Ten-thousand volts was bad enough on my body.

"Mary, this incident is purely a personal vendetta against me." Still silence. "It will be all right I just–"

"Sorry," she whispered. "I've got to go."

She hung up.

"Well, I know you're concerned about this turn of events," said Stanley, "but I missed breakfast this morning and I'm starving. Are you up for lunch?"

Being almost noon, my stomach should have been rolling, but it was more of a nauseous churning, like a plunger sucking on a toilet.

"Okay, but don't expect me to be happy about it. If Frank shows up I'll probably puke. I don't think my constitution can withstand his infernal boorishness. Just let me make a report to Dr. Tipton about a cell phone I threw out the window today."

"Not yours, I hope."

"No. A Miss Shoaven. A real ass of a student. I'm sure she'll complain to Dr. Tipton. I just want to get my licks in first."

Stan started down the hallway in his long-stride gait. If I waited too long, I would have to run to catch him.

"Hold up a minute. I think I'll lock up the lab real quick." Stanley, being intuitively curious about my behavior, came back and followed me inside.

"Do you know of anyone borrowing the digital scales?"

"No, that's not something I traditionally keep an eye on. Why?"

"Because one of them is missing from the cabinet."

I pointed at the empty shelf behind the glass door.

"There were five of them on the shelf, and one's missing. And I could swear they were all here this morning."

I quickly scanned the rest of the cabinets but noticed nothing else out of place or missing. Nothing now, that is. Things had previously disappeared, never to be seen again, but not something as costly as a digital scale.

"I'll ask around at lunch. Maybe one of the other instructors borrowed it. That thing goes for about eight-hundred dollars."

I walked heavily to the cafeteria slightly behind Stanley. How was I going to handle the students involved in the scandal? Who the hell took the scales? And what was with Damascus and his belligerent attitude?

Lunch fell like a brick to my stomach and lay there the rest of the day, a lump of glop left in a drain.

Chapter 26

L ook, Marney," I pleaded. "All I need is the lock changed on the physics lab. Some things are missing and I don't want anything else to turn up missing. We can't afford to replace what they took this time."

"You say things are missing?" He asked.

"Yeah. I lost an expensive set of digital scales."

"Well, you might as well get used to it."

"What do you mean?"

"Hey, stuff turns up missing around here all the time."

"What do you mean?"

"I mean there's stuff stolen around campus all the time. Nobody knows who does it and there ain't nobody cares."

"Why not?"

"Hey, Mac, I just work here. I ain't no cop."

I gripped the receiver tighter thinking, somewhere in my rattled head, it was Marney's throat. "Well, I still need the lock changed."

"Okay, but I got to have paperwork."

"What kind of paperwork?"

"Work order."

"What's a work order?"

"Paperwork."

"Do you mean you can't just take out a lock and slip a new one in?"

"Hey," Marney whined, "I'm only following orders from my boss. He said no locks changed without his approval. And that means I got to have the paperwork."

I sighed heavily hoping he would take the hint. Marney said nothing.

"Okay, okay. I'll get you a work order."

"Sorry professor. I hope you understand."

"Yeah, yeah, "I said. "By the way, where the hell do I get a work order?"

"Oh, yeah. I guess you'll need one of those, won't you."

"If that's what you want, then that's what I have to have."

"How about if I bring one over?"

"Fine. I'm in room –"

"Oh, I know where you are, Professor. I'll be there in a minute."

I had expected some leeway because of the immense favor I extended him by not reporting the van incident to the administration. I guess there was a grace period I didn't know about. If I could just get the lock changed, I'd be happy.

I didn't think of Marney as the running type, but it seemed like I had just hung up the phone when he popped into the office with a work order form.

"What happened to you?" He asked, staring at my left eye. "You run into something?"

"You might say that. I tend to lose my bearings."

"Yeah, well it must have had a hell of a right jab."

I filled out the form, hoping he would understand that I was finished discussing the matter.

"Thanks again, Marney. I think this will help keep our equipment safe."

"I wouldn't hold my breath, if I were you."

"About how long are we looking at?" I asked, handing him the completed form.

"I'm thinking about five days."

"For a door lock? Five days for a fifteen minute job?"

"Hey, we got to put this here thing through the mill. You know, copy it, send a copy to everybody on campus, find someone who can actually change the lock, then get it done. Five days ain't so bad in my book."

"Well, my book doesn't have that many chapters. But, if that's what it takes, then so be it. Are you going to contact me when you have the key, or should I check back with you in five days?"

"Oh, I'll bring it over when I get it."

Marney left with a grin of satisfaction on his face. I'm not sure if the satisfaction was due to having an authentic work order in his hands, or the fact that he actually had something meaningful to do.

I was feeling lucky and was determined to stop tardiness in my GPS classes, mainly the athletes. I prepared a quiz for the afternoon GPS section. If anyone showed up late, they would receive a zero for the quiz. If they were smart, it would happen only once. The athletes would soon learn that they could not take advantage of me and that they would be treated like the other students.

At precisely two-ten, whining overtook the classroom in response to my announcement of a quiz. I quickly passed out the papers and at the end of the ten-minute limit I had the papers back in hand. Then the athletes walked in.

"I'm sorry, gentlemen, you just missed a quiz."

They stopped. Their eyes had a sordid gaze that bespoke loathing and vengeance. Like a freezing blast of hatred. I wish I hadn't been so arrogant when I said it. I almost felt sorry for them. And it was sort of a dirty trick. But they were late. I hated that.

"Next class, be here on time."

They moved to their seats without taking their eyes from me, mumbling among themselves. It was like they were registering their weapons on me for a kill. They said nothing to me. That surprised me. I expected at least some whining.

I was preoccupied with Dr. Damascus for the rest of the day. What I had passed off as mystery and idle curiosity was quickly becoming more critical to my sense of well-being. It's funny how such stress can fatigue a person. What the day's challenges had not consumed of my energy, college algebra pretty much finished off. My exhausted body wanted to ignore the ringing phone. It was Claudia. It was Claudia in her nasty, nice voice. It was Claudia in her nasty, nice voice and demanding demeanor.

"August, I need to see you. Can you come to my office before you leave for the day?"

What little strength I had left rapidly escaped my command. I trudged over to the Life Sciences Building and knocked on her door only once before she responded.

"August, thank you for coming over," she said, getting up from her chair and charging around to greet me. Even though her tone was friendly, if she really could be friendly, there was something about her behavior that told me to run. She was still a witch.

"August, what in the world happened? That looks awful."
It had taken her longer than I thought for her to notice the growing blemish on my face.

"I just had a brief altercation. Nothing serious. It's certainly nothing to be worried about."

"Is that the result of a fight? Have you been fighting with one of your students?"

"No, Claudia. Any fights I have with my students are not physical. Only intellectual. And besides, I think I could take any of them."

"The faculty, then? Who is it?"

"Claudia, I am fine and I will handle this myself. There is no cause for you to be alarmed. I assure you, I will in no way damage the reputation of the Math Science Department."

I figured that was pretty safe considering that neither the department nor Hartmann had much of a reputation to damage. She sighed and resumed her station behind the desk.

"Well, I know you're probably on your way home, so I'll make this quick."

A deep breath bolstered my energy enough to fight back the fatigue.

"If you recall, I sent out surveys a couple of weeks ago to your classes."

I remembered them. Actually, I had forgotten them, until she mentioned them. Then I remembered them. Another waste of valuable class time. The students weren't too happy about them either, in spite of the fact that it spared them at least thirty minutes of my lecture. It occurred to me that at Hartmann College administrative tasks seemed to be more important than learning. Another hole in the balloon that, I thought, should have been lifting me to success. I shook my head in acknowledgement.

"Well, I got the results back this morning," she tittered.

She was almost gloating and I took that to mean that maybe there was something good about all of this. I had no idea of the significance of the surveys, and I really didn't care. The students were there to learn. I was there to teach, not to be popular.

I shook my head, again.

"Your labs, August. Your labs," she squealed, grinning like an opossum eating crap.

The spike of her voice startled me and I reeled back. Hell, she was going to nail me for incompetence. That was the only thing I could think of. I try my best to give the little brats opportunities to learn and they just spit it back in my face.

"The students love your labs."

She stood there with her hands pressed together as if praying and the smile revealed more teeth than I had ever seen at one time in the mouth of a witch. And I sat there in absolute shock of hearing what I thought I didn't hear.

"Isn't it great?" She squealed again. "The students are really liking your physics labs."

Did she expect gratitude or just a simple reply? Or something else? I tried something else.

"Well, I do expect them to learn something. And if it happens to be enjoyable for them, well, so much the better. And, I'm really not sure if my students would have made such favorable comments if I had been more careful so as to prevent some of the... mishaps."

At times my humility astounds me. I thought carefully about what I had just said and for an instant I thought the words came from another source. But being the only two people in the room, it must have been me. Her sudden exultation puzzled me and I began to study various scenarios of this meeting while she rambled on in an unrepressed state of excitement. Finally she paused long enough to exhibit some signs of rationality and I broke in.

"Excuse me, but what is this all really about?"

"Oh, yes."

She calmly put her hands flat on her desk and looked at me straight on.

"I guess I really didn't tell you about that, did I?"

"Tell me about what?"

"You see, there has been talk about your effectiveness at Hartmann and, of course, being the head of the department, I was obligated to verify or dispute the claims."

"Wait a minute," I burst in. "You mean I was about to be sacked?"

My humility transcended the common bound of self-effacement and I found myself in a dream. I was falling through the air toward the sordid depths of poverty.

"Well, I wouldn't go so far as to say that," she said.

She contorted her nose in thought and took a deep breath.

"We just like to keep tabs on anyone who is new here. You are on probation, after all. And we really don't expect everyone we hire to adapt easily to teaching in this environment. I mean, every college has its own way of doing things and we just like to make sure our faculty is more or less consistent with the philosophy and goals of the college."

Since I had already determined that the goals of Hartmann College were suspect and the philosophy was nuts, I let her explanation pass and, instead, concentrated on her gestures. Her hands were nervously working a pencil back and forth through her fingers. This could be good, but it had also been bad on occasion.

"So, why are you telling me all of this?"

"I just wanted to let you know how proud I am of your efforts here at Hartmann. This sort of thing makes the department look good, so naturally I am pleased with the results of the survey."

That meant she was getting credit for it. I would get nothing except a useless pat on the back.

"Thank you for the vote of confidence," I mumbled, trying not to sound condescending, but I think my upturned nose revealed my arrogance.

"I am curious about something, though," she said.

There it was. The real reason for the meeting. My muscles instinctively contracted and my grip on the arm of the chair tightened, ready to lunge for the door if necessary.

"Yes?"

"We usually have a very large request for physics equipment. I'm used to seeing expensive equipment on requisition and replacement parts, and such. Well, I mean we can't afford to actually buy it, you know. But that shouldn't prevent you from requesting it. But you're not even doing that. How are you managing the lab without it?"

My relief at her simple observation released the knots in my muscles and set my ego soaring. This was my chance to fully explain my approach to physics education. If I could make her a believer in my philosophy, maybe I could gain her support for changing the entire physics program to a problem-based course. I began my presentation and she listened with nervous energy thinking, I suppose, that I might actually know what I was talking about.

I summed it all up and prepared to rest my case. "What it all amounts to is that I don't need the complicated and expensive equipment to teach a physics lab. Common, ordinary items are quite enough."

"So, we have all of this expensive equipment over there that nobody's using?"

"Well, some of it I use, if it actually works, and depending on what I want them to learn. Much of the equipment I used for demonstrations during lecture. That way they don't have to worry about how to use it. They can just enjoy the results of it."

"August, that is just wonderful. I don't think anyone really understood what you were going to do with this program."

There was my chance to jump in and pitch my objective. I had a dozen things ready to say. I couldn't summon one of them. I just nodded, basking in the radiance of praise, and still trying to think of what I wanted to say.

"Well, August, I don't want to keep you. You surely would like to get home."

"There is one other thing I would like to discuss with you, however," I said.

Her mouth fell into an inquisitive line across her face, no longer a smile; almost a frown.

"The success I've had with physics is not limited to just the labs. The labs and lecture really go hand-in-hand. In fact, recent studies have shown that if the lecture and lab are combined, students learn better because they are discovering for themselves what it is they're learning."

"I'm not sure I follow you."

Here is where I unleashed my performance expounding the great plan. She listened as intently as I talked.

"Look, I can do some more research and give you some information on it. I know this can't be done overnight. It would take at least two semesters to make it happen. But that's plenty of time for us to massage the schedule."

"Well, you get me the information and we'll see."

I got up to leave, content with my presentation.

"Take care of your eye. I know it must hurt."

I quickly left before she changed her mind about physics. I didn't mention the money it would take to set up the new program. We didn't have it.

As I walked out of her office, I was thinking I could have lost my job. I could have been poverty-stricken before I even got a good start in my educational career. As if someone pulled the rug out from under my clumsy feet. The thought bore down on me with every step away from Claudia's office. I could have been fired. I would have failed. There I was, expecting students to hustle for a grade and, hell, I might not have made it myself.

The meeting with Claudia aroused my ego and I felt I had to do something to further the cause of higher education. It was smoldering under a blanket of apathy and ignorance. The problem was not a small one, and it did not affect just the imbecilic lives in Elkridge. It reached over the entire nation. I would have to do something. Something grand. Something that would reach the masses. Then I remembered Samantha Crumb.

Smantha's request for an article needled my ego to the point that I had to do it. The sacrosanct visage of academia had enjoyed enough languor in its mire of intellectual squalor. It was time for a change. I somehow felt that I would be able to do that. The written word is, as the old adage goes, mightier than the sword. However, my own experience has proven that one must ascertain the potential of the sword's threat before relying on mere prose as a viable strategy. Words are easily cut with the dullest of weapons.

Notwithstanding my own reservations, I embarked on the task of writing a firsthand critique of the sad state of education as we know it in America. With my self-endowed sense of academic prowess, I had a duty to expound the pitfalls of the secondary education system. After all, it was, in large part, responsible for the defective misfits that graced the classrooms of colleges and universities. Especially, Hartmann. And that same institution groomed the student to expect coddling and a supplied him with a plethora of excuses for why he should not have to exert effort to learn. In order to function with the expectation of a productive citizen, one must grow out of the "me" and "my" mindset and into the awareness of "one for all" and "all for one."

So, with the main thrust of the article aimed toward the heart of secondary education, I would be able to deliver a second blow with an in-depth documentary of how these same students either succeed or collapse in the small college environment. I could single-handedly awaken the public from a long and deep sleep and turn its eye toward the future, as we might know it. Or, not know it, as the case might be. I had no shortage of disappointments to convey to the innocence that lurked beyond the ivy walls, like fools that wasted away in a continuum of ignorance that perpetuated itself by fear of the unknown.

It was just before six when I finished the article. I had blasted through it like a rocket. I fired off the article to Samantha in an e-mail. The chimes struck the evening hour and my energy, sucked dry by the demands on my intellect, struck an evening low. Even the glory I had received from the stimulating pat on the back from Claudia could not resurrect my attitude. I went home to dwell on Dr. Damascus and prepare for midterm exams.

Chapter 27

I read the letter that summoned me to Dr. Tipton's office, written on college letterhead and signed in an embellished and effeminate script. After blowing through the innuendos concerning my qualifications as an instructor, I read the part about "neglecting your responsibility as a model for the students." I could take my pulse by merely counting the throbs in my head. And the part concerning my "failure to follow policy" struck a deeper nerve, since I had no idea what policy I supposedly did not follow. But what really toasted my cookies was the insinuation that I was bullying my students. Then I saw Cleeta Shoaven's name near the bottom.

Immediately after entering Dr. Tipton's outer office, a wave of nausea washed over me. Not because of anxiety or fear. I wasn't at all worried about the meeting because I knew it was going to go only one way: mine. A small file box bulging with papers pointing this way and that managed to find a home among the dense population of dreadful figurines on the secretary's desk. I winced at the gaudy wall hangings and kitsch that loomed over the room like macabre circus posters in a church sanctuary. The farther into the room I got, the worse my stomach tossed. I wondered if that office was what the inside of a mental ward might look like.

I stopped in front of the secretary, a prissy black woman. No brown or coffee color. Just black. With astonishing mahogany hair, purple lip gloss, and matching eye shadow that had apparently been applied with a roller instead of the small brush that comes in the plastic case. I didn't consider myself to be prejudiced. I suppose few people consider themselves prejudiced. It was the orange dress, though, tight and suggestive, that alarmed me to the possibility that I might be prejudiced, after all.

While she was staring at my left eye, I identified myself and she alerted Dr. Tipton that I had arrived. I was told to "enter."

"Dr. Tipton," I said approaching a huge, almost black desk, grotesquely carved in a floral motif. Had I not been standing, I might not have recognized the head and shoulders that peeked from behind the massive affair, since they were also black. I wondered why the administration at Hartmann liked large desks. She appeared much differently than when I had met her in Dr. Gaines' office. It seemed odd that a person as short as she would not use a cushion of some sort in her chair.

"Professor Lane," she said bluntly, looking up at me. "Thank you for coming." Then she also noticed my eye. "What happened to you?"

I had failed to notice before, probably because I was preoccupied with my injury, but her voice shot at the air like steel pellets against a cast iron pot. I wondered if there was one woman on the campus, aside from Mary, who had a normal voice. She did not invite me to sit, but I did, anyway.

"A minor altercation. Nothing serious."

"I see. Well, I'll get right to the point. I have received a complaint from one of your students."

She picked up a paper and held it in short stubby fingers tipped with vermillion nails that clashed dramatically, at least within my own sense of fashion, with the green and orange bracelets that were embedded in plump wrists. She rested her arms on the desk, which put them at her shoulder level like small girl sitting at the dinner table without a booster seat.

"A Miss Cleetah Shoaven."

I said nothing, but looked at her with as much disinterest as I could manage.

"Miss Shoaven claims that you confiscated her cell phone and threw it out of the window of your classroom."

I sat motionless and still said nothing. I tried not to even blink. She squinted her eyes slightly as if annoyed. I still didn't blink.

"Professor Lane, this is a very serious charge. If her phone had been damaged, the college would have been responsible for replacing it. And if someone had picked it up, they could have made hundreds of calls, running up Miss Shoaven's phone bill that the college might also have been liable for, not to mention personal information she might have had on the phone could have been compromised."

I blinked slowly, crossed my legs, and turned up my nose slightly. I still said nothing.

"You have violated this school's policy of student respect, you have risked the security of a student's personal property, and I consider your actions to be nothing less than bullying the student."

I'm sure the incident was merely an excuse for retaliation over the tongue lashing I gave her in Dr. Gaines' office. The intense pressure on my ego began to squeeze out a bit of anger. I managed to contain it.

"Fortunately," she said, looking at me from the tops or her eyes, which was difficult for her given the shortness of her neck. "Miss Shoaven was able to find her phone undamaged."

I nodded in the affirmative and crossed my arms. I still said nothing. She dropped the paper to the desk and glared at me.

"Professor Lane, are you listening to me?"

I was not able to determine from the numerous rings on her fingers if she was married, but from the tone of her voice I was fairly certain she had children. Since she asked a direct question, I pretty much had to say something in response.

"Yes, Dr. Tipton. I've heard every word you said."

"Then why don't you say something?"

"Did Miss Shoaven tell you why I confiscated her cell phone and threw it out the window?"

"Well… ah… no. She didn't."

"You didn't bother to ask?"

Her eyes narrowed atop the chubby cheeks and fell to the paper.

"No, Professor. I didn't."

"Allow me to fill in the missing details."

I sat back in my chair and rested my hands at the ends of the chair's arms.

"On two previous occasions, Miss Shoaven violated *my* class policy by using her cell phone during class. This policy is clearly stated in the syllabus and all students, including Miss Shoaven, were made aware of it on the first day of class. On the first occasion, I warned her about using the phone in class and asked her to turn it off. On the second occasion, I took the phone and kept it during class, returning it to her afterward. The third occasion was too much and I got rid of it."

Dr. Tipton seemed to rise a bit in her chair, enough so that I could distinguish the presence of breasts that apparently had been resting on the desk all the time.

"I consider Miss Shoaven's actions to be nothing less than total disregard for this school's policy, bullying the instructor, as well as, disruptive to the rest of the class."

I forced myself not to blink or move any part of my body except my mouth. I wanted to be certain that she would not be distracted from hearing what I had to say.

"In fact, I sent your office a report of her behavior after the second incident. I received no response. When the third incident occurred, I assumed there would be no action taken on your part to correct the situation, so I took matters into my own hands."

She seemed to swell up and her eyes glowed from a kind of blaze that I suppose came from the anger behind them.

"If anyone has violated a policy, Dr. Tipton, it is most certainly Miss Shoaven. I have an obligation to keep order in my classroom. If acceptable measures don't work, I will use whatever measures I deem appropriate. And Miss Shoaven appears to be impervious to policy. So I must resort to other methods."

"I never received any report from you," she said, her glare reflecting off the desktop.

"I assure you, I sent the report. I might suggest that you look on your secretary's desk. Her in-box seemed to be pretty well stuffed."

She immediately picked up the phone and called her secretary.

"Shawndra, did you receive a report from Professor Lane about a disciplinary problem in the last few days?"

Her face had not strayed from the glower that seemed to fit so well on it.

"That's all right," she barked. "I'll wait."

Her stubby hand clamped the phone against her ear while her offensive eyes kept watch on mine. Then she stared into the receiver and put it back to her ear.

"When did you get that?" Her face was sheer anger. "Well, you get that right in here. Now," she said. Pellets hitting a pan, again.

She slammed down the phone and watched the door while twisting the bracelets around her arm.

The secretary burst through the door in a half run, attempting to manage her portly body as well as she could in the orange dress that almost hobbled her at the knees. I failed to notice this before because she was sitting behind her desk. She wobbled to the desk, dropping my report in front of Dr. Tipton. Then she immediately turned and wobbled out of the office.

Dr. Tipton picked up the report and scanned it. "I guess you were right, Professor Lane."

That was all I was to receive from Dr. Tipton. Not even an actual apology. In fact, she dismissed me without so much as a thank you. On the way out, I passed by the secretary with make-up and tried not to smile too much. I figured that, under the circumstances, smiling might be a sign of prejudice. And I still didn't think I was prejudiced.

I walked past Dr. Hartmann's statute. Or, where it used to be. I saw a smile on his face. A different smile. One of contentment, perhaps. He surely must have been proud of me. My outstanding performance in the face of adversity had reeled him in. As much as I hated confrontation, I have to admit that my delight was more than just a passing pleasure. I was enthralled with triumph. And that was something I had tasted little of in the last three years. I gloated all the way to my office.

*****

"Stan, I figured you'd be gone."

He usually left the office by four each day. He did not say anything right away. When I sat at my desk, he finally came over and lowered himself into the guest chair like a stork trying to squat. His heavy face did not bear good humor.

"August, I got wind of an impending disaster."

I knew what he was going to say. Miss Parker had almost become a daily issue in my battles, like an enemy tank on the prowl for my whereabouts.

"The sexual harassment hearing is scheduled for ten-thirty in Dr. Gaines' office a week from Tuesday. I understand it's informal. Just a meeting with some interested parties."

I sunk back into my chair. "Oh, that."

I had not been thinking about the hearing and, with the mention of it, even the chimes that bellowed out across campus did nothing to relieve the sudden pang of fear that struck like the blow of an executioner's axe.

"You said informal." I said.

"That's what I hear. I was surprised that it wasn't going to be a full-fledged inquiry."

"Hmm, this is peculiar. You know, that tells me they probably don't have much. Maybe they're hoping I'll hang myself."

"Well, pal, just be careful."

"Right now, I can't very well be anything else. I suppose I'll get a letter soon."

He got up to leave.

"Stan."

He turned around, putting on his jacket.

"Thanks."

He nodded and left. Then the fear slowly gave way to indignation. And that slowly gave way to anger. And then I was pissed. I was going to get that little bitch. She was not going to win. I knew what was at stake and much of the damage would already have been done. I had to concentrate on strategy and minimize that damage. But I needed information. What did they actually have on me?

Since I hadn't yet formally received notice of the complaint, it was still in the initial stage. That would give me a little bit of time to do some snooping. I expected to see something delivered to my mailbox soon. Dr. Tipton would most likely turn the affair over to the Dean of Academic Services. So, that must be the reason for the early meeting with Dr. Gaines that Mary had told me about. I really needed to know what was going to happen in the meeting with Gaines and Damascus. And I needed to know how Mary really felt about me. I got the idea that she was suspicious and might actually believe that I was having an affair with the little tramp. What would I do about that? And what was Dr. Damascus' part in all of this?

Surely, Dr. Gaines would have some documents in his office pertaining to the hearing. Mary would probably have access to them. She could read them and relay that information to my already frayed mind. No one would know that I knew. I could put together an expedient defense. They wouldn't be expecting that. Yes, that would redirect suspicion to some other entity. I would be exonerated and would regain my status as a respected member of academia, as smudged as it was.

While I wallowed in the anticipation of victory, Mary flashed in and out of my mind. What about her? I could not put her to such shameful service. How could I have even thought about it? I would be using her like a shovel to dig a ditch. I was slipping into the clutches of my own vile ego. My God! Had my marriage also been so tainted?

Guilt clouded my walk through the campus like a violent storm ripping at the tattered shreds left of my dignity. Gloom seemed to possess each face I passed on the sidewalk, a heavy, ugly shadow that hid the innocence and admiration from my pensive eyes.

It was there, before Dr. Hartmann's station of prominence, that propriety overtook my ominous purpose and I decided that Mary would have no part in any clandestine activity. I, alone, would bear the responsibility.

That evening was warm for October and I sat on my sofa again, under the ceiling fan, naked, and graded the GPS mid-term exams from Boyd Atkins. The lowest score was a C. There was only one. The rest were A's and B's. I was pleasantly surprised. Then I had to wonder why my other students didn't perform as well. The generational thing came to mind. The students in the prison were at least old enough to have been out of school for a few years, if they had ever gotten out of school. So they had more experience than my other students. The kind of experience that sharpens the awareness and leads to success. At least the uniforms they wore did not antagonize my contempt for modern youth that swaddled themselves in tattered clothes and bare midriffs.

Chapter 28

All of the morning GPS students were in class on time except the athletes. I yanked the stack of quizzes from my notebook and the moaning began.

"This isn't fair," came from a back corner of the room.

"You should give us some warning," came from a young lady in front.

"I didn't get a chance to study last night. Can I take a make-up?" From another young man.

"I need feedback from all of you about the class," I said. "I need to know if you're having problems with any of the concepts. You rarely speak during class, so I don't know. This quiz will give me some idea, at least, where you stand."

The mumbling continued until they all discovered that the quiz wasn't really as bad as they might have feared. The quiz was, in fact, almost a joke. If they had even read the chapter title they would have answered the two questions.

Just as the last quiz paper was put on my desk, the athletes swaggered in like a procession from the World Olympics.

"Good morning, gentlemen," I said. "You just missed a quiz."

"Can we take it?" The same one asked.

"Had you been to class on time you could have." I said.

"But, we couldn't help it." One of the others said.

"If I can be here on time, so can you." I told him.

New grumbling arose while the parade marched to the back of the room and took their seats. The vivacity that normally charged my lectures fell to the ominous stares from the seven pairs of eyes at the back of the room. They watched my every move as if measuring it. Sizing it up to mount an attack. But, soon their drawn faces and helpless expressions played on my guilt. I then thought that they just might have a good reason for being late. Maybe I should check with their coach.

The afternoon section of GPS went pretty much the same. The only difference was that I had six more tardy athletes who might be on the verge of vengeance. If I allowed the situation to continue, they would gain little from the class. I resolved to discover what was going on with them.

*****

"Yeah," the voice grumbled over the phone.

"Coach Mendez," I said.

"Yeah?" The surly voice said. "That's me."

"This is August Lane." I waited for some indication that he understood who I was. There was none. "Math and science."

Still no response.

"I have several of your athletes in my GPS classes."

I could hear a repeated thud in the background. Maybe a student's head hitting the wall?

"I wondered if you had a few minutes to discuss their progress in this class."

"Are they flunking?"

"Well, no. Not yet."

"Then what's the problem?"

"They're not flunking now," I said. "But if the situation continues, they might."

"I'm here till four-thirty."

It was almost four. I had time to just make it.

"I'll be there in a minute."

The phone clicked and I was left with a dial tone. I launched myself toward the gymnasium.

I had never dealt with a coach on this level before. The succinct phone conversation did not suggest a productive meeting. I pictured Mr. Mendez as a psychopath stalking the dugout ready to launch a barrage of obscenities and violent gestures with each error made by a player on the field. But I had been through worse. My hesitation grew as I approached the gym.

Each building has its own personality. The Math Science Building was old. It looked old. It felt old when you walked in it. It even smelled old. The musty fragrance of wood saturated with nearly a century of human essence. The erosion of floors and steps from young feet treading them, the seasoned carvings in woodwork and toilet stalls embellished by happenstance artists, and the sounds emanating from deep within the structure made the building seem almost alive. It all exuded an aura of life and history.

But not all buildings lend themselves to such presence of inspiration. The gymnasium was one of those buildings. Even before I opened the door I was assaulted with the odor of musty towels. Then the swing of the door unleashed the pungency of the air that had been saturated with the sweat of thousands of young bodies hurling themselves down the basketball courts, pumping their muscles to superhuman sizes in the weight room, and distributing soaked towels and clothing at random in the locker rooms. The gymnasium definitely had a personality. Its acrid bouquet, although sweet to those of athletic endeavors, would have been offensive to those of more reticent lifestyles. As for myself, bittersweet memories lingered as I listened to the echoes of my shoes on the glistening floor. I looked for Mr. Mendez's office.

"Lane."

The sound of my name startled me and I jerked my head toward its source. There, through the door on the right just behind me sat a large, dark-skinned man with dark hair, wild, like he was sitting in a swirling wind. He looked straight at me with piercing brown eyes.

"Come on in."

It was the same surly voice that intimidated me on the phone.

"Most folks don't find me so easy, so I watch for them. You're pretty good, though. It took you less than eight minutes. And that's from the Math Science Building. That's where your office is, right?"

"Yes," I said, though not sure if I was actually in the right place. The profuse verbiage was not in character with the man who yielded such a terse phone conversation.

"Sit down," he ordered.

I sat.

"So, how deep have the boys buried themselves?"

"Oh, yes," I said, bringing myself back to the present. "I have two groups, seven in the morning GPS class and six in the afternoon."

"Yeah, I know."

"They're not too bad off right now, but they are falling behind. I think much of it is due to the fact that they show up late for class."

"Oh, that." He waved me off like I had just coughed up a lung after winning the 880 run. "Hell, what difference can a few minutes make?"

I'm sure he noticed the anger in my eyes since they stared directly at his as if the fire inside me could roast his big ass like the sacrificial cow served at their annual sports banquet.

"The same difference a few hundredths of a second can make in a race." I stared him down without flinching. "It means the difference between winning and losing. Your boys are losing."

His eyes narrowed as his head raised and he looked at me with stern concentration. I wasn't sure if the silence meant that he was plotting some way to dismember my meager body and wave the pieces in the air as a tribute to his quest for athletic dominance over education, or if he might actually be considering the meaning of what I said.

"It's that important, huh?"

I don't know if he saw my body heave a sigh of relief, but I took advantage of the situation.

"It's that important. This is a tough class. The slightest difficulty in reading, especially technical material, will put them at a severe disadvantage. If they can understand the material I present in lecture and pay attention to the demos I do in class, they can overcome part of that difficulty. The problem is, most of them don't realize it. And they're not there to see all of it."

"You're serious, aren't you?" He asked.

"Very." I gave him my tough look. The "go-to-hell" look I use on my students to bluff them into playing the game. It rarely worked, but it gave me something to do while I quietly suffered the humiliation of being beaten by their apathy.

"These athletes are good students," I continued. "Well, they can be. They're bright and inquisitive. It's just that their interests don't lie in science. They have to realize that what they're trying to accomplish in their careers as athletes is all about science. The more they understand about it, I think the better athletes they will be."

His face softened and he looked at me like he was seeing some bizarre phenomenon.

"You know, most of you professors come in here ranting and raving about the sorry-assed athletes and about how big of losers they are. They threaten me with flunking them."

I returned his inquisitive look. And then I could picture some of the faculty leveling such wild threats to the coaches.

"Mr. Mendez, I'm here to teach, just like you are. I'm responsible in large part for the knowledge these kids leave here with, just like you want them to leave as better athletes. I'm sorry if you're disappointed that I don't spar with you over their dilemmas with honor versus intellect. They should have both. And they can have it if they just get some sort of push from your end."

"Okay, Lane." He leaned forward and his face brightened. "I'll be honest with you. These kids have a PE class right before your classes.

The coaches have been keeping them late because they aren't perform-
ing up to par. I'll talk with them and make sure they get out in time to
make your class."

The sudden heaviness of guilt pulled at me and I realized I had
been a jerk. I should have known the athletes had some reason for being
late. There was still that driving stereotype of smart-assed punks. I had
to get rid of that. No more quizzes.

"Mr. Mendez, I will look forward to a successful semester for all
of the athletes in my classes. I want them to succeed as much as you
do. After all, if I flunk too many students, they sort of wonder about
my competence as an instructor."

"I imagine the same way they feel about my competence as a
coach if we lose too many games."

"Thank you," I said, getting up to leave.

He leaned back casually, and picked up a baseball. He threw it
against the brick wall where it bounced back to his desk and he caught
it.

"You're all right, Lane."

The ball hit the wall again. I nodded and left. So, it wasn't really
a student's head, after all.

*****

Green lights glared in the darkness over the empty ringing that
echoed through the room. I knew something was going on, I just didn't
know what. The lights. The ringing. Then my eyes cleared. Was that a
three on the clock? 3:17? The phone.

"Hello?"

"Professor Lane?"

A woman's voice. I could hear chimes in the background. How
grand.

"Yeah."

"Professor, I'm sorry to wake you. This is Wanda Cooper. Campus
security."

"Oh, hi, Wanda. Notwithstanding the three-seventeen on my
clock, is there something I can do for you?"

"You can do plenty. You can come down here and shut off these
infernal chimes."

"What chimes?"

"The ones you fixed. Here at the college."

"Why?"

"Don't you hear that? They playin' over and over and over. That's what you hear. I done got a call from the president. He say get those things fixed."

I listened carefully. The melody played continuously. A drone of the Westminster tune repeating itself like a chronic cough.

"Okay. I'll be right there."

I put on some old jeans and a sweatshirt and rushed to the campus risking a reckless driving charge. Even campus security was not a deterrent as I pulled past the parking spaces and drove up the maintenance access ramp and into the grounds of the Math Science Building. I parked behind the small group of observers who were watching the top of the building. Wanda was waiting for me.

"Glad you could make it."

"I'm not sure I am," I said. "How long have they been playing?"

"Let's just say the Pres probably didn't get much sleep."

"Oh."

After I got the key to open the lock, I dove into the building and ran up the stairs with Wanda trudging after me. The once pleasant knell of the chimes had become obnoxious bonging. As much as I had become attached to them, the continual toll was grating on my hazy mind. I could only wonder what the president was thinking about me.

After unlocking the door to the Cop Room, it took no less than one second to find the power button to the computer and press and hold it. The computer died and the chiming stopped immediately, but the echoes reverberated in my head for several minutes while the cheers from the small crowd outside hung in the musty air of the equipment room. When my head cleared there was nothing but emptiness, a sullen regret for having killed the source of my inspiration. Now it lay there, in a metal box, dead to the world. I felt like I had been beaten.

"You sure fixed that," Wanda said, her white teeth dominating her dark, plump face in the shadow of her cap.

"Yup."

"Well, I think maybe we can all get some sleep, now."

"I'm glad someone can."

Without knowing what went wrong, I thought it best to leave it alone until I could analyze the situation. If it did it once, it would certainly do it again. I didn't want it to happen again that night. My good name had been dragged through enough mud. It didn't need to be stomped on as well.

But, as much as I favored safety, I couldn't stand it. I had grown to rely on the chimes. They made my oppression bearable. They gave me strength to face each day. They were my inspiration. I turned on the computer.

Once up and running, I tested the program with the speakers disconnected. No problem. I reset it for the current time and let it fly. The door locked behind me and I trudged out to my car. The group was disbanding, waving kudos to me as I started the engine and drove back home to a restless night. I unplugged my phone.

Chapter 29

The article I had promised Samantha Crumb was intended to be an exposé of the stormy secondary education system and the cloudy future of higher education. By the time I had finished pouring out my frustration, the document had grown into a prize-winning piece of literature. Or, that was my opinion of it. Although I used self-restraint, I had to include some finger-pointing to accurately convey the mood of the local secondary schools systems and to settle any doubt as to the origin of the problem. I explained the reason for the legions of mathematically illiterate people walking the streets of Elkridge and populating the campus of Hartmann College. I showed no mercy, even to the parents of the incapacitated students who chose to relinquish responsibility for their children's futures to the maladroit classroom environment. I thought that would surely awaken some latent sense of duty and responsibility in the local population.

I had not spared the local colleges, either. I exposed the lack of integrity in maintaining the high standards of academic excellence, if there ever were any, which had been eroded by the indifference of administrative dimwits who consider the almighty dollar more important than a student's education. So, I had laid bare the ills of modern education in a nation that once was the epitome of learning for the world to imitate. All in a tastefully composed critique.

I submitted the article to Ms. Crumb and waited for the accolades to roll in. In the meantime, mid-term exams would fill the rest of the week and took much of my time to organize. At least the exams would spare me the embarrassment of lecture mishaps. They would not spare me the student resentment that normally followed an exam.

I had picked up a copy of the "Clodhopper Dispatch" on the way into the Math Science Building that Friday morning. I was surprised by the professional edge given to a college newspaper. I revered in the notoriety she had given my article. It exploded on the front page in all of its glory: "Generation of Misfits." I read it several times. My ego swelled larger with each read.

Late in the morning, Samantha called in a state of distress.

"August, I know I can call you by your first name," she said almost as one word, "I've done something terrible."

I immediately thought that perhaps she had committed some error with my article in the newspaper. No mind, I figured. It read just fine the way it was.

"What's the problem?"

"I just met with Dr. Dennison. He's the president of the college, you know. Well, he wanted to see me about the paper. I thought he was going to congratulate our newspaper staff on an excellent publication this month. And that's where the problem is."

I failed at that point to realize why it would be a problem for the president of the college to congratulate her on the fine newspaper she had just published, what with my article on the front page, and all.

"Yes?" I prompted.

"He instructed me to see that all of the issues of the newspaper were pulled from the distribution boxes and to retract the article you wrote."

The words seemed to pull the blood from me like a vacuum. I don't know how long I sat there unable to speak, but I eventually became aware of Samantha's voice on the phone.

"So, what's wrong with it?" I asked.

"It was the article you submitted. Dr. Dennison said that it represented a personal attack on the local community and did not reflect the views of the college. He said it reflected poorly on the college as an institution of higher learning and betrayed its mission. He said…"

I sat there, stunned, at loss for words. It was completely beyond my capacity to comprehend why my article would have been censored. In that kind of situation, I can usually run through several scenarios in my mind and find at least one that would be suspect to the circumstances. However, my mind was devoid of any circumstances that might have caused such a reaction. By this time she was almost blathering. I broke in.

"Sam, I don't understand."

"I really don't either, but I have to get those newspapers back."

"Okay, look. I'm not entirely sure what the hell is going on, but I'll pick up what papers I can find here in the Math Science Building and anywhere close."

"Oh, that would be a big help."

"What do you want me to do with them?"

"Just stash them someplace safe and I'll collect them later."

"I can do that."

"August, I'm scared."

"Samanatha, you didn't write the article," I said. "I did. If there's going to be repercussions, they should fall on me. After all, this is a college. Independent thought and idealism should be encouraged here."

"August, you don't understand."

I heard sobbing. Whenever I hear sobbing from a woman to whom I'm talking, I know I have missed something.

"What's wrong?"

"Oh, August," she almost wailed, "you're going to want to kill me. I sent the article to the Elkridge Press. It's probably already on the newsstand.

I was beyond stunned. She actually sent the article to the local newspaper. I knew she was somewhat of a twit, but I never dreamed her affliction was so severe. I caught glimpses of my world ebbing from reality and melting into the vast ocean of the unemployed. During the moment of silence I tried to think of what to say.

"Okay, I guess that's that. We'll just have to endure whatever comes of it for now. I imagine I will be getting call from Dr. Dennison."

"Oh, I'm sorry, August. I didn't realize you were waiting on a call."

"No, Samantha, I wasn't waiting on a call. It's just that if the president called you, he's damned sure going to call me."

"Oh, I see what you mean. Well, I'll let you go so you can talk to him. I mean, if the president were to call you, of course you should talk to him. It would be an insult if you –"

"Sam," I broke in. "Sam, I know what you mean. I'll talk to you later."

The line went dead and I held the receiver for a short time wondering if she really did hang up. The instant I replaced the handset, the phone rang.

"Hello, this is August."

"Professor Lane?"

"Yes."

"This is Janice Demereaux, secretary to President Dennison."

"Yes?"

"Professor Lane, Dr. Dennison would like to meet with you."

"Okay. Can you tell me the nature of the meeting, ah, just in case I might need to bring some notes along with me?"

"Yes. He wants to discuss the article you wrote for the college newspaper."

"I figured that would be it. I'll be right over."

The grilling finished just before noon. I was sent on my way before the coals burned out. I suspected the old man figured I had roasted enough. After all, I was the only person on campus who was qualified to teach physics. Had he fired me, he would have had a hell of a problem determining what to do with my physics class.

The encounter with Dr. Dennison left me in a particularly feisty mood. He had accused the faculty of insubordination, conspiring to defraud the college, and counting me liable. I carefully explained that the article specifically stated that the content was my own opinion and was in no way an official reflection of the opinions of the staff or faculty at Hartmann College. I also explained that a college environment should foster free thinking and exploration. He reluctantly agreed in theory, but was stern in his criticism of the article. Even though I would suffer no legal repercussions from the college, I had certainly fallen out of favor with Dr. Dennison. The incident with the chimes didn't help, either.

The confrontation had also inflamed my passion for arresting the spread of ignorance and laying a secure foundation for the future of our country. My God, it had spread even to the executive ranks of academia. My cause was confirmed. No path would be left unexplored. Not even the clandestine activities of the faculty at Hartmann College. If the good Doctor Hartmann could not be present to oversee the business of the college, the least I could do was conserve the old boy's legend.

The evening passed while I sat on my sofa drowning my ego in George Killian's Irish Red, a fine beer if there ever was, and wondering about the plot woven by Miss Parker. What did she have on her mind? Did someone put her up to it? The warming beer was producing violent images in my mind. I wished I'd had Glenlivet. Thinking is always better under the influence of a good single-malt.

When I am forced into a situation where I have to do much thinking, it usually turns sour. My examination of the evening's events made me question my own common sense. No matter about it that evening. I'd had enough. Tomorrow I would be in Oklahoma City for a curriculum transfer meeting, anyway. At least there I would have a chance to schmooze and find out if some of my colleagues had information that might help.

Chapter 30

It rained during the entire trip to Oklahoma City. The motor pool car I was assigned had an inoperable heater, windshield wipers that were little more than remnants of rubber that flailed from metal arms, and a driver's door that would not completely close. I arrived at the curriculum meeting late and wet and in a sour mood. But I didn't let that prevent me from schmoozing folks to learn what I could about Dr. Damascus and Dr. Gaines.

I talked to several faculty member who were acquaintances of the two scoundrels. The mere mention of their names sent their eyes rolling back into their heads. Most had worked with them. No one wanted to again. Some told me why, but most of them wouldn't because they said they didn't use that kind of language. Little was known about Mr. Bartholomew among that crowd, but I was assured that if he chose to associate with either Dr. Gaines or Dr. Damascus, he certainly was not worthy of consideration as a reputable faculty member. And Dr. O'Mally's name was mentioned more than once in concert with Dr. Damascus. I wasn't able to garner much meaning of it, but discussions of her contained serious ethical overtones. All of this from a camaraderie that should have bolstered a peer's reputation instead of slandering it. By the time the meeting was over, I had regained much of my constitution and self-esteem. It had stopped raining and I stepped aboard the cradle of death to return to Elkridge. The fuel gage showed slightly over half of a tank. If necessary, I would stop for fuel closer to Elkridge.

All of this weighed on my anxiety while I shimmied down the road with the blast of air roaring in my ear. The clock on the dash read three-sixteen even though I knew it was past seven because it was already dark. After all, I had just turned on the headlights. Just for the heck of it I reached out to set the clock. As soon as I pressed the button, the display went blank. I pushed again. Nothing. I tried another button. Nothing. I thought I had just broken the clock. In fact, it appeared that the entire dash was broken because all of the lights were out. I couldn't even read the speedometer. The only good fortune I had at that time was that the headlights were still working, notwithstanding the fact that one was illuminating the right shoulder and the other was shining upward into the air like a beacon for alien spacecraft.

So as my ton and a half lump of shuddering steel shot down the highway at, God knows what speed, my hands went nearly numb from restraining the vibrating steering wheel. My hearing was rapidly eroding from the air that roared through the crack in the door. And my agility was being replaced with fatigue. I had not eaten since lunch. I didn't want to eat. Not then. The incessant shaking and vertigo of the darkness would surely have forced any solid contents of my stomach to the floor of the car. And I had enough to contend with. I damned sure didn't need the obnoxious odor of vomit, as well.

The seemingly fourteen-hour round trip, that was actually about three, ended when I bypassed the gas station at the entrance to Hartmann College and heard the chimes while en route to the motor pool to ditch the defective steel turd. I'm not sure, but I would swear that just as I turned off the ignition, the engine seemed to sputter as if it had just exhausted its fuel supply. My only thought at that point was the sweet justice of the maintenance folks having to lug gasoline to the car to get it started again. If it would start at all. Aside from the information about Dr. Gaines and Dr. Damascus I had garnered, the revenge I had exacted on the maintenance crew with the empty fuel tank was the only other product of my journey that had any redeeming value. I felt fortunate to have two such successes to my credit. I could just as easily have come back with nothing. Or less.

As I got out of the car, I still heard the chimes. Even as I walked to my own car, I still heard the chimes. They were stuck again.

I hurried to the Math Science Building and found a gathering of people in front looking up at the roof. Wanda and Dr. Dennison seemed to be having an articulated exchange in front of the door. I approached them.

"Professor Lane, am I glad you're here," yelled Wanda.

Dr. Dennison jerked around with a glare that would have turned any ordinary mortal into stone.

"Professor Lane," he snapped, "I want these chimes stopped immediately."

"Yes sir," I acknowledged. "Right away."

I unlocked the front door and ran up the stairs to the "Cop Room". And since I was in a hurry, of course the key was a difficult fit into the lock. The intensity of the yelling from below increased, becoming more of a chant. The door finally gave way and I reached directly for the computer's power cord and yanked. The death was immediate, right in mid-stroke of the chorus. Then all was silent except for the cheers I heard through the window.

When I returned downstairs, only Wanda was waiting for me. The others, including Dr. Dennison, had gone.

"Professor Lane, I'm sure glad I ain't you tonight."

"Yes, I'm surprised my ears weren't burning."

"They sure would've been on fire if you was here listening to what I was."

"Well, Wanda, you can rest assured that there will be no further interruptions from the chimes tonight. I shut down the computer. I guess I'll leave it at that until I can talk to Ed about a new one."

"Thank the Lord for that," she said. "Have a good evening, Professor."

Being Thursday evening, I had classes the next day but I felt a compelling urge to drown my anxiety, which seemed to linger like a foul odor, in a series of single-malts.

Jim Bob's was busy, which was fine with me because I was in the kind of mood to lose myself in a crowd. Cindy was in excellent form, cavorting with an extremely effeminate couple at the bar.

"Hey, Perfessor," Cindy barked. "I go' one coming right up for ya."

I looked toward the sticky booth and, sure enough, there sat Ricky. I wandered over and invited myself into the seat opposite him.

"You keep strange company, Rick," I said.

"Sure, now that you sat down."

"So, how's the good doctor been treating you?"

"You're referring, of course, to Dr. Hartmann?"

"Yeah," I said. "I think he recently visited the motor pool."

"Hell, I thought that's where he lived." He cut loose with a ditzy laugh.

"I hadn't thought of that. But you know, it would explain a lot."

Cindy bounced to the table with a glass of Glenlivet. A double.

"Hon, I read your mind. You need this."

"Cindy," I said, "you should be a psychiatrist."

She hacked her way back to the bar, convulsing on every other step.

"I take it you're a veteran motor pool patron," I said, gasping from my first sip of some of the finest liquid God allowed man to make, should it ever be proven that there was indeed a god.

"Let's just say that I have endured virtually every form of vehicular torture known to man."

"Well, I think I can dispute that claim. I just survived an excursion in the vehicle from Hell."

Rick was in mid-drink when the mug nearly fell from his hand and he belched out a laugh.

"You poor bastard. It was two-four-three, wasn't it?"

His body convulsed in laughter and by then, everyone was staring at us.

"How the hell did you know?"

"What the hell did you do, buddy? Who did you piss off?"

I had no idea how foolish I looked at the time because I couldn't imagine what he was talking about. I hadn't pissed off anyone. Well, not anyone that was connected with the motor pool. Or, at least not that I knew.

"What are you talking about?" I asked.

"Hell, man, you made someone's shit list." He laughed again. "That particular vehicle is reserved for persona non grata."

I was dumbfounded. Who had I offended in maintenance? If anything, they owed me. I had kept Marney's ass out of the wringer and, unless I had the wrong idea, that in turn also kept everyone else in maintenance secure. Why would they have done such a thing?

I sat in silence sipping the Glenlivet and watching Rick alternate between shaking his head and raring back in a laughing fit. The whisky had lost its edge.

So, I was indeed the fool. I thought it might have been just the peculiar circumstances I often found myself in. But as I deliberated there, in the sticky booth, with the fumes of Glenlivet softening my brain, I realized that I seemed to find myself in those circumstances more often than most people. It was always that way in my marriage, as well. Alexis had called me foolish on occasion. Well, actually, more than that. One of her pet names for me was "The Fool." I thought she was using it as a term of endearment. I really was a fool.

My thoughts deepened as I reflected on why I had married her at all. She had not exactly been a knockout. Nor did she have any particular sense of decorum. And I really can't think of any one thing that had attracted me to her. At that time of my life I had been lonely, much like I was sitting there in Jim Bob's. And therein lay the answer.

Chapter 31

The experience with vehicle two-four-three ate at me like a rat gnawing on a piece of rope. The tension would be relieved once the rope was completely severed, leaving my ego in total disarray. Between calculus and GPS classes, I composed a critical e-mail concerning motor pool vehicles to Claudia, to whom I always copied anything of importance, the Business Office, and Dr. Gaines. I debated about Dr. Dennison. I normally would not have elected to go straight to the president of the college, but the humiliating experience I suffered in two-four-three required some measure of retribution, especially being compounded by the van incident earlier. However, just in case the heat from my murderous article had not cooled from his disposition, and in consideration of the embarrassing incident with the chimes, I elected to omit Dr. Dennison's name from the list.

I read my composition several times, tweaking it here and there for maximum effectiveness. It was direct and to the point. I left nothing to the imagination and barred no holds when I referred to the maintenance group as an intellectually impaired cluster of misfits.

I clicked on send. In few moments the electronic signal would make its way to those who held the power to rectify the dreadful situation. I was feeling quite proud of myself when I noticed that in the address line, instead of Cooper, was the entry, "College Faculty/Staff". The bottom fell out of my ego when I realized that my email had just been sent to every faculty and staff member of Hartmann College. All of them. I had been too quick on the mouse.

My tendency toward haste has entangled me more than once in a morass of carelessness. Even as a child I seemed to have had more than my share of unfortunate accidents, if that's what they really were. At the time I viewed them more as vindictive attempts by God, in case I should someday be disposed to acknowledge His existence, to neutralize the store of sacrilegious words and phrases I used to combat frustration with His world. And now, after my maturity to a full-fledged agnostic, I realize how foolish it was. It wasn't God who was responsible for my misgivings. It was only fate. And, so, what would fate bring to combat my misstep with the e-mail?

I had to wait no longer than ten minutes. The phone rang.

"August!"

It was a woman. I could normally recognize a voice on the phone, but the yelling rendered it indiscernible because of the unusual pitch and texture.

"Yes," I said, remaining calm.

"August, what are you doing?"

I still had no idea who it was. I wasn't used to answering calls with such impatience, anger, or whatever it was on the other end.

"What do you mean?"

"Are you nuts? You sent this e-mail to every faculty member on campus."

"Oh, that. Well, if you have something to say, you might as well be clear about it."

"August, August."

There it was. "This is Mary, isn't it?"

"Why yes. I thought you recognized my voice."

"I wasn't aware that the frantic voice belonged to you. It's still a very nice voice, by the way. Are you mad at me?"

After a longer than normal pause, she said, "No, August. I'm not mad at you."

"Well, you seem so… I don't know, mad lately?"

"I'm sorry, August. I'm just a little bit confused about your situation, right now."

So, she wasn't mad. She was just… mad. I still had a chance with her.

"So how much damage did the e-mail do at headquarters?"

"You know, this could be more serious than you think."

I had misjudged her. She was really an all right kind of girl. She had a sense of humor. At least, I hoped that's what it was. I think she was actually on my side. I couldn't afford to alienate her. I needed all the help I could get. The edge in her voice seemed to cut right through my lack of acumen.

"Perhaps you're right. What would you suggest I do?"

"Dr. Gaines just called Mr. Zewick at HR. From what little I could hear through the door, they're planning to move up your hearing date. You know, the one about the harassment charge."

"What has this e-mail got to do with that?"

"Everything if you consider that he is looking for a way to get rid of you."

Her words seemed forced, as if she was not telling me something. It lacked the cordial tone to which I was accustomed. And the recurrence of the possibility of unemployment startled me. It seemed to be happening more often.

"Yes, I'm aware that he and Dr. Damascus are cooking up something. I just don't know what."

"Oh my God, August."

Her voice deepened and I felt something very wrong in it. She paused.

"Mary?"

"You don't know about that, do you?"

"Know about what?"

"Oh, I'm sorry. I can't talk about it on the phone."

"You having lunch in the cafeteria?"

"Yes, I can meet you there."

"Okay, I'll see you around twelve-thirty. Maybe we can–"

"He's coming out. Bye."

The phone went dead and I sat there wondering what the hell just happened. Mary Einhorn, mad at me even though she said she wasn't, calling me and offering help. I was confused.

My lackluster GPS lecture did nothing for the students or me. They seemed to be able to sense the path a lecture is going to take long before the instructor. They had their books stowed and were ready to depart twenty minutes before the class was to end. I figured, what the hell? I wasn't doing any good and they weren't listening. I dismissed them and beat a path over to see Dr. Damascus.

While trying to dodge the larger cracks and upheavals of the sidewalk, I saw Shawn Crandall sitting nearby on a bench. I walked over to him. "Mr. Crandall." As I approached, his red eyes became apparent. "Are you all-right?"

The red eyes turned upward and hazily focused on what I think was me. He didn't answer.

"Is something wrong?" I sat down beside him.

He dropped his head and sniffed.

"Did something happen with Professor Bartholomew?"

He snapped his head toward me and stared with a face that held pride, but in a fearsome kind of way. "He did it." He sniffed again. "He did it."

"Did what?"

"He kicked me out of his class."

This wallop in the gut overwhelmed my state of consciousness and a mirage of Dr. Damascus floated there before me, laughing and pointing at me, and bellowing crude insults, castigating me as a callow moron.

"I did what you said," the boy squeaked. Then the tears came.

Somewhere between my contact with the bench and the boy's statement, a rage in me erupted like the fury of a pent-up volcano spewing rills of blistering guilt and incited my reticence into action.

"Shawn, you did nothing wrong. He is not going to get away with this."

I bounded from the bench landing at the door of the administration building in only a few long strides. The stairway, being no contest for my charged state, delivered me to Dr. Damascus' floor. I saw him waddling down the hall toward his office just as I topped the stairs.

"Dr. Damascus," I yelled.

He stopped and looked back toward me. I thought I heard a "humph" as he jerked his head and continued waddling toward his office.

I caught up with him at the door and followed him inside.

"I don't recall inviting you in," he snapped.

"You didn't."

"Then why are you here bothering me?"

The dour voice would have smothered the life out of any good intention. I chose to ignore it and closed the door.

"I know what you're up to, Dr. Damascus. It won't work."

He leaned over his desk. His eyes, full of evil, stared up at me through bristly eyebrows like a demon peering through the tines of his pitchfork.

"I'm sure I have no idea of what you're speaking," he said with a devilish grin.

"Oh, I think you do."

"You're mistaken."

"On the contrary, I'm very much certain. I know about your scheme with Dr. Gaines to eradicate me from the faculty, here."

I thought I saw him flinch while sorting papers on the desk. He fell into his chair.

"I don't scheme, Mr., a... who the hell are you?"

"You know damned well who I am. And I know damned well about your meeting with Dr. Gaines. You're planning to use Miss

Parker's allegations to drive a wedge between me and the college administration."

He did not respond, but smiled even wider. I continued my attack.

"If you persist in this exploit, I am prepared to enlist the testimony of certain students who can provide proof of extortion involving... ah... certain members of the faculty."

The evil in his eyes grew as if fueled by a source of vile energy. His hands quivered and he slowly rose from his chair. I had been confident until then.

"If you dare make such wanton accusations against me or this college I will surely destroy you. My reputation here is above reproach. But you... you smart-assed punk. You are nothing," he said, shaking his jowls.

I stood there slowly succumbing to his influence. My meager attempt at intimidating him was no match for his experience, power, and command. But I did not yield ground.

"Be that as it may, I believe your reign here is about to come to an end."

I don't know where that came from, because fear still lurked behind every word I said. As I left I wanted to be sure I had the last word.

"And, no sir, you will not destroy me. I will survive in any event. But you? You don't have the means to survive."

The inferno behind his rage could have unleashed the flames of Hell on me. I stared back at him, standing my ground. Then the ancient face, wrung with anger, slowly softened into a hint of doubt that begged an answer. He stood there hovering over his desk, a pathetic old man, worn from his own callous service in life. I couldn't feel sorry for the old fart. My fear of his wrath had transformed into another kind. I had felt it before. Just after my wife left me. The gnawing feeling that I had left something undone.

I paused at the top of the stairs wondering what I should do. If I reported the incident with Shawn, I would have to have strong evidence. I had only student testimony. Nothing in writing. Nothing verifiable. Only the word of a few students against that of a highly esteemed cornerstone of Hartmann College. I needed more.

Just as I started down the stairs I heard the elevator door open. As I turned to look back, Dr. O'Mally's head passed by the stairway toward Dr. Damascus' office. She hadn't seen me. Curiosity needled me and I slithered back up the steps and followed O'Mally to the office I had just left. The door closed quickly. I listened from outside.

"You know, Tim, you're going to have to be careful." Her gruff voice was low, but forceful.

"What do you mean?" Snorted Damascus. "I've got that bastard right where I want him."

"Look, I don't think you understand the potential impact of what you're trying to do."

"Hell, Susan, there is no impact. Lane is just another one of those smart-assed sons-a-bitches that thinks he can remake the world by filling these students full of his fancy science crap."

"But you don't understand."

"What's there to understand?" Damascus said. "He's just another pawn to be dealt with."

"I'm afraid that's where you're wrong."

"Susan, have I been wrong yet?"

Pause. "No. Not yet."

"Then what's the worry?"

"You haven't been wrong, yet. But you will. Everyone makes mistakes sooner or later."

Another pause. "What do you mean?" The coarse voice became testy.

"You seem awfully confident in your handling of Barholomew."

Another pause. "Bathololmew?"

"I know about him, Tim."

Pause.

"And you underestimate Professor Lane," she continued. "He has established quite a following here at Hartmann. I've been keeping tabs on his activities. He's gaining respect."

"What in hell are you talking about? I have students lined up for complaints against him, I have evidence of his philandering, further evidence of his sexual harassment of students."

"Like I said, Tim. Be careful. I am also aware of your, ah… escapades with your own students."

"What do you mean by that?"

"I am familiar with the terms of your divorce, Tim. If this situation ever goes any further, I have to warn you that your own behavior might become suspect. We've been friends for a long time. I would hate to see that jeopardized by your foolish behavior."

Then a long pause. "You wouldn't dare. Don't forget I'm the one who got you this job here."

"Just keep an eye on Bartholomew."

Footsteps were coming toward the door and I jumped in a recess in the hall opposite the direction of the stairs. The door slammed and O'Mally's feet clonked down the hall toward the stairs. I cautiously left for my office.

The sketchy conversation I had just overheard frosted the air around me and I sat there in my chair, shivering at something I couldn't even identify. If Dr. O'Mally was involved in this caper, what was her roll? It didn't exactly sound as if she were in charge. More like Dr. Damascus was running amuck. My mind billowed in the wind of befuddlement.

That afternoon, a phone marathon started.

"Professor Lane, I am Martin Worthen. I am an instructor at Cauffburn College."

"Cauffburn," I said. "I'm not familiar with Cauffburn College."

"We're about sixty-five miles south of Elkridge."

"Ah. How can I help you?"

"Actually, I just read your article in the Elkridge Press. My wife works near there, you see, and she likes to peruse their newspaper."

"Oh, I see."

"Anyway, I wanted to commend you on such a gallant stance for education. We too have students coming to us who are very ill prepared for college life."

The conversation that followed included more praise from Mr. Worthen and he vowed to follow up with a similar article about Cauffburn College. All the while I was measuring the weight of responsibility for my untimely prose that would bear upon my reputation. And I wasn't sure of the firmness of the ground beneath me.

There were several more calls from instructors, all in support of my article. Then a different call.

"Is this… ah… Perfessor… ah… Lane?"

The surly male voice conveyed a less than cordial attitude.

"Yes, this is he."

"Well, I just wanted to tell you what I think of you."

I waited, wondering what grand compliment he would render.

"I just wanted you to know that I think you're a real asshole."

I waited again, hoping I had missed something.

"Hey, are you there, asshole?"

"This is Professor Lane, if that's who you mean. What is it that you want?"

"I want you to know that you're an asshole."

"Apparently you're a little slow. You're repeating yourself."

"You know, you're a real dickhead."

"No, I didn't know that because you just said I was an asshole. Which is it? And, how would you know such a thing?"

"Anybody that calls a whole town stupid is a dickhead. You wouldn't know stupid if you saw it."

"You must be referring to the article that appeared in the paper. If that's the case you're probably illiterate as well, because that isn't what I said. Thus, you have just proven the main point of the article."

He hung up. The next call was worse.

"Hey, are you the bastard that wrote that sick bunch of shit in the paper?"

"I haven't read the paper today, so I wouldn't know."

"Well, did you call us a bunch of stupid idiots?"

"The article I wrote did not refer to anyone as stupid or as an idiot, which is redundant, by the way. And since I have no earthly notion who you are, I couldn't very well know if I called you an idiot or not."

"Now you're calling me stupid to my face?"

"Since I can't see your face I hardly think that's possible."

"You smart-assed son-of-a-bitch. I'd sure be careful, if I was you."

"Are you threatening me?"

"I'm just saying you'd better watch were you go and what you do, bud."

"And why is that?"

"Hey, dumbass, there's a lot of folks out hear that hate your guts."

"If this is your natural demeanor, I'm sure there are several people who surely feel the same about you."

"Hey, listen. I got plenty of friends. And we don't need the likes of you telling us we're stupid."

"I'm not telling you that at all."

"Well, I'm telling you we're not."

Then he hung up.

The phone immediately rang again. Not wanting to give this performance repeatedly, I left the office.

Chapter 32

Dr. Hartmann's statue, or at least the base of it, stood smartly in the bright autumn sun wielding its fanciful essence of honor and intellect toward all who passed within sight. No one except me seemed to notice. It must have been something about the nagging puzzle of my divorce that made me susceptible to his telepathy. At that instant my mind needed some sort of structural reinforcement. On to the cafeteria.

I took my place at the end of the cafeteria line behind some young ladies who apparently had forgotten part of their wardrobe. One of them, with her back to me, advertised a tattoo of a suggestive nature that seemed to point downward toward the strap of the thong that girdled her waist and disappeared behind the low-riding top of her jeans. It wasn't that her clothes were sloppy or ill fitting. She filled them out nicely. I just wasn't accustomed to seeing provocative displays in such proximity to my person.

While I was trying to make out the pattern on the thong strap, she bumped backward against me and whirled around.

"Oh, I'm so sorry," she said.

The silver bead that impaled her tongue erased any thoughts I might have had at that moment. I stared at the bead until she turned back around and continued her nonsensical conversation with her friends. Then I was staring at her thong, again. I don't know why I was so perplexed. I could not see how those things served any useful purpose other than to provoke lust in the minds of the innocent, or not so innocent, male who dared look. I wondered how a strap might feel in my own crack.

The line moved forward. I shelled out four dollars to the cashier.

"Will I actually get four dollars worth of food today?" I asked her.

Tired eyes looked out beneath grey hair. "Depends on how much you value your food," she scowled. "We ain't got no food critics here today, so I wouldn't look for a whole lot."

"Maybe I'm in the wrong line of work."

I passed on by, following the line. Just as I left I heard the cashier mutter, "If you're working here, you are."

My surly appetite overtook the fetor of the entrees, feeding my anxiety to reach the serving line that weaved near some tables filled with boisterous young men, slobs, actually. Each was competing to see who could talk with the most food in his mouth. One of them placed a hamburger between his teeth and massaged his lips around it until an entire fourth of it had been severed and deposited into the opening. When he began to talk, I moved on.

Among the labels above the serving line I spotted one that read "Pork Chops." I didn't have to look any further. I had my plate loaded with the chop, mashed potatoes and gravy, corn, and two rolls. Even if the pork chop was not edible, I could at least count on the potatoes and corn to be relatively harmless.

I had not seen Mary so I selected a table at the opposite end of the cafeteria where the old fogies ate. I tore into the pork chop. That was the only way I could get a bite-size piece of it. Dry, bland, and tough, but a pork chop, nonetheless. Not that I could have prepared one any better. It still beat the malnourishment provided by the frozen dinners to which I was accustomed.

I saw Mary in the line just coming through the door. I waved and she cast a quick glance in my direction. She maintained a more than comfortable distance from others in the line, like she, or one of them, had a contagious disease. Her austere face, a troubled one, but in an attractive sort of way, kept its bearing straight ahead. I could tell she was still angry with me.

Due to my sudden wane in popularity, there was no one else at the table. Maybe she was going to back off from me, as well. I watched her as she moved through the line. She glanced at me once more. I acknowledged it with a smile. Even as remote as she was, she was still the most attractive woman in the cafeteria. The raving beauties sporting tight pants, thongs, provocative butts, tight tummies, and firm breasts could not compare. I didn't know if Mary had any of those things. It really didn't seem important.

She lumbered toward my table with a tray laden with more food than I could have eaten in an entire day. I jumped up and pulled out a chair next to mine. Being of the old school, chivalry was still very much a worthy cause to me. After helping her set the tray down and easing her into her seat, I stared at the food in front of her.

"What's the matter," she said, not exactly in a pleasant tone. "Is something wrong with the food?"

"Oh, I'm sorry." I looked straight into her magnetic green eyes that nearly pulled me out of my seat toward her lips. I was hoping she didn't know what I was really thinking. "I'm glad to see you have such a voracious appetite."

"Oh, that," she laughed. "You know, my ex used to make fun of me all the time."

Her ex. So, she was divorced. I had never noticed the absence of a ring on her finger.

"He said I should quit eating so much. He was afraid I would get fat. The funny thing is that he's the one that got fat."

Her selections contained basically the same that I had made along with a salad, fried okra, and a large slice of cherry pie. I had missed the pie.

"I see you have good taste in food. The pork chop is a little on the dry side. And tough. But kind of edible."

She started with the salad.

"August, listen. I'm sorry I cut you off on the phone."

"I understand. No problem."

"Well, Dr. Damascus came out and handed me a letter to type. You'd better hold onto your seat."

I stopped eating and looked at her. I couldn't accept the urgency of the situation. I could only see her in my home, sitting at the table with me, eating a romantic dinner and talking about things lovers talk about. But, I'm not sure I knew what those things were. I caught glimpses of her cooking, or laughing, or doing whatever she did. I could see myself sitting beside her on the sofa watching television. Holding hands. Holding each other.

"I made a copy of it."

She slipped a folded paper under the table toward me. Our hands met and for an instant my mind went blank. I backed away from the table and read the paper I had unfolded in my lap. It was a memo to Dennis Zewick, Director of Human Resources, recommending that the hearing be moved up to a week from Tuesday and that I not be given the customary probation period should I be found guilty of sexual harassment. The memo contained numerous allegations, all false, concerning my behavior. I needed time to study each of them and develop a defense.

"Does he know you have this?"

"No. If he found out I'd be on the street."

"Mary, you shouldn't have done this."

I looked at her and she stared back at me through all of her anger with eyes that poured out sympathy. It had been a long time since anyone had looked at me that way.

"I mean, you shouldn't have put yourself in jeopardy just for my sake."

I had not seen the expression on her face before. It emitted anxiety, disgust, and blame. And since no one else was at the table, it was focused on me.

"August, did you do those things? The things in the memo?"

Her question hit me like ball bat. She actually believed I had done those things. Holy shit! Had I disgraced myself that much in her eyes? I had plummeted to an all-time low in my life. The defilement by Alexis was not enough. Obviously, fate had yet to finish with me. More indignity. More humiliation. I was indeed the fool.

"Mary…" I wasn't sure what to say. What could I have said under such circumstances? "Mary, I can't believe that you would think I did that."

The green of her eyes melted and tears formed, ready to burst forth. But before one of them fell, she jumped up and almost ran to the door, leaving behind her lunch. I watched her leave, believing, then, that I was unworthy of anyone's respect. What tiny ray of hope that illuminated my ego had just been extinguished. Wisps of spent aspiration settled as fog in my head and the weight of worthlessness pulled at my body.

I sat like a lump in my chair, lost in the complexities of humanity, and wondering how things like that kept happening to me. I shoveled stiff, clumpy mashed potatoes into my mouth. A kind of punishment.

*****

Stanley jumped me the moment I walked in the office door.

"August, are you all right?"

"I just had lunch with Mary. She brought me a copy of a memo she typed for Dr. Damascus. They're moving up the hearing date for Miss Parker."

"Do you mean she actually let you see a copy of a private memo?"

"She's all right. In fact, if you look beneath all that hair, there is real potential. Anyway, she has become one of my allies. I think."

"What do you mean, you think?"

"I think she might believe these allegations, but there is doubt, anyway."

"And that bothers you, doesn't it?"

"You've no idea how much."

"Is there something going on with you two that I don't know about, you sly dog?"

"Well, there is something strangely enticing about her."

"So, what's going on with the hearing? I haven't heard much about it lately."

"Apparently, it's gaining momentum. I had another run-in with Dr. Damascus again this morning. He wasn't too happy with my position. I suppose he thought I was just going to back down and let them have their way."

"They? Who are they?"

"That would be Dr. Damascus and Dr. O'Mally. Oh, and Bartholomew."

"Are they all in this together?"

"Well, I'm not entirely sure what the whole story is, but they are all connected to this extortion thing, somehow. In fact, the memo Mary showed me was almost an order for HR to expedite the hearing and find me guilty."

"Sounds like you'd better hunker down, Boy. What in the world have you gotten yourself into?"

I wondered the same thing. I was just minding my own business, and that of my students, and all of a sudden I'm branded as a common criminal. I had undoubtedly touched a nerve, somewhere. I had to get a defense together.

The chimes that would have nourished my ego did not ring out the start of the afternoon because I had killed them. I had severed their lifeblood and left them to waste in cold silence in the dust and litter of an abandoned office. It hurt to think that I had done that. I needed them. The defense would have to wait. It was time for afternoon classes. And then the prison.

*****

I handed my driver's license to the guard at Boyd Atkins.

"What's this for?" He asked.

"I'm teaching algebra tonight. In the Program Building."

"Not tonight, you're not. We're having inspection. No one in, no one out."

"Is Dr. Eizenhurz available?"

"No one is available, right now."

I know he was aware of my growing anger. He was probably laughing like hell behind that austere, autocratic face.

Why hadn't someone notified Hartmann of the inspection? I was making mental notes of the choice words I would have for Dr. Purdy. He should have known about this sort of thing.

I put my license back in my wallet and left. Anger is a funny thing with me. Once it grabs hold, it is very hard to turn loose. It was like barbed hook in my neck. The more I fought it, the deeper it went. This time it had me by the throat and was choking the life out of my loyalty to Hartmann College.

Chapter 33

Tuesday nights were usually lacking for excitement. In fact, most nights were lacking for excitement in Elkridge. I was surprised to hear the noise and music in the Honk-N-Holler parking lot next to Jim Bob's. I parked at the store next door because Jim Bob's lot was overflowing into the street. The boisterous ambience might be just what I needed to kick myself into gear. I lumbered toward the door and opened it onto a raucous scene of dancing and groping. My entrance sent Cindy into a hacking fit.

"Perfessor…" Hack, hack. "I got one…" Hack, hack. "...coming up for you," Hack, hack.

I waved and searched myriad strange faces and costumes for Ricky. I wasn't sure he would be attracted to noise, but I saw him there, through the throng of gyrating bodies, sitting in the sticky booth, alone. All of the other booths were overflowing, but his was strangely empty, like he had something contagious. I wormed my way toward him through the gaggle of horny males bumping butts and rubbing genitals. My own butt received several good feels. It was almost tempting.

"August," he looked up at me, beer in hand. "Sit." He motioned toward the empty seat opposite him.

I stuck myself to the seat. "I didn't know you liked the party scene."

"Hell, this is no party, my friend. This is just simple joy."

His smile was not so much from laughing, but contentment.

Hack, hack. "Here you go, Perfessor," Cindy bowed as she set the double Glenlivet on the table.

I took a large sip and the burn started immediately, soothing my wracked body.

"You seem distracted. Something wrong?" He said. "For a married man, I'd think you would be celebrating life, but here you are doubtful about your present happiness."

"I'm divorced. I don't think I could provide an honest appraisal of that situation."

"Exactly my point. Hell, even if you were still married, do you think it would have made any difference in the way you feel now?"

Ricky waved his mug in the air. Cindy saw it and waved back.

I had to think about that one. I contemplated what Alexis might have said to me in response to all of this. Then I imagined her eyes blazing at me for even getting myself into this mess at Hartmann. I would like to think that she would possibly have supported me. Not that she would have believed in me, but she might have helped. And she might not have. But, as for security? I wouldn't have felt any more secure than I would have with my testicles knotted in a rope and tied to a bucking bronco. I would still be caught in the generation gap, which had since expanded to rival the Grand Canyon. And I would still be vulnerable to Melanie Parker's attack. I hated to admit it, but Ricky was right.

"You see, you have to think about it. If there was true security in your life, you shouldn't have to blink an eye."

I shook my head in agreement then took a huge sip.

"So, August, what are you going to do about your… ah… situation?"

I filled him in on the information Mary had given me, and my talk with Dr. Damascus. I also mentioned the meeting between Dr. Damascus and Dr. O'Mally I had overheard in the hallway.

"What do you mean, you eavesdropped?" He said. "August, you old miscreant. I didn't know you had it in you." He raised his mug in a toast. "I salute you."
I responded.

"I don't think you realize just what you're up against," he said.

"And, let me guess. You do?"

"Yeah, August, I do."

"And just what would that be?"

He said nothing for a while. He just chugged the fresh beer and waved to Cindy again.

"Ah, it's like that, is it? The new boy is not to be entrusted with the sacred truths of life."

His face lost all expression and his eyes bored into mine as if drilling into my mind. Cindy brought his beer and a fresh drink for me. He never took his eyes from mine.

"August," he said at last, "I've just reached a profound conclusion." Just saying that seemed to have been a great relief for him. He sat back, completely relaxed. He took a drink. "I'm going to retire."

"What brought that on?"

"August, I've been fighting the same battle you have for too many years."

"What the hell are you talking about?"

"The battle with Damascus."

"What did you ever have to do with him?"

"He and I go way back. About twenty-five years. I got myself into a little bit of trouble back then with a lively little wench. Of course, twenty-five years ago I had not the wisdom that I have today. And had I even possessed a fraction of it, I wouldn't be sitting here offering to help you, now."

I figured I would keep still. Ricky would set the pace.

"Anyway, Damascus found out about it. Now, it would have meant nothing to him except that I could have turned him in for fraud. He had changed the exam scores of several of his students for what I thought were bribes. He challenged me and vowed to extract vengeance, and the little wench incident would have given him his opportunity. Fortunately for me, he came to me first."

He paused for a drink of beer.

"How did you know about the extortion thing?"

"Buddy, I get around more than you think I do."

I stared at him trying to discover what it was about him that was so intriguing. "So, who told you?"

"Bartholomew."

"How did you get anything out of him?"

"He came to me. He knew about the rivalry between Damascus and me. It seems that he was getting cold feet. That and a lack of nerve. He was hoping he could trade information about Damascus for my promise not to get him involved in any scandal that might result.

"And –"

"I did some snooping and discovered that Bartholomew has been doing the same thing, although, not quite so blatantly. So I told him to get lost. He's matured a lot since then."

"So, what about you and Damascus?"

"We still keep our fingers on the trigger."

"Sounds like it's a non-issue, now."

"Like I said, he came to me first. It was a standoff. If he ratted on me, I would rat on him. The only thing that saved me was that he had more to lose than I did. So the matter became dormant. It never went away, it has just lain aside over the years, gaining energy, if you will. You know all about that, though, don't you? Energy, I mean. Everyone has forgotten about the girl. No one even remembers who she was.

But changing grades? That sort of thing has immortality." He took a generous gulp from his mug. "Don't be misled by Damascus' act. He has his clutches into everything and everybody around here. So does O'Mally, but she's in a position where she is expected to be involved with the students. This poor girl who's nailing you is probably in pretty deep with the old son-of-a-bitch."

"Okay, you lost me. What does all of that have to do with your retiring?"

He picked up his mug and chugged it. He motioned me to do the same. I did, with pleasure. Then he waved at Cindy again. We sat there in silence until Cindy returned with a fresh round.

"August, I know things about Damascus that would make your hair stand on end. And maybe one other thing, as well, if you were so inclined."

I got his drift. The fact that Damascus was a crook explained a lot.

"I decided to retire because I've decided it's time for Damascus and O'Mally to retire, too. They've corrupted this poor college enough."

I still did not fully understand what was taking place.

"Let me testify at your hearing," he said, grinning.

"You? What could you possibly do to help my situation?"

"Just let me testify. I can almost assure you that nothing will come of it except a couple of resignations. Nothing that will affect you adversely, anyway."

I sat there dumbfounded wondering why he would do this for me. And wondering, what in the hell did he know? I was not so sure just how secure I was at that moment.

*****

The morning brought new e-mails that filled the screen, all addressed to me in response to an announcement by Dr. Dennison that all motor pool vehicles would be locked down until a safety inspection was completed for each of them. I was surprised at the impact my report on vehicle safety had made on the administration. It was obvious that everyone else was surprised, too. Not necessarily at the state of vehicle safety, but rather the fact that anyone would publicly say anything about it. Anyone planning a trip in the next few days was suddenly without a college vehicle. Even the athletic and judging teams were stranded unless they could find alternate means of transportation. I seemed to be the clearing point for their wrath. A few of the messages were complimentary to my sense of judgment in promoting safety. Even Horace lauded my report as essential to the foundation of Hartmann's mission, but also pointed out several errors in grammar.

The rest of the e-mails resembled some form of hate mail directed at my "unwarranted, selfish, and exaggerated" attack on the maintenance department, notwithstanding the fact that these very same people had probably been waiting since the beginning of the fall term to get the air conditioners in their offices repaired and were now suffering from chills because of the lack of heating. I blew them off and turned my attention to my next class. I just had time to hit the restroom.

My foot found the pencil on the edge of the fifth step down from the top of the stairs. After a short roll, it suddenly propelled my foot to the next step and I followed, landing on my butt and bouncing, one step at a time, to the landing. I heard footsteps coming down behind me and when I looked around and up, as I was then sitting at floor level, my view followed two shapely legs up inside Melanie Parker's skirt. Other students were pushing by us on their way either up or down the steps gawking as they passed.

"Why Professor Lane," she cooed. "I knew you had the hots for me but never thought you would go to this much trouble just to look up my skirt."

It was then that I noticed Frank at the top of the stairs staring at us and starting to choke himself into a laughing fit. The other students were staring. I also noticed Allison Boyer from my physics class behind Frank. Her face was blank with nondescript eyes, as though she were in a trance. No feeling, no awareness. Just existence.

I remembered Miss Parker standing over me. "Miss Parker, you know perfectly well I have just fallen down the steps and you should also know better than to place yourself in such a vulnerable position, unless your intentions are to advertise something."

She smiled with a wicked grin. All of a sudden, the traffic seemed to have slowed nearly to a stop, like rubber-necks driving by the scene of an accident.

"Well," she said, "if you're buying, I'll negotiate."

I picked myself up and pressed the bruise on my butt thinking it might help relieve the ache. It didn't.

"Miss Parker, please conduct yourself in a proper manner."

That is when Horace came walking up the stairs. Traffic was congested at the landing and she was slow getting to the top.

When Melanie saw her, she said, "Well that's sort of hard to do with you looking up my skirt and all."

That got Horace's attention and she stopped just sort of the landing with her mouth open and gaping eyes staring at me.

"I fell down the stairs and Miss Parker was just… a… passing by."

I turned to Melanie.

"Weren't you, Miss Parker?"

"If you say so." She smiled again and flashed her eyes.

Stifled giggles and murmurs erupted in the crowd of spectators. Still smiling, she brushed by Horace on the way down the stairs, swishing in celebration.

"What was that all about," Horace squawked.

"I fell down the stairs and when I looked up the little vixen had positioned herself strategically over my head so that I would be sure to see something I really didn't want to see."

"Isn't she the one who accused you of –"

"Yes," I said, cutting her off.

"Well, I can see why you are attracted to her."

"Horace, this incident was purely of her own making. When I fall down stairs, I'm not exactly thinking of how to arrange myself in order to view the underside of someone's skirt. I'm trying to not get killed. Her position with respect to me was merely an attempt on her part to take advantage of the circumstances." I tried to straighten my clothes. "And I'm not attracted to her."

Traffic had resumed and my bladder was telling me to focus on my original purpose for going down the stairs. The large glasses hovering over the tip of Horace's petite nose filled her face with brown eyes, staring at me, obviously with contempt. I still wondered what held the glasses in place.

I looked up to see if Frank was still around in case I needed to use him as a witness. He wasn't. But Allison Boyer, the student from my physics class, was. From the landing, she stared at me, one corner of her thin lips slightly curled upward in a devious smile. I stared back. Her eyes bore right through me like a bullet from Satan's gun, if the fellow had one. Why was she always there when something like this happened?

My butt hurt and the urinal was calling.

*****

In the afternoon I found time to visit Claudia and ask about the Boyd Atkins inspection schedule. She was not particularly pleased to have me bring it up.

"August, I don't know that much about the prison schedules," she said in an annoyed voice. "That's something you need to talk to Dr. Purdy about."

"Do you mean to tell me that a department head doesn't even know what sort of hell her faculty is going through each day?"

She pulled her face into a visage of cold stone. "August, the prison assignments are the responsibility of Dr. Purdy. That's not something I'm held accountable for." She narrowed her eyes. "And I resent your attitude." Then she raised her nose.

I was aggravated when I arrived at her office. Now I was pissed.

"And I resent yours. But I'll go see Dr. Purdy."

I turned to leave.

"Oh, and by the way," I added, "since, you're not accountable for your job, don't expect me to do anything that I'm not accountable for in my contract."

I left and went straight to Dr. Purdy's office. There must have been something in the administrator's handbook about assuming responsibility, like not to do it. He made notes about my complaint, but did nothing to rectify the situation. He did not even commit to obtaining a schedule of events at the prison so I would know when classes were not to be held. Dr. Purdy, being a true administrator, was able to blow me off with much more finesse than Claudia.

I had accomplished little by the end of the day. I hadn't even made any progress on my defense for the hearing and it appeared my ramparts were being overrun. I sulked in my office for an hour before going home to sulk some more. Still no chimes.

Chapter 34

I passed up Glenlivet in favor of a Killian's Red. I needed a clear mind to sort out what was happening. Whisky tended to open my mind and I might have been able to conjure some creative thoughts about recent events, but I needed a more logical approach. I wanted to be able to put names and times with the events. To the casual observer, the episodes would seem to have no connection. Melanie Parker, Dr. Damascus, Dr. O'Mally, Bartholomew, the theft from the lab. I had to find the connection.

Three Killians later, I wondered if I was further removed from the new generation than I thought. Nothing made sense.

I had printed out the class rosters for Damascus and Bartholomew. I went through each one of them looking for a name that might mean something. Several students were in Bartholomew's social science class and Damascus' history class. I got another Killian and studied the rosters, staring at them as if the words and numbers would rearrange themselves into a solution to the puzzle.

I looked through the rosters again. Then again. Parker's name was on Damascus' roster. So was Allison Boyer's. But what was the connection? From Miss Parker's comment in my office about Allison, I surmised that they were not good friends. But what about the "Matador girl?" By that time the beer had done its work, my mind was drifting into regions I had not anticipated. My focus was gone and with it, my sense of logic. But then I noticed that O'Mally was the advisor to both of these students. I remembered that O'Mally had also advised Shawn Crandall. O'Mally. That must be the link.

*****

The work of the five Killians continued into Friday morning, at least through the first GPS class. My lunch of beastly steak fingers, fried into dreadful brown sticks of compacted meat, resembled blistered turds that must have had some effect on the left-over Killians that were pickling my veins. It actually helped return some sense of logic to my mind, but did little for my physical dexterity. That's why I dropped the phone when I picked it up. I called Marney to check on the lock for physics lab I had requested several days before.

"Marney?"

"Yeah, that's me. What d'ya want?"

"Marney, this is August."

Click.

I dialed again.

"Marney, if you hang up again I'll not waste any more time with you, I'll just take my issue directly to Dr. Dennison."

No click.

"Several days ago I requested that the lock on the physics lab be changed. Any progress?"

"I'll have someone take care of it," he grumbled.

"Will that happen anytime soon?"

During the long pause I heard the noise of ruffled paper. Then he quietly spoke into the phone, "Lane. Lane. Here it is. You'll have it this afternoon."

"Thank you, very much, Marney. I appreciate your willingness to cooperate."

Click.

I had physics and another GPS class to endure. Despite my best efforts at scheduling course content, days like that one always sabotaged my intentions. The students would probably wind up another day behind because I had little confidence that my lectures and demonstrations would be worthy of their attention. Hell, if they wouldn't pay attention to me when I was enthusiastic and entertaining, why would they pay attention to me when I was sloshed?

Three o'clock came slowly. It was as if the rest of the world had somehow increased to relativistic speed in defiance of the great burden placed on my physiological functions, and my own reference of time stood still. The strength required to meet that challenge nearly depleted what little stores of energy my body had left after processing five Killians and blistered turds.

I just left my office and almost collided with a tall, lanky man wearing a tool belt. He was one of Marney's group.

"Marney said I should bring you this key. I just changed your lock on that room there." He said and pointed to the physics lab across the hall.

"Thank you, very much. Please give Marney my thanks."

"Yeah, sure. Oh, by the way."

I had just turned toward my office, key in hand. Curiosity made me stop and turn back around to face him.

"That there key will fit your office door, too. Marney said to key this lock so the same key would fit both locks." He lowered his eyebrows and squinted. "I don't' know why he told me to do that."

"Thanks," I said again.

He looked at me with suspicious glare, then turned and left.

A provoking thought occurred to me in the hall. I returned to my office and looked up the college records for Parker and Boyer on the computer.

Allison's records showed little in the way of family. She was listed as the responsible party for all billing. She was a Korean immigrant, although she didn't look a bit Korean. However, from the few words I had heard her speak, she did have an accent and an eastern European look about her. With a dead end there, I went to my computer and just for the hell of it typed her name into Google. Only two hits showed up, both of them from the "Los Angeles Times." And both of them in reference to a story about Kim Lee, a Korean immigrant who was arrested a year earlier for trafficking drugs and prostitution. He was currently residing at the California State Prison at Solano. The second article dealt with some of the girls that were in his employ, if that's what you actually call it. The pictures were a little blurry, but one of the girls that was shown sitting beneath the police car was a dead ringer for Allison.

She didn't live in a dormitory, but listed a post office box. I had to wonder, without parents, how she was paying for her education. Surely she must be receiving scholarships or grants or something, but no financial aid was listed in her records, or at least the ones I could see.

My curiosity prodded me to investigate Melanie, as well. She was bright, as she had one of the highest scores on the ACT. I was beleaguered by her poor grades at Hartmann and the bologna about her learning disability. Google nearly went nuts showing several thousand hits. Either it was a very popular name, or she was a very active young lady. I narrowed the search to include Elkridge and Hartmann and the screen display showed a curt three entries. The third reference was an article from the Elkridge paper about a fire at 308 West Monroe. It included a picture of the tenants being interviewed by someone. As I looked at the picture closer, I could swear they were Allison and Melanie. And sure enough, their names were listed in the article.

From the college records, Melanie also listed her address the same post office box as Allison. I thought at the time that some error had been made. But the more I thought about it, the less convinced I was. I replaced the office key on my key ring with the new one and left.

*****

The silhouette of the Math Science Building stood like a dark lump in the glow of Monday morning's new sun. The rays just broke the horizon and slowly stole the dew's privacy, leaving behind it a trail of glistening, newly ripened droplets of water. Light fog hovered over the campus filtering the buildings like an old screen door.

No one else had seen it fit to show up at six-thirty in the morning. I had spent too much time worrying about the hearing and I needed to catch up on my grading. At that hour of the morning, the front door would be locked. After futile efforts of trying my key, it remained locked. Frustration yanked at my enthusiasm. My good intentions for the day had been thwarted by a simple lock. By then, the situation evolved into more than frustration and I was losing my logical edge. I tried the key again. The frustration passed. I was pissed.

I yanked the key from the lock. The glare of the shiny metal reminded me that it was the key maintenance had given me to fit the new lock on the lab. It also fit my office door. But, apparently, it did not fit the building's entry door as my old one had. So, there I was on the doorstep of my building without an operable key. Again, the fool. My destiny in life seemed to be just that: the fool. Maybe Alexis actually realized this long before I did. After all, she really wouldn't want to be married to a fool unless she was hopelessly in love with him. I guess that was part of my problem. She wasn't.

I yelled and banged on the door hoping someone might be inside the building. Alexis always told me I had a one-track mind. She was probably right on that account, because I banged on the door several times before I realized that I was only making my hand sore.

I tried calling Security on my cell phone. No answer. Whoever was on the night shift was apparently in some other building, asleep. I called Marney. I knew he wouldn't be on campus, yet, but I tried anyway just to say that I had in case it would be necessary for me to say that. I was right. No answer there, either.

Just about the time I had decided to break into the building through a window, Wanda happened by. She kindly unlocked the door and I asked her why my key wouldn't fit.

She examined it and said, "That there is not a master key. It only fit one or two doors in the building."

"Marney gave me this one for the new lock he put on the lab. Why would he have given my such a key?" I asked. "My old one fit the front door, as well."

"You don't want to go around here messing with Marney. He can screw you up one side of the college and down the other and you won't even know what happened. Some folks even thank him for the trip." I could think of no reply. I merely stood there in a trance wondering what the hell was going on at Hartmann. I finally got my bearings and looked at Wanda.

"Okay, I'll just have to get a new key from him."

She lowered her head and looked up at me. "Uh huh."

Once in my office I forced my worries into the usual state of ignorance and started grading papers, flying through them with ease. Grading papers is not a difficult challenge, and I polished them off in good time with my usual disappointment at the grades.

I slogged through the day with misplaced direction and purpose. My students knew it. They could sense it, I suppose, just like an animal senses fear in a human. At the time I wasn't aware of their intuitions, nor did I care. After my last class I turned my attention to the hearing.

I had received a letter at my apartment on Saturday notifying me of the hearing. It offered few details, but I was aghast to read that Allison Boyer had registered a charge of sexual harassment against me. Melanie Parker's name appeared nowhere in the letter. Miss Parker's intentions I could understand. But Miss Boyer? I had no earthly idea what was going on.

The hearing would start in the morning and I had much more to do in preparation. I also had intermediate algebra at Boyd Atkins that evening. It would be a long night.

Since the inspection at Boyd Atkins the previous week had put the class another week behind, I would have to catch up on that evening's class. It would probably take a couple of weeks, and that was a conservative estimate. I arrived in time to be at the Program Building by five. I was surprised by the absence of students loitering in the hallway waiting for class to begin. Dr. Eigenhurtz's angry eyes caught me as I passed by her office. I waved and continued on to the classroom. She called my name from her doorway.

I stopped and turned to face her.

"Good evening," I said

"I waited for you for twenty minutes." The words dribbled

from her like molasses. "But I had to send the inmates back to their blocks."

"What do you mean, you waited?"

"Class was supposed to start at four-thirty."

"Why four-thirty? It starts at five. When did it change?"

"They didn't tell you?"

"Tell me what?"

"During the first week in November we change to winter hours. Classes start at four-thirty and end at seven. That way we can get the inmates back into the blocks before it gets completely dark outside."

"No. They didn't tell me."

I stood there, a beaten soul. No matter how hard I tried to play by the rules and do my job well, the rules kept changing. Of the many things that flashed through my mind in the few seconds I hung there on my facade of dignity, that of someone neglecting their job torqued my jaw. I would talk with Dr. Purdy and go all the way to the president if I had to. This crap was going to stop. If I was expected to do my job, then by God, everyone else could damn well do his.

Chapter 35

I chose not to be early to the hearing. Looking at the faces of my accusers before I could actually say anything in my defense would destroy my courage. The same thing happened with Alexis whenever I was called on the carpet for an infringement, real to her, imaginary to me. So, I waited around the corner of the hallway until I could make my entrance at exactly the time the hearing was to start.

Mary was waiting for me in the outer office. Her eyes, full of uncertainty, seemed to probe me looking for some hint of virtue.

"Has the tribunal assembled?" I asked.

"You need to watch yourself," she chided. "This is not funny."

"I realize that." I stood by the corner of her desk to get a better whiff of her perfume, which could thwart my self-induced compunction. "But, if I don't try to maintain some sense of humor, I'll go nuts."

I studied her face, watching for any clue as to her real feelings toward me. It was almost like she wanted to do something to acknowledge my predicament but was trying to avoid doing it.

Very quietly, I said, "Mary, I know this looks pretty bad. I understand that you might be thinking I'm a terrible person. And I know a lot of other folks are. Thinking I'm a terrible person, I mean."

Her head remained stationary, not a muscle moving. Not a flinch of an eyelash. But her eyes were beginning to water.

"I might be a screwed up, clumsy, arrogant bastard, but I don't cavort with teenagers. You can think of me whatever you like. But, I'm not like that."

She blinked and opened her mouth as if to speak, but paused. "Well, they're waiting for you." She motioned toward the door.

The chatter, audible through the doors, ceased the moment I entered the conference room. The enchanting fragrance I had just enjoyed was quickly displaced by a vicious smell of what seemed to be baby burp punctuated with two-year old sweat. I could not picture any sort of activity in the conference room that would account for the foul odor.

The taste of vomit came to my mouth and foreboding landed with a thump in my stomach.

Mary followed me in and took her place at the conference table by Dr. Gaines. The tailored, but well-worn, three-piece suit that normally encrusted his frail body had given way to a bluish thing frayed at the elbows and cuffs that hung from his shoulders like a wet sweater. His tie contained too much green to complement his suit and was splayed into two wrinkled ribbons of silk that turned backward at the end.

I looked around the table at the other participants, sizing them up for my plan of attack, or defense. On Dr. Gaines' right was Dr. Damascus. I wasn't exactly sure why he was present, since he had no administrative authority over such proceedings. His dour face remained focused on his hands that were busily fanning the pages of a notebook on the table in front of him. He gave no indication that he was aware of any other presence in the room.

To his right was Dennis Zewick from Human Resources. His sharp eyes darted from one of us to another while a petite beard framed thin lips that made kissing gestures. The wiry little man reminded me of a marionette I had once seen in a puppet show.

To Dr. Gaines' left was, of course, Mary. She sat erect in her chair, prim and rigid, glancing frequently toward me. What exactly was she looking at? Or for?

To her left was Claudia, clad in one of her traditional sack dresses, her stringy hair falling ungracefully around her blanched face and over her shoulders.

And on the end of the table, in a smaller chair, sat Dr. Brasserie Tipton, Dean of Student Affairs. I wondered if she selected that place since the table had a noticeable slope in that direction and the top of the table fell just enough so as to be directly beneath her two huge breasts that rested inertly upon it.

It was five to one. Fair enough, as I figured, for a kangaroo court I placed my notebook on the table and rested my hands beside it in the dust that screened the numerous scratches in the finish from the undiscerning eye. Apparently, the hearing was not significant enough to warrant thorough preparations of the conference room. That gave me reason to believe that they probably wouldn't have bothered substantiating the charges, either. Carafes of water and stacks of plastic cups along with napkins occupied the center of the table. In spite of the meager arrangements, I got the feeling that I was going to be there a long time.

Dr. Gaines started the hearing by reading the allegations.

"Professor Lane, you have been accused of sexual harassment by one Allison Boyer. You are alleged to have accosted Miss Boyer in room 315 of the Math Science Building on September ninth of this year, using inappropriate language and bodily contact."

While my mind was tiptoeing about in Oz, wondering about Allison's motive, Dr. Gaines spewed forth rot about policy and procedure of which they were required to inform me, not that I was ever given this information ahead of time, as the policy directed. A short pause followed while he arranged the papers on his desk, almost as if he was stalling. Damascus was fidgeting in his chair, obviously annoyed by the delay.

"Why don't we get these proceedings started," he grumbled. "I'm sure many of us have things to do today."

Dr. Gaines glared at him and turned his eyes toward the group.

"Excuse me," I said. "But where did Allison Boyer come into all of this?"

"Professor Lane, we have a number of pieces of evidence to support the allegations presented by Miss Boyer. Have you prepared a defense?"

"Well, Dr. Gaines, since I really didn't know what you were going to throw at me, it would seem very unlikely that I would have any sort of defense prepared, now would it? I mean when one is bushwhacked, preparation seldom precedes it."

"Oh, come now," bellowed Damascus. "Either you have a defense or you don't. If you are innocent of these charges you should have no trouble disputing them."

I looked straight at him.

"Sir," I said as calmly as I could, "I fail to see that you have any authority to bully me about. You are merely a faculty member and not a member of the administration. According to the policies of this college you hold no position of authority for disciplinary action over faculty, and you damned sure don't have any business being in this hearing."

His eyes were confined to their sockets only by the bushy eyebrows as his face distended itself like a red balloon.

Dr. Gaines' face glowed with sympathy and he seemed reluctant to continue.

"I'm afraid Professor Lane is correct, on that account," he said. "Dr. Damascus, I must ask you to refrain from any further comment."

"How about if we just take each of the allegations in turn," suggested Mr. Zewick.

"That sounds reasonable," said Dr. Gaines, obviously relieved to know what to do. "To begin with, let's take the incident in the hallway outside your classroom on September 7. It is reported that you asked Miss Parker to join you in the hallway. Following your... ah... meeting, she was seen leaving the Math Science Building in tears. She did not return to class. She reported that you physically accosted her."

He looked at me with eyes that said he didn't believe what he had just read, but he had presented it to the room, just the same. "Is this true?"

"I thought we were talking about Miss Boyer? When did Miss Parker make her appearance?"

Mr. Zewik pointed a pencil at me. "This all has to do with patterns of behavior, Professor Lane."

Dr. Gaines repeated the question.

"Not all of it," I said. "Yes, I did ask Miss Parker to meet in the hallway because she had come to class with only half of her clothes on in violation of the student dress code. I asked her to return home and put on something more appropriate."

"And did you accost her?"

I looked straight at him. For an instant I thought about revealing to the panel exactly what she had been wearing and why it had been so inappropriate. But then they might have thought that since I had paid so much attention to her wardrobe, I had fallen prey to vice merely by viewing a young lady who happened to be treated more kindly by Mother Nature than some other unfortunate young women.

"No. But what the hell has this got to do with Allison Boyer?"

"Professor Lane, we have other student accounts of this incident who will attest to your actions."

"They might be willing to attest to my actions," I said, "but not the ones I used toward Miss Parker. They would be lying because no one was in the hallway except Miss Parker and myself. There is no way anyone could have witnessed it. That's why I reprimanded her in the hallway, to spare her the embarrassment of an audience. And what does this have to do with Miss Boyer?"

"Let's move on to the next one," barked Damascus.

Mary was busy taking notes of the proceedings, frequently cutting her eyes toward Dr. Damascus in contempt. Dr. Gaines' eyes also darted toward him with jabs of ire. Then he turned toward me.

"Now we come to an incident that took place in the women's restroom of Caftan Hall on September 12. It was reported that you had entered the women's restroom and Allison Boyer found you there. You were alone with a female student in a women's restroom."

"That is correct." I dared not say too much. Wait for him to ask.

"Can you explain your presence there, Professor Lane?"

"I have no idea from whom you got your information. I had experienced an injury during physics lecture. My head was bleeding. I went to Caftan Hall in search of the nurse." I glared at Dr. Tipton. "She was not in her office in spite of the fact that the hours published by this institution indicate that she should have been. I bloodied my nose while trying to open her office door. So there I was with both the back of my head and my nose bleeding. I went to the nearest restroom to find some paper towels to stop the bleeding. I had just suffered a concussion and I was hardly in any condition to discern the gender of the restroom, much less care about it. I sensed that I had an emergency situation. While in the restroom, Miss Boyer entered. She was able to show me to a telephone where I enlisted the assistance of Ms. Einhorn to drive me to the emergency room. The student was in no danger and I certainly was in no condition to have taken advantage of her."

The panel, except for Damascus, looked stunned at my explanation and silence followed for several minutes.

Until Damascus grunted, "Get on with it."

Dr. Gaines reluctantly picked up the form in front of him and continued.

"It was also reported that you were found lying on the landing of the stairway in the Math Science Building gazing up the skirt of Miss Melanie Parker."

Mr. Zewick had already placed his hands over his face, shaking his head in what I suppose was disgust. Mary, of course, was embarrassed. I'm not sure if it was on my account, or hers. Dr. Tipton seemed indifferent to the whole affair. Almost like she expected it all. And I still had no idea where all of this was going.

I didn't realize that the expression on my face was so cross until Dr. Gaines reared back in surprise. The annoying accusations were beginning to get to me. It was becoming more and more clear that Miss Parker herself was relaying this information to Dr. Damascus, and he in turn to Dr. Gaines. But where the hell did Allison Boyer come into it?

"And exactly how did you learn of this incident?" I asked.

"That is not something this panel is obligated to tell you."

"Then, let me tell you how you learned of it. I had fallen down the stairs and was just recovering when Miss Parker appeared standing over me in a position from which I could not possibly avoid having to look up her skirt. Other students and faculty were also present and can verify my account of the story. So it had to have been Miss Parker that reported it, omitting key information. And that report, I'll wager, was made to Dr. Damascus, who then reported it to you. Is that not correct?"

Dr. Gaines turned and looked at Damascus, who ignored him and tightened his scowl toward me.

"If you doubt my word, which obviously you must or I wouldn't be here, Professor Able passed by at that time and I'm sure he will be happy to verify what really happened. And Allison Boyer was also present and can also explain what happened."

No one was going to touch that one. The silence left everyone looking for an escape.   "Shouldn't Miss Boyer be present at this hearing," I asked, "since she is obviously the one who instigated it?"

"We didn't feel that Miss Boyer's presence would be necessary unless we had some difficulty," said Dr. Gaines. "She is available should we need her."

"Well?" Said Damascus.

Dr. Gaines shot him an angry look. He continued.

"On Friday, September twenty-first you confiscated a cell phone from a Miss... ah... Shoaven and threw it out of a window."

"And I talked with Professor Lane about that incident," piped Dr. Tipton. "That girl's cell phone could have been stolen while laying out there on the ground like that. It could have even broke and she would of had to gone and get a new one."

Damascus leaned back with an evil smile on his face and glared at me.

"Was Professor Lane reprimanded?" Dr. Gaines asked.

I sat motionless in my chair, stewing about Dr.Tipton's account of that day. Each point she made was punctuated by an animated arm that jutted out toward Dr. Gaines, fingers tapping on the table as if she was trying to send a message in Morse code. I figured I would let her dig a hole before I pushed her and her testimony into it. Besides, I was being entertained by her large bosom that wiped the dust from the table each time she reached forward to tap.

"Professor Lane," Dr. Gaines said to me. "Do you have anything to say about this?"

"In the first place, I don't see where this incident has any relevance to Miss Boyer's complaint. But, in the interest of saving time and satisfying everyone's curiosity, as well as vindicating myself, I'll answer it. As I told Dr. Tipton, when I informed her that Miss Shoaven violated the policy concerning cell phones in the syllabus, she had been warned twice before, and I had sent a report to Dr. Tipton about Miss Shoaven and her cell phone, and she did not receive that report until her secretary produced it during our meeting. And then there's the apology that Dr. Tipton never extended to me for having done everything I should have according to policy and procedure."

I glared first at Dr. Tipton, who sat with her upturned nose toward no one in particular. Then I fired a nasty look toward Damascus. He had lost his smile, but the glare was fixed by the vindictiveness that controlled him. It was like staring at Satan, himself.

"Move on," he commanded.

The panel, except for Damascus, seemed to withdraw from the hearing. I could see doubt in their eyes about the allegations. Mr. Zewick spoke next.

"Professor Lane, we still have the question on the table about your harassment—"

"Excuse me, Mr. Zewick. I believe that should be alleged harassment since I haven't been proven guilty of anything, yet. And, I still haven't heard anything in the way of my conduct toward Miss Boyer."

The stress of the hearing was eating at me. It wasn't so much the hearing as the half-witted attempt by Damascus to steer the panel toward his favor. That and the collective ignorance of the rest of them. The dryness in my mouth distracted me and I couldn't afford to lose focus or acuity. I reached for the carafe of water in front of Dr. Tipton and took a cup from the top of the stack. I motioned to her in case she wanted me to pour a cup of water for her as well, but she rested her hands on the edge of the table, shook her head behind a forced smile and turned toward Mary.

I looked for a button on top of the carafe, but the cap was solid. Perhaps it was one of those automatic types that opened when it was tilted. It didn't. So, I loosened the cap. Still nothing. Loosening it more, I tried again, this time successfully. More than I wanted. The cap fell from the carafe sending a cascade of water downhill across the table toward Dr. Tipton, who was eyeing Dr. Gaines at that instant and was not aware of the flood of ice water soaking the underside of her blouse that rested on the table beneath her massive bosom. The cold shock finally registered and her body bolted backward against her chair. Apparently, the wheels hung on the rippled carpet and her momentum launched her chair backward in a peculiar arc that carried her to the floor. Still a captive of her chair, her arms flailed wildly for something to grasp and her skirt, of course, had fallen downward leaving two very stocky legs thrashing about in the air. The impact had also strained her blouse and the buttons had given way allowing the two enormous ebony breasts, which had been dislodged from her brassiere, to relocate just beneath her chin.

Everyone at the table had jumped up by that time to see if she had been injured, or to just see. Claudia rushed toward her and tried to restore her wardrobe but the thrashing arms and legs prevented her from getting close enough. Mr. Zewick arrived shortly afterward and attempted to grab hold of at least one of her arms to pull her upright. Unfortunately, it was all he could do to track the motion of her arms and he was completely unaware of the errant foot that delivered a killer blow to his groin. He fell to the floor in a heap beside the floundering Dr. Tipton whose thrashing continued to deliver blows to his incapacitated body. Dr. Gaines was frozen in both the shock of such an interruption to his hearing and to the embarrassment of such a sight. Dr. Damascus seemed only angered by the delay. Mary, in the meantime, had quietly gone to the outer office and retrieved a shawl from her desk chair, which she brought in and placed over Dr. Tipton's writhing body.

Being some distance away from the scene, there was little I could do immediately to help the situation. But I did proceed toward the activity and took Dr. Tipton's left arm while Claudia had her right and we managed to pull her upright. In the process of finding her footing, one of her feet dispatched yet another critical blow to Mr. Zewick's groin and he was pretty much done for as far as the hearing was concerned. Dr. Tipton fought feverishly to right her skirt and blouse while Mary fought to keep her concealed beneath the shawl. Mary encouraged her to retreat to the outer office where she could repair herself in private.

"I'm sorry, Dr. Tipton," I said to her as she stumbled out of the room on Mary's arm.

We all stared at poor Mr. Zewick who, with tears pouring across his face, had both hands between his legs clutching what was left of his defiled manhood and moaning a most distressful mantra that begged our sympathy. I imagine each of us felt the same pain. Sort of sympathy pains. The kind that is ingrained in a man's memory at an early age, usually when he is initiated into the vulnerability of his blossoming manhood by falling onto the crossbar of a bicycle. One never forgets that moment. And whenever I witness such an incident, the pain seems to sear through my body as if it were happening to me all over again. So, we men, except for Dr. Damascus, stood there with our hands near our crotches in some mystical attempt to prevent Mr. Zewick's misfortune from finding its way to our own frailties.

I reached down to take Mr. Zewick's arm and Dr. Gaines took the other. We got him to his feet, even though he was incapable of standing erect. Dr. Gaines told him to run along and get whatever assistance he needed. As an afterthought, he mentioned the school nurse. It was those few words that seemed to do the trick for Mr. Zewick, because he turned to look at Dr. Gaines and stood upright detaching his hands from his crotch into what I could swear was a windup to sock the doctor in the nose. The contortions of anguish in Mr. Zewick's face quickly faded into sultry contempt. But, he relaxed his fists and slowly waddled out of the room.

I mopped up what water I could with the napkins and we all took our seats.

"You really should replace these carafes," I said, holding one up as if they could see for themselves the defective nature of the design. I'm not sure Dr. Gaines had recovered completely, but Dr. Damascus seemed to have a new infusion of fire.

Mary returned to the room and Damascus stood.

"I think we should hear from Miss Boyer," he grumbled.

Dr. Gaines looked around the room.

"Does anyone have any objections to Miss Boyer addressing this hearing?"

Everyone shook his head in the negative.

"I would welcome a visit from Miss Boyer," I said. "I, for one, would like to know exactly what she thinks I have been doing."

"Professor Lane, behave yourself," cautioned Dr. Gaines. "You will treat Miss Boyer with respect."

"Of course I will," I replied.

Mary called Allison Boyer and we sat in silence waiting for the appearance of the one person who had been the cause of the assembly. I hated the prospect of enduring such insulting accusations, but I was also curious as to what lengths the poor girl would go to degrade me. I had prepared for almost anything Melanie Parker could throw at me. Not that I had a host of witnesses. I just had common sense and my integrity. Mostly integrity. That is, if integrity meant anything to the people in that room.

But I had no clue as to what Miss Boyer had in store. Or why.

Chapter 36

Sitting at the conference table, I tried not to look at the others while, I suppose, they were trying not to look at me. We waited for the return of Mr. Zewick and Dr. Tipton, if they dared show their faces after such humiliation. The heavy chin of Dr. Damascus rested upon the knot of his tie, obviously made of some exotic fabric, complemented by a white silk shirt. The light glinted from his gold cufflink. Dr. Gaines nervously tapped out distress signals with his fingernails against the desk. Mary, true to her charming nature, sat at attention, calmly studying her notes, and frequently stealing glances in my direction. And not smiling. When not watching Mary, I studied the patterns left in the fine transparent dust on the table. I even added a few designs of my own.

Miss Boyer's entrance took us by surprise. She stood cautiously for a moment in the open doorway, surveying the occupants of the room then gracefully closed the door and turned to face Dr. Gaines. She was tastefully attired in a dark blue full-length skirt, a cream chiffon blouse that buttoned to the neck, and smart navy shoes. She had obviously been coached by someone. Dr. Gaines directed her to a seat at the end of the table adjacent to him.

"I think we should recess this hearing until Dr. Tipton and Mr. Zewick can rejoin us," said Dr. Gaines.

"What good would they be?" bellowed Damascus. "They know the nature of all of this and they have nothing to add. They were just taking up space. Let's get on with it."

Mr. Zewick and Dr. Tipton stopped just inside the door, and heard his remark. They looked at each other briefly, then glared at him and moved to their seats. Dr. Tipton hesitated, then moved to the opposite end of the room and took a chair near Dr. Damascus. Mr. Zewick toddled to his seat, staying clear of Dr. Tipton.

Dr. Gaines looked disturbed at the turn of events, but proceeded with the hearing.

"Miss Boyer, you have made allegations against Professor Lane. This panel would like to hear your account of what happened."

Miss Boyer was a better actress than Melanie Parker. She played the part of the victimized female to perfection. Almost too perfectly. According to her testimony, I had ogled her, stalked her, and fondled her, and even gone so far as to remove her clothing. And she relayed in remarkable detail several incidences that involved Melanie Parker and myself, although embellished with additional details that changed the character of them into sordid affairs, making it sound as though I had ravaged the poor girl. It never occurred to the panel to ask when and where all of these events took place. They had all taken the bait and Miss Boyer was reeling them in.

I watched her production while trying to understand how this shy, innocent girl could become such a vicious predator. I had barely spoken to her directly and she had rarely spoken to me. A slender, docile scholar, with respectable grades and, I supposed, no obvious objection to learning. Why, then, this vilification?

As a final blow and as a climax to her attack, with exacting finesse, she blurted out with remarkable clarity, "...and I have his baby."

That statement was the calamity that stopped the clock. No one uttered a word. I had not seen that coming. In a fraction of a second I felt the blood drain from my head, numbness overtake my entire body, and my stomach wrench in fear. Perhaps a similar incident had been responsible for the wretched odor of vomit that hung in the room. Slowly, all eyes were trained on me as if I had just murdered someone. I looked at each of them in turn.

Dr. Tipton's eyes exploded into an expanse of brilliant whiteness that, except for the hot pink lip-gloss, masked the darkness of her face. Mary's mouth had fallen open in a less than feminine demeanor, and she appeared to be in a state of shock. Mr. Zewick's slight beard hid much of his expression, but I suspected that he was not as surprised as the rest of us. Dr. Gaines sat in a daze as though he were somewhere else, not knowing what it was he should do next. And Dr. Damascus sported a grin and a nasty twinkle in his eye.

It took several minutes to bring my shock and anger under control. I wanted to lunge across the table and choke the life out of the little bitch. I sat there, weakening from the incriminating rays radiated by the other ten eyes.

"Miss Boyer, do you honestly expect me to sit here and do nothing about your wonton accusations?"

"But you," she said, pointing at me. "You give me baby."

Sudden quiet overtook the room. The girl's eyes were drowning in tears and her face was like a cornered tiger, fierce and dangerous. Her threat stunned me and the hearing suddenly took on a new meaning. I didn't know what happened, I didn't know why, and apparently, neither did anyone else. Except for Damascus. His eyes, like those of a hunter, stared at me as if I would soon be mounted on his wall. I could even smell a faint odor of the excitement of an impending kill. He didn't even blink and I don't think he was conscious of what else was happening in the room.

Mr. Zewick finally found enough nerve to speak.

"Miss Boyer, I have a report placed in your folder from campus security that indicates you suffered an injury that required medical attention in April of this year. Is that correct?"

He lifted his nose from the file and looked at her. She didn't look at him.

Dr. Gaines tried to intervene. "Miss Boyer, is this true?"

She still gave no response.

Dr. Gaines, now becoming annoyed, turned his chair toward her and raising his voice, said, "Miss Boyer—"

"Yes," she shouted. "Yes, it true. The pig. He try to rape me. I had to defend myself."

"Who?" Asked Dr. Gaines. "Professor Lane?"

She straightened herself upward and slowly looked around the room. "He try to rape me. He follow me. We reach pond. He pounce on me like rabid dog. I took knife from purse but he take it from me and slash my wrist," she proudly stated, holding up her arm to reveal the scar. "That's when police come. He run away." She stared straight at Dr. Gaines.

I didn't know whether to believe her or not, and I suppose everyone else was thinking the same thing because no one said a word for at least three minutes. The personnel director broke the silence.

"But, the report stated that you didn't name your attacker. Why was that?"

"It no good. They come to beat me."

"They? I thought there was only one, Professor Lane. Were you attacked more than once?"

"They stick together. Cross one, they all take turns at you."

"Miss Boyer, we have the means to offer protection to you. If you'll see me after this hearing, we can arrange something for you."

She almost snarled at him. "You arrange nothing. It no work. Nobody protect me. Not against them."

"And why is that?" Asked Dr. Gaines, clearly perplexed by her statement.

"You know them." She said, snarling again. "They pigs. Just like professors. They prey on us like animals. They take away pride and dignity. Only thing left is shame. Shame of failure."

Dr. Gaines was almost beside himself and I thought I could see veins pulsating in his neck. His face was already turning red.

"Miss Boyer..." I'm sure he was trying to keep a lid on his temper. "Miss Boyer, I'm afraid I don't understand what your position is with respect to the college. Are you saying that you have been abused here?"

"I just say you all bunch of pigs. I deal with your kind all my life. Even my father was pig. All he want was to screw me like he did other girls. And steal money I make. I fight to leave from him."

The room again fell silent for several minutes. I sat back in my chair assessing her testimony with the article I read from the Los Angeles Times. Finally, Dr. Damascus spoke up.

"I think we've heard all we need to hear. Clearly, Professor Lane tried to take advantage of this poor girl, probably sensing her vulnerability. Apparently, she was easy prey for him."

"Dr. Damascus, sit down," boomed Dr. Gaines. "We have yet to hear any evidence that the incidents ever took place. All we have is Miss Boyer's word for it. I would like to get to the bottom of it."

Mr. Zewick broke in. "Miss Boyer, we still have the question of the allegation against Professor Lane."

She started up again, but with more gusto. "I no care about Professor Lane."

Then she snapped here head toward Dr. Damascus and leveled a finger at him. "But him!"

We all turned and looked at the accused, wondering what new surprise awaited. Damascus was waving off her accusations and slowly rose out of his chair, a smirk on his face.

"Now, Miss Boyer," he crooned. "What could I possibly have done to harm you?" He looked around the room, hoping someone would buy into his plea. "I have given you every opportunity to succeed in my class, and in fact, several opportunities that I have not been extended to other students. Why, I have—"

"You pig!" Allison screamed. "You filthy pig. You screw all girls in your class, you cheat them out of grades, and make us to steal for you. Melanie try to tell me but no listen. How you harm me? I come from a poor family. I try to follow rules, but you destroy everything I work for. You are—"

"Miss Boyer," Damascus shouted. "You will not address me in that manner. You will restrain yourself and—"

This is where all hell broke loose as the two had it out, each yelling accusations and flailing arms above the table with curt gestures. Finally, Dr. Gaines broke in, banging on the table.

"Shut up!" Bang, bang, bang. "Shut up!" Bang, bang, bang. "Everybody just shut the hell up!"

The silence was frightening. We all just sat there, stymied by what had just happened, and unsure of what to do. Allison's sobbing stopped momentarily as if a quick turn of the faucet had terminated the flow. For once I could read genuine surprise in her eyes. Her mouth moved but no words came out. The others in the room turned their attention on Miss Boyer. And they stared.

It was only a moment before she leaned forward, crumpled her face into a hideous contortion, and turned loose the tears again. Her drama captured the attention in the room and melted the incredulity of the panel into oozing sympathy. How good she was.

Then she jerked her head up like a veteran thespian, tears flowing like gushers, and directed her eyes toward me. I seemed to be the only person in the room not touched by her piteous condition, because her face revealed to me the madness of her accusation. And I also knew that I could not possibly be the father of her unborn child. Her stinging words broke the silent air hanging over the table like falling shards of crystal.

"But you do it. You do it to me."

She snatched a tissue from her small bag and dabbed her eyes as a gesture of true distress.

"No, Miss Boyer, I didn't do anything to you. You see, several years ago, I had a vasectomy. I'm incapable of impregnating anyone."

Every eye in the room grew larger and Miss Boyer's complexion paled, even against her stunning cream-colored blouse. Dr. Damascus wore a priceless expression of dismay, his deep eyes peering through his eyebrows as if hiding. Mr. Zewick sat back in his chair and smiled. Dr. Gaines had still not recovered from his trance and I wondered if he even heard what I had said. Mary's stare was puzzling. I wasn't sure if she was upset, offended, or somehow pleased. And poor Dr. Tipton had taken to fanning herself with her notebook.

Then silence, except for the wailing of Allison Boyer. A softer wailing. More hopeless than angry.

A welcome knock on the door broke the tension. Mary left to take care of the interruption. In a few moments, Mary returned and Ricky followed her into the room.

"Professor Smithers, this is a closed hearing," Dr. Gaines told him.

"Not for someone who has information related to the subject of this hearing," he said, taking a seat beside me. "I'm here on Professor Lane's behalf."

What little fire remained in Dr. Damascus' eyes suddenly cooled, his complexion turned pale, and nervous fingers worked the cufflink in his sleeve. I could almost see wheels turning in his head as if he might be planning another attack. Then a blaze replaced the smoldering embers in his eyes.

"You have no place in this hearing," he boomed, banging his fists on the table. "I demand that he be removed from the room." He pointed at Ricky and glared at Dr. Gaines.

"Professor Lane has every right to call witnesses in his behalf," Dr. Gaines replied. "If anyone has no place in this room, it is you, Dr. Damascus. Sit down."

They challenged each other with angry stares. Dr. Gaines' impatience with Damascus had become more evident. Damascus finally conceded. Dr. Gaines turned toward me.

"Do you wish to use Professor Smithers as witness?"

"Yes," I told him, looking at Ricky.

"In that case," said Dr. Gaines, "let's hear what he has to say."

"This is outrageous," yelled Damascus, jumping up from his chair. "This man has no business being here."

Dr. Gaines jerked his head toward him.

"Sit down, Dr. Damascus, or I will have security remove you from this room. We will hear what Professor Smithers has to say."

Damascus began banging on the table again.

"I will not have that fool ruin this hearing," he yelled.

Dr. Gaines moved toward him and tried to subdue him. Damascus rebelled and threw a punch, catching Dr. Gaines in the left eye. While holding a hand over his eye and fending off Damascus' attack, Dr. Gaines motioned to Mary.

"Mary! Wanda! Now!"

Mary jumped up and ran to the outer office.

Dr. Gaines finally managed to wrestle free and put the legs of a side chair between himself and Damascus' flailing fists. The rest of us remained in our seats. As for myself, I was afraid to do anything. I had seen enough violence that day. And I figured the two of them could duke it out. The rest probably just didn't know what they should do.

Miss Boyer had since jumped from her chair and ran to my side of the table, observing the spectacle like a child watching a tiger attack its prey.

"Dr. Damascus, this hearing will go no further," groaned Dr. Gaines, poking Damascus with the legs of the chair, "until you are removed," poke, poke, "from the room. You are not entitled to be here, yourself. I only agreed to your," poke, poke, poke, "presence because of information you had about Professor Lane." Dr. Damascus overcame the chair and landed another lucky punch to the nose.

By the time Wanda arrived, Damascus had Dr. Gaines bent backwards over the table, the chair still in Dr. Gaines' firm grasp, its legs straddling Damascus' broad belly, one of them caught beneath his ear and drawing a considerable amount of blood. He kept swinging nonetheless, and Dr. Gaines kept working the chair against his massive paunch trying to force it away from him.

Wanda rushed into the room and it took her only a moment to see what she needed to do. I had underestimated her abilities to handle her job. She moved around the table as gracefully and quickly as a large, plump cat and, with the dexterity and expertise of a trained professional, placed her arms around those of Dr. Damascus, effectively restraining his movement with her own mass. She pulled him off of Dr. Gaines, and herded him back around the table toward the door. Damascus grumbled and screamed in pain the entire time, apparently from the tight hold Wanda maintained on him.

Dr. Gaines instructed her to remove Damascus from the room and not allow him to return.

The room fell silent except for our heavy breathing and Dr. Gaines' gasps to recover his breath. We sat for a few moments watching Dr. Gaines attempt to mop the blood that streamed from his nose. I could have offered him some pointers, but I thought better of it. Confident that he had arrested the bleeding, we looked at each other, then at Ricky, each of us anticipating his purpose for interrupting the meeting.

"I apologize for that unprofessional display," began Dr. Gaines. "It won't happen again. Is everyone ready to continue?"

Miss Boyer slowly returned to her seat and sat at the end of the table, bleary-eyed and frightened.

Ricky leaned forward and rested the frayed cuffs of his jacket in the dust on the worn spot of the table in front of him. He cocked a smile to the room.

"What I have to say in this hearing should be heard by Dr. Damascus. It's just not right that the accuser should be able to spill the beans without the accused being present."

After a considerable period of silence, Dr. Gaines said, "Very well. We'll wait a few moments until Dr. Damascus has collected himself."

During the short break, I talked with Mary in the outer office.

"Do you have any idea what is going to happen in there?" She asked.

She stood in front of me and looked up into my eyes.

"Apparently he has something on Damascus, but I'm not sure exactly what he is going to say."

"Whatever it is, I'll bet it's going to be a bomb."

It was only about ten minutes before we were summoned back to the hearing. We took our seats around the table and looked at Ricky. Wanda reappeared with Dr. Damascus. She held his arm while she forced him into a chair on my side of the table, safely away from Dr. Gaines.

"I'll be right outside if you need me," she said, looking across the table.

Dr. Gaines nodded and she retreated to the outer office. Ricky began.

"I've been here a long time. Probably longer than I should. I've seen a lot of shit take place, here. A lot of it I caused. Most of it I didn't. I've pretty much kept to myself so as not to interfere with anyone else. I believe I have been a good teacher and my first concern has always been for the student's benefit. But, I'm growing tired of the charade."

I still had no idea what he was getting at, and from the looks I saw on other faces, I was sure no one else did, either, except Dr. Damascus.

"In the last several years I have seen this college fall from mediocrity to just plain terrible. I have seen greedy, power-hungry people tear it down, bit by bit. I can't watch it any longer. The students deserve better. And that's why I'm resigning my position effective at the end of this semester."

I thought I heard Dr. Gaines gasp and there seemed to be a whimper come from Mary. Damascus had a large, evil smile on his face. And poor Miss Boyer had no clue.

"The reasons are many, but the most compelling one is the lecherous incantation that has overtaken this institution. I have sadly watched Dr. Damascus pilfer through this college's cupboard, taking whatever funds he thought he could safely abscond with. How else would a professor at a second rate college, divorced and fleeced of finances, be able to afford expensive clothes and a Mercedes?"

"You liar!" Damascus bellowed. "I'll see you in Hell, you son-of-a-bitch."

Dr. Gaines jumped up from the table. "You will shut your mouth and listen or I'll call Wanda," he yelled.

Gasps, moans, and exclamations again erupted in the room. Dr. Damascus' face had drawn into anger and his chin had dropped as if a puppet's string had gone slack. Miss Boyer's face seemed to turn white for an instant and then suddenly change to crimson while she clenched her teeth. Mary, as I suspected, showed complete shock and Dr. Gaines looked as if someone had just asked him if he had pissed his pants.

Ricky stood and began pacing slowly behind the chairs. Damascus' forehead sprouted beads of sweat that glistened through the thick eyebrows and his hands wrung around themselves, a furious battle raging between them.

"Oh, I'm sure you have all heard the story about how his wife has some measure of wealth. Well, the story bears out. His wife is indeed wealthy. But the story you probably don't know is how she cut him off when she found out he was cheating on her."

More gasps filled the air and all eyes were on Dr. Damascus, who by that time had become so enraged that his hands were shaking, and the sweat began running down his face.

Dr. Gaines kept a finger pointed at him.

"It sickens me to think that I could have neglected my civic responsibility to report it. And for that, I'm probably just as guilty as he. But, it's going to be over. Because I'm going to finish it. Here and now."

Dr. Damascus jumped up and beat his hands on the table.

"You impertinent fool," he screamed. "What right have you to come in here and levy such wanton accusations against me?"

The old man stood there hunched over the table, his head lowered so as to look out from the tops of his eyes at Ricky. An accursed grin spread across his jowls, a specter of evil.

"You have no idea what you're talking about, you impudent dolt," he moaned in low guttural sounds. "I've been a professor here for almost thirty years. I have more credentials on my business card than you have in your entire vita."

I had also been caught off guard by this incredible accusation. It seemed everyone else was, too. No one dared say anything. I knew

I certainly didn't want to interrupt the show. By then Damascus had plopped back into his seat, his eyes never leaving Ricky.

"As it turns out, you see, Dr. Damascus' infidelity was not just a passing fling with an acquaintance. His tastes run toward the college student. And he has preyed on many young and innocent women as well as men here at Hartmann for many years. I have no idea what his rewards were, except that the grades of some of these victims might be suspect."

He paused to stare at Dr. Damascus, smiling like a content general might smile as his troops destroyed the enemy. Murmurs fluttered around the room.

"And that's not really the bad part of this game. He also shares his enthusiasm with a certain Professor Bartholomew, although in a slightly different light."

Gasps worked their way around the table again, one at a time. So now I began to understand what had been going on.

"I don't mean to imply that Professor Bartholomew preys on young women. No, that is not the case at all."

Ricky had confused everyone except Damascus.

"He preys on young men."

I could swear I heard Dr. Tipton squeal as her fanning notebook worked itself at blinding speed.

"Oh," continued Ricky. "Then there's this matter of sexual harassment."

The room again went mute and all eyes, showing more white than usual, were on Ricky.

"I'm afraid you folks are taking the wrong person to task for this one."

Allison Boyer and Damascus shared frightened stares.

"You see, as most you know, I live here in Elkridge. I know a lot of folks around here. And they all know us. Some of them know Dr. Damascus, here. And they love to talk about how broke he is. And how he's always hitting them up for money. They bought into it for a while and made him some extremely generous loans. Then they finally realized he never intended to pay them back and they cut him off just as his wife had. So he turned to Hartmann for his financial support. He began extorting money from his students for grades and I know for a fact that he even convinced some of the poor bastards to steal for him so he could fence the items. Well, Professor Lane, here, showed up and threatened to expose his little game and that would never do. I'm guessing Dr. Damascus staged this entire event to get rid of him."

Dr. Gaines buried his head in his hands. Mary looked faint. Dr. Tipton's mouth hung open, leaving a giant pink hole in her face. Mr. Zewick seemed to be salivating. Damascus had already crossed the line to devilry.

"You bastard," screamed Miss Boyer, looking at Dr. Damascus. "You say this easy. You promised I get scholarship. You swine, you tell me file charge. You say Melanie do all dirty stuff."

She pointed at him with an accusing finger. Then out of that sweet, petite mouth, "You go hell."

Then she turned toward me.

"And you!"

The finger, again. She stood there, thrusting her hands to her sides, tears cascading from her cheeks, her body stiff and bent, helpless and pitiful. She continued and her arms echoed her anger.

"You," she squeaked. She began crying. Then screaming. Then crying. The horrid wailing wore down into whimpers and she quietly sobbed.

"I'm sorry," she wailed. "Professor Lane, I so sorry."

I could barely understand her words beneath the cloud of sorrow that bellowed forth from this fragile being. She collapsed into her chair and fell forward on the table, holding her sobbing face in her hands.

Then we all heard, "What in the world is going on here?" as Dr. Dennison burst into the room with Wanda in tow. He looked straight at Dr. Gaines.

Silence thrust the room into a suspended state of awareness as everyone turned toward Dr. Dennison. Each of us, except for Miss Boyer who was still sobbing helplessly on the table, was surely wondering why he was there.

"I'm sorry, Dr. Gaines," said Wanda, peeking around Dr. Dennison. "I was listening just outside the door and when I heard all of that going on I figured I'd better get Dr. Dennison over here."

After the embarrassment of explaining the proceedings to Dr. Dennison, the meeting was cut short. Miss Boyer, Mary, Ricky, and I were asked to leave. Allison almost ran from the office.

"I'm sorry, August," Mary said, placing a hand on my chest. "I'm really sorry you were put through all of that."

Her hand lingered there on my chest, over my heart. I'm sure she could feel it throbbing, beating its life out because of the excitement. But more because of that simple gesture she had made.

"Yeah, you got a bad deal," said Ricky. "None of this would have happened if I had done what I should have done long ago."

"It's not your fault, Ricky," I said. "Those two in there would have found some other way to get what they wanted."

We stood in the outer office, eyes on the floor, in collective empathy. I regained the scent of Mary's perfume. My soul felt refreshed in spite of the sordid scene we had just witnessed. None of us wanted to admit that he had been victimized. None of us wanted the stigma associated with us that we were ignorant, or less than perfect. Although, I don't think it really would have bothered Ricky that much.

"Hey, listen," he said. "Let's all go out and celebrate tonight. My treat."

I looked at Mary, hoping she wouldn't find some excuse not to go.

"I think that's a fine idea," she said.

Her response infused my spirit with new energy. The company of both Ricky and Mary would be welcome. Although, I had never been in mixed company with them, there seemed to be a sort of bonding occurring, bringing us closer together into a coterie.

"And I think Jim Bob's would be an appropriate setting for our victory party," I said.

"Isn't that the gay bar?" Asked Mary.

"The very one," said Ricky.

"You don't honestly expect me to go into that place, do you?"

"Why not?" I said. "How is it different from any other bar?"

"Well... you know. Those... kind of people."

"Hey," I said, "those kind of people are some of the nicest you will ever meet."

She looked at Ricky and me with disgust.

"Well, okay. But you've got to promise me I won't get mixed up in any funny business."

"Done," I said. "Seven?"

Ricky left. Mary and I were alone in the outer office.

"Mary, I'm sorry you had to sit through this. I know it wasn't pleasant. I mean, having everyone's lives ripped open in public that way."

"No, August. I'm the one who should be apologizing to you. I doubted you. I even wondered what sort of man you really were when I know... I knew you really weren't –"

"Mary, I understand. You had no idea what to believe. It's not like you've known me all your life. You had no way of knowing what sort of jerk I would be."

"August, you're not a jerk. I just meant that –"

"I know what you meant. There's no need to apologize."

I looked into her green eyes, soft but intense, comforting but exciting. Like pools of placid water reflecting the tranquility of overhanging trees and bursting with arousal that churned just beneath the surface. I think at that point I was falling in love.

Chapter 37

From the Administration building, I looked at Dr. Hartmann's statue, or where it wasn't. It was more difficult to see from a distance so in a radical break with tradition I stepped off the sidewalk and, actually walking on the grass, crossed the lawn in the square toward the red brick monument. His vacant image was crisp against the sienna hue of the brick buildings. He seemed more chipper and his head was held high with dignity. For a moment, I thought I saw a faint likeness of myself up there in his mooring. I could almost feel the tug of the bolts on my feet as I prepared to leave. My chest had already inflated to fill the void in my shirt, and as I stepped away from the statue that wasn't there, I decided that the campus needed the routine reminder of its purpose. The silence begged for the persistent affirmation of the presence of academia. Hartmann would persevere in the absence of ivy-covered walls. But it couldn't continue to serve those who inhabited its halls without fanfare. My heart sank a bit knowing there were no chimes. The computer that stirred them to life each hour still lay dormant in the Cop Room. A brush of warm air blew past my cheek. Was the old boy trying to tell me something? I went to see Ed.

*****

"Ed, you got a minute?"

He was sitting behind his desk banging on a keyboard.

"Oh," he said, cutting his eyes toward me. "It's you. Come on in, if you have to."

"Yes, I think I really have to."

I sat down in a chair in front of the desk after wiping the dust from it with my handkerchief.

"I need a computer," I said.

"Thought you had one."

"I do. It's not for me."

"Then why do you need it?"

"It's for the chimes."

He shoved his keyboard away from him and turned to face me. "You're really a glutton for punishment, aren't you?"

"You can call me anything you like. I need a computer."

"What happened to the one I gave you?"

"It broke. Like the first one. Surely you've noticed?"

We stared at each other, neither of us speaking. Finally, he broke eye contact and got up from his chair, shaking his head in aggravation.

"You know, the campus has been pretty peaceful, lately. That is, up until this stink with Dr. Damscus." He narrowed his eyes at me. "And I guess we all have you to thank for that."

I wasn't sure if that was a good thing for him or not. His surly sense of humor hid much of his emotion.

He walked toward a wall concealed behind boxes and computer carcasses.

"I think I've got one here that will probably work for you. I'll have one of the guys bring it over."

"How about now?"

"You don't want much, do you?"

"You know it's for a very good cause. I've seen you stop and look up at the roof when they played."

He smiled for just an instant and lowered his head. "Okay. I'll get it right over to you."

*****

I waited no longer than fifteen minutes before the computer was delivered. I plugged in the cables, installed the software, turned everything on, then set the time. It would be five-o'clock in eleven minutes. I watched the computer monitor.

At exactly five-o'clock, the air vibrated with the first strain of chimes singing its Westminster tune. I looked out the window to the campus below. Students had stopped and looked toward the Math Science Building. Others walked slowly, also gazing into the air. Then the five long peals that echoed the resonance of time. The reverberations slowly died out and the people resumed their journeys across the campus. I looked at Dr. Hartmann's statue, or where it wasn't and I went back down to it.

I stood there again in front of the old boy looking up at him. I could definitely see a smile on his face this time, as if he too had shared in my triumph. And I could swear he actually looked down at me, the victory of academia that illuminated the shadows of corruption.

*****

I was walking with a higher step than usual and bounced into my office welcoming the musty air that permeated everything in the building.

"Hey, Stan, this is a banner day."

"So, how did the hearing go?"

"I'm sure there's never been, nor will there ever be, another like it."

His eyes narrowed and he tightened his lips.

"Is that good or bad?"

"For me, good. For Hartmann, good and not so good."

"What do you mean? Is everything okay or isn't it?"

"Oh, yeah. I'm great. I'm better than I have been in some time."

I smiled and passed by him to my desk and dropped the load of documents from my arm on top of the clutter on my desk.

"I'm off the hook. There is no longer any issue with sexual harassment."

He smiled and leaned back in his chair, even though it didn't.

"However," I said, "there are some other issues that will be addressed. But not with me."

He gave me his full attention while I relayed the events of the meeting.

"You really had me worried, there," he said. "I actually thought I might have to endure this office in solitude."

"Hey, we're having a celebration at Jim Bob's tonight. Why don't you come along?"

"I've never been to a gay bar."

"It's pretty much like any other bar."

"Then why is it called a gay bar instead of just a bar?"

"Because gays frequent it. But that doesn't mean no one else can."

"Who all is planning to be there?"

"So far, Ricky, Mary, and myself."

"Ricky Smithers?"

"Yup. That's him."

"You know, I don't believe I've ever socialized with him. I've seen him around, but I've never had the opportunity to really talk with him."

"Well, here's your chance. Of course, you know Mary Einhorn?"

"Yes, I know Mary. Okay, what time?"

"Seven. I thought I'd grab a bite to eat there at the bar. They have some dynamite burgers."

*****

The door to Jim Bob's squeaked open to a vast emptiness. The familiar sweet, yeasty smell of spilled beer complemented the heavy sourness of ripe, burnt grease. The bouquet hit me square in the face along with the blast of cold air from the air conditioner vent above that was missing its diffuser. Tuesday evenings were not host to big events at the establishment, the patrons were few and business slack. Ricky, sporting a huge smile that was visible even from the door, already claimed the sticky booth along with Mary. One of her hands nervously played with loose strands of her hair.

"Perfessor," barked Cindy, beaming at me from behind the bar. "Come on in. I'll 'ave one ready for ya."

I strode through the empty tables toward the booth and took a seat beside Mary. She turned her head and smiled at me as she lifted a Black Russian to her lips.

"No hats?" Ricky asked.

"No," I laughed. "No hats."

He finished off his beer just as Cindy brought my Glenlivet. He waved the mug in the air for another.

I looked at Mary, still wrapping her hair around a finger, more vigorously now. I stared at her profile peeking from behind the loose tufts. The lines of her nose, not too sharp, not too round, but a perfect companion to the gentle cheeks cascading toward expressive lips. A petite chin, more delicate than any other I had noticed, which is odd because I usually didn't notice chins. My eye was drawn to her alluring face. I hadn't really noticed how incredibly pretty she was.

"I take it this is your first visit to Jim Bob's?" I said to her.

"I can't believe you actually suggested a place like this," she said, keeping her fingers busy with her hair while her eyes slowly swept through the room.

The lines of her ear, just visible beneath the swooping bun of hair, teased me like an exotic dancer revealing tantalizing flashes of leg. Of course, being a leg man, this was highly symbolic. She was wearing that perfume, a fresh dose, I guessed. I was swallowing harder than usual.

"It's merely a bar," I said, not sure I was aware of what was happening. "Pretty much like any other."

I inhaled more deeply than necessary just so I could savor the piquant delight of the fragrance.

"No, it's not," she said in a loud whisper and turning her face toward me. "This is a… a… gay bar," she said, emphasizing the gay.

She had difficulty getting that word out. My sudden attraction to her swelled with comedy at her naive regard for a strange culture. A large lump settled in my throat, tasting vaguely of adolescence.

"Do you know any gay people?" I asked her.

"No."

"Are you sure?"

"What do you mean?"

"I mean, how do you know that none of the people you know aren't gay?"

"Well… they just aren't."

"Okay, I'll let you indulge in your fantasies. The folks here are really quite docile and very pleasant."

The door squealed and a male couple entered the bar holding hands and led each other to a table across the room. Mary stared at them from behind her hair. Ricky was chuckling.

"Well, I suppose you have a point," she admitted. "I just get all… upset when the subject comes up."

"That's a perfectly natural emotion for most folks. There's really no fundamental difference between a gay person and anyone else."

They both looked at me in a queer sort of way. Perhaps it was my arrogance.

"All right, there is a difference. Hell, there are probably lots of differences. The point I'm trying to make is that they're people just like us. They just happen to get off on the same gender." I looked at them smugly. "That's all."

We all turned toward the squeal of the door to see Stanley poke his head in. After a careful look about, he slid inside and stood there canvassing the room. He finally spotted us, waved, and cautiously made his way toward us, like a cat creeping past a sleeping dog. He sat next to Ricky. When he tried to scoot across the seat, he didn't move.

"What is this all over the seat? It's sticky with something."

"Oh, that's just so we can't fall out of the booth," Ricky said. "After a few belts one tends to get lost under the table."

Stanley gave Ricky a curious look. "Hi, Ricky. I don't get to see much of you on campus."

"Welcome to Jim bob's," said Ricky. "Glad you could join us."

Stan looked at Mary. "Hi. I don't get to see you too often, either. This is really a pleasure."

"Well, I'm not sure how much of a pleasure it is in this adhesive booth," she said. "But I'm glad to see you, too."

Cindy suddenly showed up at the end of our table. She stood there with a towel over her face hacking out God knows what. We all patiently waited for the violence to subside.

"Hey, we've got another new face tonight," she barked, looking at Stanely. "Welcome to Jim Bob's. What can I get for you?"

"Just whatever Ricky's having," he said, pointing to the mug.

"Comin' right up."

"And why don't you bring everyone a burger," said Ricky. "The fat one with cheese and fries."

She turned and hacked her way back to the bar.

"I propose a toast to today's victory," said Ricky. "And to my retirement."

We all smiled and looked at him as he continued.

"Hartmann College has been the sight of many years of happiness and misery. For me and everyone else who has ventured through her ivyless doors. It is with sound regret that I part in such sweet delight. I shall not miss her, nor shall she miss me. It will be a good parting."

Cindy arrived with Stan's beer.

"Now, drink up in haste," ordered Ricky. "We have much more to celebrate this evening."

We threw back our heads and consumed the first toast.

"And now, the second order of business. Our victory. The triumph over decadence and evil. Not that Hartmann will be the better for it. In fact, she might falter a bit until she gets her bearings. But in the long run I would say it is for the best."

He sat straight back in his seat and raised his mug high.

"I salute you, Dr. Hartmann. And I salute you, Professor August Lane. And your chimes. Here's to a long and… well, here's to a long life at Hartmann."

We all lifted our glasses and mugs and again sipped down another tribute.

"By the way," said Stanley, "what about this Dr. Damascus thing?"

Ricky perked up and leaned into the table.

"I have it from reliable sources that Dr. Damascus has left the building."

"You mean he's gone? From Hartmann?" Asked Stanley.

"As a matter of fact, sometime during the afternoon he cleaned out his office, and parts of some others, and no one has seen him since."

Stanley leaned forward. "As I was leaving campus, the police were around the Administration Building. Something about Dr. O'Mally barricading herself inside her office."

"Well, what about Damascus' classes?" I asked.

Mary jumped in. "Dr. Gaines has already asked me to find substitute teachers for him and Professor Bartholomew. I thought it was because Dr. Damascus was busy preparing for the charges Dr. Dennison was bringing against him. I had no idea he just left."

"And Bartholomew?" Asked Stanley.

"Oh, he was a part of all of this, too. Probably somewhere with Dr. Damascus."

Ricky continued the exposé while the three of us listened.

"My sources also told me that Dr. Dennison has placed Dr. Gaines on probation. Somehow," he smiled broadly when he said that, "word about this incident has leaked to the board of regents and the North Central Association. Now even Dr. Dennison has some explaining to do. He might not be with us much longer."

"And Shawn Crandall?" I asked.

"Oh, yes," said Mary. "Dr Damascus had him suspended. I suppose he will be reinstated immediately."

She smiled again. A smile of trust.

"Well," I said. "I guess there is justice to be had, even in the world of academia. The dominion of bells and statues. And Melanie Parker? Allison Boyer?"

Mary took the lead on this one.

"As it turns out, Allison has been taken into custody for her own safety. I think they're trying to arrange some sort of investigation into her parents and how she actually got admitted to the college."

"What, they arrested her?" I asked.

"No, they didn't arrest her. They just moved her into the county detention center near Tulsa until they can figure out what's going on with her. Sort of holding her. It seems that her step-father was a scam artist in California and her mother was a prostitute. She ran away and neither of them made any attempt to find her. She's been living on whatever she could find in the dumpsters and trash cans, and what little Dr. Damascus provided her."

"What about Melanie?"

"Well, I understand that the Department of Human Services is taking on her case. They're trying to find her a job nearby where she can at least help pay her way through school."

The evening passed in tribute after tribute and replays of the events in the hearing. After the second beer, Stanley would have slid beneath the table in fits of laughter had it not been for the adhesive that bonded him to the seat. During our presence, a few other patrons wandered in and kept attentive eyes toward out booth, for they, too, were enjoying our merriment.

Cindy brought the burgers and shoved a plate in front of each of us. And a stack of napkins. Each of us picked up his monster burger and took a mouthful of the toasted, sweet bun, thick beef patty, oozing cheese, grilled onions, lettuce, and tomatoes, and, the best part, the grease that dripped onto our chins and down our wrists. The plump, crispy fries almost snapped with the first bite and the sweet, soft meat of the potatoes filled our mouths with familiar essence of carb heaven. Life couldn't get any better.

As joyous as we were, Cindy was not without her own exuberance as more folks entered the bar and business picked up. The frivolity of our booth spread throughout the room, warming up the cash register.

We were lost in our own good will and celebration. I was lost in Mary. Sitting next to her, I felt a different sort of pleasure, unlike that which follows victory. It was more like the delirious state that follows several drinks. Something I had not felt for a long time. In fact, I couldn't ever remember feeling like that.

Her auburn hair rested neatly in the bun on top of her head with only the few strands having fallen loose, which hid her eyes, and the other strands she twirled by her ear. A few more fell as she continued curling them with her fingers. I studied the crisp profile of her small nose and perfectly formed lips, especially when she sipped the Black Russian, and imagined her lips against my own. The smell of her hair, her clothes, and… just her, blew away my loneliness.

I felt the joy of companionship, although she really did not qualify as a companion. I felt an attraction like a magnet pulling me to her, and the fear that always came with such attraction. But I also felt the thrill. And I didn't know what I should do. That was where I excused myself to go the restroom.

Chapter 38

The heady aroma of beer that followed me out the front door sweetened the acrid smell of the parking lot, a gourmet gutter filled with flashy cars and beat up trucks. There were also some junk heaps that appeared to have been rescued from the salvage yard. I wandered over the cracked and stained asphalt, avoiding the large holes filled with water and antifreeze and God knows what else, contemplating what had really happened that day. After replaying the hearing several times in my mind, little of it made sense. What had driven Miss Boyer and Miss Parker to do what they did? How had Damascus continued his charade for so long undetected? And, aside from my arrogance, clumsiness, and stupidity, what else was wrong with me?

The questions raced through my mind, battering my brain, now pretty well sloshed with whisky. I searched through my recollection of the hearing to piece things together. But few of the events fit. The biggest question was me. I seemed to be playing a game. I didn't know the rules and had no idea what the objective was.

I leaned against a red, blue, and green car, an assemblage of parts from other vehicles. The student parking decal on the windshield reminded me of my college days and my fellow students. I usually have no trouble remembering the major events that had an impact on my life. I struggled to find memories of the little things, the small, insignificant bits of misery and delight that fuse into the college experience and shape one's character into the person he will eventually become. Then I realized that at that time in my life, I wasn't thinking about my future all that much.

Having no distractions other than the blinking sign near the highway, visions of my youth flashed in front of me. Within the reckless and carefree voyage through college that's undertaken by many of the students I went to school with, there seemed to be a propensity for abandoning responsibility. It was almost like a code of conduct for new students. A pact that bound them all to a collective lack of ambition. They were in college mainly because that's what was expected. They had no idea what they were going to do with the rest of their lives and that made it impossible to determine what to study, if they studied at all.

I saw the same attributes in many of my own students. Or, at least the ones who weren't doing well. It was like a tiny window had opened into the world of studentdom. I couldn't think of a thing I could do to change it. Even being the best teacher in the world would not motivate some of these students enough to learn. The world in which I came of age was much different than the world my students were facing. I wouldn't want to be a student today, where things changed too fast. There are too many dangers. More than when I was there. Given today's environment, with constant nurturing and encouragement, they might make it. But that sort of ideal is impossible for a teacher. I couldn't possibly do that for all of them. Nurturing was not something I knew how to do. Alexis would certainly attest to that.

"I wondered where you went."

I hadn't heard Mary approach behind me.

"We were all a little worried about you." She took a place beside me on the fender of the red, blue, and green car.

"And why would my esteemed colleagues be worried about me?" I said, wryly.

"Not that we thought you might do yourself in. But, after the hearing today, we didn't know exactly what to expect of you."

"Mary, you are full of surprises."

"What surprises?"

I knew she would ask that, and now I had to explain.

"I don't know you very well," I said, twirling the last bit of Glenlivet in my glass. "It's not that I don't want to. It's just that I never thought about making the effort, I guess."

That was stupid. Now she probably thought I was a jerk. "And that's not because you're not the kind of woman I wouldn't want to know. It's just that –" God help me, my foot was starting toward my mouth.

"August, you're rambling."

"Oh. Yes, I guess I am. But you see, that's why you're surprising."

She shook her head and looked at me for an explanation.

"You just seem to have this effect on me. I don't know why. It… it's just there."

She smiled. Not just a smile. An "I like it" kind of smile.

"I mean, when I first met you I figured you to be some holy roller who would dismiss me as a distasteful bite of humanity. Not many people can stand my arrogance and self-righteousness."

"Well, I must say, you really know how to throw a girl a compliment."

I felt grateful that she couldn't see my red face beneath the glare of the blinking sign. I turned to look at her. She was staring at my eyes, still smiling, the blinking light flashing through her glasses; eyes – lens – eyes – lens. Even the bizarre conditions of the parking lot could not mask her beauty.

"Mary, I'm sorry. What I meant was that I misjudged you. But, then, I do that a lot."

"Obviously."

We resumed our places side by side on the fender of the red, blue, and green car, surveying the parking lot. It was comfortable. It felt right, leaning on the car with Mary. As if I belonged there, next to her. I began to wonder why she was still there.

"You know," she said, staring at the blinking sign, "Bill, my ex, used to tell me that I was a… forgive me for saying this, but… a bitch. He would get all huffy, throw down a beer, then tell me how much he hated me. He said he didn't even know why he married me."

I was stunned by her revealing confession. I couldn't image any man thinking such things of her. "He must be a real jerk," I offered as consolation.

"He is. I used to love him, but that ended when I took the job here at Hartmann. I worked for four years at night to finish my degree and he resented every minute of it. But I discovered something important about people."

"What's that?"

"They need someone."

"Didn't think I needed anyone," I said. "Not until now. You know, I have to wonder why you decided to come to my aid. I mean, here you are, a very attractive lady, working for a prestigious figure in the college, probably a very good job, and in a position to make a lot of good contacts. Why would you jeopardize all of that for me?"

"Well, I have to admit that I was beginning to have doubts after reading all of the memos and notes for the hearing."

"So, do you still have doubts?"

"No, August. I should never have had them in the first place."

"You mean you jeopardized your career for the sake of an arrogant, self-righteous jerk?"

"It's not that I'm putting anything in jeopardy. I'm merely look-

ing out for you. I happen to believe you're a very good teacher. And
a pretty nice man. Contrary to what you might believe, I have heard
some nice things about you."

"You're right. I find that hard to believe."

"It was from the students."

"And just how would you know about that? I certainly haven't
been privy to any sort of complimentary remarks. In fact, I have been
the brunt of much discontent among the students. And faculty."

"August, you might not realize it, but you're somewhat of a hero
among the faculty. And, as it turns out, the students, too."

I jerked my head around toward her and narrowed my eyes.

"What in the world ever gave you that idea? They despise me.
They go out of their way to avoid being seen with me."

"Aside from your good traits, you are also the most cynical man
I know."

"Oh, yeah, that's another of my many virtues."

"You must really have it in for this place," she scolded. "And
yourself."

I stopped snapping and thought seriously about what she said.
Even the Glenlivet couldn't compete with the graveness of that last
allegation. She was right. I did have it in for Hartmann College. Not
even one semester had passed and I had already turned my resolve from
Hartmann's mission, condemning the very purpose of its existence. And
myself? Yeah, I didn't think much of me, either. It was clear, there on
the fender of the red, blue, and green car, that I had driven my learned
chariot into a wall of befuddlement. What wasn't clear was why.

Then I listened in unmistakable chagrin as she extolled my many
virtues that I had not taken the time to see. I had sailed into academia,
that exalted ivy-league presence in American culture, on a whim of
fantasy thinking it would cure everything that was wrong with me. But,
where was the ivy? I must have missed it. And I began to hear something else in her mellow, sweet, voice. A sudden infusion of strength
awakened my ego and I realized that Mary was damned near telling me
that she thought I could walk on water. That old feeling of being human
wandered back to me. There on the green fender of the red, blue, and
green car. I felt human again.

The aroma of her hair overcame the sweet and sour staleness of
the parking lot. Her presence was exotic and soothing. Like the smell
of cinnamon and vanilla made me feel when I walked into my grand-
mother's kitchen. Comfort. Safety.

"Well," I said turning toward her, "that just goes to show you how gullible some people can be." I turned my glass up hoping for another drop of whisky. "And I'll tell you another thing. I looked directly into those emerald eyes. "I guess I kind of need you. I've never said that to anyone before. But I'm saying it to you."

Of course, everything I had said was true. I'd told her I'd become obsolete, and that I'd failed. Any hint of masculine aptitude that I might have presented up until then just drained from me like water through holes in a bucket. I don't know why I even thought I had a chance with someone like her, the college, or anyone. Maybe I just needed to go back into Jim Bob's and pick up the first guy who grabbed my ass. He probably wouldn't care that I was a loser. I sort of poured myself onto the green fender and waited for... I don't know what. Somehow I found the courage to say it to the person I feared most.

Her eyes seemed to float there in the parking lot away from everything else. Just float there as if they weren't a part of anything. Just eyes. Knowing eyes.

"August..." Here, she hesitated. I felt the rejection building. I was ready for it. "Ever since Bill left I didn't think I would ever need anyone again, either. But you opened the door for me to see what I was missing." She placed her hand on mine, laying flat on the green fender. "You're a fine, decent man, and I care about you. I care about the things you care about."

Here it comes, I thought.

"This semester has been confusing to me. Until now."

I braced myself. Could she feel the tension in my hand?

"I need you, August. I... I think I'm falling in love with you."

That one got me. I swallowed. Hard, like a golf ball had been shoved down my throat. Did she just say that? She loves me?

I grabbed her like a warm lifebuoy in the Arctic Ocean. We squeezed each other paying no mind to any ribs that might have cracked. The warmth spread between us, neither of us wanting to be the first to let go. I figured I would have to be the brave one. I loosened my grasp and looked at her.

"You know, if it weren't for my stoical ego, I would actually admit that I love you, too."

"I knew that the first time I saw you," she said with authority.

"At least one of us knows what's going on."

"That's you, August. You've always known what's going on. You came here with a marvelous vision. And now, because the clouds got in the way, you think the sun has quit shining."

"That's very poetic. I've never written a poem."

"The sun is still there. You just have to wait until the storm passes."

"Well, you're right about one thing. We are in the middle of a storm."

"Don't run away. These kids need to know that someone actually cares about their futures. If you expect more of someone, they begin to believe because you believe they can do it. Give them that chance."

No matter how frustrated I was with the college, the students, the administration, I couldn't argue with her logic. It was true. That had been my life's philosophy. How easily we let our own ideals fall behind whims.

I had just enough resolve for at least one more drink. I was nearly looped as it was and I had some misgivings about my ability to recall what I had decided that evening. Maybe one more Glenlivet would drive the point home. We turned from the red, blue, and green car and I felt the smile on my face as we wandered toward the door to Jim Bob's, hand in hand.

"I think I know how you must feel about this," she said. "The college and all."

"I just believe that Dr. Hartmann had a great idea. And he has given a lot of people chances to do what they couldn't have done otherwise."

"You're a true visionary, Professor Lane." She looked at me with a curious expression, then came toward me and looked directly into my eyes. Her hand reached for her head and unleashed that beautiful auburn hair that fell gracefully to her shoulders. She leaned closer and kissed me. Through the din of traffic and music we heard the faint chimes from the college. They hung in the air like a cloud of music.

Her eyes glowed a mysterious green. An ethereal glow, like some essence of life unknown to me. At that moment I couldn't accept the fact that she could actually be so common as an employee of Hartmann College. This wonderful woman who seemed to find within me what I had denied to myself all of my life. And there she was, with me, looking into my eyes with a magical gaze. I could not remember such a feeling of reverie.

We kissed again. Not just a kiss. More like the joining of souls. Two souls that had searched an eternity for what was then to be ours. Our lips were drawn to each other like a great force of nature that holds together the inimitable particles of the atom. A force, timeless and unceasing. Like the statue of Dr. Johanus Avery Hartmann that, even though not really there, was there. And like the chimes, timeless and unceasing, that bellowed forth their melody, over and over, stuck again in the fallibility of technology. I didn't care what Dr. Dennison might be thinking about them, then. Or me.

THE END

www.ingramcontent.com/pod-product-compliance
Lightning Source LLC
Chambersburg PA
CBHW060535260626
47161CB00003B/915